THE MAN WHO WOULD
BE KING

AND OTHER STORIES

RUDYARD KIPLING (1865–1936) was born in Bombay in December 1865. He returned to India from England in the autumn of 1882, shortly before his seventeenth birthday, to work as a journalist first on the *Civil and Military Gazette* in Lahore, then on the *Pioneer* at Allahabad. The poems and stories he wrote over the next seven years laid the foundation of his literary reputation, and soon after his return to London in 1889 he found himself world-famous. Throughout his life his works enjoyed great acclaim and popularity, but he came to seem increasingly controversial because of his political opinions, and it has been difficult to reach literary judgements unclouded by partisan feeling. The Oxford World's Classics series, published half a century after Kipling's death, provides the opportunity for reconsidering his remarkable achievement.

LOUIS L. CORNELL has taught English literature and philology at Dartmouth College and Columbia University. The author of *Kipling in India*, he currently lives and farms in Vermont.

OXFORD WORLD'S CLASSICS

For over 100 years Oxford World's Classics have brought
readers closer to the world's great literature. Now with over 700
titles—from the 4,000-year-old myths of Mesopotamia to the
twentieth century's greatest novels—the series makes available
lesser-known as well as celebrated writing.

The pocket-sized hardbacks of the early years contained
introductions by Virginia Woolf, T. S. Eliot, Graham Greene,
and other literary figures which enriched the experience of reading.
Today the series is recognized for its fine scholarship and
reliability in texts that span world literature, drama and poetry,
religion, philosophy and politics. Each edition includes perceptive
commentary and essential background information to meet the
changing needs of readers.

OXFORD WORLD'S CLASSICS

RUDYARD KIPLING

The Man who would be King
and Other Stories

Edited with an Introduction and Notes by
LOUIS L. CORNELL

OXFORD
UNIVERSITY PRESS

OXFORD
UNIVERSITY PRESS

Great Clarendon Street, Oxford OX2 6DP

Oxford University Press is a department of the University of Oxford.
It furthers the University's objective of excellence in research, scholarship,
and education by publishing worldwide in

Oxford New York

Athens Auckland Bangkok Bogotá Buenos Aires Cape Town
Chennai Dar es Salaam Delhi Florence Hong Kong Istanbul Karachi
Kolkata Kuala Lumpur Madrid Melbourne Mexico City Mumbai Nairobi
Paris São Paulo Shanghai Singapore Taipei Tokyo Toronto Warsaw

with associated companies in Berlin Ibadan

Oxford is a registered trade mark of Oxford University Press
in the UK and in certain other countries

Published in the United States
by Oxford University Press Inc., New York

Introduction, Note on the Text, and Explanatory Notes
© Louis L. Cornell 1987

General Preface, Select Bibliography, and Chronology
© Andrew Rutherford 1987
Updated Bibliography
© Andrew Rutherford 1996

British Library Cataloguing in Publication Data

Data available

Library of Congress Cataloging in Publication Data

Kipling, Rudyard, 1865–1936.
The man who would be king and other stories.
(Oxford world's classics).
Bibliography: p.
I. Cornell, Louis L.   II. Title.
PR4854.M16   1987   823'.8   86–16444

ISBN–13: 978–0–19–283629–8
ISBN–10: 0–19–283629–3

10

Printed in Great Britain by
Clays Ltd, St Ives plc

CONTENTS

GENERAL PREFACE

RUDYARD KIPLING (1865–1936) was for the last decade of the nineteenth century and at least the first two decades of the twentieth the most popular writer in English, in both verse and prose, throughout the English-speaking world. Widely regarded as the greatest living English poet and story-teller, winner of the Nobel Prize for Literature, recipient of honorary degrees from the Universities of Oxford, Cambridge, Edinburgh, Durham, McGill, Strasbourg, and the Sorbonne, he also enjoyed popular acclaim that extended far beyond academic and literary circles.

He stood, it can be argued, in a special relation to the age in which he lived. He was primarily an artist, with his individual vision and techniques, but his was also a profoundly representative consciousness. He seems to give expression to a whole phase of national experience, symbolizing in appropriate forms (as Lascelles Abercrombie said the epic poet must do) the 'sense of the significance of life he [felt] acting as the unconscious metaphysic of the time'.[1] He is in important ways a spokesman for his age, with its sense of imperial destiny, its fascinated contemplation of the unfamiliar world of soldiering, its confidence in engineering and technology, its respect for craftsmanship, and its dedication to Carlyle's gospel of work. That age is one about which many Britons—and to a lesser extent Americans and West Europeans—now feel an exaggerated sense of guilt; and insofar as Kipling was its spokesman, he has become our scapegoat. Hence, in part at least, the tendency in recent decades to dismiss him so contemptuously, so unthinkingly, and so mistakenly. Whereas if we approach him more historically, less hysterically, we shall find in this very relation to his age a cultural phenomenon of absorbing interest.

Here, after all, we have the last English author to appeal to readers of all social classes and all cultural groups, from

---

[1] Cited in E. M. W. Tillyard, *The Epic Strain in the English Novel*, London, 1958, p. 15.

viii GENERAL PREFACE

lowbrow to highbrow; and the last poet to command a mass
audience. He was an author who could speak directly to the
man in the street, or for that matter in the barrack-room or
factory, more effectively than any left-wing writer of the
'thirties or the present day, but who spoke just as directly and
effectively to literary men like Edmund Gosse and Andrew
Lang; to academics like David Masson, George Saintsbury,
and Charles Eliot Norton; to the professional and service
classes (officers and other ranks alike) who took him to their
hearts; and to creative writers of the stature of Henry James,
who had some important reservations to record, but who
declared in 1892 that 'Kipling strikes me personally as the
most complete man of genius (as distinct from fine intelligence) that I have ever known', and who wrote an
enthusiastic introduction to *Mine Own People* in which he
stressed Kipling's remarkable appeal to the sophisticated
critic as well as to the common reader.[2]

An innovator and a virtuoso in the art of the short story,
Kipling does more than any of his predecessors to establish it
as a major genre. But within it he moves confidently between
the poles of sophisticated simplicity (in his earliest tales) and
the complex, closely organized, elliptical and symbolic mode
of his later works which reveal him as an unexpected con-
tributor to modernism.

He is a writer who extends the range of English literature
in both subject-matter and technique. He plunges readers
into new realms of imaginative experience which then
become part of our shared inheritance. His anthropological
but warmly human interest in mankind in all its varieties
produces, for example, sensitive, sympathetic vignettes of
Indian life and character which culminate in *Kim*. His
sociolinguistic experiments with proletarian speech as an
artistic medium in *Barrack-Room Ballads* and his rendering
of the life of private soldiers in all their unregenerate humanity gave a new dimension to war literature. His portrayal of

---

[2] See *Kipling: The Critical Heritage*, ed. Roger Lancelyn Green, London,
1971, pp. 159–60. *Mine Own People*, published in New York in 1891, was a
collection of stories nearly all of which were to be subsumed in *Life's
Handicap* later that year.

Anglo-Indian life ranges from cynical triviality in some of the *Plain Tales from the Hills* to the stoical nobility of the best things in *Life's Handicap* and *The Day's Work*. Indeed Mrs Hauksbee's Simla, Mulvaney's barrack-room, Dravot and Carnehan's search for a kingdom in Kafiristan, Holden's illicit, star-crossed love, Stalky's apprenticeship, Kim's Grand Trunk Road, 'William''s famine relief expedition, and the Maltese Cat's game at Umballa, establish the vanished world of Empire for us (as they established the unknown world of Empire for an earlier generation), in all its pettiness and grandeur, its variety and energy, its miseries, its hardships, and its heroism.

In a completely different vein Kipling's genius for the animal fable as a means of inculcating human truths opens up a whole new world of joyous imagining in the two *Jungle Books*. In another vein again there are the stories in which he records his delighted discovery of the English countryside, its people and traditions, after he had settled at Bateman's in Sussex: England, he told Rider Haggard in 1902, 'is the most wonderful foreign land I have ever been in';[3] and he made it peculiarly his own. Its past gripped his imagination as strongly as its present, and the two books of Puck stories show what Eliot describes as 'the development of the imperial . . . into the historical imagination.'[4]

In another vein again he figures as the bard of engineering and technology. From the standpoint of world history, two of Britain's most important areas of activity in the nineteenth century were those of industrialism and imperialism, both of which had been neglected by literature prior to Kipling's advent. There is a substantial body of work on the Condition of England Question and the socioeconomic effects of the Industrial Revolution; but there is comparatively little imaginative response in literature (as opposed to painting) to the extraordinary inventive energy, the dynamic creative power, which manifests itself in (say) the work of engineers like Telford, Rennie, Brunel, and the brothers Stephenson—

[3] *Rudyard Kipling to Rider Haggard*, ed. Morton Cohen, London, 1965, p. 51.
[4] T. S. Eliot, *On Poetry and Poets*, London, 1957, p. 247.

men who revolutionized communications within Britain by
their road, rail and harbour systems, producing in the
process masterpieces of industrial art, and who went on to
revolutionize ocean travel as well. Such achievements are
acknowledged on a sub-literary level by Samuel Smiles in his
best-selling *Lives of the Engineers* (1861–2). They are acknowledged also by Carlyle, who celebrates the positive as well as
denouncing the malign aspects of the transition from the
feudal to the industrial world, insisting as he does that the
true modern epic must be technological, not military: 'For
we are to bethink us that the Epic verily is not *Arms and the
Man*, but *Tools and the Man*,—an infinitely wider kind of
Epic.'[5] That epic has never been written in its entirety, but
Kipling came nearest to achieving its aims in verses like
'McAndrew's Hymn' (*The Seven Seas*) and stories like 'The
Ship that Found Herself' and 'Bread upon the Waters' (*The
Day's Work*) in which he shows imaginative sympathy with
the machines themselves as well as sympathy with the men
who serve them. He comes nearer, indeed, than any other
author to fulfilling Wordsworth's prophecy that

If the labours of men of Science should ever create any material
revolution, direct or indirect, in our condition, and in the
impressions which we habitually receive, the Poet will sleep then no
more than at present, but he will be ready to follow the steps of the
Man of Science, not only in those general indirect effects, but he will
be at his side, carrying sensation into the midst of the objects of the
Science itself.[6]

This is one aspect of Kipling's commitment to the world of
work, which as C. S. Lewis observes 'imaginative literature
in the eighteenth and nineteenth centuries had [with a few
exceptions] quietly omitted, or at least thrust into the background', though it occupies most of the waking hours of most
men:

And this did not merely mean that certain technical aspects of life
were unrepresented. A whole range of strong sentiments and

[5] *Past and Present* (1843), Book iv, ch.1. cf. ibid., Book iii, ch.5.
[6] *Lyrical Ballads*, ed. R. L. Brett and A. R. Jones, London, 1963, pp.
253–4.

emotions—for many men, the strongest of all—went with them . . . .
It was Kipling who first reclaimed for literature this enormous
territory.[7]

He repudiates the unspoken assumption of most novelists
that the really interesting part of life takes place outside
working hours: men at work or talking about their work are
among his favourite subjects. The qualities men show in their
work, and the achievements that result from it (bridges built,
ships salvaged, pictures painted, famines relieved) are the
very stuff of much of Kipling's fiction. Yet there also runs
through his *œuvre*, like a figure in the carpet, a darker, more
pessimistic vision of the impermanence, the transience—but
not the worthlessness—of all achievement. This underlies his
delighted engagement with contemporary reality, and gives a
deeper resonance to his finest work in which human
endeavour is celebrated none the less because it must
ultimately yield to death and mutability.

ANDREW RUTHERFORD

[7] *'Kipling's World'*, *Literature and Life: Addresses to the English Association*,
London, 1948, pp. 59–60.

INTRODUCTION

I

In the summer of 1889 two cheaply produced paperbound
volumes found their way from the railway bookstalls of
Allahabad to the London desk of Andrew Lang. Writing
them up for the *Saturday Review*,[1] the eminent critic greeted
In Black and White and *Under the Deodars* with surprise and
enthusiasm. The author—'so clever, so fresh, and so cynical
that he must be young'—spoke in a new and authentic voice
of strong emotions and exotic lands. It was a pity the little
books were as yet so inaccessible to English readers. 'There is
a new and enjoyable talent at work in Anglo-Indian
literature,' Lang concluded; the English reading public were
quick to agree.

Though Rudyard Kipling was indeed young—only
twenty-three at the time of Lang's review—he was already on
his way to becoming a seasoned man of letters. His first book,
privately printed in India at his parents' expense, had
appeared before his sixteenth birthday; since then he had
collaborated with members of his family on two further
collections of prose and verse. The first books he could call
his own—*Departmental Ditties* (1886) and *Plain Tales from the
Hills* (1888)—were culled from a body of journalism that had
already made his name widely known in British India. Their
success was quickly exploited: 1888 saw the launching of the
Indian Railway Library with six new Kipling titles. Besides
the two already mentioned, these were *Soldiers Three*, *The
Story of the Gadsbys*, *The Phantom 'Rickshaw*, and *Wee Willie
Winkie*. In more substantial format but with only slight
variations in content, the six little books have remained in
print from Lang's day to the present.

The original volumes contained a total of thirty-seven
stories divided according to subject or theme—tales of

[1] See Kipling: *The Critical Heritage*, ed. Roger Lancelyn Green (1971),
pp. 44–6.

wonder in *The Phantom 'Rickshaw*, stories about children in *Wee Willie Winkie*, and so forth. This is how they have appeared in all later editions, but it is not the way Kipling originally conceived them. With the exception of *The Story of the Gadsbys*, which began as five linked tales and grew into a short novel in parts, the stories were published independently of each other in the newspapers Kipling worked for, or in special supplements. Then, when the Indian Railway Library volumes were put together, Kipling added at least one new piece to each book; most of the later additions were weightier and more considered than the reprinted tales.

In this selection from the six volumes, I have arranged the stories in the order of their original appearance. During the three years that separate the earliest of the tales from the latest, Kipling's skills were developing with extraordinary speed: a chronological arrangement reveals his growing mastery. At the same time, important thematic concerns, obscured by the Railway Library division, may now be traced through a sequence of stories that mark stages in the growth of a strong and individual imagination.

The circumstances of first publication can be sketched briefly. Two early tales—'The Strange Ride of Morrowbie Jukes' and 'The Phantom 'Rickshaw'—stand apart from the rest. Written in 1885, they were printed in December of that year in *Quartette*, a Christmas supplement to the *Civil and Military Gazette* produced entirely by the Kipling parents and their two children. After a year devoted chiefly to light verse, Rudyard began a series of very short stories the following November. These condensed narratives, written for the *Civil and Military* during 1886 and the first half of 1887 under the series title of 'Plain Tales from the Hills', were brought together in a volume of that name in January, 1888. A few stragglers found place in later collections, authorized and otherwise.

In June, 1887, Kipling brought the 'Plain Tales' series to an end; that autumn he moved from Lahore to Allahabad and a host of new responsibilities. Among them was the editorship of the *Week's News*, a weekly supplement to the *Pioneer*.

In his autobiography Kipling identified himself with Browning's Fra Lippo Lippi, another enthusiastic novice granted an unexpected opportunity:

There was to be a weekly edition of the *Pioneer* for Home consumption. Would I edit it, additional to ordinary work? Would I not? There would be fiction—syndicated serial-matter bought by the running foot from agencies at Home. That would fill one whole big page . . . Why buy Bret Harte, I asked, when I was prepared to supply home-grown fiction on the hoof? And I did.

My editing of the *Weekly* may have been a shade casual—it was but a re-hash of news and views after all. My head was full of, to me, infinitely more important material. Henceforth no mere twelve-hundred[-word] Plain Tales jammed into rigid frames, but three- or five-thousand-word cartoons once a week. So did young Lippo Lippi, whose child I was, look on the blank walls of his monastery when he was bidden decorate them! 'Twas 'ask and have; Choose, for more's ready', with a vengeance.[2]

The new series of longer tales began the first week of January, 1888; the four stories Kipling published that month included one of his best, the brilliant 'Wayside Comedy'. As the months went on, Kipling extended the series to a total of thirty-five, concluding in mid-September with the author's formal farewell to his creations in an uncollected sketch called 'The Last of the Stories'.[3] But Kipling's creative energy was by no means exhausted. He had 'Baa Baa, Black Sheep' ready in December for the Christmas supplement to the *Week's News*; and, when the Indian Railway Library volumes began to appear near the end of that year, they included, along with other new material, three stories finer than anything he had yet written: 'Black Jack', 'On the City Wall', and 'The Man who would be King'.

With a very few exceptions, then, the seventeen stories

[2] *Something of Myself* (1937), pp. 70–1.
[3] Published 15 September, reprinted in the collection *Abaft the Funnel* (1909). Kipling missed a few weeks; on the other hand, one item in verse, 'The Ballad of Boh Da Thone', belongs to the series, and one issue of the *Week's News* ran two of his stories. In the mean time, he was publishing travel letters, poems, and sketches in the *Pioneer* and *Civil and Military Gazette* at a furious rate.

presented in this anthology were written in Kipling's twenty-third year. As he later recalled, 'When I came out of that furious spell of work towards the end of '88 I rearranged myself'.[4] This meant a trip around the world, a return to London, marriage to an American, and all the varied experiences of a wandering life. But though some of the greatest of Kipling's Indian tales were written later, the stories of '88 hold a special place, representing as they do the week-by-week record of the struggles of a young genius with the literary medium he was to make uniquely his own.

II

Browning's Fra Lippo may have been offered acres of monastery wall to decorate, but he was obliged to paint in full sight of his fellow monks, who expressed strong views concerning matters of subject and technique. Kipling had come out to India with only the slenderest experience in journalism; the literary ambitions of his schoolboy years were based, rather, on the new poetry of the 'aesthetic' 1870s. But when he arrived in Lahore, he had to cope with the taste of a reading public very different from the London avant-garde. Writing under the eye of the overworked officials who frequented the Punjab Club, he soon concluded that romantic verse in the style of Swinburne and D. G. Rossetti was of no interest to the readers of the *Civil and Military Gazette*.

Appealing to this readership called for a certain tact. The British community was neither stupid nor uneducated: competitive examinations for the Indian Civil Service weeded out all but a handful of aspirants. Nevertheless, the feeling was widespread that British India was a cultural wasteland. When Mrs Hauksbee (in 'The Education of Otis Yeere') proposes to set up a salon in Simla, Mrs Mallowe quickly dissuades her: not only is a man's mental energy entirely absorbed by his official work—'"You can't focus anything in India"'; there isn't enough social stability to support an intellectual culture.

[4] *Something of Myself*, p. 74.

Free of both the support and the constraints of a literary establishment, Kipling adapted his style and voice to the tastes of his newspaper readers. Like Lippi's fellow-monks, they were quick to pass judgement on his work. At the same time, his own need to find a place for himself in a closed, stratified society made the young journalist especially sensitive to their criticism. Busy men all, they placed a high value on speed: encouraged by the tight format imposed by the *Civil and Military Gazette*, Kipling achieved a compression hitherto unknown in nineteenth-century English letters. Doers rather than theorists, they looked for a fiction that engaged the everyday world: Kipling went to his French and American contemporaries for lessons in the new realism, adopting from Maupassant and Zola a disillusioned scepticism and from Mark Twain and Bret Harte a disarming good humour and colloquial ease of diction. Literate if not literary, the men of the Punjab Club welcomed a prose that captured the pace and wit of good club talk: Kipling embellished the surfaces of his fiction with irony and allusion, appealing to his readers with the flattering knowingness that soon became his trademark.

Kipling developed his characteristic voice in the 'Plain Tales from the Hills' of 1886 and 1887. The presiding teller of those tales is the breezy, cynical reporter, the knowing observer of a community to which he himself belongs. The model was Mark Twain in his role of frontier journalist, the Mark Twain of *Roughing It*, whose tall stories both celebrate and poke fun at the eccentricities of frontier life. But though Kipling never abandoned all the stylistic mannerisms of these early tales, he soon began to show signs of impatience with the limitations this voice imposed. Already in the 'Plain Tales' he had begun to experiment with the more romantic voice of Mulvaney and with a deepening of feeling in the reporter's own treatment of love and death.[5]

[5] I have discussed the development of Kipling's prose at greater length in *Kipling in India* (1966); see especially chapters 4 and 5. The present discussion of narrative voice—and of the soldier stories in general—owes much to a penetrating essay by J. H. Fenwick, 'Soldiers Three', in *Kipling's Mind and Art*, ed. Andrew Rutherford (1964).

The stories of '88 highlight the importance Kipling attached to voice—each tale can be seen as an experiment in presentation. Kipling's first challenge was to get his own narrative voice out of the stories. An extreme solution was to present the material entirely in dialogue, as in 'The Hill of Illusion' and *The Story of the Gadsbys*. But this technique invites awkward questions: are we meant to be eavesdropping on the characters; should we consider ourselves readers of a play script? More effectively dramatic are the monologues of the Indian speakers—the device, learned from Robert Browning, of having the monologist address himself to an implied listener gives ironic humour to the chicanery of 'Gemini' and unprecedented force to the heroic and obsessed narrators of 'In Flood Time' and 'Dray Wara Yow Dee'. Here we never ask why the speaker chooses to tell his tale: as in the best of Browning's monologues, he is driven to speak from the sheer pressure of his personality; he must sing the song of himself in order to ease his heart of its burden.

Contrast 'Dray Wara Yow Dee' with 'At Twenty-Two'. Kipling could have told the story of the mine disaster using the voice of one of the principals. Instead, he employs a detached narration that drastically lowers the emotional temperature. The effect of chill is similar in other stories told in the same manner, whether the tone is comic, as in 'The Education of Otis Yeere' and 'The Judgment of Dungara', or sardonic, as in 'At the Pit's Mouth' and 'A Wayside Comedy'. Taking the narrator out of the action seems to remove an essential source of control: the Hauskbee–Mallowe conversations go on too long, Bobby Wick's devotion to duty is too single-minded, the Tertium Quid's death is as unmotivated as it is nasty. At the same time, we miss the knowingness, the sentimentality, the self-directed irony of the youthful reporter. It is significant that in the last three stories in this volume—among the finest Kipling ever wrote—the presence of the narrator and his complex relation to characters and events immeasurably deepen the richness of effect.

There remains the case of 'Baa Baa, Black Sheep'. Here alone an omniscient narrator stands outside the tale, in the

manner of Dickens, so as to recruit the reader to an overtly
held moral position. But though 'Baa Baa, Black Sheep'
succeeds in enlisting our sympathy, the narrative mode does
not show Kipling at his best: the pressure to take sides with
Punch is too relentless. Allowance must be made for
Kipling's closeness to the autobiographical raw material. We
know he felt the weight of the experience as he wrote; we may
speculate that the awkwardness of the narrative stance comes
in part from the unacknowledged presence of the two readers
for whom the tale was, consciously or unconsciously,
designed: the author's mother and father.

III

Whatever its aesthetic merits, 'Baa Baa, Black Sheep' provides an indispensable key to the attitudes and themes
expressed in Kipling's fiction.[6] The outline of the story is
faithful to the crucial experience of the author's childhood.
Little Punch is taken by his parents from India—where he
has enjoyed a life of ease, affection, and beauty—and
deposited, without explanation, in a strange English household that he finds, from the outset, physically and morally
repulsive. Here he is first deprived of the love he has come to
expect, then subjected to a baffling and humiliating discipline. The woman of the house mounts a relentless attack on
his selfhood, an attack motivated by the inexplicable
demands of her harsh Evangelicalism. Is he, in some obscure
way, responsible for his own predicament? Aunty Rosa's
creed, in which guilt and suffering play a central role,
encourages him to accept this intolerable suggestion. Finally,
after he has lost all hope that he will awaken from the

---

[6] Kipling's three versions of the Southsea years—the other two are given
in *The Light that Failed* and *Something of Myself*—have been discussed by all
his biographers. My own view of the effect of the experience on his writings
has been chiefly influenced by Elliot L. Gilbert's thoughtful essay, 'To
Whom Does Kipling Speak Today?' in the *Kipling Journal* (December,
1965). My earlier conclusions about the bleakness of Kipling's world view
were strongly reinforced by Alan Sandison's masterly study of the imperial
idea, *The Wheel of Empire* (1967).

nightmare, he is rescued from the House of Desolation by the
same loving mother who first abandoned him there.

The pressure of feeling that gives emotional impact to 'Baa
Baa, Black Sheep' lends its power to a number of Kipling's
fictions. 'The Strange Ride of Morrowbie Jukes' and 'The
Phantom 'Rickshaw'—the earliest of the stories in this
volume—concern men who find themselves abandoned.
Trapped at the bottom of a sand-pit, Jukes is deprived,
through the most arbitrary of accidents, of proper food,
decent shelter, and suitable companions. Reduced to a bare
struggle for existence, he has become as dependent as a child
upon the ministrations of a man for whom he feels nothing
but hostility and contempt. On the face of it Jack Pansay's
predicament seems quite unrelated. And yet he, too, finds
himself trapped, isolated from his fellows in a world between
life and death, doomed to wander forever in 'the dark
labyrinths of doubt, misery, and utter despair'. Both victims
yearn only for a return to the ordinary pleasures of the
daylight world.

These are nightmare stories: clumsily motivated, they rely
on the author's ability to make his readers feel the effect of his
own bad dreams. As Kipling's gifts matured, he learned to
embody the theme of abandonment, of isolation, in more
plausible situations. Durga Dass, the hoodwinked money-
lender of 'Gemini', robbed of his cash and accounts, is fully
exposed to the hatred and contempt of the villagers. 'At
Twenty-Two' traps the protagonists in the depths of the
earth; they extricate themselves from the mine shaft by skill
and energy but remain trapped in an age-old pattern of lust
and greed. The Pathan horse-dealer of 'Dray Wara Yow Dee'
scours the north of India in search of his rival; isolated by his
obsession from all human relationships, he is the trapped and
helpless victim of his society's code of vengeance.

Compare 'The Phantom 'Rickshaw' with 'The Hill of
Illusion'. The eloping couple of the later story, proposing to
cut themselves off from society, look forward with dismay to
a lifetime of mutual distrust. No supernatural machinery is
required to isolate them from their fellows: they are the
architects of their own trap. Otis Yeere seems almost ready to

scramble out of the pit of his own mediocrity when a natural impulse of affection for his would-be deliverer frightens Mrs Hauksbee into abandoning him to the isolation of his dreary Bengal district. Chance has thrown together the ill-assorted European residents of Kashima; now they are held fast within the rock-tipped circle of the Dosehri hills, trapped as surely as Jukes at the bottom of his sand pit. They have not been snatched, like Jukes, from the everyday world of Anglo-Indian society and thrust into a nightmare. On the contrary, for them the everyday world is their nightmare, their own society the beginning and end of their doom.

Written in 1888, 'Baa Baa, Black Sheep' helps knit together these earlier explorations of the theme of isolation and abandonment. The kinship of the little boy in the House of Desolation with the engineer in the sand-pit has not gone unrecognized; but it should be clear by now that Kipling's imagination sought and found many ways of expressing indirectly the meaning of that central childhood experience.

And yet he did not—more probably could not—address the autobiographical material directly until he had moved from the parental home in Lahore. Though no record of their reaction is known to me, the son must have recognized that the parents could not have read an account of his childhood suffering without pain. The fact that he did write it supports the conclusion the narrator draws: 'When young lips have drunk deep of the bitter waters of Hate, Suspicion, and Despair, all the Love in the world will not wholly take away that knowledge.' This is not to say that the tale is an indictment of the parents. Acting, as they believed, for the best, they did only what was sanctioned by Anglo-Indian custom; son and parents remained on loving terms as long as the parents lived. But if a loved and loving parent cannot be blamed for the infliction of such memorable suffering, the indictment must be directed elsewhere. It can only be that the order of the world is deeply flawed. If human love, whether between mother and son or man and woman, renders us so vulnerable, then our lives must be subject to an inscrutable authority very different from the traditional God of benevolence and justice. Under these obscure auspices, any of us might, at any time, be snatched up and locked away in the House of Desolation, there to wear out an indefinite sentence from which there is no appeal.

IV

'Baa Baa, Black Sheep' concludes on a sombre note, but the effect of the story is the reverse of dispiriting. Although Punch's antagonists bring all their force to bear upon their helpless victim, they are unable to break his will. With no expectation of rescue, he not only defies his tormentors but persists in his loyalty to his sister and in the development of his own intellect and imagination. At the same time, there is no suggestion that the happy ending is the consequence of his refusal to give in: arbitrarily abandoned, he is as arbitrarily rescued; the only reward for his fortitude is the reader's sympathetic admiration. In that sense, the ending is irrelevant to the meaning of the story: what counts is the child's successful struggle to maintain his integrity in a world devoid of hope or solace.

Most of the stories in the present collection focus on the actions of men and women who find themselves isolated, like Punch, in just such a desolate and hostile world. The scenes are set in India, where the conditions of existence pose specific problems for both Indian natives and British invaders; but Kipling's India is unmistakably situated in the larger intellectual world of the late nineteenth century, when alert and sensitive thinkers recognized that the God of Things as They Should Be—the personal God of the Christian centuries—had withdrawn in favour of the God of Things as They Are.

This stern divinity is given a name and cult in 'The Judgment of Dungara', a tale more complex than might first appear. Justus Krenk of the Tübingen Mission competes with Athon Dazé, priest of Dungara, the God of Things as They Are, for the souls of the 'naked, good-tempered, timid, shameless, lazy Buria Kol'. Holding many of Western society's strong cards—agriculture and medicine, logical argument and humanitarian concern—Justus wins the first few hands. But Athon Dazé has an ace up his sleeve. When he plays it, the God of Things as They Should Be suffers a spectacular defeat: Justus departs, determined to study botany, and the little mission reverts to jungle.

On one level 'The Judgment of Dungara' is a simple fable of colonial rule. In contrast to the Krenks, Gallio, the English Assistant Collector, knows and accepts the conditions of life in his remote district. Claiming indifference to religious beliefs, he accepts the jurisdiction of the God of Things as They Are, colluding with Athon Dazé and intervening in the lives of the Buria Kol only to protect them from the most pressing dangers. On the face of it, he would seem to be an early version of Kipling's ideal colonial officer, benign, dedicated, realistic to the point of cynicism. From the perspective of Indian administration, he is right and the Krenks are wrong. The mission fails, not just because the Krenks are ignorant of the properties of the local flora, but because they have deluded themselves into believing that they can change cultural patterns almost as profound as human nature itself. They are judged by the God of Things as They Are and found wanting, for Dungara is but another name for the Gods of the Copybook Headings, the lords of everyday reality, who 'showed us each in turn / That Water would certainly wet us, as Fire would certainly burn'.[7]

But for all the slapstick comedy of the dénouement, the game is being played for high stakes. Gallio—'with a longing for absolute power which his undesirable District gratified'—is named, of course, for the imperial official who refused to intervene in the dispute between Saint Paul and the Jews of Corinth, a type, with Pilate, of the worldly man damned for refusing to take sides.[8] The modern Gallio may be a shrewd administrator, but under his authority the Buria Kol will continue to feud with their neighbours and leave their surplus children to die. The missionaries, though Kipling mocks their childlike enthusiasm, are granted a large

[7] *The Definitive Edition of Rudyard Kipling's Verse* (1940), p. 793.

[8] For Kipling's continuing interest in the biblical Gallio, see Angus Wilson's helpful analysis in *The Strange Ride of Rudyard Kipling* (1977), pp. 337–40.

measure of sympathy. The warmth of their humanity, like the strength of their commitment, is never called into question. Five paragraphs at the beginning of the story invoke the loneliness of the calling—'isolation that weighs upon the waking eyelids and drives you by force headlong into the labours of the day'. Gallio laughs at the desertion of the converts, but then the laughter dies out of his eyes. From the perspective of the author of 'Baa Baa, Black Sheep', in other words, the administrator acknowledges his kinship with the innocent missionaries. Committed to a life of isolation and misunderstanding, all three are inmates of the House of Desolation. Like Punch, they earn our sympathetic admiration not in proportion to their success but because they act resolutely in the face of a world that mocks or ignores their lonely endeavours.

V

Gallio may prosper in the short term because he recognizes in Dungara a genuine if crude avatar of the God of Things as They Are; but Justus will study his botany and return to the lonely struggle in some other undesirable District, his enthusiasm perhaps backed by a greater respect for the conditions of everyday existence. Nor will Kipling reject the possibility that in the long run Justus may have a deeper insight than Gallio into the shape of ultimate reality.[9] But in the interval there remains the problem of what constitutes meaningful action on this earth, in the India of the 1880s, within the specific constraints imposed by nationality, sex, age, profession, and caste.

The isolation of Kipling's protagonists does not liberate them from these constraints. On the contrary, what is

---

[9] That is, although Kipling emphasizes the need to see the facts of life in this world as clearly as possible, he does not rule out the possibility that—as the great religions teach us—the earth we know may be but a shadow of the true reality. At the end of time, when the world's genuine artists are liberated from the need to work for money and fame, 'each for the joy of the working, and each, in his separate star, / Shall draw the Thing as he sees It for the God of Things as They are!' ('When Earth's Last Picture Is Painted', 1892).

required of the man in the trap is that he obey the laws of his caste or calling despite the pressure to break them. There is little to Morrowbie Jukes beyond the conventional prejudices of a pukka sahib—his profession of engineer underscores his lack of imagination—but he remains true to these simple standards throughout his ordeal: Pansay, by contrast, insists on his failures as a lover and a gentleman, and under the pressure of his haunting his personality collapses. Excuses are made for Judy in 'Baa Baa, Black Sheep'—she is a little girl of winning manners, too young to be fully subject to the conditions of her upbringing—but the story projects a clear sense of disappointment that she can be so easily won over to Aunty Rosa's side. If Punch's resistance is to succeed, he must remain the unrepentant sahib, scornfully dismissive of Negroes, Jews, and the sons of shopkeepers. For him to relinquish these prejudices would be to put his integrity at risk: crude armatures, they must be accepted as part of the bracing necessary to his present survival.

The Indian setting of the early stories emphasizes the need to stick by the laws of caste. Everyday life in India imposed extraordinary strains; nature and society presented the harshest conditions to rulers and subjects alike. The English suffered under almost intolerable burdens of frustration and overwork; the Indians passively accepted a social and economic order that condemned most of them to a life of grinding hardship. Such strains appeared supportable only by the most rigid of structures. Kipling's world is braced by an elaborate gridwork consisting of the barriers that separate women from men, Indians from Europeans, civilians from soldiers, Hindus from Muslims, rich from poor, tribe from tribe, caste from caste. These barriers might give occasion for regret—some of Kipling's most moving stories celebrate love's defiance of all prohibitions—but they are breached at peril: so much rigidity is built into the structure that no individual can threaten its integrity and hope to prevail.

In the more common situation, the individual is confronted with the strain that gave rise to the barriers in the first place; success or failure is measured in terms of his ability to maintain the values of his caste or calling in the face of the challenge presented by Indian life. Either outcome serves to confirm the need for the structure, not the individual's right to question or subvert it. At its most schematic, this framework allows for little flexibility in the delineation of character. Bobby Wick, the hero of 'Only a Subaltern', has no choice but to act out his role as exemplary junior officer, first seeing Private Dormer through a personal crisis, then nursing him during an attack of cholera at the cost of his own life. Responsibility entails sacrifice: this, Kipling tells us, is the code of honour that enables a small band of soldiery to garrison a hostile subcontinent. The larger question of whether it is honourable for the British to govern by force is never allowed to arise; Bobby maintains the ideals of his caste and calling; no more is asked of him.

The guardian of the ford embodies an even simpler idea of heroism. His test in the flooded Barhwi confirms the value of his code: his youthful ardour is a match for the river; he endures better than the railway bridge, even though in the end traffic will desert the ford for the greater efficiency of the fire-chariots. The Pathan horse-dealer and the avaricious old miner present a less simple affirmation. Though the codes they live by are narrow in the extreme, they hold to them with a tenacity that entails a kind of moral heroism. It is futile to argue, as some have done, that they represent false and biased portraits of the Indian character. Inhabitants of a world simplified to the point of bleakness, they look forward to the barely humanized machines and animals of Kipling's middle period, whose only function is to fulfil with integrity the roles assigned to them in a world of whose outlines they are scarcely conscious.

When Kipling shifts his focus from Indian to English society, there is a modest gain in the complexity of his characters and the situations in which they find themselves. The heroism of Bobby Wick carries weightier implications than the heroism of the keeper of the ford. 'At Twenty-Two' treats the adulterous relationship of Kundoo and Unda with cool irony; it is far otherwise with the English civilians who play tennis with the Seventh Commandment: theirs are stories of conspicuous moral failure. Subverting the rules of

their caste and creed, they threaten the rigid monogamy that
alone can preserve the family against the terrible strains of
Indian life. In terms that seem excessively harsh for an
admirer of Thomas Hardy and a coeval of W. B. Yeats,
Kipling virtually dismisses the claims of individual passion.
Least sympathy is granted to the Man's Wife and the
Tertium Quid: they flout the rules; their punishment is
arbitrary, brutal, and swift. Kurrell and the Boultes are
granted a trace more understanding—the strain of life in
Kashima might almost excuse behaviour that would be
reprehensible among the frivolities of Simla, where Mrs
Hauksbee can manipulate the career and affections of Otis
Yeere with impunity, so long as the proprieties are strictly
observed. 'The Hill of Illusion', for all the stilted character of
its dialogue, represents an honourable attempt to explore the
implications of a painful moral choice. But for the most part,
the stories I have discussed so far allow only the narrowest
scope for significant action. Their protagonists, whether
Indian or British, confront a meaningless world with the
bewilderment of the man in the sand-pit or the little boy in
the House of Desolation. Condemned to Indian life as if by
the will of an incomprehensible deity, Kipling's men and
women have no choice but to affirm or reject the rigid code
that alone will ensure their survival. They fight their lonely
battles in a moral universe that allows for little or no complexity of feeling. Escape remains a remote possibility;
assertion of the self, or even a deepened awareness of the
possibilities of being, are all but out of the question.

VI

Of the stories Kipling wrote in India, the more interesting
involve characters who do not merely affirm the rules of caste
and calling. Compare 'Only a Subaltern' and 'With the Main
Guard'. Both stories are about the soldier's vocation, with its
demand for sacrifice off the battlefield as well as on it, but
there the resemblance ends. Behind Bobby Wick lies all the
weight of a tradition that obliges him to take grave risks for
the sake of his subordinates. By sacrificing his life for Private

Dormer he affirms the military code. But though the circumstances are carefully rendered, the action is viewed from a
distance; the hero's ordeal, though difficult, is not complex,
and the conclusion is never in doubt. In order to be moved by
the action, we have to suspend an uncomfortable feeling that
Kipling is reading us a tract.

With Mulvaney we are on different ground. Kipling's
social affinities were with the officer class, yet none of his
subalterns really comes to life; wary of questioning the code
they live by, he views them as if through a haze of uncritical
approval. But though he might be flattered by the good
opinion of the Other Ranks, the young reporter knew he
would not be called to account for misrepresenting what was
for him and his Indian readers almost an alien caste. Mulvaney, Ortheris, and Learoyd are creatures of his imagination: he is free not only to make them larger than life, but to
place them in ambiguous relations with their military calling.

In their earliest appearance in the 'Plain Tales' the three
are introduced as tricksters and scamps, 'the worst men in
the regiment, so far as genial blackguardism goes'. It soon
becomes clear, however, that they pose no real threat to the
military establishment. Their first victim is a pretentious
globe-trotter; Lungtungpen is taken, however eccentrically;
an unsuitable elopement is frustrated; drunken recruits are
kept in order; the victim of Learoyd's dog-stealing deserves
to be defrauded. Like Stalky and his mates, with whom they
are often compared, the three stand for a healthy irreverence
that mocks the establishment while advancing its cause by
unconventional means.

But unlike the three schoolboys, for whom the College is a
training field they know better than to take seriously, the
soldiers are grown men committed to a life that assigns them
the lowest rank in a service that polite society holds in
contempt. Alongside the stories that celebrate their imaginative knavery runs a far more impressive series that
emphasizes the hardship of their lot. Beginning with 'The
Daughter of the Regiment' and 'The Madness of Private
Ortheris', continuing through 'Black Jack' and 'With the
Main Guard', culminating in 'The Courting of Dinah Shadd'

and 'On Greenhow Hill', these tales of sorrow and loss provide a sombre counterpoint to what would otherwise be a sequence of light-hearted escapades.

That these men are trapped in a desolate world goes almost without saying. Desertion, the only escape route, is tested and rejected in 'The Madness of Private Ortheris'; progress through the ranks is scarcely a possibility for Ortheris and Learoyd, and in Mulvaney's case is thwarted by his inability to overcome his need for drink. In these bleak circumstances the three assert themselves, like so many of Kipling's characters, by a resolute adherence to their professional code; masters of the soldier's arts, they are sustained by a fierce pride in their craft. But this is not the whole story. Kipling found in them, and especially in Mulvaney, a scope for moral action denied to most of his other protagonists, and with this broadening of scope comes a new depth of feeling and complexity of theme.

I have referred to 'With the Main Guard' in terms of the sacrifice demanded of the soldier in time of peace; comparison with 'Only a Subaltern' reveals the difference in quality. There is nothing singular about the ordeal described in 'With the Main Guard': fort duty on a stifling June night, with the narrator suffering alongside his friends. A threat of death—by heat exhaustion or suicide—hovers in the thick air. Putting aside his own discomfort, Mulvaney distracts them with his story of the fight at Silver's Theatre. It is a brilliant stroke. The style and wit of his narrative bring the battle vividly to life; the circumstances of the telling overcome our natural resistance to the bloodthirstiness he describes. Afterwards, the encounter with the child—however difficult for the modern reader to accept—has the effect of leaving Ortheris and Learoyd thoroughly cheered up. But at the very end the story takes a darker turn, for Mulvaney's effort has left him exhausted.

He looked at me wearily; his eyes were sunk in his head, and his face was drawn and white. 'Eyah!' said he; 'I've blandandhered thim through the night somehow, but can thim that helps others help thimsilves? Answer me that, sorr!'

And over the bastions of Fort Amara broke the pitiless day.

xxx   INTRODUCTION

This sombre ending confirms the story's deeper intention. For Mulvaney is dedicated not to the soldier's calling alone. His gifts as a story-teller, together with his willingness to use them to solace his companions, give him a significance that Kipling grants to few of his characters. Mulvaney has come to represent the artist. The night at Fort Amara stands for all the boredom and hopelessness of life, not just for the private soldier in India but for every inhabitant of Kipling's bleak world. Condemned along with the rest of us to this House of Desolation, the artist can still choose, as Mulvaney does, to employ his gift to comfort his fellows, at whatever cost to himself. 'With the Main Guard' joins 'The Children of the Zodiac' in asserting Kipling's deepest convictions about the moral significance of the artist's vocation.

'Black Jack' illuminates the storyteller's art from a different angle. As with the earlier tale, Mulvaney's narrative is set in a rather elaborate frame. In both cases the young reporter meets his friends in circumstances that emphasize the harshness of the soldier's lot. But whereas in 'With the Main Guard' the relation of frame to inner narrative is one of simple contrast—the stifling inactivity of the fort against the violence of the battle—in 'Black Jack' the relation is of another order of complexity. Unjustly condemned to punishment duty and prevented by the laws of his calling from taking revenge on his superior, Mulvaney deflects his feelings into a reminiscence of his years in the Black Tyrone. It is a complex story of conspiracy and vengeance. Vulmea and his fellows make an attempt on the life of Sergeant O'Hara, planning to put the blame on Mulvaney; Mulvaney turns the tables, incidentally avenging himself upon Vulmea. On one level, then, 'Black Jack' shows how Mulvaney can overcome his frustration by recalling a situation that gave him scope for vigorous and successful action.

But the inner narrative of plot and counter-plot is set within the wider context of O'Hara's story. Like Mulvaney a strong man and a fine soldier, he will not be turned aside from his fatal course by Mulvaney's prudent advice:

'"Ye're a bould man," sez he, breathin' harrd. "A very bould man.

But I am a bould man tu. Do you go your ways, Privit Mulvaney, an'
I will go mine."'

In the end O'Hara's way leads him to death at the hands of
Rafferty, who kills him in yet another stroke of vengeance:
'"He wint his own way too well—Eyah, too well!"'
Mulvaney's judgement takes us to the heart of the story. For
the purpose of the tale is not just to relieve the teller's
feelings. 'Black Jack' is a meditation on the theme of revenge;
but Mulvaney has thought long and hard about the larger
problem of moral action within the rigid framework of army
life: the story of O'Hara and Vulmea embodies the wisdom
the harsh years have brought. Ortheris seizes the point with
characteristic quickness; Mulvaney, he recognizes, has told
the story in order to remind them all, himself included, that
the laws governing their lives forbid them to go their own
way, however great the need to prove their manhood. The
story-teller, in other words, is no mere entertainer. Through
the medium of his narrative art he conveys to his fellows
whatever understanding of reality his sufferings have helped
him to achieve.

Unlike the other protagonists of the stories Kipling wrote
in India, Mulvaney transcends the condition of isolation and
abandonment in which he finds himself. He does not merely
endure. Unable to change his world or escape it, he has come
to terms with it through intellectual analysis and imaginative
representation. His stories, like those of his creator, help
sustain us by defining the limits and celebrating the renewals
that life in the House of Desolation affords.

VII

The last two stories in the present collection—'On the City
Wall' and 'The Man who would be King'—differ in significant ways from the other fiction Kipling wrote in India. The
theme of entrapment is no longer expressed through concrete
images. Gone are the sand-pit and the mine shaft, the stifling
guard room and the rock-tipped circle of the Dosehri Hills.
These stories take us out of the sphere of private suffering

and determined endurance: their protagonists are given a larger measure of freedom; the author addresses public themes of conquest and rule, authority and justice.

No House of Desolation, Lalun's apartment on the City wall commands an extensive view.

If you fell from the broad window-seat you dropped thirty feet sheer into the City Ditch. But if you stayed where you should and looked forth, you saw all the cattle of the City being driven down to water, the students of the Government College playing cricket, the high grass and trees that fringed the river-bank, the great sand-bars that ribbed the river, the red tombs of dead Emperors beyond the river, and very far away through the blue heat-haze a glint of the snows of the Himalayas.

Wali Dad spends hours at a time gazing from Lalun's window, brooding over a prospect that symbolizes the past and present of his native Punjab. Between the City Ditch and the faraway mountains lies the river, where the peasants still drive their cattle down to water next to the playing fields of the anglicized students of the Government College. Emblem of both continuity and division, the river links the Himalayan snows to the fertile meadows outside the walls, where bucolic tradition rubs shoulders with hybrid modernity; but at the same time the river divides the ancient tombs of the Mughal Emperors from the teeming nineteenth-century city where the action of the story takes place.

Unique among Kipling's Indian tales, 'On the City Wall' addresses itself to contemporary politics. The scene is set in Lahore, capital of the Punjab, which had been annexed to the Raj in 1849 against fierce Sikh resistance. In 1872 Sikh fundamentalists rose against the British; the leader of the revolt, Ram Singh, was exiled to Burma, where he died in 1885. 'On the City Wall' takes place against the background of these events. The plot turns on a conspiracy to free an aged rebel named Khem Singh, recently repatriated from Burma, and use him as the spearhead of a new rising. The rescue of Khem Singh succeeds, but the planned rebellion falls flat: the days of armed mutiny belong irrevocably to a vanished past. When he discovers that the younger generation of

Indians would rather co-operate with the Raj than die with their back to the mouth of a gun, the old warrior returns peaceably to a comfortable detention in Fort Amara.

At the centre of this complex story stands Wali Dad. He personifies the dilemma forced upon talented young Indians by the British occupation. High intelligence and a European education have left him disdainful of his own countrymen, yet he sees with bitter clarity that collaboration with the conquerors would only bring him a lifetime of humiliating slights. Rejecting both worlds, he spends his time with Lalun the courtesan, gazing from her window and composing poems. The view he observes reflects his own situation. He dreams of great men and heroic deeds; but between the red tombs of dead Emperors and the modern City runs the river, dividing the prosaic students and peasants of the 1880s from the martial past. Khem Singh is a relic of that past, '"an Interesting Survival"', as Wali Dad describes him. '"He was once a great man. There will never be any more great men in India."' But despite the young poet's cynical conclusion, he is led by romantic nostalgia to join the conspiracy; and then, caught up in the turmoil of the Mohurrum festival, he abandons both his modern scepticism and his responsibility to the conspirators in an orgy of sectarian fervour.

Kipling's feelings about his protagonist are uncharacteristically complex. As in most of the stories of this period, the hero is faced with a test. But unlike characters in parallel situations, Wali Dad is not required to affirm or reject the rules of his profession or tribe. Wandering between two worlds, he has no valid set of rules to fall back on. His European education has detached him from his own tradition, yet he cannot unlearn what he knows; when he does revert to the religion of his childhood, he fails the conspiracy. Though Kipling insists that the conspiracy is a futile and pernicious dream, he shares Wali Dad's fascination with a life of martial action: the story clearly suggests that the young poet might have done better to have played his part in this bad cause than revert to childish religious excitement.

To put it another way, Kipling allows his protagonist unusual freedom of choice but grants him no acceptable options. For the story implicitly rejects the one possibility that would provide scope for Wali Dad's combination of gifts: a life of public responsibility in an independent modern India. India, the narrator asserts, 'will never stand alone'.

But the idea is a pretty one, and men are willing to die for it, and yearly the work of pushing and coaxing and scolding and petting the country into good living goes forward. If an advance be made all credit is given to the native, while the Englishmen stand back and wipe their foreheads. If a failure occurs the Englishmen step forward and take the blame. Overmuch tenderness of this kind has bred a strong belief among many natives that the native is capable of administering the country, and many devout Englishmen believe this also, because the theory is stated in beautiful English with all the latest political colours.

Thus Kipling reduces the dream of an independent India to the level of the other delusive choices facing Wali Dad. The young Muslim ends where he began, gazing from Lalun's window at a homeland he can only observe, never possess, writing witty subversive poems about his one futile venture into the life of action.

There are significant points of comparison between 'On the City Wall' and 'The Man who would be King'. Like Wali Dad, Daniel Dravot and Peachey Carnehan are adrift between worlds: though they despise the native Indians, they are not accepted as citizens of the British raj, for they have cut loose from the network of responsibility and privilege that holds the European community together. Granted a large measure of freedom, they are not called upon to prove themselves worthy of any caste or profession. Though they share Wali Dad's cynical view of Indian politics, they commit themselves, as he does, to a harebrained scheme of conquest. The narrator's comment on the Indian conspirators could apply equally to Dan and Peachey: 'There are other men who, though uneducated, see visions and dream dreams, and they, too, hope to administer the country in their own way—that is to say, with a garnish of Red Sauce.' All three set their dreams against reality, which strikes them down in retaliation.

'"Perhaps he wishes to be a King,"' says Wali Dad of

Khem Singh: 'The Man who would be King' explores the proposition that two strong men, free of the constraints of the Pax Britannica, might succeed in creating a veritable kingdom out of a blank spot on the map. As with 'On the City Wall', the action is played against a backdrop of recent history: Dan and Peachey imagine themselves emulating the almost legendary exploits of Sir James Brooke, the English soldier who pacified Borneo and ended as Rajah of Sarawak. But Kipling looks with grave scepticism upon such efforts to impose imaginative visions upon the real world. Peachey and Dan are allowed to succeed for a time, provided they recognize and act upon the facts of their situation. The Contrack, which binds them to resist their weakness for liquor and women, represents such a recognition; by facing up to their limitations they gain power over themselves. In the wild lands, where the artificial rules of civilization no longer hold them back, their real skill at disguise, diplomacy, and battle gives them the advantage over the primitive tribesmen.

But they are not as free from societal restraints as might first appear. They are linked to society, in a curious way, by their membership in the masonic order, an alternative society that nevertheless requires strict obedience to its own rules. At the beginning of the tale they exploit the masonic connection to win a favour from the narrator, overcoming his reluctance to help a pair of desperadoes who reject the sahibs' code. Later they discover that against all probability, the Kafiristani tribesmen too practise a form of Freemasonry. Once again they exploit their membership in the order, but this time they violate the rules, claiming a masonic rank to which they have no shadow of a title.

'At the levee which was held that night on the hillside with big bonfires, Dravot gives out that him and me were Gods and sons of Alexander, and Past Grand-Masters in the Craft, and was come to make Kafiristan a country where every man should eat in peace and drink in quiet, and 'specially obey us.'

By making these wildly inflated claims, which the tribesmen accept as truth, Dan and Peachey violate not only the masonic code but the actualities of their situation. Reality asserts itself with ferocious suddenness. The moment the fact of their humanity is exposed, the whole basis of their authority collapses; the tribesmen revolt, Dan is killed, and Peachey is driven forth to bring the extraordinary tale back to the humdrum world of the newspaper office.

In the manner of the telling, 'The Man who would be King' is beyond praise. Kipling never surpassed himself; every touch contributes to the effect of the whole. But though the outlines are so clear that the story has been made into a successful action film, the meaning remains rich and complex. This complexity derives not so much from the characters of Peachey and Dan—they are drawn with broad and simple strokes—as from the issues the tale presents. Ruthless in the pursuit of his ambition, Dravot possesses at the same time extraordinary gifts of will and imagination. Not only does he make a kingdom: by acknowledging the responsibilities that accompany power, he grows towards a validation of the authority his arms have won. The two adventurers embody the idea of the conquistador, the military commander who imposes a superior culture upon his defeated enemies, and thus they arouse the contradictory feelings that inevitably attach to this figure. Against the prosaic background of an India kept in order by an efficient civil service, knit together by the railway, linked to Europe by telegraph, Dravot and Carnehan stand for the martial energy and imperial will that established the raj in an earlier day.

At the same time, Dravot poses the contradiction of the tragic hero. Larger than life, though neither good nor just he compels our admiration and involves us in his fate. Like the heroes of Greek tragedy, he is guilty of sacrilege; but the god he defies is neither pagan nor Christian: it is the presiding deity of the sceptical nineteenth century, the shadowy but omnipotent divinity that Kipling names the God of Things as They Are. Dravot's sin, like that of the conspirators surrounding Khem Singh, is to attempt to impose upon modern reality the dreams that belong properly to poetry, history, and legend. What propels Dan and Peachey into their adventure is a refusal to admit what is obvious to all around them: the fact that they are a couple of boastful vagabonds whose lack of self-discipline has condemned them to a shifty existence beyond the pale of Anglo-Indian society. And yet, what reader has ever thought the less of them for their refusal? In Kipling's view they are enmeshed in the toils of the ultimate trap, the human condition as revealed once and for all to the little boy abandoned by his parents in the House of Desolation. The heroic are those who refuse to capitulate, but the only mode of heroism presented to most of Kipling's characters is a life of dutiful service followed by an obscure death. Peachey and Dan are granted a larger fate. Their crazy defiance of the God of Things as They Are opens the door to a world beyond the confines of the trap, a world where will and energy can be expressed, for once, in meaningful action, even though the consequences involve the actors in a catastrophic downfall.

NOTE ON THE TEXT

THE textual history of the tales collected in the present volume is somewhat complex. The general circumstances of first publication are set forth in the Introduction, and specific details may be found in the Explanatory Notes to the individual stories. Most of the stories were first printed in provincial Indian newspapers and reprinted soon after in the six volumes of Wheeler's *Indian Railway Library* (1888–9): the texts of the reprinted stories were revised—in the case of the earliest, quite extensively—for the new format. The six Railway Library titles were reprinted separately in England (1890), then collected into two volumes with reset type (1892) under the titles *Soldiers Three / The Story of the Gadsbys / In Black and White*, and *Wee Willie Winkie / Under the Deodars / The Phantom 'Rickshaw / and other Stories*.

In 1895 Macmillan & Co. brought out a revised and reset text in the two-volume format; this text persisted through the many printings of Macmillan's *Uniform Edition* (1899–1947). Meanwhile, shortly before his death in 1936, Kipling revised all his works for the (limited) *Sussex Edition*; this was published in 1937–9 and stands as the definitive embodiment of his final intentions.

Commencing in 1949, Macmillan replaced their *Uniform Edition* with the *Library Edition*; the two volumes from which the present collection is drawn were published in 1950 and 1951. Though Macmillan's noted that the types were reset for this edition, nothing in the books called attention to substantive changes from the earlier *Uniform Edition* text, and the identity of the two editions has long been assumed.

Nevertheless, such changes were made. Though a full collation did not appear practicable, spot comparisons of *Library* with *Uniform* and *Sussex* strongly suggested that the texts of at least some of the stories were altered in 1950–1 so as to correspond to Kipling's final version. In the case of 'The Man who would be King', in particular, *Sussex / Library* clearly presents better readings than *Uniform*. In view of the technical problems attending the use of the *Sussex Edition*, the text of the *Library Edition* was chosen as the basis for the present anthology. At the same time, it was decided not to annotate textual variants, as the complexity of such an apparatus would be inappropriate for a reader's edition.

SELECT BIBLIOGRAPHY

THE standard bibliography is J. McG. Stewart's *Rudyard Kipling: A Bibliographical Catalogue*, ed. A. W. Yeats (1959). Reference may also be made to two earlier works: Flora V. Livingston's *Bibliography of the Works of Rudyard Kipling* (1927) with its *Supplement* (1938), and Lloyd H. Chandler's *Summary of the Work of Rudyard Kipling, Including Items ascribed to Him* (1930). We still await a bibliography which will take account of the findings of modern scholarship over the last quarter-century.

The official biography, authorized by Kipling's daughter Elsie, is Charles Carrington's *Rudyard Kipling: His Life and Work* (1955; 3rd edn., revised, 1978). Other full-scale biographies are Lord Birkenhead's *Rudyard Kipling* (1978) and Angus Wilson's *The Strange Ride of Rudyard Kipling* (1977). Briefer, copiously illustrated surveys are provided by Martin Fido's *Rudyard Kipling* (1974) and Kingsley Amis's *Rudyard Kipling and his World* (1975), which combine biography and criticism, as do the contributions to *Rudyard Kipling: the man, his work and his world* (also illustrated), ed. John Gross (1972). Information on particular periods of his life is also to be found in such works as A. W. Baldwin, *The Macdonald Sisters* (1960); Alice Macdonald Fleming (*née* Kipling), 'Some Childhood Memories of Rudyard Kipling' and 'More Childhood Memories of Rudyard Kipling', *Chambers Journal*, 8th series, vol. 8 (1939); L. C. Dunsterville, *Stalky's Reminiscences* (1928); G. C. Beresford, *Schooldays with Kipling* (1936); E. Kay Robinson, 'Kipling in India', *McClure's Magazine*, vol. 7 (1896); Edmonia Hill, 'The Young Kipling', *Atlantic Monthly*, vol. 157 (1936); *Kipling's Japan*, ed. Hugh Cortazzi and George Webb (1988); H. C. Rice, *Rudyard Kipling in New England* (1936); Frederic Van de Water, *Rudyard Kipling's Vermont Feud* (1937); Julian Ralph, *War's Brighter Side* (1901); Angela Thirkell, *Three Houses* (1931); *Rudyard Kipling to Rider Haggard: The Record of a Friendship*, ed. Morton Cohen (1965); and *'O Beloved Kids': Rudyard Kipling's Letters to his Children*, ed. Elliot L. Gilbert (1983). Useful background on the India he knew is provided by 'Philip Woodruff' (Philip Mason) in *The Men Who Ruled India* (1954), and by Pat Barr and Ray Desmond in their illustrated *Simla: A Hill Station in British India* (1978). Kipling's own autobiography, *Something of Myself* (1937), is idiosyncratic but indispensable.

The early reception of Kipling's work is usefully documented in

Kipling: The Critical Heritage, ed. Roger Lancelyn Green (1971). Richard Le Gallienne's *Rudyard Kipling: A Criticism* (1900), Cyril Falls's *Rudyard Kipling: A Critical Study* (1915), André Chevrillon's *Three Studies in English Literature* (1923) and *Rudyard Kipling* (1936), Edward Shanks's *Rudyard Kipling: A Study in Literature and Political Ideas* (1940), and Hilton Brown's *Rudyard Kipling: A New Appreciation* (1945) were all serious attempts at reassessment; while Ann M. Weygandt's study of *Kipling's Reading and Its Influence on His Poetry* (1939), and (in more old-fashioned vein) Ralph Durand's *Handbook to the Poetry of Rudyard Kipling* (1914) remain useful pieces of scholarship.

T. S. Eliot's introduction to *A Choice of Kipling's Verse* (1941; see *On Poetry and Poets*, 1957) began a period of more sophisticated reappraisal. There are influential essays by Edmund Wilson (1941; see *The Wound and the Bow*), George Orwell (1942; see his *Critical Essays*, 1946), Lionel Trilling (1943; see *The Liberal Imagination*, 1951), W. H. Auden (1943; see *New Republic*, vol. 109), and C. S. Lewis (1948; see *They Asked for a Paper*, 1962). These were followed by a series of important book-length studies which include J. M. S. Tompkins, *The Art of Rudyard Kipling* (1959); C. A. Bodelsen, *Aspects of Kipling's Art* (1964); Roger Lancelyn Green, *Kipling and the Children* (1965); Louis L. Cornell, *Kipling in India* (1966); and Bonamy Dobrée, *Rudyard Kipling: Realist and Fabulist* (1967), which follows on from his earlier studies in *The Lamp and the Lute* (1929) and *Rudyard Kipling* (1951). There were also two major collections of critical essays: *Kipling's Mind and Art*, ed. Andrew Rutherford (1964); and *Kipling and the Critics*, ed. Elliot L. Gilbert (1965). Nirad C. Chaudhuri's essay on *Kim* as 'The Finest Story about India—in English' (1957) is reprinted in John Gross's collection (see above). *The Readers' Guide to Rudyard Kipling's Work*, ed. R. E. Harbord (8 vols., privately printed, 1961–72) is an eccentric compilation, packed with useful information but by no means infallible.

Other studies devoted in whole or in part to Kipling include Richard Faber, *The Vision and the Need: Late Victorian Imperialist Aims* (1966); T. R. Henn, *Kipling* (1967); Alan Sandison, *The Wheel of Empire* (1967); Herbert L. Sussman, *Victorians and the Machine: The Literary Response to Technology* (1968); P. J. Keating, *The Working Classes in Victorian Fiction* (1971); Elliot L. Gilbert, *The Good Kipling: Studies in the Short Story* (1972); Jeffrey Meyers, *Fiction and the Colonial Experience* (1972); Shamsul Islam, *Kipling's 'Law'* (1975); J. S. Bratton, *The Victorian Popular Ballad* (1975); Philip Mason, *Kipling: The Glass, The Shadow and The Fire* (1975); John

Bayley, *The Uses of Division* (1976); M. Van Wyk Smith, *Drummer Hodge: The Poetry of the Anglo-Boer War 1899–1902* (1978); Stephen Prickett, *Victorian Fantasy* (1979); Martin Green, *Dreams of Adventure, Deeds of Empire* (1980); J. A. McClure, *Kipling and Conrad* (1981); R. F. Moss, *Rudyard Kipling and the Fiction of Adolescence* (1982); S. S. Azfar Husain, *The Indianness of Rudyard Kipling: A Study in Stylistics* (1983); Norman Page, *A Kipling Companion* (1984); B. J. Moore-Gilbert, *Kipling and 'Orientalism'* (1986); Sandra Kemp, *Kipling's Hidden Narratives* (1988); Norah Crook, *Kipling's Myths of Love and Death* (1989); and Ann Parry, *The Poetry of Rudyard Kipling* (1992); while further collections of essays include *Rudyard Kipling*, ed. Harold Bloom (1987); *Kipling Considered*, ed. Philip Mallett (1989); and *Critical Essays on Rudyard Kipling*, ed. Harold Orel (1989). Among the most important recent studies are Edward Said, *Culture and Imperialism* (1991); Sara Suleri, *The Rhetoric of English India* (1992); Zorah T. Sullivan, *Narratives of Empire: The Fictions of Rudyard Kipling* (1993); and Peter Keating, *Kipling the Poet* (1994).

Two important additions to the available corpus of Kipling's writings are *Kipling's India: Uncollected Sketches*, ed. Thomas Pinney (1986); and *Early Verse by Rudyard Kipling 1879–1889: Unpublished, Uncollected and Rarely Collected Poems*, ed. Andrew Rutherford (1986). Indispensable is Pinney's edition of *The Letters of Rudyard Kipling*, available in four volumes.

A CHRONOLOGY OF KIPLING'S LIFE AND WORKS

THE dates given here for Kipling's works are those of first authorized publication in volume form, whether this was in India, America, or England. (The dates of subsequent editions are not listed.) It should be noted that individual poems and stories collected in these volumes had in many cases appeared in newspapers or magazines of earlier dates. For full details see James McG. Stewart, *Rudyard Kipling: A Bibliographical Catalogue*, ed. A. W. Yeats, Toronto, 1959; but see also the editors' notes in this Oxford World's Classics series.

1865 Rudyard Kipling born at Bombay on 30 December, son of John Lockwood Kipling and Alice Kipling (*née* Macdonald).

1871 In December Rudyard and his sister Alice Macdonald Kipling ('Trix'), who was born in 1868, are left in the charge of Captain and Mrs Holloway at Lorne Lodge, Southsea ('The House of Desolation'), while their parents return to India.

1877 Alice Kipling returns from India in March/April and removes the children from Lorne Lodge, though Trix returns there subsequently.

1878 Kipling is admitted in January to the United Services College at Westward Ho! in Devon. First visit to France with his father that summer. (Many visits later in his life.)

1880 Meets and falls in love with Florence Garrard, a fellow-boarder of Trix's at Southsea and prototype of Maisie in *The Light that Failed*.

1881 Appointed editor of the *United Services College Chronicle*. *Schoolboy Lyrics* privately printed by his parents in Lahore, for limited circulation.

1882 Leaves school at end of summer term. Sails for India on 20 September; arrives Bombay on 18 October. Takes up post as assistant-editor of the *Civil and Military Gazette* in Lahore in the Punjab, where his father is now Principal of the Mayo College of Art and Curator of the Lahore Museum. Annual leaves from 1883 to 1888 are spent at Simla, except in 1884 when the family goes to Dalhousie.

1884 *Echoes* (by Rudyard and Trix, who has now rejoined the family in Lahore).

1885 *Quartette* (a Christmas Annual by Rudyard, Trix, and their parents).

1886 *Departmental Ditties*.

1887 Transferred in the autumn to the staff of the *Pioneer*, the *Civil and Military Gazette*'s sister-paper, in Allahabad in the North-West Provinces. As special correspondent in Rajputana he writes the articles later collected as 'Letters of Marque' in *From Sea to Sea*. Becomes friendly with Professor and Mrs Hill, and shares their bungalow.

1888 *Plain Tales from the Hills*. Takes on the additional responsibility of writing for the *Week's News*, a new publication sponsored by the *Pioneer*.

1888–9 *Soldiers Three*; *The Story of the Gadsbys*; *In Black and White*; *Under the Deodars*; *The Phantom 'Rickshaw*; *Wee Willie Winkie*.

1889 Leaves India on 9 March; travels to San Francisco with Professor and Mrs Hill via Rangoon, Singapore, Hong Kong, and Japan. Crosses the United States on his own, writing the articles later collected in *From Sea to Sea*. Falls in love with Mrs Hill's sister Caroline Taylor. Reaches Liverpool in October, and makes his début in the London literary world.

1890 Enjoys literary success, but suffers breakdown. Visits Italy. *The Light that Failed*.

1891 Visits South Africa, Australia, New Zealand, and (for the last time) India. Returns to England on hearing of the death of his American friend Wolcott Balestier. *Life's Handicap*.

1892 Marries Wolcott's sister Caroline Starr Balestier ('Carrie') in January. (The bride is given away by Henry James.) Their world tour is cut short by the loss of his savings in the collapse of the Oriental Banking Company. They establish their home at Brattleboro in Vermont, on the Balestier family estate. Daughter Josephine born in December. *The Naulahka* (written in collaboration with Wolcott Balestier). *Barrack-Room Ballads*.

1893 *Many Inventions*.

1894 *The Jungle Book*.

1895 *The Second Jungle Book*.

1896 Second daughter Elsie born in February. Quarrel with brother-in-law Beatty Balestier and subsequent court case end their stay in Brattleboro. Return to England (Torquay). *The Seven Seas.*

1897 Settles at Rottingdean in Sussex. Son John born in August. *Captains Courageous.*

1898 The first of many winters at Cape Town. Meets Sir Alfred Milner and Cecil Rhodes who becomes a close friend. Visits Rhodesia. *The Day's Work.*

1899 Disastrous visit to the United States. Nearly dies of pneumonia in New York. Death of Josephine. Never returns to USA. *Stalky and Co.*; *From Sea to Sea.*

1900 Helps for a time with army newspaper *The Friend* in South Africa during Boer War. Observes minor action at Karee Siding.

1901 *Kim.*

1902 Settles at 'Bateman's' at Burwash in Sussex. *Just So Stories.*

1903 *The Five Nations.*

1904 *Traffics and Discoveries.*

1906 *Puck of Pook's Hill.*

1907 Nobel Prize for Literature. Visit to Canada. *Collected Verse.*

1909 *Actions and Reactions*; *Abaft the Funnel.*

1910 *Rewards and Fairies.* Death of Kipling's mother.

1911 Death of Kipling's father.

1913 Visit to Egypt. *Songs from Books.*

1914–18 Visits to the Front and to the Fleet. *The New Army in Training, France at War, Sea Warfare,* and other war pamphlets.

1915 John Kipling reported missing on his first day in action with the Irish Guards in the Battle of Loos on 27 September. His body was never found.

1917 *A Diversity of Creatures.* Kipling becomes a member of the Imperial War Graves Commission.

1919 *The Years Between*; *Rudyard Kipling's Verse: Inclusive Edition.*

1920 *Letters of Travel.*

1923 *The Irish Guards in the Great War; Land and Sea Tales for Scouts and Guides.*

1924 Daughter Elsie marries Captain George Bambridge, MC.

1926 *Debits and Credits*.

1927 Voyage to Brazil.

1928 *A Book of Words*.

1930 *Thy Servant a Dog*. Visit to the West Indies.

1932 *Limits and Renewals*.

1933 *Souvenirs of France*.

1936 Kipling's death, 18 January.

1937 *Something of Myself For My Friends Known and Unknown*.

1937–9 *The Complete Works of Rudyard Kipling*, Sussex Edition. Prepared by Kipling in the last years of his life, this edition contains some previously uncollected items; but in spite of its title it does not include all his works.

1939 Death of Mrs Kipling.

1940 *The Definitive Edition of Rudyard Kipling's Verse*. This is the last of the series of 'Inclusive Editions' of his verse published in 1919, 1921, 1927, and 1933. In spite of its title the edition is far from definitive in terms of its inclusiveness or textual authority.

1948 Death of Kipling's sister Trix (Mrs John Fleming).

1976 Death of Kipling's daughter Elsie (Mrs George Bambridge).

The Man who would
be King
and Other Stories

The Strange Ride of
Morrowbie Jukes

Alive or dead—there is no other way.
Native Proverb

THERE is no invention about this tale. Jukes by accident
stumbled upon a village that is well known to exist, though he
is the only Englishman who has been there. A somewhat
similar institution used to flourish on the outskirts of Calcutta, and there is a story that if you go into the heart of
Bikanir, which is in the heart of the Great Indian Desert, you
shall come across, not a village, but a town where the Dead
who did not die, but may not live, have established their
headquarters. And, since it is perfectly true that in the same
Desert is a wonderful city where all the rich money-lenders
retreat after they have made their fortunes (fortunes so vast
that the owners cannot trust even the strong hand of the
Government to protect them, but take refuge in the waterless
sands), and drive sumptuous C-spring barouches, and buy
beautiful girls, and decorate their palaces with gold and ivory
and Minton* tiles and mother-o'-pearl, I do not see why
Jukes's tale should not be true. He is a Civil Engineer, with a
head for plans and distances and things of that kind, and he
certainly would not take the trouble to invent imaginary
traps. He could earn more by doing his legitimate work. He
never varies the tale in the telling, and grows very hot and
indignant when he thinks of the disrespectful treatment he
received. He wrote this quite straightforwardly at first, but
he has touched it up in places and introduced Moral Reflec-
tions: thus:—

In the beginning it all arose from a slight attack of fever.
My work necessitated my being in camp for some months
between Pakpattan and Mubarakpur—a desolate sandy
stretch of country as every one who has had the misfortune to
go there may know. My coolies were neither more nor less

exasperating than other gangs, and my work demanded sufficient attention to keep me from moping, had I been inclined to so unmanly a weakness.

On the 23rd December 1884 I felt a little feverish. There was a full moon at the time, and, in consequence, every dog near my tent was baying it. The brutes assembled in twos and threes and drove me frantic. A few days previously I had shot one loud-mouthed singer and suspended his carcass *in terrorem** about fifty yards from my tent-door, but his friends fell upon, fought for, and ultimately devoured the body; and, as it seemed to me, sang their hymns of thanksgiving afterwards with renewed energy.

The light-headedness which accompanies fever acts differently on different men. My irritation gave way, after a short time, to a fixed determination to slaughter one huge black-and-white beast who had been foremost in song and first in flight throughout the evening. Thanks to a shaking hand and a giddy head I had already missed him twice with both barrels of my shot-gun, when it struck me that my best plan would be to ride him down in the open and finish him off with a hog-spear. This, of course, was merely the semi-delirious notion of a fever-patient; but I remember that it struck me at the time as being eminently practical and feasible.

I therefore ordered my groom to saddle Pornic and bring him round quietly to the rear of my tent. When the pony was ready, I stood at his head prepared to mount and dash out as soon as the dog should again lift up his voice. Pornic, by the way, had not been out of his pickets for a couple of days; the night air was crisp and chilly; and I was armed with a specially long and sharp pair of persuaders* with which I had been rousing a sluggish cob that afternoon. You will easily believe, then, that when he was let go he went quickly. In one moment, for the brute bolted as straight as a die, the tent was left far behind, and we were flying over the smooth sandy soil at racing speed. In another we had passed the wretched dog, and I had almost forgotten why it was that I had taken horse and hog-spear.

The delirium of fever and the excitement of rapid motion

through the air must have taken away the remnant of my senses. I have a faint recollection of standing upright in my stirrups, and of brandishing my hog-spear at the great white moon that looked down so calmly on my mad gallop; and of shouting challenges to the camelthorn bushes as they whizzed past. Once or twice, I believe, I swayed forward on Pornic's neck, and literally hung on by my spurs—as the marks next morning showed.

The wretched beast went forward like a thing possessed, over what seemed to be a limitless expanse of moonlit sand. Next, I remember, the ground rose suddenly in front of us, and as we topped the ascent I saw the waters of the Sutlej shining like a silver bar below. Then Pornic blundered heavily on his nose, and we rolled together down some unseen slope.

I must have lost consciousness, for when I recovered I was lying on my stomach in a heap of soft white sand, and the dawn was beginning to break dimly over the edge of the slope down which I had fallen. As the light grew stronger I saw I was at the bottom of a horseshoe-shaped crater of sand, opening on one side directly on to the shoals of the Sutlej. My fever had altogether left me, and, with the exception of a slight dizziness in the head, I felt no bad effects from the fall overnight.

Pornic, who was standing a few yards away, was naturally a good deal exhausted, but had not hurt himself in the least. His saddle, a favourite polo one, was much knocked about, and had been twisted under his belly. It took me some time to put him to rights, and in the meantime I had ample opportunities of observing the spot into which I had so foolishly dropped.

At the risk of being considered tedious, I must describe it at length; inasmuch as an accurate mental picture of its peculiarities will be of material assistance in enabling the reader to understand what follows.

Imagine then, as I have said before, a horseshoe-shaped crater of sand with steeply-graded sand walls about thirty-five feet high. (The slope, I fancy, must have been about 65°.) This crater enclosed a level piece of ground about fifty yards long by thirty at its broadest part, with a rude well in the centre. Round the bottom of the crater, about three feet from the level of the ground proper, ran a series of eighty-three semicircular, ovoid, square, and multilateral holes, all about three feet at the mouth. Each hole on inspection showed that it was carefully shored internally with drift-wood and bamboos, and over the mouth a wooden drip-board projected, like the peak of a jockey's cap, for two feet. No sign of life was visible in these tunnels, but a most sickening stench pervaded the entire amphitheatre—a stench fouler than any which my wanderings in Indian villages have introduced me to.

Having remounted Pornic, who was as anxious as I to get back to camp, I rode round the base of the horseshoe to find some place whence an exit would be practicable. The inhabitants, whoever they might be, had not thought fit to put in an appearance, so I was left to my own devices. My first attempt to 'rush' Pornic up the steep sand-banks showed me that I had fallen into a trap exactly on the same model as that which the ant-lion sets for its prey. At each step the shifting sand poured down from above in tons, and rattled on the drip-boards of the holes like small shot. A couple of ineffectual charges sent us both rolling down to the bottom, half choked with the torrents of sand; and I was constrained to turn my attention to the river-bank.

Here everything seemed easy enough. The sand-hills ran down to the river edge, it is true, but there were plenty of shoals and shallows across which I could gallop Pornic, and find my way back to *terra firma* by turning sharply to the right or the left. As I led Pornic over the sands I was startled by the faint pop of a rifle across the river; and at the same moment a bullet dropped with a sharp '*whit*' close to Pornic's head.

There was no mistaking the nature of the missile—a regulation Martini-Henry 'picket'.* About five hundred yards away a country-boat was anchored in mid-stream; and a jet of smoke drifting away from its bows in the still morning air showed me whence the delicate attention had come. Was ever a respectable gentleman in such an *impasse*? The treacherous sand-slope allowed no escape from a spot which I had visited most involuntarily, and a promenade on the river frontage was the signal for a bombardment from some insane native in a boat. I'm afraid that I lost my temper very much indeed.

Another bullet reminded me that I had better save my breath to cool my porridge; and I retreated hastily up the sands and back to the horseshoe, where I saw that the noise of the rifle had drawn sixty-five human beings from the badger-holes which I had up till that point supposed to be untenanted. I found myself in the midst of a crowd of spectators—about forty men, twenty women, and one child who could not have been more than five years old. They were all scantily clothed in that salmon-coloured cloth which one associates with Hindu mendicants, and, at first sight, gave me the impression of a band of loathsome *fakirs*. The filth and repulsiveness of the assembly were beyond all description, and I shuddered to think what their life in the badger-holes must be.

Even in these days, when local self-government* has destroyed the great part of a native's respect for a Sahib, I have been accustomed to a certain amount of civility from my inferiors, and on approaching the crowd naturally expected that there would be some recognition of my presence. As a matter of fact there was, but it was by no means what I had looked for.

The ragged crew actually laughed at me—such laughter I hope I may never hear again. They cackled, yelled, whistled, and howled as I walked into their midst; some of them literally throwing themselves down on the ground in convulsions of unholy mirth. In a moment I had let go Pornic's head, and, irritated beyond expression at the morning's adventure, commenced cuffing those nearest to me with all the force I could. The wretches dropped under my blows like ninepins, and the laughter gave place to wails for mercy; while those yet untouched clasped me round the knees, imploring me in all sorts of uncouth tongues to spare them.

In the tumult, and just when I was feeling very much ashamed of myself for having thus easily given way to my temper, a thin high voice murmured in English from behind my shoulder: 'Sahib! Sahib! Do you not know me? Sahib, it is Gunga Dass, the telegraph-master.'

I spun round quickly and faced the speaker.

Gunga Dass (I have, of course, no hesitation in mentioning the man's real name) I had known four years before as a Deccanee Brahmin* lent by the Punjab Government to one of the Khalsia States. He was in charge of a branch telegraph-office there, and when I had last met him was a jovial, full-stomached, portly Government servant with a marvellous capacity for making bad puns in English—a peculiarity which made me remember him long after I had forgotten his services to me in his official capacity. It is seldom that a Hindu makes English puns.

Now, however, the man was changed beyond all recognition. Caste-mark, stomach, slate-coloured continuations,* and unctuous speech were all gone. I looked at a withered skeleton, turbanless and almost naked, with long matted hair and deep-set codfish-eyes. But for a crescent-shaped scar on the left cheek—the result of an accident for which I was responsible—I should never have known him. But it was indubitably Gunga Dass, and—for this I was thankful—an English-speaking native who might at least tell me the meaning of all that I had gone through that day.

The crowd retreated to some distance as I turned towards the miserable figure and ordered him to show me some method of escaping from the crater. He held a freshly-plucked crow in his hand, and in reply to my question climbed slowly to a platform of sand which ran in front of the holes, and commenced lighting a fire there in silence. Dried bents, sand-poppies, and driftwood burn quickly; and I derived much consolation from the fact that he lit them with an ordinary sulphur match. When they were in a bright glow and the crow was neatly spitted in front thereof, Gunga Dass began without a word of preamble:—

'There are only two kinds of men, sar—the alive and the dead. When you are dead you are dead, but when you are alive you live.' (Here the crow demanded his attention for an instant as it twirled before the fire in danger of being burnt to a cinder.) 'If you die at home and do not die when you come to the ghat to be burnt you come here.'

The nature of the reeking village was made plain now, and all that I had known or read of the grotesque and the horrible paled before the fact just communicated by the ex-Brahmin. Sixteen years ago, when I first landed in Bombay, I had been told by a wandering Armenian of the existence, somewhere in India, of a place to which such Hindus as had the misfortune to recover from trance or catalepsy were conveyed and kept, and I recollect laughing heartily at what I was then pleased to consider a traveller's tale. Sitting at the bottom of the sand-trap, the memory of Watson's Hotel, with its swinging punkahs, white-robed servants, and the sallow-faced Armenian, rose up in my mind as vividly as a photograph, and I burst into a loud fit of laughter. The contrast was too absurd!

Gunga Dass, as he bent over the unclean bird, watched me curiously. Hindus seldom laugh, and his surroundings were not such as to move him that way. He removed the crow solemnly from the wooden spit and as solemnly devoured it. Then he continued his story, which I give in his own words:—

'In epidemics of the cholera you are carried to be burnt almost before you are dead. When you come to the riverside the cold air, perhaps, makes you alive, and then, if you are only a little alive, mud is put on your nose and mouth and you die conclusively. If you are rather more alive, more mud is put; but if you are too lively, they let you go and take you away. I was too lively, and made protestation with anger against the indignities that they endeavoured to press upon me. In those days I was Brahmin and proud man. Now I am dead man and eat'—here he eyed the well-gnawed breast-bone with the first sign of emotion that I had seen in him since we met—'crows, and—other things. They took me from my sheets when they saw that I was too lively and gave me medicines for one week, and I survived successfully. Then they sent me by rail from my place to Okara Station, with a man to take care of me; and at Okara Station we met two other men, and they conducted us three on camels, in the night, from Okara Station to this place, and they propelled me from the top to the bottom, and the other two succeeded, and I have been here ever since two and a half years. Once I was Brahmin and proud man, and now I eat crows.'

'There is no way of getting out?'

'None of what kind at all. When I first came I made experiments frequently, and all the others also, but we have always succumbed to the sand which is precipitated upon our heads.'

'But surely,' I broke in at this point, 'the river-front is open, and it is worth while dodging the bullets; while at night——'

I had already matured a rough plan of escape which a natural instinct of selfishness forbade me sharing with Gunga Dass. He, however, divined my unspoken thought almost as soon as it was formed; and, to my intense astonishment, gave vent to a long low chuckle of derision—the laughter, be it understood, of a superior or at least of an equal.

'You will not'—he had dropped the 'sir' after his first sentence—'make any escape that way. But you can try. I have tried. Once only.'

The sensation of nameless terror which I had in vain attempted to strive against overmastered me completely. My long fast—it was now close upon ten o'clock, and I had eaten nothing since tiffin on the previous day—combined with the violent agitation of the ride had exhausted me, and I verily believe that, for a few minutes, I acted as one mad. I hurled myself against the sand-slope. I ran round the base of the crater, blaspheming and praying by turns. I crawled out among the sedges of the river-front, only to be driven back each time in an agony of nervous dread by the rifle-bullets which cut up the sand round me—for I dared not face the death of a mad dog among that hideous crowd—and so fell, spent and raving, at the curb of the well. No one had taken the slightest notice of an exhibition which makes me blush hotly even when I think of it now.

Two or three men trod on my panting body as they drew water, but they were evidently used to this sort of thing, and had no time to waste upon me. Gunga Dass, indeed, when he had banked the embers of his fire with sand, was at some pains to throw half a cupful of fetid water over my head, an attention for which I could have fallen on my knees and thanked him, but he was laughing all the while in the same mirthless, wheezy key that greeted me on my first attempt to force the shoals. And so, in a half-fainting state, I lay till noon. Then, being only a man after all, I felt hungry, and said as much to Gunga Dass, whom I had begun to regard as my natural protector. Following the impulse of the outer world when dealing with natives, I put my hand into my pocket and drew out four annas. The absurdity of the gift struck me at once, and I was about to replace the money.

Gunga Dass, however, cried: 'Give me the money, all you have, or I will get help, and we will kill you!'

A Briton's first impulse, I believe, is to guard the contents of his pockets; but a moment's thought showed me the folly of differing with the one man who had it in his power to make me comfortable; and with whose help it was possible that I might eventually escape from the crater. I gave him all the money in my possession, Rs. 9–8–5—nine rupees, eight annas, and five pice—for I always keep small change as *bakshish* when I am in camp. Gunga Dass clutched the coins, and hid them at once in his ragged loin-cloth, looking round to assure himself that no one had observed us.

'*Now* I will give you something to eat,' said he.

What pleasure my money could have given him I am unable to say; but inasmuch as it did please him I was not sorry that I had parted with it so readily, for I had no doubt that he would have had me killed if I had refused. One does not protest against the doings of a den of wild beasts; and my companions were lower than any beasts. While I ate what Gunga Dass had provided, a coarse *chapatti** and a cupful of the foul well-water, the people showed not the faintest sign of curiosity—that curiosity which is so rampant, as a rule, in an Indian village.

I could even fancy that they despised me. At all events they treated me with the most chilling indifference, and Gunga Dass was nearly as bad. I plied him with questions about the terrible village, and received extremely unsatisfactory answers. So far as I could gather, it had been in existence from time immemorial—whence I concluded that it was at least a century old—and during that time no one had ever been known to escape from it. (I had to control myself here with both hands, lest the blind terror should lay hold of me a second time and drive me raving round the crater.) Gunga Dass took a malicious pleasure in emphasizing this point and in watching me wince. Nothing that I could do would induce him to tell me who the mysterious 'They' were.

'It is so ordered,' he would reply, 'and I do not yet know any one who has disobeyed the orders.'

'Only wait till my servants find that I am missing,' I retorted, 'and I promise you that this place shall be cleared off the face of the earth, and I'll give you a lesson in civility, too, my friend.'

'Your servants would be torn in pieces before they came near this place; and, besides, you are dead, my dear friend. It is not your fault, of course, but none the less you are dead *and* buried.'

At irregular intervals supplies of food, I was told, were dropped down from the land side into the amphitheatre, and the inhabitants fought for them like wild beasts. When a man felt his death coming on he retreated to his lair and died there. The body was sometimes dragged out of the hole and thrown on to the sand, or allowed to rot where it lay.

The phrase 'thrown on to the sand' caught my attention, and I asked Gunga Dass whether this sort of thing was not likely to breed a pestilence.

'That,' said he, with another of his wheezy chuckles, 'you may see for yourself subsequently. You will have much time to make observations.'

Whereat, to his great delight, I winced once more and hastily continued the conversation: 'And how do you live here from day to day? What do you do?' The question elicited exactly the same answer as before—coupled with the information that 'this place is like your European Heaven*; there is neither marrying nor giving in marriage.'

Gunga Dass had been educated at a Mission School, and, as he himself admitted, had he only changed his religion 'like a wise man,' might have avoided the living grave which was now his portion. But as long as I was with him I fancy he was happy.

Here was a Sahib, a representative of the dominant race, helpless as a child and completely at the mercy of his native neighbours. In a deliberate lazy way he set himself to torture me as a schoolboy would devote a rapturous half-hour to watching the agonies of an impaled beetle, or as a ferret in a blind burrow might glue himself comfortably to the neck of a rabbit. The burden of his conversation was that there was no escape 'of no kind whatever,' and that I should stay here till I died and was 'thrown on to the sand.' If it were possible to forejudge the conversation of the Damned on the advent of a new soul in their abode, I should say that they would speak as Gunga Dass did to me throughout that long afternoon. I was powerless to protest or answer; all my energies being devoted to a struggle against the inexplicable terror that threatened to overwhelm me again and again. I can compare the feeling to nothing except the struggles of a man against the overpowering nausea of the Channel passage—only my agony was of the spirit and infinitely more terrible.

As the day wore on, the inhabitants began to appear in full strength to catch the rays of the afternoon sun, which were now sloping in at the mouth of the crater. They assembled by little knots, and talked among themselves without even throwing a glance in my direction. About four o'clock, so far as I could judge, Gunga Dass rose and dived into his lair for a moment, emerging with a live crow in his hands. The wretched bird was in a most draggled and deplorable condition, but seemed to be in no way afraid of its master. Advancing cautiously to the river-front, Gunga Dass stepped from tussock to tussock until he had reached a smooth patch of sand directly in the line of the boat's fire. The occupants of the boat took no notice. Here he stopped, and, with a couple of dexterous turns of the wrist, pegged the bird on its back with outstretched wings. As was only natural, the crow began to shriek at once and beat the air with its claws. In a few seconds the clamour had attracted the attention of a bevy of wild crows on a shoal a few hundred yards away, where they were discussing something that looked like a corpse. Half-a-dozen crows flew over at once to see what was going on, and also, as it proved, to attack the pinioned bird. Gunga Dass, who had lain down on a tussock, motioned to me to be quiet, though I fancy this was a needless precaution. In a moment, and before I could see how it happened, a wild crow, which had grappled with the shrieking and helpless bird, was entangled in the latter's claws, swiftly disengaged by Gunga Dass, and pegged down beside its companion in adversity. Curiosity, its seemed, overpowered the rest of the flock, and almost before Gunga Dass and I had time to withdraw to the tussock, two more captives were struggling in the upturned claws of the decoys. So the chase—if I can give it so dignified a name—continued until Gunga Dass had captured seven crows. Five of them he throttled at once, reserving two for further operations another day. I was a good deal impressed by this, to me, novel method of securing food, and complimented Gunga Dass on his skill.

'It is nothing to do,' said he. 'To-morrow you must do it for me. You are stronger than I am.'

This calm assumption of superiority upset me not a little, and I answered peremptorily: 'Indeed, you old ruffian? What do you think I have given you money for?'

'Very well,' was the unmoved reply. 'Perhaps not to-morrow, nor the day after, nor subsequently; but in the end, and for many years, you will catch crows and eat crows, and you will thank your European God that you have crows to catch and eat.'

I could have cheerfully strangled him for this, but judged it best under the circumstances to smother my resentment. An hour later I was eating one of the crows; and, as Gunga Dass had said, thanking my God that I had a crow to eat. Never as long as I live shall I forget that evening meal. The whole population were squatting on the hard sand platform opposite their dens, huddled over tiny fires of refuse and dried rushes. Death, having once laid his hand upon these men and forborne to strike, seemed to stand aloof from them now; for most of our company were old men, bent and worn and twisted with years, and women aged to all appearance as the Fates themselves. They sat together in knots and talked—God only knows what they found to discuss—in low equable tones, curiously in contrast to the strident babble with which natives are accustomed to make day hideous. Now and then an access of that sudden fury which had possessed me in the morning would lay hold on a man or woman; and with yells and imprecations the sufferer would attack the steep slope until, baffled and bleeding, he fell back on the platform incapable of moving a limb. The others would never even raise their eyes when this happened, as men too well aware of the futility of their fellows' attempts and wearied with their useless repetition. I saw four such outbursts in the course of that evening.

Gunga Dass took an eminently businesslike view of my situation, and while we were dining—I can afford to laugh at the recollection now, but it was painful enough at the time—propounded the terms on which he would consent to 'do' for me. My nine rupees eight annas, he argued, at the rate of three annas a day, would provide me with food for fifty-one days, or about seven weeks; that is to say, he would be willing to cater for me for that length of time. At the end of it I was to look after myself. For a further consideration—*videlicet* my boots—he would be willing to allow me to occupy the den next to his own, and would supply me with as much dried grass for bedding as he could spare.

'Very well, Gunga Dass,' I replied; 'to the first terms I cheerfully agree, but, as there is nothing on earth to prevent my killing you as you sit here and taking everything that you have' (I thought of the two invaluable crows at the time), 'I flatly refuse to give you my boots and shall take whichever den I please.'

The stroke was a bold one, and I was glad when I saw that it had succeeded. Gunga Dass changed his tone immediately, and disavowed all intention of asking for my boots. At the time it did not strike me as at all strange that I, a Civil Engineer, a man of thirteen years' standing in the Service, and, I trust, an average Englishman, should thus calmly threaten murder and violence against the man who had, for a consideration it is true, taken me under his wing. I had left the world, it seemed, for centuries. I was as certain then as I am now of my own existence, that in the accursed settlement there was no law save that of the strongest; that the living dead men had thrown behind them every canon of the world which had cast them out; and that I had to depend for my own life on my strength and vigilance alone. The crew of the ill-fated *Mignonette** are the only men who would understand my frame of mind. 'At present,' I argued to myself, 'I am strong and a match for six of these wretches. It is imperatively necessary that I should, for my own sake, keep both health and strength until the hour of my release comes—if it ever does.'

Fortified with these resolutions, I ate and drank as much as I could, and made Gunga Dass understand that I intended to be his master, and that the least sign of insubordination on his part would be visited with the only punishment I had it in my power to inflict—sudden and violent death. Shortly after this I went to bed. That is to say, Gunga Dass gave me a double armful of dried bents which I thrust down the mouth of the lair to the right of his, and followed myself, feet foremost; the hole running about nine feet into the sand with a slight downward inclination, and being neatly shored with timbers. From my den, which faced the river-front, I was able to watch the waters of the Sutlej flowing past under the light of a young moon and compose myself to sleep as best I might.

The horrors of that night I shall never forget. My den was nearly as narrow as a coffin, and the sides had been worn smooth and greasy by the contact of innumerable naked bodies, added to which it smelt abominably. Sleep was altogether out of the question to one in my excited frame of mind. As the night wore on, it seemed that the entire amphitheatre was filled with legions of unclean devils that, trooping up from the shoals below, mocked the unfortunates in their lairs.

Personally I am not of an imaginative temperament—very few Engineers are—but on that occasion I was as completely prostrated with nervous terror as any woman. After half an hour or so, however, I was able once more to calmly review my chances of escape. Any exit by the steep sand walls was, of course, impracticable. I had been thoroughly convinced of this some time before. It was possible, just possible, that I might, in the uncertain moonlight, safely run the gauntlet of the rifle shots. The place was so full of terror for me that I was prepared to undergo any risk in leaving it. Imagine my delight, then, when after creeping stealthily to the river-front I found that the infernal boat was not there. My freedom lay before me in the next few steps!

By walking out to the first shallow pool that lay at the foot of the projecting left horn of the horseshoe, I could wade across, turn the flank of the crater, and make my way inland. Without a moment's hesitation I marched briskly past the tussocks where Gunga Dass had snared the crows, and out in the direction of the smooth white sand beyond. My first step from the tufts of dried grass showed me how utterly futile was any hope of escape; for, as I put my foot down, I felt an indescribable drawing, sucking motion of the sand below. Another moment and my leg was swallowed up nearly to the knee. In the moonlight the whole surface of the sand seemed to be shaken with devilish delight at my disappointment. I struggled clear, sweating with terror and exertion, back to the tussocks behind me and fell on my face.

My only means of escape from the semicircle was protected by a quicksand!

How long I lay I have not the faintest idea; but I was roused at last by the malevolent chuckle of Gunga Dass at my ear. 'I would advise you, Protector of the Poor' (the ruffian was speaking English), 'to return to your house. It is unhealthy to lie down here. Moreover, when the boat returns you will most certainly be rifled at.' He stood over me in the dim light of the dawn, chuckling and laughing to himself. Suppressing my first impulse to catch the man by the neck and throw him on to the quicksand, I rose sullenly and followed him to the platform below the burrows.

Suddenly, and futilely, as I thought while I spoke, I asked: 'Gunga Dass, what is the good of the boat if I can't get out *anyhow*?' I recollect that even in my deepest trouble I had been speculating vaguely on the waste of ammunition in guarding an already well-protected foreshore.

Gunga Dass laughed again and made answer: 'They have the boat only in daytime. It is for the reason that *there is a way*. I hope we shall have the pleasure of your company for much longer time. It is a pleasant spot when you have been here some years and eaten roast crow long enough.'

I staggered, numbed and helpless, towards the fetid burrow allotted to me, and fell asleep. An hour or so later I was awakened by a piercing scream—the shrill, high-pitched scream of a horse in pain. Those who have once heard that will never forget the sound. I found some little difficulty in scrambling out of the burrow. When I was in the open, I saw Pornic, my poor old Pornic, lying dead on the sandy soil. How they had killed him I cannot guess. Gunga Dass explained that horse was better than crow, and 'greatest good of greatest number is political maxim. We are now Republic, Mister Jukes, and you are entitled to a fair share of the beast. If you like, we will pass a vote of thanks. Shall I propose?'

Yes, we were a Republic indeed! A Republic of wild beasts penned at the bottom of a pit, to eat and fight and sleep till we died. I attempted no protest of any kind, but sat down and stared at the hideous sight in front of me. In less time almost than it takes me to write this, Pornic's body was divided, in some unclean way or other; the men and women had dragged the fragments on to the platform and were preparing their morning meal. Gunga Dass cooked mine. The almost irresistible impulse to fly at the sand walls until I was wearied laid hold of me afresh, and I had to struggle against it with all my might. Gunga Dass was offensively jocular till I told him that if he addressed another remark of any kind whatever to me I should strangle him where he sat. This silenced him till the silence became insupportable, and I bade him say something.

'You will live here till you die like the other Feringhi,'* he said coolly, watching me over the fragment of gristle that he was gnawing.

'What other Sahib, you swine? Speak at once, and don't stop to tell me a lie.'

'He is over there,' answered Gunga Dass, pointing to a burrow-mouth about four doors to the left of my own. 'You can see for yourself. He died in the burrow as you will die, and I will die, and as all these men and women and the one child will also die.'

'For pity's sake, tell me all you know about him. Who was he? When did he come, and when did he die?'

This appeal was a weak step on my part. Gunga Dass only leered and replied: 'I will not—unless you give me something first.'

Then I recollected where I was, and struck the man between the eyes, partially stunning him. He stepped down from the platform at once, and, cringing and fawning and weeping and attempting to embrace my feet, led me round to the burrow which he had indicated.

'I know nothing whatever about the gentleman. Your God be my witness that I do not. He was as anxious to escape as you were, and he was shot from the boat, though we all did all things to prevent him from attempting. He was shot here.' Gunga Dass laid his hand on his lean stomach and bowed to the earth.

'Well, and what then? Go on!'

'And then—and then, Your Honour, we carried him into his house and gave him water, and put wet cloths on the wound, and he laid down in his house and gave up the ghost.'

'In how long? In how long?'

'About half an hour after he received his wound. I call Vishnu* to witness,' yelled the wretched man, 'that I did everything for him. Everything which was possible, that I did!'

He threw himself down on the ground and clasped my ankles. But I had my doubts about Gunga Dass's benevolence, and kicked him off as he lay protesting.

'I believe you robbed him of everything he had. But I can find out in a minute or two. How long was the Sahib here?'

'Nearly a year and a half. I think he must have gone mad. But hear me swear, Protector of the Poor! Won't Your Honour hear me swear that I never touched an article that belonged to him? What is Your Worship going to do?'

I had taken Gunga Dass by the waist and had hauled him on to the platform opposite the deserted burrow. As I did so I thought of my wretched fellow-prisoner's unspeakable misery among all these horrors for eighteen months, and the final agony of dying like a rat in a hole, with a bullet-wound in the stomach. Gunga Dass fancied I was going to kill him and howled pitifully. The rest of the population, in the plethora that follows a full flesh meal, watched us without stirring.

'Go inside, Gunga Dass,' said I, 'and fetch it out.'

I was feeling sick and faint with horror now. Gunga Dass nearly rolled off the platform and howled aloud.

'But I am Brahmin, Sahib—a high-caste Brahmin. By your soul, by your father's soul, do not make me do this thing!'

'Brahmin or no Brahmin, by my soul and my father's soul, in you go!' I said, and, seizing him by the shoulders, I crammed his head into the mouth of the burrow, kicked the rest of him in, and, sitting down, covered my face with my hands.

At the end of a few minutes I heard a rustle and a creak; then Gunga Dass in a sobbing, choking whisper speaking to himself; then a soft thud—and I uncovered my eyes.

The dry sand had turned the corpse entrusted to its keeping into a yellow-brown mummy. I told Gunga Dass to stand off while I examined it. The body—clad in an olive-green hunting-suit much stained and worn, with leather pads on the shoulders—was that of a man between thirty and forty, above middle height, with light sandy hair, long moustache, and a rough unkempt beard. The left canine of the upper jaw was missing, and a portion of the lobe of the right ear was gone. On the second finger of the left hand was a ring—a shield-shaped bloodstone set in gold, with a monogram that might have been either 'B. K.' or 'B. L.' On the third finger of the right hand was a silver ring in the shape of a coiled cobra, much worn and tarnished. Gunga Dass deposited a handful of trifles he had picked out of the burrow at my feet, and, covering the face of the body with my handkerchief, I turned to examine these. I give the full list in the hope that it may lead to the identification of the unfortunate man:—

1. Bowl of a briarwood pipe, serrated at the edge; much worn and blackened; bound with string at the screw.

2. Two patent-lever keys; wards of both broken.

3. Tortoise-shell-handled penknife, silver or nickel, name-plate marked with monogram 'B. K.'

4. Envelope, postmark undecipherable, bearing a Victorian stamp, addressed to 'Miss Mon——' (rest illegible)—'ham'—'nt.'

5. Imitation crocodile-skin notebook with pencil. First forty-five pages blank; four and a half illegible; fifteen others filled with private memoranda relating chiefly to three persons—a Mrs L. Singleton, abbreviated several times to 'Lot Single', 'Mrs S. May', and 'Garmison', referred to in places as 'Jerry' or 'Jack'.

6. Handle of small-sized hunting-knife. Blade snapped short. Buck's horn, diamond-cut, with swivel and ring on the butt; fragment of cotton cord attached.

It must not be supposed that I inventoried all these things on the spot as fully as I have here written them down. The notebook first attracted my attention, and I put it in my pocket with a view to studying it later on. The rest of the articles I conveyed to my burrow for safety's sake, and there, being a methodical man, I inventoried them. I then returned to the corpse and ordered Gunga Dass to help me to carry it out to the river-front. While we were engaged in this, the exploded shell of an old brown cartridge dropped out of one of the pockets and rolled at my feet. Gunga Dass had not seen it; and I fell to thinking that a man does not carry exploded cartridge-cases, especially 'browns', which will not bear loading twice, about with him when shooting. In other words, that cartridge-case had been fired inside the crater. Consequently there must be a gun somewhere. I was on the verge of asking Gunga Dass, but checked myself, knowing that he would lie. We laid the body down on the edge of the quicksand by the tussocks. It was my intention to push it out and let it be swallowed up—the only possible mode of burial that I could think of. I ordered Gunga Dass to go away.

Then I gingerly put the corpse out on the quicksand. In doing so—it was lying face downward—I tore the frail and rotten khaki shooting-coat open, disclosing a hideous cavity in the back. I have already told you that the dry sand had, as it were, mummified the body. A moment's glance showed that the gaping hole had been caused by a gunshot wound; the gun must have been fired with the muzzle almost touching the back. The shooting-coat, being intact, had been drawn over the body after death, which must have been instantaneous. The secret of the poor wretch's death was plain to me in a flash. Some one of the crater, presumably Gunga Dass, must have shot him with his own gun—the gun that fitted the brown cartridges. He had never attempted to escape in the face of the rifle-fire from the boat.

I pushed the corpse out hastily, and saw it sink from sight literally in a few seconds. I shuddered as I watched. In a dazed, half-conscious way I turned to peruse the notebook. A stained and discoloured slip of paper had been inserted between the binding and the back, and dropped out as I opened the pages. This is what it contained: '*Four out from crow-clump; three left; nine out; two right; three back; two left; fourteen out; two left; seven out; one left; nine back; two right; six back; four right; seven back.*'* The paper had been burnt and charred at the edges. What it meant I could not understand. I sat down on the dried bents turning it over and over between my fingers, until I was aware of Gunga Dass standing immediately behind me with glowing eyes and outstretched hands.

'Have you got it?' he panted. 'Will you not let me look at it also? I swear that I will return it.'

'Got what? Return what?' I asked.

'That which you have in your hands. It will help us both.' He stretched out his long bird-like talons, trembling with eagerness.

'I could never find it,' he continued. 'He had secreted it about his person. Therefore I shot him, but nevertheless I was unable to obtain it.'

Gunga Dass had quite forgotten his little fiction about the rifle-bullet. I heard him calmly. Morality is blunted by consorting with the Dead who are alive.

'What on earth are you raving about? What is it you want me to give you?'

'The piece of paper in the notebook. It will help us both.

Oh, you fool! You fool! Can you not see what it will do for us? We shall escape!'

His voice rose almost to a scream, and he danced with excitement before me. I own I was moved at the chance of getting away.

'Do you mean to say that this slip of paper will help us? What does it mean?'

'Read it aloud! Read it aloud! I beg and I pray to you to read it aloud.'

I did so. Gunga Dass listened delightedly, and drew an irregular line in the sand with his fingers.

'See now! It was the length of his gun-barrels without the stock. I have those barrels. Four gun-barrels out from the place where I caught crows. Straight out; do you mind me? Then three left. Ah! Now well I remember how that man worked it out night after night. Then nine out, and so on. Out is always straight before you across the quicksand to the north. He told me so before I killed him.'

'But if you knew all this why didn't you get out before?'

'I did *not* know it. He told me that he was working it out a year and a half ago, and how he was working it out night after night when the boat had gone away, and he could get out near the quicksand safely. Then he said that we would get away together. But I was afraid that he would leave me behind one night when he had worked it all out, and so I shot him. Besides, it is not advisable that the men who once get in here should escape. Only I, and *I* am a Brahmin.'

The hope of escape had brought Gunga Dass's caste back to him. He stood up, walked about, and gesticulated violently. Eventually I managed to make him talk soberly, and he told me how this Englishman had spent six months night after night in exploring, inch by inch, the passage across the quicksand; how he had declared it to be simplicity itself up to within about twenty yards of the river-bank after turning the flank of the left horn of the horseshoe. This much he had evidently not completed when Gunga Dass shot him with his own gun.

In my frenzy of delight at the possibilities of escape I recollect shaking hands wildly with Gunga Dass, after we had

decided that we were to make an attempt to get away that
very night. It was weary work waiting throughout the
afternoon.

About ten o'clock, as far as I could judge, when the moon
had just risen above the lip of the crater, Gunga Dass made a
move for his burrow to bring out the gun-barrels whereby to
measure our path. All the other wretched inhabitants had
retired to their lairs long ago. The guardian boat had drifted
down-stream some hours before, and we were utterly alone
by the crow-clump. Gunga Dass, while carrying the gun-
barrels, let slip the piece of paper which was to be our guide. I
stooped down hastily to recover it, and, as I did so, I was
aware that the creature was aiming a violent blow at the back
of my head with the gun-barrels. It was too late to turn
round. I must have received the blow somewhere on the nape
of the neck, for I fell senseless at the edge of the quicksand.

When I recovered consciousness the moon was going
down, and I was sensible of intolerable pain in the back of my
head. Gunga Dass had disappeared and my mouth was full of
blood. I lay down again and prayed that I might die without
more ado. Then the unreasoning fury which I have before
mentioned laid hold upon me, and I staggered inland towards
the walls of the crater. It seemed that some one was calling to
me in a whisper—'Sahib! Sahib! Sahib!' exactly as my bearer
used to call me in the mornings. I fancied that I was delirious
until a handful of sand fell at my feet. Then I looked up and
saw a head peering down into the amphitheatre—the head of
Dunnoo, my dog-boy, who attended to my collies. As soon as
he had attracted my attention, he held up his hand and
showed a rope. I motioned, staggering to and fro the while,
that he should throw it down. It was a couple of leather
punkah-ropes knotted together, with a loop at one end. I
slipped the loop over my head and under my arms; heard
Dunnoo urge something forward; was conscious that I was
being dragged, face downward, up the steep sand-slope, and
the next instant found myself choked and half-fainting on the
sand-hills overlooking the crater. Dunnoo, with his face
ashy-grey in the moonlight, implored me not to stay, but to
get back to my tent at once.

It seems that he had tracked Pornic's footprints fourteen miles across the sands to the crater; had returned and told my servants, who flatly refused to meddle with any one, white or black, once fallen into the hideous Village of the Dead; whereupon Dunnoo had taken one of my ponies and a couple of punkah-ropes, returned to the crater, and hauled me out as I have described.

The Phantom 'Rickshaw*

May no ill dreams disturb my rest,
Nor Powers of Darkness me molest.
*Evening Hymn**

ONE of the few advantages that India has over England is a great Knowability. After five years' service a man is directly or indirectly acquainted with the two or three hundred Civilians* in his Province, all the Messes of ten or twelve Regiments and Batteries, and some fifteen hundred other people of the non-official caste. In ten years his knowledge should be doubled, and at the end of twenty he knows, or knows something about, every Englishman in the Empire, and may travel anywhere and everywhere without paying hotel-bills.

Globe-trotters who expect entertainment as a right, have, even within my memory, blunted this open-heartedness, but none the less to-day, if you belong to the Inner Circle and are neither a Bear nor a Black Sheep, all houses are open to you, and our small world is very, very kind and helpful.

Rickett of Kamartha stayed with Polder of Kumaon some fifteen years ago. He meant to stay two nights, but was knocked down by rheumatic fever, and for six weeks disorganized Polder's establishment, stopped Polder's work, and nearly died in Polder's bedroom. Polder behaves as though he had been placed under eternal obligation by Rickett, and yearly sends the little Ricketts a box of presents and toys. It is the same everywhere. The men who do not take the trouble to conceal from you their opinion that you are an incompetent ass, and the women who blacken your character and misunderstand your wife's amusements, will work themselves to the bone in your behalf if you fall sick or into serious trouble.

Heatherlegh, the Doctor, kept, in addition to his regular practice, a hospital on his private account—an arrangement of loose-boxes* for Incurables, his friends called it—but it was really a sort of fitting-up shed for craft that had been damaged by stress of weather. The weather in India is often sultry, and since the tale of bricks* is always a fixed quantity, and the only liberty allowed is permission to work overtime and get no thanks, men occasionally break down and become as mixed as the metaphors in this sentence.

Heatherlegh is the dearest doctor that ever was, and his invariable prescription to all his patients is, 'Lie low, go slow, and keep cool.' He says that more men are killed by overwork than the importance of this world justifies. He maintains that overwork slew Pansay, who died under his hands about three years ago. He has, of course, the right to speak authoritatively, and he laughs at my theory that there was a crack in Pansay's head and a little bit of the Dark World came through and pressed him to death. 'Pansay went off the handle,' says Heatherlegh, 'after the stimulus of long leave at Home. He may or he may not have behaved like a blackguard to Mrs Keith-Wessington. My notion is that the work of the Katabundi Settlement ran him off his legs, and that he took to brooding and making much of an ordinary P. & O.* flirtation. He certainly was engaged to Miss Mannering, and she certainly broke off the engagement. Then he took a feverish chill and all that nonsense about ghosts developed. Overwork started his illness, kept it alight, and killed him, poor devil. Write him off to the System that uses one man to do the work of two and a half men.'

I do not believe this. I used to sit up with Pansay sometimes when Heatherlegh was called out to patients and I happened to be within claim. The man would make me most unhappy by describing, in a low, even voice, the procession that was always passing at the bottom of his bed. He had a sick man's command of language. When he recovered I suggested that he should write out the whole affair from beginning to end, knowing that ink might assist him to ease his mind.

He was in a high fever while he was writing, and the blood-and-thunder magazine diction he adopted did not calm him. Two months afterwards he was reported fit for duty, but, in spite of the fact that he was urgently needed to help an undermanned Commission stagger through a deficit, he preferred to die; vowing at the last that he was hag-ridden. I got his manuscript before he died, and this is his version of the affair, dated 1885, exactly as he wrote it:—

My doctor tells me that I need rest and change of air. It is not improbable that I shall get both ere long—rest that neither the red-coated messenger nor the mid-day gun can break, and change of air far beyond that which any homeward-bound steamer can give me. In the meantime I am resolved to stay where I am; and, in flat defiance of my doctor's orders, to take all the world into my confidence. You shall learn for yourselves the precise nature of my malady, and shall, too, judge for yourselves whether any man born of woman on this weary earth was ever so tormented as I.

Speaking now as a condemned criminal might speak ere the drop-bolts are drawn, my story, wild and hideously improbable as it may appear, demands at least attention. That it will ever receive credence I utterly disbelieve. Two months ago I should have scouted as mad or drunk the man who had dared tell me the like. Two months ago I was the happiest man in India. To-day, from Peshawur to the sea,* there is no one more wretched. My doctor and I are the only two who know this. His explanation is that my brain, digestion, and eyesight are all slightly affected; giving rise to my frequent and persistent 'delusions'. Delusions, indeed! I call him a fool; but he attends me still with the same unwearied smile, the same bland professional manner, the same neatly-trimmed red whiskers, till I begin to suspect that I am an ungrateful, evil-tempered invalid. But you shall judge for yourselves.

Three years ago it was my fortune—my great misfortune— to sail from Gravesend to Bombay, on return from long leave, with one Agnes Keith-Wessington, wife of an officer on the Bombay side. It does not in the least concern you to know what manner of woman she was. Be content with the knowledge that, ere the voyage had ended, both she and I were desperately and unreasoningly in love with one another. Heaven knows that I can make the admission now without one particle of vanity! In matters of this sort there is always

one who gives and another who accepts. From the first day of
our ill-omened attachment, I was conscious that Agnes's
passion was a stronger, a more dominant, and—if I may use
the expression—a purer sentiment than mine. Whether she
recognized the fact then, I do not know. Afterwards it was
bitterly plain to both of us.

Arrived at Bombay in the spring of the year, we went our
respective ways, to meet no more for the next three or four
months, when my leave and her love took us both to Simla.
There we spent the season together; and there my fire of
straw burnt itself out to a pitiful end with the closing year. I
attempt no excuse. I make no apology. Mrs Wessington had
given up much for my sake, and was prepared to give up all.
From my own lips, in August 1882, she learnt that I was sick
of her presence, tired of her company, and weary of the
sound of her voice. Ninety-nine women out of a hundred
would have wearied of me as I wearied of them; seventy-five
of that number would have promptly avenged themselves by
active and obtrusive flirtation with other men. Mrs Wessington was the hundredth. On her neither my openly-
expressed aversion nor the brutalities with which I garnished
our interviews had the least effect.

'Jack, darling!' was her one eternal cuckoo-cry: 'I'm sure
it's all a mistake—a hideous mistake; and we'll be good
friends again some day. *Please* forgive me, Jack, dear.'

I was the offender, and I knew it. That knowledge trans-
formed my pity into passive endurance, and, eventually, into
blind hate—the same instinct, I suppose, which prompts a
man to stamp savagely on the spider he has but half killed.
And with this hate in my bosom the season of 1882 came to an
end.

Next year we met again at Simla—she with her mon-
otonous face and timid attempts at reconciliation, and I with
loathing of her in every fibre of my frame. Several times I
could not avoid meeting her alone; and on each occasion her
words were identically the same. Still the unreasoning wail
that it was all a 'mistake'; and still the hope of eventually
'making friends'. I might have seen, had I cared to look, that
that hope only was keeping her alive. She grew more wan and

thin month by month. You will agree with me, at least, that such conduct would have driven any one to despair. It was uncalled-for; childish; unwomanly. I maintain that she was much to blame. And again, sometimes, in the black, fever-stricken, night-watches, I have begun to think that I might have been a little kinder to her. But that really *is* a 'delusion'. I could not have continued pretending to love her when I didn't; could I? It would have been unfair to us both.

Last year we met again—on the same terms as before. The same weary appeals, and the same curt answers from my lips. At least I would make her see how wholly wrong and hopeless were her attempts at resuming the old relationship. As the season wore on, we fell apart—that is to say, she found it difficult to meet me, for I had other and more absorbing interests to attend to. When I think it over quietly in my sick-room, the season of 1884 seems a confused nightmare wherein light and shade were fantastically intermingled: my courtship of little Kitty Mannering; my hopes, doubts, and fears; our long rides together; my trembling avowal of attachment; her reply; and now and again a vision of a white face flitting by in the 'rickshaw with the black-and-white liveries I once watched for so earnestly; the wave of Mrs Wessington's gloved hand; and, when she met me alone, which was but seldom, the irksome monotony of her appeal. I loved Kitty Mannering; honestly, heartily loved her, and with my love for her grew my hatred for Agnes. In August Kitty and I were engaged. The next day I met those accursed 'magpie' *jhampanis* at the back of Jakko,* and, moved by some passing sentiment of pity, stopped to tell Mrs Wessington everything. She knew it already!

'So I hear you're engaged, Jack, dear.' Then, without a moment's pause: 'I'm sure it's all a mistake—a hideous mistake. We shall be as good friends some day, Jack, as we ever were.'

My answer might have made even a man wince. It cut the dying woman before me like the blow of a whip. 'Please forgive me, Jack. I didn't mean to make you angry; but it's true, it's true!'

And Mrs Wessington broke down completely. I turned

away and left her to finish her journey in peace, feeling, but only for a moment or two, that I had been an unutterably mean hound. I looked back, and saw that she had turned her 'rickshaw with the idea, I suppose, of overtaking me.

The scene and its surroundings were photographed on my memory. The rain-swept sky (we were at the end of the wet weather), the sodden, dingy pines, the muddy road, and the black powder-riven cliffs formed a gloomy background against which the black-and-white liveries of the *jhampanis*, the yellow-panelled 'rickshaw, and Mrs Wessington's down-bowed golden head stood out clearly. She was holding her handkerchief in her left hand and was leaning back exhausted against the 'rickshaw cushions. I turned my horse up a bypath near the Sanjaolie Reservoir and literally ran away. Once I fancied I heard a faint call of 'Jack!' This may have been imagination. I never stopped to verify it. Ten minutes later I came across Kitty on horseback; and, in the delight of a long ride with her, forgot all about the interview.

A week later Mrs Wessington died, and the inexpressible burden of her existence was removed from my life. I went Plainsward perfectly happy. Before three months were over I had forgotten all about her, except that at times the discovery of some of her old letters reminded me unpleasantly of our bygone relationship. By January I had disinterred what was left of our correspondence from among my scattered belongings and had burnt it. At the beginning of April of this year, 1885, I was at Simla—semi-deserted Simla—once more, and was deep in lovers' talks and walks with Kitty. It was decided that we should be married at the end of June. You will understand, therefore, that, loving Kitty as I did, I am not saying too much when I pronounce myself to have been, at that time, the happiest man in India.

Fourteen delightful days passed almost before I noticed their flight. Then, aroused to the sense of what was proper among mortals circumstanced as we were, I pointed out to Kitty that an engagement ring was the outward and visible sign of her dignity as an engaged girl; and that she must forthwith come to Hamilton's to be measured for one. Up to that moment, I give you my word, we had completely forgotten so trivial a matter. To Hamilton's we accordingly went on the 15th of April, 1885. Remember that—whatever my doctor may say to the contrary—I was then in perfect health, enjoying a well-balanced mind and an *absolutely* tranquil spirit. Kitty and I entered Hamilton's shop together, and there, regardless of the order of affairs, I measured Kitty for the ring in the presence of the amused assistant. The ring was a sapphire with two diamonds. We then rode out down the slope that leads to the Combermere Bridge and Peliti's shop.

While my Waler* was cautiously feeling his way over the loose shale, and Kitty was laughing and chattering at my side,—while all Simla, that is to say, as much of it as had then come from the Plains, was grouped round the Reading-room and Peliti's veranda,—I was aware that some one, apparently at a vast distance, was calling me by my Christian name. It struck me that I had heard the voice before, but when and where I could not at once determine. In the short space it took to cover the road between the path from Hamilton's shop and the first plank of the Combermere Bridge I had thought over half-a-dozen people who might have committed such a solecism, and had eventually decided that it must have been some singing in my ears. Immediately opposite Peliti's* shop my eye was arrested by the sight of four *jhampanis* in 'magpie' livery, pulling a yellow-panelled, cheap, bazar 'rickshaw. In a moment my mind flew back to the previous season and Mrs Wessington with a sense of irritation and disgust. Was it not enough that the woman was dead and done with, without her black-and-white servitors reappearing to spoil the day's happiness? Whoever employed them now I thought I would call upon, and ask as a personal favour to change her *jhampanis*' livery. I would hire the men myself, and, if necessary, buy their coats from off their backs. It is impossible to say here what a flood of undesirable memories their presence evoked.

'Kitty,' I cried, 'there are poor Mrs Wessington's *jhampanis* turned up again! I wonder who has them now?'

Kitty had known Mrs Wessington slightly last season, and had always been interested in the sickly woman.

'What? Where?' she asked. 'I can't see them anywhere.'

Even as she spoke, her horse, swerving from a laden mule, threw himself directly in front of the advancing 'rickshaw. I had scarcely time to utter a word of warning when, to my unutterable horror, horse and rider passed *through* men and carriage as if they had been thin air!

'What's the matter?' cried Kitty. 'What made you call out so foolishly, Jack? If I *am* engaged I don't want all creation to know about it. There was lots of space between the mule and the veranda; and, if you think I can't ride—There!'

Whereupon wilful Kitty set off, her dainty little head in the air, at a hand-gallop in the direction of the Bandstand; fully expecting, as she herself afterwards told me, that I should follow her. What was the matter? Nothing indeed. Either that I was mad or drunk, or that Simla was haunted with devils. I reined in my impatient cob, and turned round. The 'rickshaw had turned too, and now stood immediately facing me, near the left railing of the Combermere Bridge.

'Jack! Jack, darling!' (There was no mistake about the words this time. They rang through my brain as if they had been shouted in my ear.) 'It's some hideous mistake, I'm sure. *Please* forgive me, Jack, and let's be friends again.'

The 'rickshaw-hood had fallen back, and inside, as I hope and pray daily for the death I dread by night, sat Mrs Keith-Wessington, handkerchief in hand, and golden head bowed on her breast.

How long I stared motionless I do not know. Finally, I was aroused by my *sais** taking the Waler's bridle and asking whether I was ill. From the horrible to the commonplace is but a step. I tumbled off my horse and dashed, half fainting, into Peliti's for a glass of cherry-brandy. There two or three couples were gathered round the coffee-tables discussing the gossip of the day. Their trivialities were more comforting to me just then than the consolations of religion could have been. I plunged into the midst of the conversation at once; chatted, laughed, and jested with a face (when I caught a glimpse of it in a mirror) as white and drawn as that of a corpse. Three or four men noticed my condition; and, evidently setting it down to the results of over-many pegs,

charitably endeavoured to draw me apart from the rest of the
loungers. But I refused to be led away. I wanted the company
of my kind—as a child rushes into the midst of the dinner-
party after a fright in the dark. I must have talked for about
ten minutes or so, though it seemed an eternity to me, when I
heard Kitty's clear voice outside inquiring for me. In another
minute she had entered the shop, prepared to upbraid me for
failing so signally in my duties. Something in my face
stopped her.

'Why, Jack,' she cried, 'what *have* you been doing? What
has happened? Are you ill?' Thus driven into a direct lie, I
said that the sun had been a little too much for me. It was
close upon five o'clock of a cloudy April afternoon, and the
sun had been hidden all day. I saw my mistake as soon as the
words were out of my mouth; attempted to recover it;
blundered hopelessly, and followed Kitty in a regal rage out
of doors, amid the smiles of my acquaintances. I made some
excuse (I have forgotten what) on the score of my feeling
faint; and cantered away to my hotel, leaving Kitty to finish
the ride by herself.

In my room I sat down and tried calmly to reason out the
matter. Here was I, Theobald Jack Pansay, a well-educated
Bengal Civilian in the year of grace 1885, presumably sane,
certainly healthy, driven in terror from my sweetheart's side
by the apparition of a woman who had been dead and buried
eight months ago. These were facts that I could not blink.
Nothing was farther from my thought than any memory of
Mrs Wessington when Kitty and I left Hamilton's shop.
Nothing was more utterly commonplace than the stretch of
wall opposite Peliti's. It was broad daylight. The road was
full of people; and yet here, look you, in defiance of every law
of probability, in direct outrage of Nature's ordinance, there
had appeared to me a face from the grave.

Kitty's Arab had gone *through* the 'rickshaw: so that my
first hope that some woman marvellously like Mrs Wessington had hired the carriage and the coolies with their old
livery was lost. Again and again I went round this treadmill of
thought; and again and again gave up baffled and in despair.
The voice was as inexplicable as the apparition. I had

originally some wild notion of confiding it all to Kitty; of begging her to marry me at once, and in her arms defying the ghostly occupant of the 'rickshaw. 'After all,' I argued, 'the presence of the 'rickshaw is in itself enough to prove the existence of a spectral illusion. One may see ghosts of men and women, but surely never coolies and carriages. The whole thing is absurd. Fancy the ghost of a hillman!'

Next morning I sent a penitent note to Kitty, imploring her to overlook my strange conduct of the previous afternoon. My Divinity was still very wroth, and a personal apology was necessary. I explained, with a fluency born of night-long pondering over a falsehood, that I had been attacked with a sudden palpitation of the heart—the result of indigestion. This eminently practical solution had its effect; and Kitty and I rode out that afternoon with the shadow of my first lie dividing us.

Nothing would please her save a canter round Jakko. With my nerves still unstrung from the previous night I feebly protested against the notion, suggesting Observatory Hill, Jutogh, the Boileaugunge road—anything rather than the Jakko round. Kitty was angry and a little hurt; so I yielded from fear of provoking further misunderstanding, and we set out together towards Chota Simla. We walked a greater part of the way, and, according to our custom, cantered from a mile or so below the Convent to the stretch of level road by the Sanjaolie Reservoir. The wretched horses appeared to fly, and my heart beat quicker and quicker as we neared the crest of the ascent. My mind had been full of Mrs Wessington all the afternoon; and every inch of the Jakko road bore witness to our old-time walks and talks. The boulders were full of it; the pines sang it aloud overhead; the rain-fed torrents giggled and chuckled unseen over the shameful story; and the wind in my ears chanted the iniquity aloud.

As a fitting climax, in the middle of the level men call the Ladies' Mile the Horror was awaiting me. No other 'rickshaw was in sight—only the four black-and-white *jhampanis*, the yellow-panelled carriage, and the golden head of the woman within—all apparently just as I had left them eight months and one fortnight ago! For an instant I fancied that Kitty *must* see what I saw—we were so marvellously sympathetic in all things. Her next words undeceived me: 'Not a soul in sight! Come along, Jack, and I'll race you to the Reservoir buildings!' Her wiry little Arab was off like a bird, my Waler following close behind, and in this order we dashed under the cliffs. Half a minute brought us within fifty yards of the 'rickshaw. I pulled my Waler and fell back a little. The 'rickshaw was directly in the middle of the road; and once more the Arab passed through it, my horse following. 'Jack! Jack, dear! *Please* forgive me,' rang with a wail in my ears, and, after an interval: 'It's all a mistake, a hideous mistake!'

I spurred my horse like a man possessed. When I turned my head at the Reservoir works the black-and-white liveries were still waiting—patiently waiting—under the grey hillside, and the wind brought me a mocking echo of the words I had just heard. Kitty bantered me a good deal on my silence throughout the remainder of the ride. I had been talking up till then wildly and at random. To save my life I could not speak afterwards naturally, and from Sanjaolie to the Church wisely held my tongue.

I was to dine with the Mannerings that night, and had barely time to canter home to dress. On the road to Elysium Hill I overheard two men talking together in the dusk.—'It's a curious thing,' said one, 'how completely all trace of it disappeared. You know, my wife was insanely fond of the woman (never could see anything in her myself), and wanted me to pick up her old 'rickshaw and coolies if they were to be got for love or money. Morbid sort of fancy I call it; but I've got to do what the Memsahib tells me. Would you believe that the man she hired it from tells me that all four of the men—they were brothers—died of cholera on the way to Hardwar, poor devils; and the 'rickshaw has been broken up by the man himself! Told me he never used a dead Memsahib's 'rickshaw. Spoilt his luck. Queer notion, wasn't it? Fancy poor little Mrs Wessington spoiling any one's luck except her own!' I laughed aloud at this point; and my laugh jarred on me as I uttered it. So there *were* ghosts of 'rickshaws after all, and ghostly employments in the other world! How much did Mrs Wessington give her men? What were their hours? Where did they go?

And for visible answer to my last question I saw the infernal Thing blocking my path in the twilight. The dead travel fast, and by short cuts unknown to ordinary coolies. I laughed aloud a second time and checked my laughter suddenly, for I was afraid I was going mad. Mad to a certain extent I must have been, for I recollect that I reined in my horse at the head of the 'rickshaw, and politely wished Mrs Wessington 'Good evening.' Her answer was one I knew only too well. I listened to the end; and replied that I had heard it all before, but should be delighted if she had anything further to say. Some malignant devil stronger than I must have entered into me that evening, for I have a dim recollection of talking the commonplaces of the day for five minutes to the Thing in front of me.

'Mad as a hatter, poor devil—or drunk. Max, try and get him to come home.'

Surely *that* was not Mrs Wessington's voice! The two men had overheard me speaking to the empty air, and had returned to look after me. They were very kind and considerate, and from their words evidently gathered that I was extremely drunk. I thanked them confusedly and cantered away to my hotel, there changed, and arrived at the Mannerings' ten minutes late. I pleaded the darkness of the night as an excuse; was rebuked by Kitty for my un-loverlike tardiness; and sat down.

The conversation had already become general; and, under cover of it, I was addressing some tender small talk to my sweetheart when I was aware that at the farther end of the table a short, red-whiskered man was describing, with much broidery, his encounter with a mad unknown that evening.

A few sentences convinced me that he was repeating the incident of half an hour ago. In the middle of the story he looked round for applause, as professional story-tellers do, caught my eye, and straightway collapsed. There was a moment's awkward silence, and the red-whiskered man muttered something to the effect that he had 'forgotten the rest,' thereby sacrificing a reputation as a good story-teller which he had built up for six seasons past. I blessed him from the bottom of my heart, and—went on with my fish.

In the fullness of time that dinner came to an end; and with genuine regret I tore myself away from Kitty—as certain as I was of my own existence that It would be waiting for me outside the door. The red-whiskered man, who had been introduced to me as Dr Heatherlegh of Simla, volunteered to bear me company as far as our roads lay together. I accepted his offer with gratitude.

My instinct had not deceived me. It lay in readiness in the Mall, and, in what seemed devilish mockery of our ways, with a lighted head-lamp. The red-whiskered man went to the point at once, in a manner that showed he had been thinking over it all dinner-time.

'I say, Pansay, what the deuce was the matter with you this evening on the Elysium Road?' The suddenness of the question wrenched an answer from me before I was aware.

'That!' said I, pointing to It.

'*That* may be either D.T. or Eyes for aught I know. Now, you don't liquor. I saw as much at dinner, so it can't be D.T. There's nothing whatever where you're pointing, though you're sweating and trembling with fright like a scared pony. Therefore, I conclude that it's Eyes. And I ought to understand all about them. Come along home with me. I'm on the Blessington lower road.'

To my intense delight the 'rickshaw, instead of waiting for us, kept about twenty yards ahead—and this, too, whether we walked, trotted, or cantered. In the course of that long night ride I had told my companion almost as much as I have told you here.

'Well, you've spoilt one of the best tales I've ever laid tongue to,' said he, 'but I'll forgive you for the sake of what you've gone through. Now come home and do what I tell you; and when I've cured you, young man, let this be a lesson to you to steer clear of women and indigestible food till the day of your death.'

The 'rickshaw kept steadily in front; and my red-whiskered friend seemed to derive great pleasure from my account of its exact whereabouts.

'Eyes, Pansay—all Eyes, Brain, and Stomach. And the greatest of these three is Stomach. You've too much conceited Brain, too little Stomach, and thoroughly unhealthy Eyes. Get your Stomach straight and the rest follows. And all that's French for a liver pill. I'll take sole medical charge of you from this hour, for you're too interesting a phenomenon to be passed over.'

By this time we were deep in the shadow of the Blessington lower road, and the 'rickshaw came to a dead stop under a pine-clad, overhanging shale cliff. Instinctively I halted too, giving my reason. Heatherlegh rapped out an oath.

'Now, if you think I'm going to spend a cold night on the hillside for the sake of a Stomach-*cum*-Brain-*cum*-Eye illusion——Lord, ha' mercy! What's that?'

There was a muffled report, a blinding smother of dust just in front of us, a crack, the noise of rent boughs, and about ten yards of the cliff-side—pines, undergrowth, and all—slid down into the road below, completely blocking it up. The uprooted trees swayed and tottered for a moment like drunken giants in the gloom, and then fell prone among their fellows with a thunderous crash. Our two horses stood motionless and sweating with fear. As soon as the rattle of falling earth and stone had subsided, my companion muttered: 'Man, if we'd gone forward we should have been ten feet deep in our graves by now. "There are more things in heaven and earth" . . . Come home, Pansay, and thank God. I want a peg badly.'

We retraced our way over the Church Ridge, and I arrived at Dr Heatherlegh's house shortly after midnight.

His attempts towards my cure commenced almost immediately, and for a week I never left his sight. Many a time in the course of that week did I bless the good-fortune which had thrown me in contact wth Simla's best and kindest doctor. Day by day my spirits grew lighter and more equable. Day by day, too, I became more and more inclined to fall in with Heatherlegh's 'spectral illusion' theory, implicating eyes, brain, and stomach. I wrote to Kitty, telling her that a slight sprain caused by a fall from my horse kept me indoors for a few days; and that I should be recovered before she had time to regret my absence.

Heatherlegh's treatment was simple to a degree. It consisted of liver pills, cold-water baths, and strong exercise, taken in the dusk or at early dawn—for, as he sagely observed: 'A man with a sprained ankle doesn't walk a dozen miles a day, and your young woman might be wondering, if she saw you.'

At the end of the week, after much examination of pupil and pulse, and strict injunctions as to diet and pedestrianism, Heatherlegh dismissed me as brusquely as he had taken charge of me. Here is his parting benediction: 'Man, I certify to your mental cure, and that's as much as to say I've cured most of your bodily ailments. Now, get your traps out of this as soon as you can; and be off to make love to Miss Kitty.'

I was endeavouring to express my thanks for his kindness. He cut me short.

'Don't think I did this because I like you. I gather that you've behaved like a blackguard all through. But, all the same, you're a phenomenon, and as queer a phenomenon as you are a blackguard. No!'—checking me a second time—'not a rupee, please. Go out and see if you can find the eyes-brain-and-stomach business again. I'll give you a lakh* for each time you see it.'

Half an hour later I was in the Mannerings' drawing-room with Kitty—drunk with the intoxication of present happiness and the foreknowledge that I should never more be troubled with Its hideous presence. Strong in the sense of my new-found security, I proposed a ride at once; and, by preference, a canter round Jakko.

Never had I felt so well, so overladen with vitality and mere animal spirits, as I did on the afternoon of the 30th of April. Kitty was delighted at the change in my appearance, and complimented me on it in her delightfully frank and outspoken manner. We left the Mannerings' house together, laughing and talking, and cantered along the Chota Simla road as of old.

I was in haste to reach the Sanjaolie Reservoir and there

make my assurance doubly sure. The horses did their best, but seemed all too slow to my impatient mind. Kitty was astonished at my boisterousness. 'Why, Jack!' she cried at last, 'you are behaving like a child. What are you doing?'

We were just below the Convent, and from sheer wantonness I was making my Waler plunge and curvet across the road as I tickled it with the loop of my riding-whip.

'Doing?' I answered; 'nothing, dear. That's just it. If you'd been doing nothing for a week except lie up, you'd be as riotous as I.

> 'Singing and murmuring in your feastful mirth,
>   Joying to feel yourself alive;
> Lord over Nature, Lord of the visible Earth,
>   Lord of the senses five.'*

My quotation was hardly out of my lips before we had rounded the corner above the Convent, and a few yards farther on could see across to Sanjaolie. In the centre of the level road stood the black-and-white liveries, the yellow-panelled 'rickshaw, and Mrs Keith-Wessington. I pulled up, looked, rubbed my eyes, and, I believe, must have said something. The next thing I knew was that I was lying face downward on the road, with Kitty kneeling above me in tears.

'Has it gone, child?' I gasped. Kitty only wept more bitterly.

'Has *what* gone, Jack, dear? What does it all mean? There must be a mistake somewhere, Jack. A hideous mistake.' Her last words brought me to my feet—mad—raving for the time being.

'Yes, there *is* a mistake somewhere,' I repeated, 'a hideous mistake. Come and look at It.'

I have an indistinct idea that I dragged Kitty by the wrist along the road up to where It stood, and implored her for pity's sake to speak to It; to tell It that we were betrothed; that neither Death nor Hell could break the tie between us; and Kitty only knows how much more to the same effect. Now and again I appealed passionately to the Terror in the 'rickshaw to bear witness to all I had said, and to release me from a torture that was killing me. As I talked I suppose I must have told Kitty of my old relations with Mrs Wessington, for I saw her listen intently with white face and blazing eyes.

'Thank you, Mr Pansay,' she said, 'that's *quite* enough. *Sais, ghora láo* [bring my horse].'

The *saises*, impassive as Orientals always are, had come up with the recaptured horses; and as Kitty sprang into her saddle I caught hold of her bridle, entreating her to hear me out and forgive. My answer was the cut of her riding-whip across my face from mouth to eye, and a word or two of farewell that even now I cannot write down. So I judged, and judged rightly, that Kitty knew all; and I staggered back to the side of the 'rickshaw. My face was cut and bleeding, and the blow of the riding-whip had raised a livid blue weal on it. I had no self-respect. Just then, Heatherlegh, who must have been following Kitty and me at a distance, cantered up.

'Doctor,' I said, pointing to my face, 'here's Miss Mannering's signature to my order of dismissal, and——I'll thank you for that lakh as soon as convenient.'

Heatherlegh's face, even in my abject misery, moved me to laughter.

'I'll stake my professional reputation——' he began.

'Don't be a fool,' I whispered. 'I've lost my life's happiness and you'd better take me home.'

As I spoke the 'rickshaw was gone. Then I lost all knowledge of what was passing. The crest of Jakko seemed to heave and roll like the crest of a cloud and fall in upon me.

Seven days later (on the 7th of May, that is to say) I was aware that I was lying in Heatherlegh's room as weak as a little child. Heatherlegh was watching me intently from behind the papers on his writing-table. His first words were not encouraging; but I was too far spent to be much moved by them.

'Here's Miss Kitty has sent back your letters. You corresponded a good deal, you young people. Here's a packet that looks like a ring, and a cheerful sort of a note from Mannering Papa, which I've taken the liberty of reading and burning. The old gentleman's not pleased with you.'

'And Kitty?' I asked dully.

'Rather more drawn than her father from what she says. By the same token, you must have been letting out any number of queer reminiscences just before I met you. Says that a man who would have behaved to a woman as you did to Mrs Wessington ought to kill himself out of sheer pity for his kind. She's a hot-headed little virago, your girl. Will have it too that you were suffering from D.T. when that row on the Jakko road turned up. Says she'll die before she ever speaks to you again.'

I groaned and turned over on the other side.

'Now you've got your choice, my friend. This engagement has to be broken off; and the Mannerings don't want to be too hard on you. Was it broken through D.T. or epileptic fits? Sorry I can't offer you a better exchange unless you'd prefer hereditary insanity. Say the word and I'll tell 'em it's fits. All Simla knows about that scene on the Ladies' Mile. Come! I'll give you five minutes to think over it.'

During those five minutes I believe that I explored thoroughly the lowest circles of the Inferno which it is permitted man to tread on earth. And at the same time I myself was watching myself faltering through the dark labyrinths of doubt, misery, and utter despair. I wondered, as Heatherlegh in his chair might have wondered, which dreadful alternative I should adopt. Presently I heard myself answering in a voice that I hardly recognized:—

'They're confoundedly particular about morality in these parts. Give 'em fits, Heatherlegh, and my love. Now let me sleep a bit longer.'

Then my two selves joined, and it was only I (half-crazed, devil-driven I) that tossed in my bed tracing step by step the history of the past month.

'But I am in Simla,' I kept repeating to myself. 'I, Jack Pansay, am in Simla, and there are no ghosts here. It's unreasonable of that woman to pretend there are. Why couldn't Agnes have left me alone? I never did her any harm. It might just as well have been me as Agnes. Only I'd never have come back on purpose to kill *her*. Why can't I be left alone—left alone and happy?'

It was high noon when I first awoke; and the sun was low in the sky before I slept—slept as the tortured criminal sleeps on his rack, too worn to feel further pain.

Next day I could not leave my bed. Heatherlegh told me in the morning that he had received an answer from Mr Mannering, and that, thanks to his (Heatherlegh's) friendly offices, the story of my affliction had travelled through the length and breadth of Simla, where I was on all sides much pitied.

'And that's rather more than you deserve,' he concluded pleasantly, 'though the Lord knows you've been going through a pretty severe mill. Never mind; we'll cure you yet, you perverse phenomenon.'

I declined firmly to be cured. 'You've been much too good to me already, old man,' said I; 'but I don't think I need trouble you further.'

In my heart I knew that nothing Heatherlegh could do would lighten the burden that had been laid upon me.

With that knowledge came also a sense of hopeless, impotent rebellion against the unreasonableness of it all. There were scores of men no better than I whose punishments had at least been reserved for another world; and I felt that it was bitterly, cruelly unfair that I alone should have been singled out for so hideous a fate. This mood would in time give place to another when it seemed that the 'rickshaw and I were the only realities in a world of shadows; that Kitty was a ghost; that Mannering, Heatherlegh, and all the other men and women I knew were all ghosts; and the great grey hills themselves but vain shadows devised to torture me. From mood to mood I tossed backwards and forwards for seven weary days; my body growing daily stronger and stronger, until the bedroom looking-glass told me that I had returned to everyday life, and was as other men once more. Curiously enough my face showed no signs of the struggle I had gone through. It was pale indeed, but as expressionless and commonplace as ever. I had expected some permanent alteration—visible evidence of the disease that was eating me away. I found nothing.

On the 15th of May I left Heatherlegh's house at eleven

o'clock in the morning; and the instinct of the bachelor drove me to the Club. There I found that every man knew my story as told by Heatherlegh, and was, in clumsy fashion, abnormally kind and attentive. Nevertheless I recognized that for the rest of my natural life I should be among but not of my fellows; and I envied very bitterly indeed the laughing coolies on the Mall below. I lunched at the Club, and at four o'clock wandered aimlessly down the Mall in the vague hope of meeting Kitty. Close to the Bandstand the black-and-white liveries joined me; and I heard Mrs Wessington's old appeal at my side. I had been expecting this ever since I came out, and was only surprised at her delay. The phantom 'rickshaw and I went side by side along the Chota Simla road in silence. Close to the bazar, Kitty and a man on horseback overtook and passed us. For any sign she gave I might have been a dog in the road. She did not even pay me the compliment of quickening her pace, though the rainy afternoon might have served for excuse.

So Kitty and her companion, and I and my ghostly Light-o'-Love, crept round Jakko in couples. The road was streaming with water; the pines dripped like roof-pipes on the rocks below, and the air was full of fine driving rain. Two or three times I found myself saying to myself almost aloud: 'I'm Jack Pansay on leave at Simla—*at Simla!* Everyday, ordinary Simla. I mustn't forget that—I mustn't forget that.' Then I would try to recollect some of the gossip I had heard at the Club: the prices of So-and-So's horses—anything, in fact, that related to the workaday Anglo-Indian world I knew so well. I even repeated the multiplication-table rapidly to myself, to make quite sure that I was not taking leave of my senses. It gave me much comfort, and must have prevented my hearing Mrs Wessington for a time.

Once more I wearily climbed the Convent slope and entered the level road. Here Kitty and the man started off at a canter, and I was left alone with Mrs Wessington. 'Agnes,' said I, 'will you put back your hood and tell me what it all means?' The hood dropped noiselessly, and I was face to face with my dead and buried mistress. She was wearing the dress in which I had last seen her alive; carried the same tiny handkerchief in her right hand, and the same card-case in her left. (A woman nine months dead with a card-case!) I had to pin myself down to the multiplication-table, and to set both hands on the stone parapet of the road, to assure myself that that at least was real.

'Agnes,' I repeated, 'for pity's sake tell me what it all means.' Mrs Wessington leaned forward, with that odd, quick turn of the head I used to know so well, and spoke.

If my story had not already so madly over-leaped the bounds of all human belief I should apologize to you now. As I know that no one—no, not even Kitty, for whom it is written as some sort of justification of my conduct—will believe me, I will go on. Mrs Wessington spoke, and I walked with her from the Sanjaolie road to the turning below the Commander-in-Chief's house as I might walk by the side of any living woman's 'rickshaw, deep in conversation. The second and most tormenting of my moods of sickness had suddenly laid hold upon me, and, like the Prince in Tennyson's poem, 'I seemed to move among a world of ghosts.'* There had been a garden-party at the Commander-in-Chief's, and we two joined the crowd of homeward-bound folk. As I saw them it seemed that *they* were the shadows—impalpable fantastic shadows—that divided for Mrs Wessington's 'rickshaw to pass through. What we said during the course of that weird interview I cannot—indeed, I dare not—tell. Heatherlegh's comment would have been a short laugh and a remark that I had been 'mashing* a brain-eye-and-stomach chimera'. It was a ghastly and yet in some indefinable way a marvellously dear experience. Could it be possible, I wondered, that I was in this life to woo a second time the woman I had killed by my own neglect and cruelty?

I met Kitty on the homeward road—a shadow among shadows.

If I were to describe all the incidents of the next fortnight in their order, my story would never come to an end, and your patience would be exhausted. Morning after morning and evening after evening the ghostly 'rickshaw and I used to wander through Simla together. Wherever I went there the four black-and-white liveries followed me and bore me company to and from my hotel. At the Theatre I found them amid the crowd of yelling *jhampanis*; outside the Club veranda, after a long evening of whist; at the Birthday Ball, waiting patiently for my reappearance; and in broad daylight when I went calling. Save that it cast no shadow, the 'rickshaw was in every respect as real to look upon as one of wood and iron. More than once, indeed, I have had to check myself from warning some hard-riding friend against cantering over it. More than once I have walked down the Mall deep in conversation with Mrs Wessington, to the unspeakable amazement of the passers-by.

Before I had been out and about a week I learned that the 'fit' theory had been discarded in favour of insanity. However, I made no change in my mode of life. I called, rode, and dined out as freely as ever. I had a passion for the society of my kind which I had never felt before. I hungered to be among the realities of life; and at the same time I felt vaguely unhappy when I had been separated too long from my ghostly companion. It would be almost impossible to describe my varying moods from the 15th of May up to to-day.

The presence of the 'rickshaw filled me by turns with horror, blind fear, a dim sort of pleasure, and utter despair. I dared not leave Simla; though I knew that my stay there was killing me. I knew, moreover, that it was my destiny to die slowly and a little every day. My only anxiety was to get the penance over as quietly as might be. Alternately I hungered for a sight of Kitty, and watched her outrageous flirtations with my successor—to speak more accurately, my successors—with amused interest. She was as much out of my life as I was out of hers. By day I wandered with Mrs Wessington almost content. By night I implored Heaven to let me return to the world as I used to know it. Above all these varying moods lay the sensation of dull, numbing wonder that the seen and the Unseen should mingle so strangely on this earth to hound one poor soul to its grave.

* * * * *

August 27.—Heatherlegh has been indefatigable in his attendance on me; and only yesterday told me that I ought to send in an application for sick leave. An application to escape the company of a phantom! A request that the Government would graciously permit me to get rid of five ghosts and an airy 'rickshaw by going to England! Heatherlegh's proposition moved me to almost hysterical laughter. I told him that I should await the end quietly at Simla; and I am sure that the end is not far off. Believe me that I dread its advent more than any word can say; and I torture myself nightly with a thousand speculations as to the manner of my death.

Shall I die in my bed decently and as an English gentleman should die; or, in one last walk on the Mall, will my soul be wrenched from me to take its place for ever and ever by the side of that ghastly phantasm? Shall I return to my old lost allegiance in the next world, or shall I meet Agnes loathing her and bound to her side through all eternity? Shall we two hover over the scene of our lives till the end of Time? As the day of my death draws nearer, the intense horror that all living flesh feels toward escaped spirits from beyond the grave grows more and more powerful. It is an awful thing to go down quick among the dead with scarcely one-half of your life completed. It is a thousand times more awful to wait as I do in your midst, for I know not what unimaginable terror. Pity me, at least on the score of my 'delusion,' for I know you will never believe what I have written here. Yet as surely as ever a man was done to death by the Powers of Darkness, I am that man.

In justice, too, pity her. For as surely as ever woman was killed by man, I killed Mrs Wessington. And the last portion of my punishment is even now upon me.

Gemini*

Great is the justice of the White Man—
greater the power of a lie.
Native Proverb

THIS is your English Justice, Protector of the Poor. Look at
my back and loins which are beaten with sticks—heavy
sticks! I am a poor man, and there is no justice in Courts.

There were two of us, and we were born of one birth, but I
swear to you that I was born the first, and Ram Dass is the
younger by three full breaths. The astrologer said so, and it is
written in my horoscope—the horoscope of Durga Dass.

But we were alike—I and my brother, who is a beast
without honour—so alike that none knew, together or apart,
which was Durga Dass. I am a Mahajun* of Pali in Marwar,
and an honest man. This is true talk. When we were men, we
left our father's house in Pali, and went to the Punjab, where
all the people are mud-heads and sons of asses. We took shop
together in Isser Jang—I and my brother—near the big well
where the Governor's camp draws water. But Ram Dass,
who is without truth, made quarrel with me, and we were
divided. He took his books, and his pots, and his Mark, and
became a *bunnia*—a money-lender—in the long street of Isser
Jang, near the gateway of the road that goes to Montgomery.
It was not my fault that we pulled each other's turban. I am a
Mahajun of Pali, and I *always* speak true talk. Ram Dass was
the thief and the liar.

Now no man, not even the little children, could at one
glance see which was Ram Dass and which was Durga Dass.
But all the people of Isser Jang—may they die without
sons!—said that we were thieves. They used much bad talk,
but I took money on their bedsteads and their cooking-pots,
and the standing crop and the calf unborn, from the well in
the big square to the gate of the Montgomery road. They
were fools, these people—unfit to cut the toe-nails of a
Marwari from Pali. I lent money to them all. A little, very
little only—here a pice and there a pice.* God is my witness

that I am a poor man! The money is all with Ram Dass—may his sons turn Christian, and his daughter be a burning fire and a shame in the house from generation to generation! May she die unwed, and be the mother of a multitude of bastards! Let the light go out in the house of Ram Dass, my brother. This I pray daily twice—with offerings and charms.

Thus the trouble began. We divided the town of Isser Jang between us—I and my brother. There was a landholder beyond the gates, living but one short mile out, on the road that leads to Montgomery, and his name was Mohammed Shah, son of a Nawab.* He was a great devil and drank wine. So long as there were women in his house, and wine and money for the marriage-feasts, he was merry and wiped his mouth. Ram Dass lent him the money, a lakh* or half a lakh—how do I know!—and so long as the money was lent, the landholder cared not what he signed.

The people of Isser Jang were my portion, and the land-holder and the out-town were the portion of Ram Dass; for so we had arranged. I was the poor man, for the people of Isser Jang were without wealth. I did what I could, but Ram Dass had only to wait without the door of the landholder's garden-court, and to lend him the money, taking the bonds from the hand of the steward.

In the autumn of the year after the lending, Ram Dass said to the landholder: 'Pay me my money,' but the landholder gave him abuse. But Ram Dass went into the Courts with the papers and the bonds—all correct—and took out decrees against the landholder; and the name of the Government was across the stamps of the decrees. Ram Dass took field by field, and mango-tree by mango-tree, and well by well; putting in his own men—debtors of the out-town of Isser Jang—to cultivate the crops. So he crept up across the land, for he had the papers, and the name of the Government was across the stamps, till his men held the crops for him on all sides of the big white house of the landholder. It was well done; but when the landholder saw these things he was very angry and cursed Ram Dass after the manner of the Mohammedans.

And thus the landholder was angry, but Ram Dass laughed

and claimed more fields, as was written upon the bonds. This was in the month of Phagun.* I took my horse and went out to speak to the man who makes lac-bangles* upon the road that leads to Montgomery, because he owed me a debt. There was in front of me, upon his horse, my brother Ram Dass. And when he saw me he turned aside into the high crops, because there was hatred between us. And I went forward till I came to the orange-bushes by the landholder's house. The bats were flying, and the evening smoke was low down upon the land. Here met me four men—swashbucklers and Mohammedans—with their faces bound up, laying hold of my horse's bridle and crying out: 'This is Ram Dass! Beat!' Me they beat with their staves—heavy staves bound about with wire at the end, such weapons as those swine of Punjabis use—till, having cried for mercy, I fell down senseless. But these shameless ones still beat me, saying: 'O Ram Dass, this is your interest—well-weighed and counted into your hand, Ram Dass.' I cried aloud that I was not Ram Dass, but Durga Dass, his brother, yet they only beat me the more, and when I could make no more outcry they left me. But I saw their faces. There was Elahi Baksh who runs by the side of the landholder's white horse, and Nur Ali the keeper of the door, and Wajib Ali the very strong cook, and Abdul Latif the messenger—all of the household of the landholder. These things I can swear on the Cow's Tail if need be, but—*Ahi! Ahi!*—they have been already sworn, and I am a poor man whose honour is lost.

When these four had gone away laughing, my brother Ram Dass came out of the crops and mourned over me as one dead. But I opened my eyes, and prayed him to get me water. When I had drunk, he carried me on his back, and by byways brought me into the town of Isser Jang. My heart was turned to Ram Dass, my brother, in that hour because of his kindness, and I lost my enmity.

But a snake is a snake till it is dead; and a liar is a liar till the Judgment of the Gods takes hold of his heel. I was wrong in that I trusted my brother—the son of my mother.

When we had come to his house and I was a little restored, I told him my tale, and he said: 'Without doubt, it is me whom they would have beaten. But the Law Courts are open, and there is the Justice of the Sirkar* above all; and to the Law Courts do thou go when this sickness is overpast.'

Now when we two had left Pali in the old years, there fell a famine that ran from Jeysulmir to Gurgaon and touched Gogunda in the south. At that time the sister of my father came away and lived with us in Isser Jang; for a man must above all see that his folk do not die of want. When the quarrel between us twain came about, the sister of my father—a lean she-dog without teeth—said that Ram Dass had the right, and went with him. Into her hands—because she knew medicines and many cures—Ram Dass, my brother, put me faint with the beating, and much bruised even to the pouring of blood from the mouth. When I had two days' sickness the fever came upon me; and I set aside the fever to the account written in my mind against the landholder.

The Punjabis of Isser Jang are all the sons of Belial* and a she-ass, but they are very good witnesses, bearing testimony unshakenly whatever the pleaders may say. I would purchase witnesses by the score, and each man should give evidence, not only against Nur Ali, Wajib Ali, Abdul Latif, and Elahi Baksh, but against the landholder, saying that he upon his white horse had called his men to beat me; and, further, that they had robbed me of two hundred rupees. For the latter testimony, I would remit a little of the debt of the man who sold the lac-bangles, and he should say that he had put the money into my hands, and had seen the robbery from afar, but, being afraid, had run away. This plan I told to my brother Ram Dass; and he said that the arrangement was good, and bade me take comfort and make swift work to be abroad again. My heart was opened to my brother in my sickness, and I told him the names of those whom I would call as witnesses—all men in my debt, but of that the Magistrate Sahib could have no knowledge, nor the landholder. The fever stayed with me, and after the fever I was taken with colic and gripings very terrible. In that day I thought that my end was at hand, but I know now that she who gave me the medicines, the sister of my father—a widow with a widow's heart—had brought about my second sickness. Ram Dass, my brother, said that my house was shut and locked, and brought me the big door-key and my books, together with all the moneys that were in my house—even the money that was buried under the floor; for I was in great fear lest thieves should break in and dig. I speak true talk; there was but very little money in my house. Perhaps ten rupees—perhaps twenty. How can I tell? God is my witness that I am a poor man.

One night, when I had told Ram Dass all that was in my heart of the lawsuit that I would bring against the landholder, and Ram Dass had said that he had made the arrangements with the witnesses, giving me their names written, I was taken with a new great sickness, and they put me on the bed. When I was a little recovered—I cannot tell how many days afterwards—I made inquiry for Ram Dass, and the sister of my father said that he had gone to Montgomery upon a lawsuit. I took medicine and slept very heavily without waking. When my eyes were opened there was a great stillness in the house of Ram Dass, and none answered when I called—not even the sister of my father. This filled me with fear, for I knew not what had happened.

Taking a stick in my hand, I went out slowly, till I came to the great square by the well, and my heart was hot in me against the landholder because of the pain of every step I took.

I called for Jowar Singh, the carpenter, whose name was first upon the list of those who should bear evidence against the landholder, saying: 'Are all things ready, and do you know what should be said?'

Jowar Singh answered: 'What is this, and whence do you come, Durga Dass?'

I said: 'From my bed, where I have so long lain sick because of the landholder. Where is Ram Dass, my brother, who was to have made the arrangement for the witnesses? Surely you and yours know these things!'

Then Jowar Singh said: 'What has this to do with us, O Liar? I have borne witness and I have been paid, and the landholder has, by the order of the Court, paid both the five

hundred rupees that he robbed from Ram Dass and yet other
five hundred because of the great injury he did to your
brother.'

The well and the jujube-tree above it and the square of
Isser Jang became dark in my eyes, but I leaned on my stick
and said: 'Nay! This is child's talk and senseless. It was I who
suffered at the hands of the landholder, and I am come to
make ready the case. Where is my brother Ram Dass?'

But Jowar Singh shook his head, and a woman cried:
'What lie is here? What quarrel had the landholder with you,
bunnia? It is only a shameless one and one without faith who
profits by his brother's smarts. Have these *bunnias* no
bowels?'

I cried again, saying: 'By the Cow—by the Oath of the
Cow, by the Temple of the Blue-throated Mahadeo,* I and I
only was beaten—beaten to the death! Let your talk be
straight, O people of Isser Jang, and I will pay for the
witnesses.' And I tottered where I stood, for the sickness and
the pain of the beating were heavy upon me.

Then Ram Narain, who has his carpet spread under the
jujube-tree by the well, and writes all letters for the men of
the town, came up and said: 'To-day is the one-and-fortieth
day since the beating, and since these six days the case has
been judged in the Court, and the Assistant Commissioner
Sahib has given it for your brother Ram Dass, allowing the
robbery, to which, too, I bore witness, and all things else as
the witnesses said. There were many witnesses, and twice
Ram Dass became senseless in the Court because of his
wounds, and the Stunt Sahib—the *baba* Stunt Sahib*—gave
him a chair before all the pleaders. Why do you howl, Durga
Dass? These things fell as I have said. Was it not so?'

And Jowar Singh said: 'That is truth. I was there, and
there was a red cushion in the chair.'

And Ram Narain said: 'Great shame has come upon the
landholder because of this judgment, and, fearing his anger,
Ram Dass and all his house have gone back to Pali. Ram Dass
told us that you also had gone first, the enmity being healed
between you, to open a shop in Pali. Indeed, it were well for
you that you go even now, for the landholder has sworn that if

he catch any one of your house, he will hang him by the heels
from the well-beam, and, swinging him to and fro, will beat
him with staves till the blood runs from his ears. What I have
said in respect to the case is true, as these men here can
testify—even to the five hundred rupees.'

I said: 'Was it five hundred?' And Kirpa Ram, the Jat,*
said: 'Five hundred; for I bore witness also.'

And I groaned, for it had been in my heart to have said two
hundred only.

Then a new fear came upon me and my bowels turned to
water, and, running swiftly to the house of Ram Dass, I
sought for my books and my money in the great wooden chest
under my bedstead. There remained nothing—not even a
cowrie's value. All had been taken by the devil who said he
was my brother. I went to my own house also and opened the
boards of the shutters; but there also was nothing save the
rats among the grain-baskets. In that hour my senses left me,
and, tearing my clothes, I ran to the well-place, crying out for
the Justice of the English on my brother Ram Dass, and, in
my madness, telling all that the books were lost. When men
saw that I would have jumped down the well they believed
the truth of my talk, more especially because upon my back
and bosom were still the marks of the staves of the
landholder.

Jowar Singh the carpenter withstood me, and turning me
in his hands—for he is a very strong man—showed the scars
upon my body, and bowed down with laughter upon the
well-curb. He cried aloud so that all heard him, from the
well-square to the Caravanserai of the Pilgrims: 'Oho! The
jackals have quarrelled, and the grey one has been caught in
the trap. In truth, this man has been grievously beaten, and
his brother has taken the money which the Court decreed!
Oh, *bunnia*, this shall be told for years against you! The
jackals have quarrelled, and, moreover, the books are
burned. O people indebted to Durga Dass—and I know that
ye be many—the books are burned!'

Then all Isser Jang took up the cry that the books were
burned—*Ahi! Ahi!* that in my folly I had let that escape my
mouth—and they laughed throughout the city. They gave

me the abuse of the Punjabi, which is a terrible abuse and very hot; pelting me also with sticks and cow-dung till I fell down and cried for mercy.

Ram Narain, the letter-writer, bade the people cease, for fear that the news should get into Montgomery, and the Policemen might come down to inquire. He said, using many bad words: 'This much mercy will I do to you, Durga Dass, though there was no mercy in your dealings with my sister's son over the matter of the dun heifer. Has any man a pony on which he sets no store, that this fellow may escape? If the landholder hears that one of the twain (and God knows whether he beat one or both, but this man is certainly beaten) be in the city, there will be a murder done, and then will come the Police, making inquisition into each man's house and eating the sweet-seller's stuff all day long.'

Kirpa Ram, the Jat, said: 'I have a pony very sick. But with beating he can be made to walk for two miles. If he dies, the hide-sellers will have the body.'

Then Chumbo, the hide-seller, said: 'I will pay three annas for the body, and will walk by this man's side till such time as the pony dies. If it be more than two miles, I will pay two annas only.'

Kirpa Ram said: 'Be it so.' Men brought out the pony, and I asked leave to draw a little water from the well, because I was dried up with fear.

Then Ram Narain said: 'Here be four annas. God has brought you very low, Durga Dass, and I would not send you away empty, even though the matter of my sister's son's dun heifer be an open sore between us. It is a long way to your own country. Go, and if it be so willed, live; but, above all, do not take the pony's bridle, for that is mine.'

And I went out of Isser Jang amid the laughing of the huge-thighed Jats, and the hide-seller walked by my side waiting for the pony to fall dead. In one mile it died, and being full of fear of the landholder, I ran till I could run no more, and came to this place.

But I swear by the Cow, I swear by all things whereon Hindus and Mohammedans, and even the Sahibs swear, that I, and not my brother, was beaten by the landholder. But the case is shut, and the doors of the Law Courts are shut, and God knows where the *baba* Stunt Sahib—the mother's milk is not dry upon his hairless lip—is gone. *Ahi! Ahi!* I have no witnesses, and the scars will heal, and I am a poor man. But, on my Father's Soul, on the oath of a Mahajun from Pali, I, and not my brother, I was beaten by the landholder!

What can I do? The Justice of the English is as a great river. Having gone forward, it does not return. Howbeit, do you, Sahib, take a pen and write clearly what I have said, that the Dipty Sahib* may see, and reprove the Stunt Sahib, who is a colt yet unlicked by the mare, so young is he. I, and not my brother, was beaten, and he is gone to the west—I do not know where.

But, above all things, write—so that the Sahibs may read, and his disgrace be accomplished—that Ram Dass, my brother, son of Purun Dass, Mahajun of Pali, is a swine and a night-thief, a taker of life, an eater of flesh, a jackal-spawn without beauty, or faith, or cleanliness, or honour!

A Wayside Comedy

Because to every purpose there is time and
judgment, therefore the misery of man is
great upon him.—*Ecclesiastes* viii. 6

FATE and the Government of India have turned the Station of
Kashima into a prison; and, because there is no help for the
poor souls who are now lying there in torment, I write this
story, praying that the Government of India may be moved to
scatter the European population to the four winds.

Kashima is bounded on all sides by the rock-tipped circle
of the Dosehri hills. In spring, it is ablaze with roses. In
summer, the roses die and the hot winds blow from the hills.
In autumn, the white mists from the *jhils** cover the place as
with water, and in winter, the frosts nip everything young
and tender to earth-level. There is but one view in
Kashima—a stretch of perfectly flat pasture and plough-
land, running up to the grey-blue scrub of the Dosehri hills.

There are no amusements, except snipe and tiger shooting;
but the tigers have been long since hunted from their lairs in
the rock-caves, and the snipe only come once a year.
Narkarra—one hundred and forty-three miles by road—is
the nearest Station to Kashima. But Kashima never goes to
Narkarra, where there are at least twelve English people. It
stays within the circle of the Dosehri hills.

All Kashima acquits Mrs Vansuythen of any intention to
do harm; but all Kashima knows that she, and she alone,
brought about their pain.

Boulte, the Engineer, Mrs Boulte, and Captain Kurrell
know this. They are the English population of Kashima, if
we except Major Vansuythen, who is of no importance
whatever, and Mrs Vansuythen, who is the most important
of all.

You must remember, though you will not understand, that
all laws weaken in a small and hidden community where
there is no public opinion. When a man is absolutely alone in
a Station he runs a certain risk of falling into evil ways. This

risk is multiplied by every addition to the population up to twelve—the Jury-number. After that, fear and consequent restraint begin, and human action becomes less grotesquely jerky.

There was deep peace in Kashima till Mrs Vansuythen arrived. She was a charming woman, every one said so everywhere; and she charmed every one. In spite of this, or, perhaps, because of this, since Fate is so perverse, she cared only for one man, and he was Major Vansuythen. Had she been plain or stupid, this matter would have been intelligible to Kashima. But she was a fair woman, with very still grey eyes, the colour of a lake just before the light of the sun touches it. No man who had seen those eyes could, later on, explain what fashion of woman she was to look upon. The eyes dazzled him. Her own sex said that she was 'not bad-looking, but spoilt by pretending to be so grave.' And yet her gravity was natural. It was not her habit to smile. She merely went through life, looking at those who passed; and the women objected while the men fell down and worshipped.

She knows and is deeply sorry for the evil she has done to Kashima; but Major Vansuythen cannot understand why Mrs Boulte does not drop in to afternoon tea at least three times a week. 'When there are only two women in one Station, they ought to see a great deal of each other,' says Major Vansuythen.

Long and long before ever Mrs Vansuythen came out of those far-away places where there is society and amusement, Kurrell had discovered that Mrs Boulte was the one woman in the world for him and—you dare not blame them. Kashima was as out of the world as Heaven or the Other Place, and the Dosehri hills kept their secret well. Boulte had no concern in the matter. He was in camp for a fortnight at a time. He was a hard, heavy man, and neither Mrs Boulte nor Kurrell pitied him. They had all Kashima and each other for their very, very own; and Kashima was the Garden of Eden in those days. When Boulte returned from his wanderings he would slap Kurrell between the shoulders and call him 'old fellow', and the three would dine together. Kashima was happy then when the Judgment of God seemed almost as distant as Narkarra or the railway that ran down to the sea. But the Government sent Major Vansuythen to Kashima, and with him came his wife.

The etiquette of Kashima is much the same as that of a desert island. When a stranger is cast away there, all hands go down to the shore to make him welcome. Kashima assembled at the masonry platform close to the Narkarra Road, and spread tea for the Vansuythens. That ceremony was reckoned a formal call, and made them free of the Station, its rights and privileges. When the Vansuythens settled down they gave a tiny housewarming to all Kashima; and that made Kashima free of their house, according to the immemorial usage of the Station.

Then the Rains came, when no one could go into camp, and the Narkarra Road was washed away by the Kasun River, and in the cup-like pastures of Kashima the cattle waded knee-deep. The clouds dropped down from the Dosehri hills and covered everything.

At the end of the Rains Boulte's manner towards his wife changed and became demonstratively affectionate. They had been married twelve years, and the change startled Mrs Boulte, who hated her husband with the hate of a woman who has met with nothing but kindness from her mate, and, in the teeth of this kindness, has done him a great wrong. Moreover, she had her own trouble to fight with—her watch to keep over her own property, Kurrell. For two months the Rains had hidden the Dosehri hills and many other things besides; but, when they lifted, they showed Mrs Boulte that her man among men, her Ted—for she called him Ted in the old days when Boulte was out of earshot—was slipping the links of the allegiance.

'The Vansuythen Woman has taken him,' Mrs Boulte said to herself; and when Boulte was away, wept over her belief, in the face of the over-vehement blandishments of Ted. Sorrow in Kashima is as fortunate as Love because there is nothing to weaken it save the flight of Time. Mrs Boulte had never breathed her suspicion to Kurrell because she was not certain; and her nature led her to be very certain before she took steps in any direction. That is why she behaved as she did.

Boulte came into the house one evening, and leaned against the door-post of the drawing-room, chewing his moustache. Mrs Boulte was putting some flowers into a vase. There is a pretence of civilization even in Kashima.

'Little woman,' said Boulte quietly, 'do you care for me?'

'Immensely,' said she, with a laugh. 'Can you ask it?'

'But I'm serious,' said Boulte. '*Do* you care for me?'

Mrs Boulte dropped the flowers, and turned round quickly. 'Do you want an honest answer?'

'Ye-es, I've asked for it.'

Mrs Boulte spoke in a low, even voice for five minutes, very distinctly, that there might be no misunderstanding her meaning. When Samson broke the pillars of Gaza, he did a little thing, and one not to be compared with the deliberate pulling down of a woman's homestead about her own ears. There was no wise female friend to advise Mrs Boulte, the singularly cautious wife, to hold her hand. She struck at Boulte's heart, because her own was sick with suspicion of Kurrell, and worn out with the long strain of watching alone through the Rains. There was no plan or purpose in her speaking. The sentences made themselves; and Boulte listened, leaning against the door-post with his hands in his pockets. When all was over, and Mrs Boulte began to breathe through her nose before breaking out into tears, he laughed and stared straight in front of him at the Dosehri hills.

'Is that all?' he said. 'Thanks, I only wanted to know, you know.'

'What are you going to do?' said the woman, between her sobs.

'Do! Nothing. What should I do? Kill Kurrell, or send you Home, or apply for leave to get a divorce? It's two days' *dâk** into Narkarra.' He laughed again and went on: 'I'll tell you what *you* can do. You can ask Kurrell to dinner to-morrow—no, on Thursday, that will allow you time to pack—and you can bolt with him. I give you my word I won't follow.'

He took up his helmet and went out of the room, and Mrs Boulte sat till the moonlight streaked the floor, thinking and thinking and thinking. She had done her best upon the spur of the moment to pull the house down; but it would not fall. Moreover, she could not understand her husband, and she was afraid. Then the folly of her useless truthfulness struck her, and she was ashamed to write to Kurrell, saying, 'I have gone mad and told everything. My husband says that I am free to elope with you. Get a *dâk* for Thursday, and we will fly after dinner.' There was a cold-bloodedness about that procedure which did not appeal to her. So she sat still in her own house and thought.

At dinner-time Boulte came back from his walk, white and worn and haggard, and the woman was touched at his distress. As the evening wore on she muttered some expression of sorrow, something approaching to contrition. Boulte came out of a brown study and said, 'Oh, *that*! I wasn't thinking about that. By the way, what does Kurrell say to the elopement?'

'I haven't seen him,' said Mrs Boulte. 'Good God, is that all?'

But Boulte was not listening, and her sentence ended in a gulp.

The next day brought no comfort to Mrs Boulte, for Kurrell did not appear, and the new life that she, in the five minutes' madness of the previous evening, had hoped to build out of the ruins of the old, seemed to be no nearer.

Boulte ate his breakfast, advised her to see her Arab pony fed in the veranda, and went out. The morning wore through, and at mid-day the tension became unendurable. Mrs Boulte could not cry. She had finished her crying in the night, and now she did not want to be left alone. Perhaps the Vansuythen Woman would talk to her; and, since talking opens the heart, perhaps there might be some comfort to be found in her company. She was the only other woman in the Station. —

In Kashima there are no regular calling-hours. Every one can drop in upon every one else at pleasure. Mrs Boulte put on a big *terai* hat,* and walked across to the Vansuythens' house to borrow last week's *Queen*.* The two compounds touched, and instead of going up the drive, she crossed through the gap in the cactus-hedge, entering the house from the back. As she passed through the dining-room, she heard, behind the *purdah*** that cloaked the drawing-room door, her husband's voice, saying:—

'But on my Honour! On my Soul and Honour, I tell you she doesn't care for me. She told me so last night. I would have told you then if Vansuythen hadn't been with you. If it is for *her* sake that you'll have nothing to say to me, you can make your mind easy. It's Kurrell——'

'What?' said Mrs Vansuythen, with a hysterical little laugh. 'Kurrell! Oh, it can't be! You two must have made some horrible mistake. Perhaps you—you lost your temper, or misunderstood, or something. Things *can't* be as wrong as you say.'

Mrs Vansuythen had shifted her defence to avoid the man's pleading and was desperately trying to keep him to a side-issue.

'There must be some mistake,' she insisted, 'and it can be all put right again.'

Boulte laughed grimly.

'It can't be Captain Kurrell! He told me that he had never taken the least—the least interest in your wife, Mr Boulte. Oh, *do* listen! He said he had not. He swore he had not,' said Mrs Vansuythen.

The *purdah* rustled, and the speech was cut short by the entry of a little thin woman, with big rings round her eyes. Mrs Vansuythen stood up with a gasp.

'What was that you said?' asked Mrs Boulte. 'Never mind that man. What did Ted say to you? What did he say to you? What did he say to you?'

Mrs Vansuythen sat down helplessly on the sofa, over-borne by the trouble of her questioner.

'He said—I can't remember exactly what he said—but I understood him to say—that is——But really, Mrs Boulte, isn't it rather a strange question?'

'*Will* you tell me what he said?' repeated Mrs Boulte. Even a tiger will fly before a bear robbed of her whelps, and Mrs Vansuythen was only an ordinarily good woman. She began in a sort of desperation: 'Well, he said that he never cared for you at all, and, of course, there was not the least reason why he should have, and—and—that was all.'

'You said he *swore* he had not cared for me. Was that true?'

'Yes,' said Mrs Vansuythen very softly.

Mrs Boulte wavered for an instant where she stood, and then fell forward fainting.

'What did I tell you?' said Boulte, as though the conversation had been unbroken. 'You can see for yourself. She cares for *him*.' The light began to break into his dull mind, and he went on: 'And he—what was *he* saying to you?'

But Mrs Vansuythen, with no heart for explanations or impassioned protestations, was kneeling over Mrs Boulte.

'Oh, you brute!' she cried. 'Are *all* men like this? Help me to get her into my room—and her face is cut against the table. Oh, *will* you be quiet, and help me to carry her? I hate you, and I hate Captain Kurrell. Lift her up carefully, and now—go! Go away!'

Boulte carried his wife into Mrs Vansuythen's bedroom, and departed before the storm of that lady's wrath and disgust, impenitent and burning with jealousy. Kurrell had been making love to Mrs Vansuythen—would do Vansuythen as great a wrong as he had done Boulte, who caught himself considering whether Mrs Vansuythen would faint if she discovered that the man she loved had forsworn her.

In the middle of these meditations, Kurrell came cantering along the road and pulled up with a cheery 'Good mornin'. Been mashing Mrs Vansuythen as usual, eh? Bad thing for a sober, married man, that. What will Mrs Boulte say?'

Boulte raised his head and said slowly: 'Oh, you liar!' Kurrell's face changed. 'What's that?' he asked quickly.

'Nothing much,' said Boulte. 'Has my wife told you that you two are free to go off whenever you please? She has been good enough to explain the situation to me. You've been a true friend to me, Kurrell—old man—haven't you?'

Kurrell groaned, and tried to frame some sort of idiotic sentence about being willing to give 'satisfaction'. But his interest in the woman was dead, had died out in the Rains, and, mentally, he was abusing her for her amazing indiscretion. It would have been so easy to have broken off the thing

gently and by degrees, and now he was saddled with——
Boulte's voice recalled him.

'I don't think I should get any satisfaction from killing
you, and I'm pretty sure you'd get none from killing me.'

Then in a querulous tone, ludicrously disproportioned to
his wrongs, Boulte added:—

'Seems rather a pity that you haven't the decency to keep to
the woman, now you've got her. You've been a true friend to
her too, haven't you?'

Kurrell stared long and gravely. The situation was getting
beyond him.

'What do you mean?' he said.

Boulte answered, more to himself than the questioner:
'My wife came over to Mrs Vansuythen's just now; and it
seems you'd been telling Mrs Vansuythen that you'd never
cared for Emma. I suppose you lied, as usual. What had Mrs
Vansuythen to do with you, or you with her? Try to speak the
truth for once in a way.'

Kurrell took the double insult without wincing, and
replied by another question: 'Go on. What happened?'

'Emma fainted,' said Boulte simply. 'But, look here, what
had you been saying to Mrs Vansuythen?'

Kurrell laughed. Mrs Boulte had, with unbridled tongue,
made havoc of his plans; and he could at least retaliate by
hurting the man in whose eyes he was humiliated and shown
dishonourable.

'Saying to her? What *does* a man tell a lie like that for? I
suppose I said pretty much what you've said, unless I'm a
good deal mistaken.'

'I spoke the truth,' said Boulte, again more to himself than
Kurrell. 'Emma told me she hated me. She has no right in
me.'

'No! I suppose not. You're only her husband, y'know.
And what did Mrs Vansuythen say after you had laid your
disengaged heart at her feet?'

Kurrell felt almost virtuous as he put the question.

'I don't think that matters,' Boulte replied; 'and it doesn't
concern you.'

'But it does! I tell you it does'—began Kurrell shamelessly.

The sentence was cut by a roar of laughter from Boulte's lips. Kurrell was silent for an instant, and then he, too, laughed—laughed long and loudly, rocking in his saddle. It was an unpleasant sound—the mirthless mirth of these men on the long white line of the Narkarra Road. There were no strangers in Kashima, or they might have thought that captivity within the Dosehri hills had driven half the European population mad. The laughter ended abruptly, and Kurrell was the first to speak.

'Well, what are you going to do?'

Boulte looked up the road, and at the hills. 'Nothing,' said he quietly. 'What's the use? It's too ghastly for anything. We must let the old life go on. I can only call you a hound and a liar, and I can't go on calling you names for ever. Besides which, I don't feel that I'm much better. We can't get out of this place. What *is* there to do?'

Kurrell looked round the rat-pit of Kashima and made no reply. The injured husband took up the wondrous tale.

'Ride on, and speak to Emma if you want to. God knows *I* don't care what you do.'

He walked forward, and left Kurrell gazing blankly after him. Kurrell did not ride on either to see Mrs Boulte or Mrs Vansuythen. He sat in his saddle and thought, while his pony grazed by the roadside.

The whir of approaching wheels roused him. Mrs Vansuythen was driving home Mrs Boulte, white and wan, with a cut on her forehead.

'Stop, please,' said Mrs Boulte. 'I want to speak to Ted.'

Mrs Vansuythen obeyed, but as Mrs Boulte leaned forward, putting her hand upon the splash-board of the dog-cart, Kurrell spoke.

'I've seen your husband, Mrs Boulte.'

There was no necessity for any further explanation. The man's eyes were fixed, not upon Mrs Boulte, but her companion. Mrs Boulte saw the look.

'Speak to him!' she pleaded, turning to the woman at her side. 'Oh, speak to him! Tell him what you told me just now. Tell him you hate him! Tell him you hate him!'

She bent forward and wept bitterly, while the *sais*,*

impassive, went forward to hold the horse. Mrs Vansuythen turned scarlet and dropped the reins. She wished to be no party to such unholy explanations.

'I've nothing to do with it,' she began coldly; but Mrs Boulte's sobs overcame her, and she addressed herself to the man. 'I don't know what I am to say, Captain Kurrell. I don't know what I can call you. I think you've—you've behaved abominably, and she has cut her forehead terribly against the table.'

'It doesn't hurt. It isn't anything,' said Mrs Boulte feebly. '*That* doesn't matter. Tell him what you told me. Say you don't care for him. Oh, Ted, *won't* you believe her?'

'Mrs Boulte has made me understand that you were—that you were fond of her once upon a time,' went on Mrs Vansuythen.

'Well!' said Kurrell brutally. 'It seems to me that Mrs Boulte had better be fond of her own husband first.'

'Stop!' said Mrs Vansuythen. 'Hear me first. I don't care— I don't want to know anything about you and Mrs Boulte; but I want *you* to know that I hate you, that I think you are a cur, and that I'll never, *never* speak to you again. Oh, I don't dare to say what I think of you, you——man!'

'I want to speak to Ted,' moaned Mrs Boulte, but the dog-cart rattled on, and Kurrell was left on the road, shamed, and boiling with wrath against Mrs Boulte.

He waited till Mrs Vansuythen was driving back to her own house, and, she being freed from the embarrassment of Mrs Boulte's presence, learned for the second time her opinion of himself and his actions.

In the evenings it was the wont of all Kashima to meet at the platform on the Narkarra Road, to drink tea and discuss the trivialities of the day. Major Vansuythen and his wife found themselves alone at the gathering-place for almost the first time in their remembrance; and the cheery Major, in the teeth of his wife's remarkably reasonable suggestion that the rest of the Station might be sick, insisted upon driving round to the two bungalows and unearthing the population.

'Sitting in the twilight!' said he, with great indignation, to the Boultes. 'That'll never do! Hang it all, we're one family here! You *must* come out, and so must Kurrell. I'll make him bring his banjo.'

So great is the power of honest simplicity and a good digestion over guilty consciences that all Kashima did turn out, even down to the banjo; and the Major embraced the company in one expansive grin. As he grinned, Mrs Vansuythen raised her eyes for an instant and looked at all Kashima. Her meaning was clear. Major Vansuythen would never know anything. He was to be the outsider in that happy family whose cage was the Dosehri hills.

'You're singing villainously out of tune, Kurrell,' said the Major truthfully. 'Pass me that banjo.'

And he sang in excruciating wise till the stars came out and all Kashima went to dinner.

*   *   *   *   *

That was the beginning of the New Life of Kashima—the life that Mrs Boulte made when her tongue was loosened in the twilight.

Mrs Vansuythen has never told the Major; and since he insists upon keeping up a burdensome geniality, she has been compelled to break her vow of not speaking to Kurrell. This speech, which must of necessity preserve the semblance of politeness and interest, serves admirably to keep alight the flame of jealousy and dull hatred in Boulte's bosom, as it awakens the same passions in his wife's heart. Mrs Boulte hates Mrs Vansuythen because she has taken Ted from her, and, in some curious fashion, hates her because Mrs Vansuythen—and here the wife's eyes see far more clearly than the husband's—detests Ted. And Ted—that gallant captain and honourable man—knows now that it is possible to hate a woman once loved, to the verge of wishing to silence her for ever with blows. Above all is he shocked that Mrs Boulte cannot see the error of her ways.

Boulte and he go out tiger-shooting together in all friendship. Boulte has put their relationship on a most satisfactory footing.

'You're a blackguard,' he says to Kurrell, 'and I've lost any self-respect I may ever have had; but when you're with me, I can feel certain that you are not with Mrs Vansuythen, or making Emma miserable.'

Kurrell endures anything that Boulte may say to him. Sometimes they are away for three days together, and then the Major insists upon his wife going over to sit with Mrs Boulte; although Mrs Vansuythen has repeatedly declared that she prefers her husband's company to any in the world. From the way in which she clings to him, she would certainly seem to be speaking the truth.

But of course, as the Major says, 'in a little Station we must all be friendly.'

At Twenty-Two

Narrow as the womb, deep as the Pit, and
dark as the heart of a man.—*Sonthal**
Miners' Proverb

'A WEAVER went out to reap but stayed to unravel the corn-stalks. Ha! ha! ha! Is there any sense in a weaver?'

Janki Meah* glared at Kundoo, but, as Janki Meah was blind, Kundoo was not impressed. He had come to argue with Janki Meah, and, if chance favoured, to make love to the old man's pretty young wife.

This was Kundoo's grievance, and he spoke in the name of all the five men who, with Janki Meah, composed the gang in Number Seven gallery of Twenty-Two. Janki Meah had been blind for the thirty years during which he had served the Jimahari Colliery with pick and crowbar. All through those thirty years he had regularly, every morning before going down, drawn from the overseer his allowance of lamp-oil—just as if he had been an eyed miner. What Kundoo's gang resented, as hundreds of gangs had resented before, was Janki Meah's selfishness. He would not add the oil to the common stock of his gang, but would save and sell it.

'I knew these workings before you were born,' Janki Meah used to reply. 'I don't want the light to get my coal out by, and I am not going to help you. The oil is mine, and I intend to keep it.'

A strange man in many ways was Janki Meah, the white-haired, hot-tempered, sightless weaver who had turned pit-man. All day long—except on Sundays and Mondays when he was usually drunk—he worked in the Twenty-Two shaft of the Jimahari Colliery as cleverly as a man with all the senses. At evening he went up in the great steam-hauled cage to the pit-bank, and there called for his pony—a rusty, coal-dusty beast, nearly as old as Janki Meah. The pony would come to his side, and Janki Meah would clamber on to its back and be taken at once to the plot of land which he, like the other miners, received from the Jimahari Company. The pony knew that place, and when, after six years, the Company changed all the allotments to prevent the miners from acquiring proprietary rights, Janki Meah represented, with tears in his eyes, that were his holding shifted he would never be able to find his way to the new one. 'My horse only knows that place,' pleaded Janki Meah, and so he was allowed to keep his land.

On the strength of this concession and his accumulated oil-savings, Janki Meah took a second wife—a girl of the Jolaha main stock of the Meahs, and singularly beautiful. Janki Meah could not see her beauty; wherefore he took her on trust, and forbade her to go down the pit. He had not worked for thirty years in the dark without knowing that the pit was no place for pretty women. He loaded her with ornaments—not brass or pewter, but real silver ones—and she rewarded him by flirting outrageously with Kundoo of Number Seven gallery gang. Kundoo was really the head of the gang, but Janki Meah insisted upon all the work being entered in his own name, and chose the men that he worked with. Custom—stronger even than the Jimahari Company—dictated that Janki, by right of his years, should manage these things, and should, also, work despite his blindness. In Indian mines, where they cut into the solid coal with the pick and clear it out from floor to ceiling, he could come to no great harm. At Home, where they undercut the coal and bring it down in crashing avalanches from the roof, he would never have been allowed to set foot in a pit. He was not a popular man because of his oil-savings; but all the gangs admitted that Janki knew all the *khads*, or workings, that had ever been sunk or worked since the Jimahari Company first started operations on the Tarachunda fields.

Pretty little Unda only knew that her old husband was a fool who could be managed. She took no interest in the colliery except in so far as it swallowed up Kundoo five days out of the seven, and covered him with coal-dust. Kundoo was a great workman, and did his best not to get drunk, because, when he had saved forty rupees, Unda was to steal everything that she could find in Janki's house and run with Kundoo to a land where there were no mines, and every one

kept three fat bullocks and a milch-buffalo. While this
scheme ripened it was his custom to drop in upon Janki and
worry him about the oil-savings. Unda sat in a corner and
nodded approval. On the night when Kundoo had quoted
that objectionable proverb about weavers, Janki grew angry.

'Listen, you pig,' said he. 'Blind I am, and old I am, but,
before ever you were born, I was grey among the coal. Even
in the days when the Twenty-Two *khad* was unsunk, and
there were not two thousand men here, I was known to have
all knowledge of the pits. What *khad* is there that I do not
know, from the bottom of the shaft to the end of the last
drive? Is it the Baromba *khad*, the oldest, or the Twenty-Two
where Tibu's gallery runs up to Number Five?'

'Hear the old fool talk!' said Kundoo, nodding to Unda.
'No gallery of Twenty-Two will cut into Five before the end
of the Rains. We have a month's solid coal before us. The
Babuji* says so.'

'Babuji! Pigji! Dogji! What do these fat slugs from Calcutta know? He draws and draws and draws, and talks and
talks and talks, and his maps are all wrong. I, Janki, know
that this is so. When a man has been shut up in the dark for
thirty years God gives him knowledge. The old gallery that
Tibu's gang made is not six feet from Number Five.'

'Without doubt God gives the blind knowledge,' said
Kundoo, with a look at Unda. 'Let it be as you say. I, for my
part, do not know where lies the gallery of Tibu's gang, but *I*
am not a withered monkey who needs oil to grease his joints
with.'

Kundoo swung out of the hut laughing, and Unda giggled.
Janki turned his sightless eyes towards his wife and swore. 'I
have land, and I have sold a great deal of lamp-oil,' mused
Janki, 'but I was a fool to marry this child.'

A week later the Rains set in with a vengeance, and the
gangs paddled about in coal-slush at the pit-banks. Then the
big mine-pumps were made ready, and the Manager of the
Colliery ploughed through the wet towards the Tarachunda
River swelling between its soppy banks. 'Lord send that this
beastly beck* doesn't misbehave,' said the Manager piously,
and he went to take counsel with his Assistant about the
pumps.

But the Tarachunda misbehaved very much indeed. After a fall of three inches of rain in an hour it was obliged to do something. It topped its bank and joined the flood-water that was hemmed between two low hills just where the embankment of the Colliery main line crossed. When a large part of a rain-fed river, and a few acres of flood-water, make a dead set for a nine-foot culvert, the culvert may spout its finest, but the water cannot *all* get out. The Manager pranced upon one leg with excitement, and his language was improper.

He had reason to swear, because he knew that one inch of water on land meant a pressure of one hundred tons to the acre; and here was about five feet of water forming, behind the railway embankment, over the shallower workings of Twenty-Two. You must understand that, in a coal-mine, the coal nearest the surface is worked first from the central shaft. That is to say, the miners may clear out the stuff to within ten, twenty, or thirty feet of the surface, and, when all is worked out, leave only a skin of earth upheld by some few pillars of coal. In a deep mine, where they know that they have any amount of material at hand, men prefer to get all their mineral out at one shaft, rather than make a number of little holes to tap the comparatively unimportant surface-coal.

And the Manager watched the flood.

The culvert spouted a nine-foot gush; but the water still formed, and word was sent to clear the men out of Twenty-Two. The cages came up crammed and crammed again with the men nearest the pit's-eye, as they call the place where you can see daylight from the bottom of the main shaft. All away and away up the long black galleries the flare-lamps were winking and dancing like so many fireflies, and the men and the women waited for the clanking, rattling, thundering cages to come down and fly up again. But the out-workings were very far off, and word could not be passed quickly, though the heads of the gangs and the Assistant shouted and swore and tramped and stumbled. The Manager kept one eye on the great troubled pool behind the embankment, and prayed that the culvert would give way and let the water through in time. With the other eye he watched the cages come up and saw the headman counting the roll of the gangs.

With all his heart and soul he swore at the winder who controlled the iron drum that wound up the wire rope on which hung the cages.

In a little time there was a down-draw in the water behind the embankment—a sucking whirlpool, all yellow and yeasty. The water had smashed through the skin of the earth and was pouring into the old shallow workings of Twenty-Two.

Deep down below, a rush of black water caught the last gang waiting for the cage, and as they clambered in, the whirl was about their waists. The cage reached the pit-bank, and the Manager called the roll. The gangs were all safe except Gang Janki, Gang Mogul, and Gang Rahim, eighteen men, with perhaps ten basket-women who loaded the coal into the little iron carriages that ran on the tramways of the main galleries. These gangs were in the out-workings, three-quarters of a mile away, on the extreme fringe of the mine. Once more the cage went down, but with only two Englishmen in it, and dropped into a swirling, roaring current that had almost touched the roof of some of the lower side-galleries. One of the wooden balks with which they had propped the old workings shot past on the current, just missing the cage.

'If we don't want our ribs knocked out, we'd better go,' said the Manager. 'We can't even save the Company's props.'

The cage drew out of the water with a splash, and a few minutes later it was officially reported that there was at least ten feet of water in the pit's-eye. Now ten feet of water there meant that all other places in the mine were flooded except such galleries as were more than ten feet above the level of the bottom of the shaft. The deep working would be full, the main galleries would be full, but in the high workings reached by inclines from the main roads there would be a certain amount of air cut off, so to speak, by the water and squeezed up by it. The little science-primers explain how water behaves when you pour it down test-tubes. The flooding of Twenty-Two was an illustration on a large scale.

* * * * *

'By the Holy Grove, what has happened to the air?' It was a

Sonthal gangman of Gang Mogul in Number Nine gallery, and he was driving a six-foot way through the coal. Then there was a rush from the other galleries, and Gang Janki and Gang Rahim stumbled up with their basket-women.

'Water has come in the mine,' they said, 'and there is no way of getting out.'

'I went down,' said Janki—'down the slope of my gallery, and I felt the water.'

'There has been no water in the cutting in our time,' clamoured the women. 'Why cannot we go away?'

'Be silent!' said Janki. 'Long ago, when my father was here, water came to Ten—no, Eleven—cutting, and there was great trouble. Let us get away to where the air is better.'

The three gangs and the basket-women left Number Nine gallery and went farther up Number Sixteen. At one turn of the road they could see the pitchy black water lapping on the coal. It had touched the roof of a gallery that they knew well—a gallery where they used to smoke their pipes and manage their flirtations. Seeing this, they called aloud upon their Gods, and the Meahs, who are thrice bastard Mohammedans, strove to recollect the name of the Prophet. They came to a great open square whence nearly all the coal had been extracted. It was the end of the out-workings, and the end of the mine.

Far away down the gallery a small pumping-engine, used for keeping dry a deep working and fed with steam from above, was throbbing faithfully. They heard it cease.

'They have cut off the steam,' said Kundoo hopefully. 'They have given the order to use all the steam for the pit-bank pumps. They will clear out the water.'

'If the water has reached the smoking-gallery,' said Janki, 'all the Company's pumps can do nothing for three days.'

'It is very hot,' moaned Jasoda, the Meah basket-woman. 'There is a very bad air here because of the lamps.'

'Put them out,' said Janki. 'Why do you want lamps?' The lamps were put out, and the company sat still in the utter dark. Somebody rose quietly and began walking over the coals. It was Janki, who was touching the walls with his hands. 'Where is the ledge?' he murmured to himself.

'Sit, sit!' said Kundoo. 'If we die, we die. The air is very bad.'

But Janki still stumbled and crept and tapped with his pick upon the walls. The women rose to their feet.

'Stay all where you are. Without the lamps you cannot see, and I—I am always seeing,' said Janki. Then he paused, and called out: 'O you who have been in the cutting more than ten years, what is the name of this open place? I am an old man and I have forgotten.'

'Bullia's Room,' answered the Sonthal who had complained of the vileness of the air.

'Again,' said Janki.

'Bullia's Room.'

'Then I have found it,' said Janki. 'The name only had slipped my memory. Tibu's gang's gallery is here.'

'A lie,' said Kundoo. 'There have been no galleries in this place since my day.'

'Three paces was the depth of the ledge,' muttered Janki without heeding—'and—oh, my poor bones!—I have found it! It is here, up this ledge. Come all you, one by one, to the place of my voice, and I will count you.'

There was a rush in the dark, and Janki felt the first man's face hit his knees as the Sonthal scrambled up the ledge.

'Who?' cried Janki.

'I, Sunua Manji.'

'Sit you down,' said Janki. 'Who next?'

One by one the women and the men crawled up the ledge which ran along one side of 'Bullia's Room'. Degraded Mohammedan, pig-eating Musahr, and wild Sonthal, Janki ran his hand over them all.

'Now follow after,' said he, 'catching hold of my heel, and the women catching the men's clothes.' He did not ask whether the men had brought their picks with them. A miner, black or white, does not drop his pick. One by one, Janki leading, they crept into the old gallery—a six-foot way with a scant four feet from thill to roof.

'The air is better here,' said Jasoda. They could hear her heart beating in thick, sick bumps.

'Slowly, slowly,' said Janki. 'I am an old man, and I forget many things. This is Tibu's gallery, but where are the four bricks where they used to put their hookah fire on when the Sahibs never saw? Slowly, slowly, O you people behind.'

They heard his hands disturbing the small coal on the floor of the gallery and then a dull sound. 'This is one unbaked brick, and this is another and another. Kundoo is a young man—let him come forward. Put a knee upon this brick and strike here. When Tibu's gang were at dinner on the last day before the good coal ended, they heard the men of Five on the other side, and Five worked *their* gallery two Sundays later—or it may have been one. Strike there, Kundoo, but give me room to go back.'

Kundoo, doubting, drove the pick, but the first soft crush of the coal was a call to him. He was fighting for his life and for Unda—pretty little Unda with rings on all her toes—for Unda and the forty rupees. The women sang the Song of the Pick—the terrible, slow, swinging melody with the muttered chorus that repeats the sliding of the loosened coal, and, to each cadence, Kundoo smote in the black dark. When he could do no more, Sunua Manji took the pick, and struck for his life and his wife, and his village beyond the blue hills over the Tarachunda River. An hour the men worked, and then the women cleared away the coal.

'It is farther than I thought,' said Janki. 'The air is very bad; but strike, Kundoo, strike hard.'

For the fifth time Kundoo took up the pick as the Sonthal crawled back. The song had scarcely recommenced when it was broken by a yell from Kundoo that echoed down the gallery: '*Par hua! Par hua!* We are through, we are through!' The imprisoned air in the mine shot through the opening, and the women at the far end of the gallery heard the water rush through the pillars of 'Bullia's Room' and roar against the ledge. Having fulfilled the law under which it worked, it rose no farther. The women screamed and pressed forward. 'The water has come—we shall be killed! Let us go.'

Kundoo crawled through the gap and found himself in a propped gallery by the simple process of hitting his head against a beam.

'Do I know the pits or do I not?' chuckled Janki. 'This is

the Number Five; go you out slowly, giving me your names. Ho, Rahim! count your gang! Now let us go forward, each catching hold of the other as before.'

They formed line in the darkness and Janki led them—for a pitman in a strange pit is only one degree less liable to err than an ordinary mortal underground for the first time. At last they saw a flare-lamp, and Gangs Janki, Mogul, and Rahim of Twenty-two stumbled dazed into the glare of the draught-furnace at the bottom of Five: Janki feeling his way and the rest behind.

'Water has come into Twenty-Two. God knows where are the others. I have brought these men from Tibu's gallery in our cutting, making connection through the north side of the gallery. Take us to the cage,' said Janki Meah.

* * * * *

At the pit-bank of Twenty-Two some thousand people clamoured and wept and shouted. One hundred men—one thousand men—had been drowned in the cutting. They would all go to their homes to-morrow. Where were their men? Little Unda, her cloth drenched with the rain, stood at the pit-mouth calling down the shaft for Kundoo. They had swung the cages clear of the mouth, and her only answer was the murmur of the flood in the pit's-eye two hundred and sixty feet below.

'Look after that woman! She'll chuck herself down the shaft in a minute,' shouted the Manager.

But he need not have troubled; Unda was afraid of death. She wanted Kundoo. The Assistant was watching the flood and seeing how far he could wade into it. There was a lull in the water, and the whirlpool had slackened. The mine was full, and the people at the pit-bank howled.

'My faith, we shall be lucky if we have five hundred hands on the place to-morrow!' said the Manager. 'There's some chance yet of running a temporary dam across that water. Shove in anything—tubs and bullock-carts if you haven't enough bricks. Make them work *now* if they never worked before. Hi! you gangers! make them work.'

Little by little the crowd was broken into detachments, and pushed towards the water with promises of overtime.

The dam-making began, and when it was fairly under way, the Manager thought that the hour had come for the pumps. There was no fresh inrush into the mine. The tall, red, iron-clamped pump-beam rose and fell, and the pumps snored and guttered and shrieked as the first water poured out of the pipe.

'We must run her all to-night,' said the Manager wearily, 'but there's no hope for the poor devils down below. Look here, Gur Sahai, if you are proud of your engines, show me what they can do now.'

Gur Sahai grinned and nodded, with his right hand upon the lever and an oil-can in his left. He could do no more than he was doing, but he could keep that up till the dawn. Were the Company's pumps to be beaten by the vagaries of that troublesome Tarachunda River? Never, never! And the pumps sobbed and panted: 'Never, never!' The Manager sat in the shelter of the pit-bank roofing, trying to dry himself by the pump-boiler fire, and, in the dreary dusk, he saw the crowds on the dam scatter and fly.

'That's the end,' he groaned. "'Twill take us six weeks to persuade 'em that we haven't tried to drown their mates on purpose. Oh for a decent, rational Geordie!'*

But the flight had no panic in it. Men had run over from Five with astounding news, and the foremen could not hold their gangs together. Presently, surrounded by a clamorous crew, Gangs Rahim, Mogul, and Janki, and ten basket-women, walked up to report themselves, and pretty little Unda stole away to Janki's hut to prepare his evening meal.

'Alone I found the way,' explained Janki Meah, 'and now will the Company give me pension?'

The simple pit-folk shouted and leaped and went back to the dam, reassured in their old belief that, whatever happened, so great was the power of the Company whose salt they ate, none of them could be killed. But Gur Sahai only bared his white teeth, and kept his hand upon the lever and proved his pumps to the uttermost.

* * * * *

'I say,' said the Assistant to the Manager, a week later, 'do you recollect *Germinal*?'

'Yes. Queer thing. I thought of it in the cage when that balk went by. Why?'

'Oh, this business seems to be *Germinal* upside-down.* Janki was in my veranda all this morning, telling me that Kundoo had eloped with his wife—Unda or Anda, I think her name was.'

'Hillo! And those were the cattle you risked your life for to clear out of Twenty-Two!'

'No—I was thinking of the Company's props, not the Company's men.'

'Sounds better to say so *now*; but I don't believe you, old fellow.'

The Education of Otis Yeere

I

In the pleasant orchard-closes
'God bless all our gains,' say we;
But 'May God bless all our losses'
Better suits with our degree.
                    *E. B. Browning**

THIS is the history of a failure; but the woman who failed said that it might be an instructive tale to put into print for the benefit of the younger generation. The younger generation does not want instruction, being perfectly willing to instruct if any one will listen to it. None the less, here begins the story where every right-minded story should begin, that is to say at Simla, where all things begin and many come to an evil end.

The mistake was due to a very clever woman making a blunder and not retrieving it. Men are licensed to stumble, but a clever woman's mistake is outside the regular course of Nature and Providence; since all good people know that a woman is the only infallible thing in this world, except Government Paper of the '79 issue, bearing interest at four and a half per cent. Yet, we have to remember that six consecutive days of rehearsing the leading part of *The Fallen Angel,** at the New Gaiety Theatre* where the plaster is not yet properly dry, might have brought about an unhingement of spirits which, again, might have led to eccentricities.

Mrs Hauksbee came to 'The Foundry' to tiffin with Mrs Mallowe, her one bosom friend, for she was in no sense 'a woman's woman'. And it was a woman's tiffin, the door shut to all the world; and they both talked *chiffons*, which is French for Mysteries.

'I've enjoyed an interval of sanity,' Mrs Hauksbee announced, after tiffin was over and the two were comfortably settled in the little writing-room that opened out of Mrs Mallowe's bedroom.

'My dear girl, what has *he* done?' said Mrs Mallowe

sweetly. It is noticeable that ladies of a certain age call each other 'dear girl', just as Commissioners of twenty-eight years' standing address their equals in the Civil List as 'my boy'.

'There's no *he* in the case. Who am I that imaginary men should be always credited to me? Am I an Apache?'

'No, dear, but somebody's scalp is generally drying at your wigwam-door. Soaking rather.'

This was an allusion to the Hawley Boy, who was in the habit of riding all across Simla in the Rains, to call on Mrs Hauksbee. That lady laughed.

'For my sins, the Aide at Tyrconnel last night told me off to The Mussuck.* Hsh! Don't laugh. One of my most devoted admirers. When the duff came—some one really ought to teach them to make puddings at Tyrconnel—The Mussuck was at liberty to attend to me.'

'Sweet soul! I know his appetite,' said Mrs Mallowe. 'Did he, oh, *did* he, begin his wooing?'

'By a special mercy of Providence, *no*. He explained his importance as a Pillar of the Empire. I didn't laugh.'

'Lucy, I don't believe you.'

'Ask Captain Sangar; he was on the other side. Well, as I was saying, The Mussuck dilated.'

'I think I can see him doing it,' said Mrs Mallowe pensively, scratching her fox-terrier's ears.

'I was properly impressed. Most properly. I yawned openly. "Strict supervision, and play them off one against the other," said The Mussuck, shovelling down his ice by *tureenfuls*, I assure you. "*That*, Mrs Hauksbee, is the secret of Government."'

Mrs Mallowe laughed long and merrily. 'And what did you say?'

'Did you ever know me at loss for an answer yet? I said: "So I have observed in my dealings with you." The Mussuck swelled with pride. He is coming to call on me to-morrow. The Hawley Boy is coming too.'

'"Strict supervision and play them off one against the other. *That*, Mrs Hauksbee, is the secret of *our* Government." And I daresay if we could get to The Mussuck's heart, we should find that he considers himself a man of the world.'

'As he is of the other two things.* I like The Mussuck, and I won't have you call him names. He amuses me.'

'He has reformed you, too, by what appears. Explain the interval of sanity, and hit Tim on the nose with the paper-cutter, please. That dog is too fond of sugar. Do you take milk in yours?'

'No, thanks. Polly, I'm wearied of this life. It's hollow.'

'Turn religious, then. I always said that Rome would be your fate.'

'Only exchanging half-a-dozen *attachés* in red for one in black, and if I fasted, the wrinkles would come, and never, *never* go. Has it ever struck you, dear, that I'm getting old?'

'Thanks for your courtesy. I'll return it. Ye-es, we are both not exactly—how shall I put it?'

'What we have been. "I feel it in my bones," as Mrs Crossley says. Polly, I've wasted my life.'

'As how?'

'Never mind how. I feel it. I want to be a Power before I die.'

'Be a Power, then. You've wits enough for anything—and beauty!'

Mrs Hauksbee pointed a teaspoon straight at her hostess. 'Polly, if you heap compliments on me like this, I shall cease to believe that you're a woman. Tell me how I am to be a Power.'

'Inform The Mussuck that he is the most fascinating and slimmest man in Asia, and he'll tell you anything and everything you please.'

'Bother The Mussuck! I mean an intellectual Power—not a gas-power. Polly, I'm going to start a *salon*.'

Mrs Mallowe turned lazily on the sofa and rested her head on her hand. 'Hear the words of the Preacher, the son of Baruch,'* she said.

'*Will* you talk sensibly?'

'I will, dear, for I see that you are going to make a mistake.'

'I never made a mistake in my life—at least, never one that I couldn't explain away afterwards.'

'Going to make a mistake,' went on Mrs Mallowe composedly. 'It is impossible to start a *salon* in Simla. A bar would be much more to the point.'

'Perhaps, but why? It seems so easy.'

'Just what makes it so difficult. How many clever women are there in Simla?'

'Myself and yourself,' said Mrs Hauksbee, without a moment's hesitation.

'Modest woman! Mrs Feardon would thank you for that. And how many clever men?'

'Oh—er—hundreds,' said Mrs Hauksbee vaguely.

'What a fatal blunder! Not one. They are all bespoke by the Government. Take my husband, for instance. Jack *was* a clever man, though I say so who shouldn't. Government has eaten him up. All his ideas and powers of conversation—he really used to be a good talker, even to his wife, in the old days—are taken from him by this—this kitchen-sink of a Government. That's the case with every man up here who is at work. I don't suppose a Russian convict under the knout is able to amuse the rest of his gang; and all our men-folk here are gilded convicts.'

'But there are scores——'

'I know what you're going to say. Scores of idle men up on leave. I admit it, but they are all of two objectionable sets. The Civilian who'd be delightful if he had the military man's knowledge of the world and style, and the military man who'd be adorable if he had the Civilian's culture.'

'Detestable word! *Have* Civilians culchaw? I never studied the breed deeply.'

'Don't make fun of Jack's Service. Yes. They're like the teapoys* in the Lakka Bazar—good material but not polished. They can't help themselves, poor dears. A Civilian only begins to be tolerable after he has knocked about the world for fifteen years.'

'And a military man?'

'When he has had the same amount of service. The young of both species are horrible. You would have scores of them in your *salon*.'

'I would *not*!' said Mrs Hauksbee fiercely. 'I would tell the bearer to *darwaza band* [not at home] them. I'd put their own Colonels and Commissioners at the door to turn them away. I'd give them to the Topsham Girl to play with.'

'The Topsham Girl would be grateful for the gift. But to go back to the *salon*. Allowing that you had gathered all your men and women together, what would you do with them? Make them talk? They would all with one accord begin to flirt. Your *salon* would become a glorified Peliti's—a "Scandal Point" by lamplight.'

'There's a certain amount of wisdom in that view.'

'There's all the wisdom in the world in it. Surely twelve Simla seasons ought to have taught you that you can't focus anything in India; and a *salon*, to be any good at all, must be permanent. In two seasons your roomful would be scattered all over Asia. We are only little bits of dirt on the hillsides— here one day and blown down the *khud** the next. We have lost the art of talking—at least our men have. We have no cohesion——'

'George Eliot* in the flesh,' interpolated Mrs Hauksbee wickedly.

'And collectively, my dear scoffer, we, men and women alike, have *no* influence. Come into the veranda and look at the Mall!'

The two looked down on the now rapidly filling road, for all Simla was abroad to steal a stroll between a shower and a fog.

'How do you propose to fix that river? Look! There's The Mussuck—head of goodness knows what. He is a power in the land, though he *does* eat like a costermonger. There's Colonel Blone, and General Grucher, and Sir Dugald Delane, and Sir Henry Haughton, and Mr Jellalatty. All Heads of Departments, and all powerful.'

'And all my fervent admirers,' said Mrs Hauksbee piously. 'Sir Henry Haughton raves about me. But go on.'

'One by one, these men are worth something. Collectively, they're just a mob of Anglo-Indians. Who cares for what Anglo-Indians say? Your *salon* won't weld the Departments together and make you mistress of India, dear. And these creatures won't talk administrative "shop" in a crowd—your *salon*—because they are so afraid of the men in the lower ranks overhearing it. They have forgotten what of Literature and Art they ever knew, and the women——'

'Can't talk about anything except the last Gymkhana, or the sins of their last nurse. I was calling on Mrs Derwills this morning.'

'You admit that? They can talk to the subalterns, though, and the subalterns can talk to them. Your *salon* would suit their views admirably, if you respected the religious prejudices of the country and provided plenty of *kala juggahs* [cosy corners].'

'Plenty of *kala juggahs*.* Oh, my poor little idea! *Kala juggahs* in a *salon*! But who made you so awfully clever?'

'Perhaps I've tried myself; or perhaps I know a woman who has. I have preached* and expounded the whole matter, and the conclusion thereof——'

'You needn't go on. "Is Vanity." Polly, I thank you. These vermin'—Mrs Hauksbee waved her hand from the veranda to two men in the crowd below who had raised their hats to her—'these vermin shall not rejoice in a new Scandal Point or an extra Peliti's. I will abandon the notion of a *salon*. It did seem so tempting, though. But what shall I do? I must do something.'

'Why? Are not Abana and Pharpar——'*

'Jack has made you nearly as bad as himself! I want to, of course. I'm tired of everything and everybody, from a moonlight picnic at Seepee to the blandishments of The Mussuck.'

'Yes—that comes, too, sooner or later. Have you nerve enough to make your bow yet?'

Mrs Hauksbee's mouth shut grimly. Then she laughed. 'I think I see myself doing it. Big pink placards on the Mall: "Mrs Hauksbee! Positively her last appearance on *any* stage! This is to give notice!" No more dances; no more rides; no more luncheons; no more theatricals with supper to follow; no more sparring with one's dearest, dearest friend; no more fencing with an inconvenient man who hasn't wit enough to clothe what he's pleased to call his sentiments in passable speech; no more parading of The Mussuck while Mrs Tarkass calls all round Simla, spreading horrible stories about me! No more of anything that is thoroughly wearying, abominable, and detestable, but, all the same, makes life worth the having. Yes! I see it all! Don't interrupt, Polly. I'm inspired. A mauve-and-white striped "cloud" round my excellent shoulders, a seat in the fifth row of the Gaiety, and *both* horses sold. Delightful vision! A comfortable arm-chair, situated in three different draughts, at every ball-room; and nice, large, sensible shoes for all the couples to stumble over as they go into the veranda! Then at supper. Can't you imagine the scene? The greedy mob gone away. Reluctant subaltern, pink all over like a newly-powdered baby,—they really ought to *tan* subalterns before they are exported, Polly,—sent back by the hostess to do his duty. Slouches up to me across the room, tugging at a glove two sizes too large for him—I *hate* a man who wears gloves like overcoats—and trying to look as if he'd thought of it from the first. "May I ah-have the pleasure 'f takin' you 'nt' supper?" Then I get up with a hungry smile. Just like this.'

'Lucy, how *can* you be so absurd?'

'And sweep out on his arm. So! After supper I shall go away early, you know, because I shall be afraid of catching cold. No one will look for my 'rickshaw. *Mine*, so please you! I shall stand, always with that mauve-and-white "cloud" over my head, while the wet soaks into my dear, old, venerable feet, and Tom swears and shouts for the Memsahib's *gharri*.* Then home to bed at half-past eleven! Truly excellent life—helped out by the visits of the Padre, just fresh from burying somebody down below there.' She pointed through the pines toward the Cemetery, and continued with vigorous dramatic gesture:—

'Listen! I see it all—down, down even to the stays! *Such* stays! Six-eight a pair, Polly, with red flannel—or list,* is it?—that they put into the tops of those fearful things. I'll draw you a picture of them.'

'Lucy, for Heaven's sake, don't go waving your arms about in that idiotic manner! Recollect every one can see you from the Mall.'

'Let them see! They'll think I am rehearsing for *The Fallen Angel*. Look! There's The Mussuck. How badly he rides! There!'

She blew a kiss to the venerable Indian administrator with infinite grace.

'Now,' she continued, 'he'll be chaffed about that at the

Club in the delicate manner those brutes of men affect, and the Hawley Boy will tell me all about it—softening the details for fear of shocking me. That boy is too good to live, Polly. I've serious thoughts of recommending him to throw up his commission and go into the Church. In his present frame of mind he would obey me. Happy, happy child!'

'Never again,' said Mrs Mallowe, with an affectation of indignation, 'shall you tiffin here! "Lucindy, your behaviour is scand'lus."'

'All your fault,' retorted Mrs Hauksbee, 'for suggesting such a thing as my abdication. No! *Jamais!* nevaire! I will act, dance, ride, frivol, talk scandal, dine out, and appropriate the legitimate captives of any woman I choose, until I d-r-r-rop, or a better woman than I puts me to shame before all Simla,—and it's dust and ashes in my mouth while I'm doing it!'

She swept into the drawing-room. Mrs Mallowe followed and put an arm round her waist.

'I'm *not*!' said Mrs Hauksbee defiantly, rummaging for her handkerchief. 'I've been dining out the last ten nights, and rehearsing in the afternoon. You'd be tired yourself. It's only because I'm tired.'

Mrs Mallowe did not offer Mrs Hauksbee any pity or ask her to lie down, but gave her another cup of tea, and went on with the talk.

'I've been through that, too, dear,' she said.

'I remember,' said Mrs Hauksbee, a gleam of fun on her face. 'In '84, wasn't it? You went out a great deal less next season.'

Mrs Mallowe smiled in a superior and Sphinx-like fashion.

'I became an Influence,' said she.

'Good gracious, child, you didn't join the Theosophists* and kiss Buddha's big toe, did you? I tried to get into their set once, but they cast me out for a sceptic—without a chance of improving my poor little mind, too.'

'No, I didn't Theosophilander. Jack says——'

'Never mind Jack. What a husband says is known before. What did you do?'

'I made a lasting impression.'

'So have I—for four months. But that didn't console me in the least. I hated the man. *Will* you stop smiling in that inscrutable way and tell me what you mean?'

Mrs Mallowe told.

* * * * *

'And—you—mean—to—say that it is absolutely Platonic on both sides?'

'Absolutely, or I should never have taken it up.'

'And his last promotion was due to you?'

Mrs Mallowe nodded.

'And you warned him against the Topsham Girl?'

Another nod.

'And told him of Sir Dugald Delane's private memo about him?'

A third nod.

'*Why?*'

'What a question to ask a woman! Because it amused me at first. I am proud of my property now. If I live, he shall continue to be successful. Yes, I will put him upon the straight road to Knighthood, and everything else that a man values. The rest depends upon himself.'

'Polly, you are a most extraordinary woman.'

'Not in the least. I'm concentrated, that's all. You diffuse yourself, dear; and though all Simla knows your skill in managing a team——'

'Can't you choose a prettier word?'

'*Team*, of half-a-dozen, from The Mussuck to the Hawley Boy, you gain nothing by it. Not even amusement.'

'And you?'

'Try my recipe. Take a man, not a boy, mind, but an almost mature, unattached man, and be his guide, philosopher, and friend. You'll find it *the* most interesting occupation that you ever embarked on. It can be done—you needn't look like that—because I've done it.'

'There's an element of risk about it that makes the notion attractive. I'll get such a man and say to him, "Now, understand that there must be no flirtation. Do exactly what I tell you, profit by my instruction and counsels, and all will yet be well." Is that the idea?'

' More or less,' said Mrs Mallowe, with an unfathomable smile. 'But be sure he understands.'

II

> Dribble-dribble—trickle-trickle—
> What a lot of raw dust!
> My dollie's had anaccident
> And out came all the sawdust!
> *Nursery Rhyme**

So Mrs Hauksbee, in 'The Foundry' which overlooks Simla Mall, sat at the feet of Mrs Mallowe and gathered wisdom. The end of the Conference was the Great Idea upon which Mrs Hauksbee so plumed herself.

'I warn you,' said Mrs Mallowe, beginning to repent of her suggestion, 'that the matter is not half so easy as it looks. Any woman—even the Topsham Girl—can catch a man, but very, *very* few know how to manage him when caught.'

'My child,' was the answer, 'I've been a female St Simon Stylites* looking down upon men for these—these years past. Ask The Mussuck whether I can manage them.'

Mrs Hauksbee departed humming, '*I'll go to him and say to him in manner most ironical.*'* Mrs Mallowe laughed to herself. Then she grew suddenly sober. 'I wonder whether I've done well in advising that amusement? Lucy's a clever woman, but a thought too careless.'

A week later the two met at a Monday Pop. 'Well?' said Mrs Mallowe.

'I've caught him!' said Mrs Hauksbee: her eyes were dancing with merriment.

'Who is it, mad woman? I'm sorry I ever spoke to you about it.'

'Look between the pillars. In the third row; fourth from the end. You can see his face now. Look!'

'Otis Yeere! Of *all* the improbable and impossible people! I don't believe you.'

'Hsh! Wait till Mrs Tarkass begins murdering Milton Wellings,* and I'll tell you all about it. *S-s-ss!* That woman's voice always reminds me of an Underground train coming into Earl's Court with the brakes on. Now listen. It is *really* Otis Yeere.'

'So I see, but does it follow that he is your property?'

'He *is*! By right of trove. I found him, lonely and unbe-friended, the very next night after our talk, at the Dugald Delanes' *burra-khana** [dinner]. I liked his eyes, and I talked to him. Next day he called. Next day we went for a ride together, and to-day he's tied to my 'rickshaw-wheels hand and foot. You'll see when the concert's over. He doesn't know I'm here yet.'

'Thank goodness you haven't chosen a boy. What are you going to do with him, assuming that you've got him?'

'Assuming, indeed! Does a woman—do *I*—ever make a mistake in that sort of thing? First'—Mrs Hauksbee ticked off the items ostentatiously on her little gloved fingers—'First, my dear, I shall dress him properly. At present his raiment is a disgrace, and he wears a dress-shirt like a crumpled sheet of the *Pioneer*.* Secondly, after I have made him presentable, I shall form his manners—his morals are above reproach.'

'You seem to have discovered a great deal about him considering the shortness of your acquaintance.'

'Surely *you* ought to know that the first proof a man gives of his interest in a woman is by talking to her about his own sweet self. If the woman listens without yawning, he begins to like her. If she flatters the animal's vanity, he ends by adoring her.'

'In some cases.'

'Never mind the exceptions. I know which one you are thinking of. Thirdly, and lastly, after he is polished and made pretty, I shall, as you said, be his guide, philosopher, and friend, and he shall become a success—as great a success as your friend. I always wondered how that man got on. *Did* The Mussuck come to you with the Civil List and, dropping on one knee,—no, two knees, *à la* Gibbon*—hand it to you and say, "Adorable angel, choose your friend's appointment"?'

'Lucy, your long experiences of the Military Department

have demoralized you. One doesn't do that sort of thing on the Civil Side.'

'No disrespect meant to Jack's Service, my dear. I only asked for information. Give me three months, and see what changes I shall work in my prey.'

'Go your own way since you must. But I'm sorry that I was weak enough to suggest the amusement.'

'"I am all discretion, and may be trusted to an in-fin-ite extent,"' quoted Mrs Hauksbee from *The Fallen Angel*; and the conversation ceased with Mrs Tarkass's last, long-drawn war-whoop.

Her bitterest enemies—and she had many—could hardly accuse Mrs Hauksbee of wasting her time. Otis Yeere was one of those wandering 'dumb' characters, foredoomed through life to be nobody's property. Ten years in Her Majesty's Bengal Civil Service, spent, for the most part, in undesirable Districts, had given him little to be proud of, and nothing to bring confidence. Old enough to have lost the first fine careless rapture that showers on the immature 'Stunt* imaginary Commissionerships and Stars, and sends him into the collar with coltish earnestness and abandon; too young to be yet able to look back upon the progress he had made, and thank Providence that under the conditions of the day he had come even so far, he stood upon the dead-centre of his career. And when a man stands still he feels the slightest impulse from without. Fortune had ruled that Otis Yeere should be, for the first part of his service, one of the rank and file who are ground up in the wheels of the Administration; losing heart and soul, and mind and strength, in the process. Until steam replaces manual power in the working of the Empire, there must always be this percentage—must always be the men who are used up, expended, in the mere mechanical routine. For these promotion is far off and the mill-grind of every day very instant. The Secretariats know them only by name; they are not the picked men of the Districts with Divisions and Collectorates awaiting them. They are simply the rank and file—the food for fever—sharing with the *ryot** and the plough-bullock the honour of being the plinth on which the State rests. The older ones have lost their aspirations; the younger are putting theirs aside with a sigh. Both learn to endure patiently until the end of the day. Twelve years in the rank and file, men say, will sap the hearts of the bravest and dull the wits of the most keen.

Out of this life Otis Yeere had fled for a few months; drifting, in the hope of a little masculine society, into Simla. When his leave was over he would return to his swampy, sour-green, undermanned Bengal District; to the native Assistant, the native Doctor, the native Magistrate, the steaming, sweltering Station, the ill-kempt City, and the undisguised insolence of the Municipality that babbled away the lives of men. Life was cheap, however. The soil spawned humanity, as it bred frogs in the Rains, and the gap of the sickness of one season was filled to overflowing by the fecundity of the next. Otis was unfeignedly thankful to lay down his work for a little while and escape from the seething, whining, weakly hive, impotent to help itself, but strong in its power to cripple, thwart, and annoy the sunken-eyed man who, by official irony, was said to be 'in charge' of it.

* * * * *

'I knew there were women-dowdies in Bengal. They come up here sometimes. But I didn't know that there were men-dowds, too.'

Then, for the first time, it occurred to Otis Yeere that his clothes wore rather the mark of the ages. It will be seen that his friendship with Mrs Hauksbee had made great strides.

As that lady truthfully says, a man is never so happy as when he is talking about himself. From Otis Yeere's lips Mrs Hauksbee, before long, learned everything that she wished to know about the subject of her experiment: learned what manner of life he had led in what she vaguely called 'those awful cholera districts'; learned, too, but this knowledge came later, what manner of life he had purposed to lead and what dreams he had dreamed in the year of grace '77, before the reality had knocked the heart out of him. Very pleasant are the shady bridle-paths round Prospect Hill for the telling of such confidences.

'Not yet,' said Mrs Hauksbee to Mrs Mallowe. 'Not yet. I must wait until the man is properly dressed, at least. Great

Heavens, is it possible that he doesn't know what an honour it is to be taken up by *Me*!'

Mrs Hauksbee did not reckon false modesty as one of her failings.

'Always with Mrs Hauksbee!' murmured Mrs Mallowe, with her sweetest smile, to Otis. 'Oh, you men, you men! Here are our Punjabis* growling because you've monopolized the nicest woman in Simla. They'll tear you to pieces on the Mall, some day, Mr Yeere.'

Mrs Mallowe rattled downhill, having satisfied herself, by a glance through the fringe of her sunshade, of the effect of her words.

The shot went home. Of a surety Otis Yeere was somebody in this bewildering whirl of Simla—had monopolized the nicest woman in it, and the Punjabis were growling. The notion justified a mild glow of vanity. He had never looked upon his acquaintance with Mrs Hauksbee as a matter for general interest.

The knowledge of envy was a pleasant feeling to the man of no account. It was intensified later in the day when a luncher at the Club said spitefully, 'Well, for a debilitated Ditcher,* Yeere, you *are* going it. Hasn't any kind friend told you that she's the most dangerous woman in Simla?'

Yeere chuckled and passed out. When, oh, when would his new clothes be ready? He descended into the Mall to inquire; and Mrs Hauksbee, coming over the Church Ridge in her 'rickshaw, looked down upon him approvingly. 'He's learning to carry himself as if he were a man, instead of a piece of furniture, and'—she screwed up her eyes to see the better through the sunlight—'he *is* a man when he holds himself like that. O blessed Conceit, what should we be without you?'

With the new clothes came a new stock of self-confidence. Otis Yeere discovered that he could enter a room without breaking into a gentle perspiration—could cross one, even to talk to Mrs Hauksbee, as though rooms were meant to be crossed. He was for the first time in nine years proud of himself, and contented with his life, satisfied with his new clothes, and rejoicing in the friendship of Mrs Hauksbee.

'Conceit is what the poor fellow wants,' she said in confidence to Mrs Mallowe. 'I believe they must use Civilians to plough the fields with in Lower Bengal. You see, I have to begin from the very beginning—haven't I? But you'll admit, won't you, dear, that he is immensely improved since I took him in hand. Only give me a little more time and he won't know himself.'

Indeed, Yeere was rapidly beginning to forget what he had been. One of his own rank and file put the matter brutally when he asked Yeere, in reference to nothing, 'And who has been making *you* a Member of Council lately? You carry the side of half-a-dozen of 'em.'

'I—I'm awf'ly sorry. I didn't mean it, you know,' said Yeere apologetically.

'There'll be no holding you,' continued the old stager grimly. 'Climb down, Otis—climb down, and get all that beastly affectation knocked out of you with fever! Three thousand a month wouldn't support it.'

Yeere repeated the incident to Mrs Hauksbee. He had come to look upon her as his Mother Confessor.

'And you apologized!' she said. 'Oh, shame! I *hate* a man who apologizes. Never apologize for what your friend called "side". *Never!* It's a man's business to be insolent and overbearing until he meets with a stronger. Now, you bad boy, listen to me.'

Simply and straightforwardly, as the 'rickshaw loitered round Jakko, Mrs Hauksbee preached to Otis Yeere the Great Gospel of Conceit, illustrating it with living pictures encountered during their Sunday afternoon stroll.

'Good gracious!'—she ended with the personal argument—'you'll apologize next for being my *attaché!*'

'Never!' said Otis Yeere. 'That's another thing altogether. I shall always be——'

'What's coming?' thought Mrs Hauksbee.

'Proud of that,' said Otis.

'Safe for the present,' she said to herself.

'But I'm afraid I have grown conceited. Like Jeshurun,* you know. When he waxed fat, then he kicked. It's the having no worry on one's mind and the Hill air, I suppose.'

'Hill air, indeed!' said Mrs Hauksbee to herself. 'He'd have been hiding in the Club till the last day of his leave, if I hadn't discovered him.' And aloud——

'Why shouldn't you be? You have every right to.'

'I! Why?'

'Oh, hundreds of things. I'm not going to waste this lovely afternoon by explaining; but I know you have. What was that heap of manuscript you showed me about the grammar of the aboriginal—what's their names?'

'Gullals.* A piece of nonsense. I've far too much work to do to bother over Gullals now. You should see my District. Come down with your husband some day and I'll show you round. Such a lovely place in the Rains! A sheet of water with the railway-embankment and the snakes sticking out, and, in the summer, green flies and green squash. The people would die of fear if you shook a dogwhip at 'em. But they know you're forbidden to do that, so they conspire to make your life a burden to you. My District's worked by some man at Darjeeling,* on the strength of a native pleader's* false reports. Oh, it's a heavenly place!'

Otis Yeere laughed bitterly.

'There's not the least necessity that you should stay in it. Why do you?'

'Because I must. How'm I to get out of it?'

'How! In a hundred and fifty ways. If there weren't so many people on the road I'd like to box your ears. Ask, my dear boy, *ask*! Look! There is young Hexarly with six years' service and half your talents. He asked for what he wanted, and he got it. See, down by the Convent! There's McArthurson, who has come to his present position by asking—sheer, downright asking—after he had pushed himself out of the rank and file. One man is as good as another in your Service— believe me. I've seen Simla for more seasons than I care to think about. Do you suppose men are chosen for appointments because of their special fitness *beforehand*? You have all passed a high test—what do you call it?—in the beginning, and, except for the few who have gone altogether to the bad, you can all work hard. Asking does the rest. Call it cheek, call it insolence, call it anything you like, but *ask*! Men argue—

THE EDUCATION OF OTIS YEERE

yes, I know what men say—that a man, by the mere audacity of his request, *must* have some good in him. A weak man doesn't say: "Give me this and that." He whines: "Why haven't I been given this and that?" If you were in the Army, I should say learn to spin plates or play a tambourine with your toes. As it is—*ask*! You belong to a Service that ought to be able to command the Channel Fleet, or set a leg at twenty minutes' notice, and *yet* you hesitate over asking to escape from a squashy green District where you *admit* you are not master. Drop the Bengal Government altogether. Even Darjeeling is a little out-of-the-way hole. I was there once, and the rents were extortionate. Assert yourself. Get the Government of India to take you over. Try to get on the Frontier, where *every* man has a grand chance if he can trust himself. *Go* somewhere! *Do* something! You have twice the wits and three times the presence of the men up here, and, and'—Mrs Hauksbee paused for breath; then continued— 'and in *any* way you look at it, you *ought* to. *You* who could go so far!'

'I don't know,' said Yeere, rather taken aback by the unexpected eloquence. 'I haven't such a good opinion of myself.'

It was not strictly Platonic, but it was Policy. Mrs Hauksbee laid her hand lightly upon the ungloved paw that rested on the turned-back 'rickshaw-hood, and looking the man full in the face, said tenderly, almost too tenderly, '*I* believe in you if you mistrust yourself. Is that enough, my friend?'

'It is enough,' answered Otis very solemnly.

He was silent for a long time, redreaming the dreams that he had dreamed eight years ago, but through them all ran, as sheet-lightning through golden cloud, the light of Mrs Hauksbee's violet eyes.

Curious and impenetrable are the mazes of Simla life—the only existence in this desolate land worth the living. Gradually it went abroad among men and women, in the pauses between dance, play, and Gymkhana, that Otis Yeere, the man with the newly-lit light of self-confidence in his eyes, had 'done something decent' in the wilds whence he came.

He had brought an erring Municipality to reason, appropriated the funds on his own responsibility, and saved the lives of hundreds. He knew more about the Gullals than any living man. Had a vast knowledge of the aboriginal tribes; was, in spite of his juniority, the greatest authority on the aboriginal Gullals. No one quite knew who or what the Gullals were till The Mussuck, who had been calling on Mrs Hauksbee, and prided himself upon picking people's brains, explained they were a tribe of ferocious hillmen, somewhere near Sikkim, whose friendship even the Great Indian Empire would find it worth her while to secure. Now we know that Otis Yeere had showed Mrs Hauksbee his MS. notes of six years' standing on these same Gullals. He had told her, too, how, sick and shaken with the fever their negligence had bred, crippled by the loss of his pet clerk, and savagely angry at the desolation in his charge, he had once damned the collective eyes of his 'intelligent local board' for a set of *haramzadas* [scoundrels]. Which act of 'brutal and tyrannous oppression' won him a Reprimand Royal from the Bengal Government; but in the anecdote as amended for Northern consumption we find no record of this. Hence we are forced to conclude that Mrs Hauksbee edited his reminiscences before sowing them in idle ears, ready, as she well knew, to exaggerate good or evil. And Otis Yeere bore himself as befitted the hero of many tales.

'You can talk to *me* when you don't fall into a brown study. Talk now, and talk your brightest and best,' said Mrs Hauksbee.

Otis needed no spur. Look to a man who has the counsel of a woman of or above the world to back him. So long as he keeps his head, he can meet both sexes on equal ground—an advantage never intended by Providence, who fashioned Man on one day and Woman on another, in sign that neither should know more than a very little of the other's life. Such a man goes far, or, the counsel being withdrawn, collapses suddenly while his world seeks the reason.

Generalled by Mrs Hauksbee, who, again, had all Mrs Mallowe's wisdom at her disposal, proud of himself, and, in the end, believing in himself because he was believed in, Otis

Yeere stood ready for any fortune that might befall, certain that it would be good. He would fight for his own hand, and intended that this second struggle should lead to better issue than the first helpless surrender of the bewildered 'Stunt.

What might have happened it is impossible to say. This lamentable thing befell, bred directly by a statement of Mrs Hauksbee that she would spend the next season in Darjeeling.

'Are you certain of that?' said Otis Yeere.

'Quite. We're writing about a house now.'

Otis Yeere 'stopped dead,' as Mrs Hauksbee put it in discussing the relapse with Mrs Mallowe.

'He has behaved,' she said angrily, 'just like Captain Kerrington's pony—only Otis is a donkey—at the last Gymkhana. Planted his forefeet and refused to go on another step. Polly, my man's going to disappoint me. What shall I do?'

As a rule, Mrs Mallowe does not approve of staring, but on this occasion she opened her eyes to the utmost.

'You have managed cleverly so far,' she said. 'Speak to him, and ask him what he means.'

'I will—at to-night's dance.'

'No—o, not at a dance,' said Mrs Mallowe cautiously. 'Men are never themselves quite at dances. Better wait till to-morrow morning.'

'Nonsense. If he's going to 'vert in this insane way there isn't a day to lose. Are you going? No? Then sit up for me, there's a dear. I shan't stay longer than supper under any circumstances.'

Mrs Mallowe waited through the evening, looking long and earnestly into the fire, and sometimes smiling to herself.

* * * * *

'Oh! oh! oh! The man's an idiot! A raving, positive idiot! I'm sorry I ever saw him!'

Mrs Hauksbee burst into Mrs Mallowe's house, after midnight, almost in tears.

'What in the world has happened?' said Mrs Mallowe, but her eyes showed that she had guessed an answer.

'Happened! Everything has happened! He was there. I went to him and said, "Now, what does this nonsense mean?" Don't laugh, dear, I can't bear it. But you know what I mean I said. Then it was a square, and I sat it out with him and wanted an explanation, and *he* said—Oh! I haven't patience with such idiots. You know what I said about going to Darjeeling next year? It doesn't matter to me *where* I go. I'd have changed the Station and lost the rent to have saved this. He said, in so many words, that he wasn't going to try to work up any more, because—because he would be shifted into a province away from Darjeeling, and his own District, where these creatures are, is within a day's journey——'

'Ah—hh!' said Mrs Mallowe, in a tone of one who has sucessfully tracked an obscure word through a large dictionary.

'Did you ever *hear* of anything so mad—so absurd? And he had the ball at his feet. He had only to kick it! I would have made him *anything*! Anything in the wide world. He could have gone to the world's end. I would have helped him. I made him, didn't I, Polly? Didn't I *create* that man? Doesn't he owe everything to me? And to reward me, just when everything was nicely arranged, by this lunacy that spoilt everything!'

'Very few men understand your devotion thoroughly.'

'Oh, Polly, *don't* laugh at me! I give men up from this hour. I could have killed him then and there. What *right* had this man—this *Thing* I had picked out of his filthy paddy-fields— to make love to me?'

'He did that, did he?'

'He did. I don't remember half he said, I was so angry. Oh, but such a funny thing happened! I can't help laughing at it now, though I felt nearly ready to cry with rage. He raved and I stormed—I'm afraid we must have made an awful noise in our *kala juggah*. Protect my character, dear, if it's all over Simla by to-morrow—and then he bobbed forward in the middle of this insanity—I *firmly* believe the man's demented—and kissed me.'

'Morals above reproach,' purred Mrs Mallowe.

'So they were—so they are! It was the most absurd kiss. I don't believe he'd ever kissed a woman in his life before. I threw my head back, and it was a sort of slidy, pecking dab, just on the end of the chin—here.' Mrs Hauksbee tapped her masculine little chin with her fan. 'Then, of course, I was *furiously* angry, and told him that he was no gentleman, and I was sorry I'd ever met him, and so on. He was crushed so easily that I couldn't be *very* angry. Then I came away straight to you.'

'Was this before or after supper?'

'Oh! before—oceans before. Isn't it perfectly disgusting?'

'Let me think. I withhold judgment till to-morrow. Morning brings counsel.'

But morning brought only a servant with a dainty bouquet of Annandale roses for Mrs Hauksbee to wear at the dance at Viceregal Lodge that night.

'He doesn't seem to be very penitent,' said Mrs Mallowe. 'What's the *billet-doux* in the centre?'

Mrs Hauksbee opened the neatly-folded note,—another accomplishment that she had taught Otis,—read it, and groaned tragically.

'Last wreck of a feeble intellect! Poetry! Is it his own, do you think? Oh, that I ever built my hopes on such a maudlin idiot!'

'No. It's a quotation from Mrs Browning, and in view of the facts of the case, as Jack says, uncommonly well chosen. Listen:—

> 'Sweet, thou hast trod on a heart,
>   Pass! There's a world full of men;
> And women as fair as thou art
>   Must do such things now and then.
>
> 'Thou only hast stepped unaware—
>   Malice not one can impute;
> And why should a heart have been there,
>   In the way of a fair woman's foot?'*

'I didn't—I didn't—I didn't!' said Mrs Hauksbee angrily, her eyes filling with tears. 'There was no malice at all. Oh, it's *too* vexatious!'

'You've misunderstood the compliment,' said Mrs Mallowe. 'He clears you completely and—ahem!—I should think by this that *he* has cleared completely too. My experience of men is that when they begin to quote poetry they are going to flit. Like swans singing before they die, you know.'

'Polly, you take my sorrows in a most unfeeling way.'

'Do I? Is it so terrible? If he's hurt your vanity, I should say that you've done a certain amount of damage to his heart.'

'Oh, you can never tell about a man!' said Mrs Hauksbee.

The Hill of Illusion

What rendered vain their deep desire?
A God, a God their severance ruled,
And bade between their shores to be
The unplumbed, salt, estranging sea.*
                                    Matthew Arnold

HE. Tell your *jhampanis** not to hurry so, dear. They forget I'm fresh from the Plains.

SHE. Sure proof that *I* have not been going out with any one. Yes, they *are* an untrained crew. Where do we go?

HE. As usual—to the world's end. No, Jakko.

SHE. Have your pony led after you, then. It's a long round.

HE. And for the last time, thank Heaven!

SHE. Do you mean *that* still? I didn't dare to write to you about it—all these months.

HE. Mean it! I've been shaping my affairs to that end since autumn. What makes you speak as though it had occurred to you for the first time?

SHE. I? Oh! I don't know. I've had long enough to think, too.

HE. And you've changed your mind?

SHE. No. You ought to know that I am a miracle of constancy. What are your—arrangements?

HE. *Ours*, Sweetheart, please.

SHE. Ours be it then. My poor boy, how the prickly heat has marked your forehead! Have you ever tried sulphate of copper in water?

HE. It'll go away in a day or two up here. The arrangements are simple enough. Tonga* in the early morning—reach Kalka at twelve—Umballa at seven—down, straight by night train, to Bombay, and then the steamer of the 21st for Rome. That's my idea. The Continent and Sweden— a ten-week honeymoon.

SHE. Ssh! Don't talk of it in that way. It makes me afraid. Guy, how long have we two been insane?

HE.   Seven months and fourteen days. I forget the odd hours exactly, but I'll think.

SHE.   I only wanted to see if you remembered. Who are those two on the Blessington Road?

HE.   Eabrey and the Penner Woman. What do they matter to *us*? Tell me everything that you've been doing and saying and thinking.

SHE.   Doing little, saying less, and thinking a great deal. I've hardly been out at all.

HE.   That was wrong of you. You haven't been moping?

SHE.   Not very much. Can you wonder that I'm disinclined for amusement?

HE.   Frankly, I do. Where was the difficulty?

SHE.   In this only. The more people I know and the more I'm known here, the wider spread will be the news of the crash when it comes. I don't like that.

HE.   Nonsense. We shall be out of it.

SHE.   You think so?

HE.   I'm sure of it, if there is any power in steam or horseflesh to carry us away. Ha! ha!

SHE.   And the *fun* of the situation comes in—where, my Lancelot?

HE.   Nowhere, Guinevere. I was only thinking of something.

SHE.   They say men have a keener sense of humour than women. Now *I* was thinking of the scandal.

HE.   Don't think of anything so ugly. We shall be beyond it.

SHE.   It will be there all the same—in the mouths of all Simla—telegraphed over India, and talked of at the dinners—and when He goes out they will stare at Him to see how He takes it. And we shall be dead, Guy, dear—dead and cast into the outer darkness where there is——

HE.   Love at least. Isn't that enough?

SHE.   I have said so.

HE.   And you think so still?

SHE.   What do *you* think?

HE.   What have I *done*? It means equal ruin to me, as the world reckons it—outcasting, the loss of my appointment, the breaking off my life's work. I pay my price too.

SHE.   And are you so much above the world that you can afford to pay it? Am I?

HE.   My Divinity—what else?

SHE.   A very ordinary woman, I'm afraid, but so far, respectable. How d'you do, Mrs Middleditch? Your husband? I think he's riding down to Annandale with Colonel Statters. Yes, isn't it divine after the rain?—Guy, how long am I to be allowed to bow to Mrs Middleditch? Till the 17th?

HE.   Frowzy Scotchwoman! What is the use of bringing her into the discussion? You were saying?

SHE.   Nothing. Have you ever seen a man hanged?

HE.   Yes. Once.

SHE.   What was it for?

HE.   Murder, of course.

SHE.   Murder. Is *that* so great a sin after all? I wonder how he felt before the drop fell.

HE.   I don't think he felt much. What a gruesome little woman it is this evening! You're shivering. Put on your cape, dear.

SHE.   I think I will. Oh! Look at the mist coming over Sanjaolie; and I thought we should have sunshine on the Ladies' Mile! Let's turn back.

HE.   What's the good? There's a cloud on Elysium Hill, and that means it's foggy all down the Mall. We'll go on. It'll blow away before we get to the Convent, perhaps. Jove! It *is* chilly.

SHE.   You feel it, fresh from below. Put on your ulster. What do you think of my cape?

HE.   Never ask a man his opinion of a woman's dress when he is desperately and abjectly in love with the wearer. Let me look. Like everything else of yours it's perfect. Where did you get it from?

SHE.   He gave it me, on Wednesday—our wedding-day, you know.

HE.   The Deuce He did! He's growing generous in his old age. D'you like all that frilly, bunchy stuff at the throat? I don't.

SHE.   Don't you?

> Kind Sir, o' your courtesy,
>   As you go by the town, Sir,
> Pray you, o' your love for me,
>   Buy me a russet gown, Sir.*

HE.   I won't say: 'Keek into the draw-well, Janet, Janet.'* Only wait a little, darling, and you shall be stocked with russet gowns and everything else.

SHE.   And when the frocks wear out you'll get me new ones—and everything else?

HE.   Assuredly.

SHE.   I wonder!

HE.   Look here, Sweetheart, I didn't spend two days and two nights in the train to hear you wonder. I thought we'd settled all that at Shaifazehat.

SHE (*dreamily*).   At Shaifazehat? Does the Station go on still? That was ages and *ages* ago. It must be crumbling to pieces. All except the Amirtollah *kutcha** road. I don't believe *that* could crumble till the Day of Judgment.

HE.   You think so? What *is* the mood now?

SHE.   I can't tell. How cold it is! Let us get on quickly.

HE.   Better walk a little. Stop your *jhampanis* and get out. What's the matter with you this evening, dear?

SHE.   Nothing. You must grow accustomed to my ways. If I'm boring you I can go home. Here's Captain Congleton coming, I daresay he'll be willing to escort me.

HE.   Goose! Between *us*, too! *Damn* Captain Congleton!

SHE.   Chivalrous Knight! Is it your habit to swear much in talking? It jars a little, and you might swear at me.

HE.   My angel! I didn't know what I was saying; and you changed so quickly that I couldn't follow. I'll apologize in dust and ashes.

SHE.   There'll be enough of those later on——Good night, Captain Congleton. Going to the singing-quadrilles already? What dances am I giving you next week? No! You must have written them down wrong. Five and Seven, *I* said. If you've made a mistake, I certainly don't intend to suffer for it. You must alter your programme.

HE. I thought you told me that you had not been going out much this season?

SHE. Quite true, but when I do I dance with Captain Congleton. He dances very nicely.

HE. And sit out with him, I suppose?

SHE. Yes. Have you any objection? Shall I stand under the chandelier in future?

HE. What does he talk to you about?

SHE. What do men talk about when they sit out?

HE. Ugh! Don't! Well, now I'm up, you must dispense with the fascinating Congleton for a while. I don't like him.

SHE (*after a pause*). Do you know what you have said?

HE. Can't say that I do exactly. I'm not in the best of tempers.

SHE. So I see,—and feel. My true and faithful lover, where is your 'eternal constancy,' 'unalterable trust,' and 'reverent devotion'? I remember those phrases; you seem to have forgotten them. I mention a man's name——

HE. A good deal more than that.

SHE. Well, speak to him about a dance—perhaps the last dance that I shall ever dance in my life before I—before I go away; and you at once distrust and insult me.

HE. I never said a word.

SHE. How much did you imply? Guy, is *this* amount of confidence to be our stock to start the new life on?

HE. No, of course not. I didn't mean that. On my word and honour, I didn't. Let it pass, dear. Please let it pass.

SHE. This once—yes—and a second time, and again and again, all through the years when I shall be unable to resent it. You want too much, my Lancelot, and—you know too much.

HE. How do you mean?

SHE. That is a part of the punishment. There *cannot* be perfect trust between us.

HE. In Heaven's name, why not?

SHE. Hush! The Other Place is quite enough. Ask yourself.

HE. I don't follow.

SHE. You trust me so implicitly that when I look at

another man—Never mind. Guy, have you ever made love to a girl—a *good* girl?

HE.   Something of the sort. Centuries ago—in the Dark Ages, before I ever met you, dear.

SHE.   Tell me what you said to her.

HE.   What does a man say to a girl? I've forgotten.

SHE.   *I* remember. He tells her that he trusts her and worships the ground she walks on, and that he'll love and honour and protect her till her dying day; and so she marries in that belief. At least, I speak of one girl who was *not* protected.

HE.   Well, and then?

SHE.   And then, Guy, and then, that girl needs *ten* times the love and trust and honour—yes, *honour*—that was enough when she was only a mere wife if—if—the other life she chooses to lead is to be made even bearable. Do you understand?

HE.   Even bearable! It'll be Paradise.

SHE.   Ah! Can you give me all I've asked for—not now, nor a few months later, but when you begin to think of what you might have done if you had kept your own appointment and your caste here—when you begin to look upon me as a drag and a burden? I shall want it most then, Guy, for there will be no one in the wide world but you.

HE.   You're a little over-tired to-night, Sweetheart, and you're taking a stage view of the situation. After the necessary business in the Courts, the road is clear to——

SHE.   'The holy state of matrimony!' Ha! ha! ha!

HE.   Ssh! Don't laugh in that horrible way!

SHE.   I—I—c-c-c-can't help it! Isn't it too absurd! Ah! Ha! ha! ha! Guy, stop me quick or I shall—l-l-laugh till we get to the Church.

HE.   For goodness sake, stop! Don't make an exhibition of yourself. What *is* the matter with you?

SHE.   N-nothing. I'm better now.

HE.   That's all right. One moment, dear. There's a little wisp of hair got loose from behind your right ear and it's straggling over your cheek. So!

SHE.   Thank 'oo. I'm 'fraid my hat's on one side, too.

HE.   What do you wear these huge dagger bonnet-skewers for? They're big enough to kill a man with.

SHE.   Oh! don't kill *me*, though. You're sticking it into my head! Let *me* do it. You men are so clumsy!

HE.   Have you had many opportunities of comparing us—in this sort of work?

SHE.   Guy, what is my name?

HE.   Eh! I don't follow.

SHE.   Here's my card-case. Can you read?

HE.   Yes. Well?

SHE.   Well, that answers your question. You know the other man's name. Am I sufficiently humbled, or would you like to ask me if there is any one else?

HE.   I see now. My darling, I never meant that for an instant. I was only joking. There! Lucky there's no one on the road. They'd be scandalized.

SHE.   They'll be more scandalized before the end.

HE.   Do-on't! I don't like you to talk in that way.

SHE.   Unreasonable man! Who asked me to face the situation and accept it?—Tell me, do I look like Mrs Penner? *Do* I look like a naughty woman? *Swear* I don't! Give me your word of honour, my *honourable* friend, that I'm not like Mrs Buzgago. That's the way she stands, with her hands clasped at the back of her head. D'you like that?

HE.   Don't be affected.

SHE.   I'm not. I'm Mrs Buzgago. Listen!

> Pendant une anné' toute entière
> Le régiment n'a pas r'paru.
> Au Ministère de la Guerre
> On le r'porta comme perdu.
>
> On se r'nonçait à r'trouver sa trace,
> Quand un matin subitement
> On le vit r'paraître sur la place,
> L'Colonel toujours en avant.*

That's the way she rolls her r's. *Am* I like her?

HE.   No, but I object when you go on like an actress and sing stuff of that kind. Where in the world did you pick up the *Chanson du Colonel*? It isn't a drawing-room song. It isn't proper.

SHE.   Mrs Buzgago taught it me. She is both drawing-room and proper, and in another month she'll shut her drawing-room to me, and thank God she isn't as improper as I am. Oh, Guy, Guy! I wish I was like some women and had no scruples about—What is it Keene* says?—'wearing a corpse's hair and being false to the bread they eat.'

HE.   I am only a man of limited intelligence, and, just now, very bewildered. When you have *quite* finished flashing through all your moods tell me, and I'll try to understand the last one.

SHE.   Moods, Guy! I haven't any. I'm sixteen years old and you're just twenty, and you've been waiting for two hours outside the school in the cold. And now I've met you, and now we're walking home together. Does *that* suit you, My Imperial Majesty?

HE.   No. We aren't children. Why can't you be rational?

SHE.   He asks me that when I'm going to commit suicide for his sake, and, and—I don't want to be French and rave about my mother, but have I never told you that I have a mother, and a brother who was my pet before I married? He's married now. Can't you imagine the pleasure that the news of the elopement will give him? Have *you* any people at Home, Guy, to be pleased with your performances?

HE.   One or two. One can't make omelets without breaking eggs.

SHE *(slowly)*.   I don't see the necessity——

HE.   Hah! What do you mean?

SHE.   Shall I speak the truth?

HE.   Under the circumstances, perhaps it *would* be as well.

SHE.   Guy, I'm afraid.

HE.   I thought we'd settled all that. What of?

SHE.   Of you.

HE.   Oh, damn it all! The old business! This is *too* bad!

SHE.   Of *you*.

HE.   And what now?

SHE.   What do you think of me?

HE.   Beside the question altogether. What do you intend to do?

SHE.   I daren't risk it. I'm afraid. If I could only cheat——

HE.   *À la Buzgago?* No, *thanks*. That's the one point on which I have any notion of Honour. I won't eat His salt and steal too. I'll loot openly or not at all.

SHE.   I never meant anything else.

HE.   Then why in the world do you pretend not to be willing to come?

SHE.   It's *not* pretence, Guy. I *am* afraid.

HE.   Please explain.

SHE.   It can't last, Guy. It can't last. You'll get angry, and then you'll swear, and then you'll get jealous, and then you'll mistrust me—you do *now*—and you yourself will be the best reason for doubting. And I—what shall *I* do? I shall be no better than Mrs Buzgago found out—no better than any one. And you'll *know* that. Oh, Guy, can't you *see*?

HE.   I see that you are desperately unreasonable, little woman.

SHE.   There! The moment I begin to object, you get angry. What will you do when I am only your property—stolen property? It can't be, Guy. It can't be! I thought it could, but it *can't*. You'll get tired of me.

HE.   I tell you I shall *not*. Won't anything make you understand that?

SHE.   There, can't you see? If you speak to me like that now, you'll call me horrible names later, if I don't do everything as you like. And if you were cruel to me, Guy, where should I go?—where should I go? I can't trust you. Oh! I *can't* trust you!

HE.   I suppose I ought to say that I *can* trust you. I've ample reason.

SHE.   *Please* don't, dear. It hurts as much as if you hit me.

HE.   It isn't exactly pleasant for *me*.

SHE.   I can't help it. I wish I were dead! I can't trust you, and I don't trust myself. Oh, Guy, let it die away and be forgotten!

HE.   Too late now. I don't understand you—I won't—

and I can't trust myself to talk this evening. May I call to-morrow?

SHE.   Yes. *No!* Oh, give me time! The day after. I get into my 'rickshaw here and meet Him at Peliti's. You ride.

HE.   I'll go on to Peliti's too. I think I want a drink. My world's knocked about my ears and the stars are falling. Who are those brutes howling in the Old Library?

SHE.   They're rehearsing the singing-quadrilles for the Fancy Ball. Can't you hear Mrs Buzgago's voice? She has a solo. It's quite a new idea. Listen!

MRS BUZGAGO (*in the Old Library, con molt. exp.*).

> See-saw! Margery Daw!
> Sold her bed to lie upon straw.
> Wasn't she a silly slut
> To sell her bed and lie upon dirt?*

Captain Congleton, I'm going to alter that to 'flirt'. It sounds better.

HE.   No, I've changed my mind about the drink. Good night, little lady. I shall see you to-morrow?

SHE.   Ye—es. Good night, Guy. *Don't* be angry with me.

HE.   Angry! You *know* I trust you absolutely. Good night and—God bless you!

(*Three seconds later. Alone.*) Hmm! I'd give something to discover whether there's another man at the back of all this.

Dray Wara Yow Dee

For jealousy is the rage of a man: therefore
he will not spare in the day of vengeance.—
Proverbs vi. 34

ALMONDS and raisins, Sahib? Grapes from Kabul? Or a pony
of the rarest if the Sahib will only come with me. He is
thirteen-three,* Sahib, plays polo, goes in a cart, carries a
lady and—Holy Kurshed and the Blessed Imams, it is the
Sahib himself! My heart is made fat and my eye glad. May
you never be tired! As is cold water in the Tirah, so is the
sight of a friend in a far place. And what do *you* in this
accursed land? South of Delhi, Sahib, you know the saying—
'Rats are the men and trulls the women.' It was an order?
Ahoo! An order is an order till one is strong enough to
disobey. O my brother, O my friend, we have met in an
auspicious hour! Is all well in the heart and the body and the
house? In a lucky day have we two come together again.

I am to go with you? Your favour is great. Will there be
picket-room in the compound? I have three horses and the
bundles and the horse-boy. Moreover, remember that the
police here hold me a horse-thief. What do these Lowland
bastards know of horse-thieves? Do you remember that time
in Peshawur when Kamal hammered on the gates of
Jumrud—mountebank that he was—and lifted the Colonel's
horses all in one night? Kamal is dead now, but his nephew
has taken up the matter, and there will be more horses a-
missing if the Khyber Levies do not look to it.

The Peace of God and the favour of His Prophet be upon
this house and all that is in it! Shafiz Ullah, rope the mottled
mare under the tree and draw water. The horses can stand in
the sun, but double the felts over the loins. Nay, my friend,
do not trouble to look them over. They are to sell to the
Officer-fools who know so many things of the horse. The
mare is heavy in foal; the grey is a devil unlicked; and the
dun—but you know the trick of the peg. When they are sold I
go back to Pubbi, or, it may be, the Valley of Peshawur.

O friend of my heart, it is good to see you again. I have
been bowing and lying all day to the Officer-Sahibs in respect
to those horses; and my mouth is dry for straight talk.
Auggrh! Before a meal tobacco is good. Do not join me, for we
are not in our own country. Sit in the veranda and I will
spread my cloth here. But first I will drink. *In the name of God
returning thanks, thrice!* This is sweet water, indeed—sweet as
the water of Sheoran when it comes from the snows.

They are all well and pleased in the North—Khoda Baksh
and the others. Yar Khan has come down with the horses
from Kurdistan—six-and-thirty head only, and a full half
pack-ponies—and has said openly in the Kashmir Serai* that
you English should send guns and blow the Amir* into Hell.
There are *fifteen* tolls now on the Kabul road; and at Dakka,
when he thought he was clear, Yar Khan was stripped of all
his Balkh stallions by the Governor! This is a great injustice,
and Yar Khan is hot with rage. And of the others: Mahbub
Ali is still at Pubbi, writing God knows what. Tugluq Khan is
in jail for the business of the Kohat Police Post. Faiz Beg
came down from Ismail-ki-Dhera with a Bokhariot belt for
thee, my brother, at the closing of the year, but none knew
whither thou hadst gone: there was no news left behind. The
Cousins have taken a new run near Pakpattan to breed mules
for the Government carts, and there is a story in the Bazar of a
priest. Oho! Such a salt tale! Listen——

Sahib, why do you ask that? My clothes are fouled because
of the dust on the road. My eyes are sad because of the glare of
the sun. My feet are swollen because I have washed them in
bitter water, and my cheeks are hollow because the food here
is bad. Fire burn your money! What do I want with it? I am
rich. I thought you were my friend. But you are like the
others—a Sahib. Is a man sad? Give him money, say the
Sahibs. Is he dishonoured? Give him money, say the Sahibs.
Hath he a wrong upon his head? Give him money, say the
Sahibs. Such are the Sahibs, and such art thou—even thou.

Nay, do not look at the feet of the dun. Pity it is that I ever
taught you to know the legs of a horse. Footsore? Be it so.
What of that? The roads are hard. And the mare footsore?
She bears a double burden, Sahib.

And now, I pray you, give me permission to depart. Great favour and honour has the Sahib done me, and graciously has he shown his belief that the horses are stolen. Will it please him to send me to the Thana?* To call a sweeper and have me led away by one of these lizard-men? I am the Sahib's friend. I have drunk water in the shadow of his house, and he has blackened my face.* Remains there anything more to do? Will the Sahib give me eight annas to make smooth the injury and—complete the insult——?

Forgive me, my brother. I knew not—I know not now— what I say. Yes, I lied to you! I will put dust on my head—and I am an Afridi! The horses have been marched footsore from the Valley to this place, and my eyes are dim, and my body aches for the want of sleep, and my heart is dried up with sorrow and shame. But as it was my shame, so by God the Dispenser of Justice—by Allah-al-Mumīt!—it shall be my own revenge!

We have spoken together with naked hearts before this, and our hands have dipped into the same dish, and thou hast been to me as a brother. Therefore I pay thee back with lies and ingratitude—as a Pathan.* Listen now! When the grief of the soul is too heavy for endurance it may be a little eased by speech; and, moreover, the mind of a true man is as a well, and the pebble of confession dropped therein sinks and is no more seen. From the Valley have I come on foot, league by league, with a fire in my chest like the fire of the Pit. And why? Hast thou, then, so quickly forgotten our customs, among this folk who sell their wives and their daughters for silver? Come back with me to the North and be among men once more. Come back, when this matter is accomplished and I call for thee! The bloom of the peach-orchards is upon all the Valley, and *here* is only dust and a great stink. There is a pleasant wind among the mulberry trees, and the streams are bright with snow-water, and the caravans go up and the caravans go down, and a hundred fires sparkle in the gut of the Pass, and tent-peg answers hammer-nose, and pack-horse squeals to pack-horse across the drift-smoke of the evening. It is good in the North now. Come back with me. Let us return to our own people! Come!

* * * * *

Whence is my sorrow? Does a man tear out his heart and
make fritters thereof over a slow fire for aught other than a
woman? Do not laugh, friend of mine, for your time will also
be. A woman of the Abazai was she, and I took her to wife to
staunch the feud between our village and the men of Ghor. I
am no longer young? The lime has touched my beard? True.
I had no need of the wedding? Nay, but I loved her. What
saith Rahman?* 'Into whose heart Love enters, there is Folly
and naught else. By a glance of the eye she hath blinded thee;
and by the eyelids and the fringe of the eyelids taken thee into
the captivity without ransom, *and naught else.*' Dost thou
remember that song at the sheep-roasting in the Pindi camp*
among the Uzbegs of the Amir?

The Abazai are dogs and their women the servants of sin.
There was a lover of her own people, but of that her father
told me naught. My friend, curse for me in your prayers, as I
curse at each praying from the Fakr to the Isha, the name of
Daoud Shah, Abazai, whose head is still upon his neck,
whose hands are still upon his wrists, who has done me
dishonour, who has made my name a laughing-stock among
the women of Little Malikand.

I went into Hindustan at the end of two months—to
Cherat. I was gone twelve days only; but I had said that I
would be fifteen days absent. This I did to try her, for it is
written: 'Trust not the incapable.' Coming up the gorge
alone in the falling of the light, I heard the voice of a man
singing at the door of my house; and it was the voice of Daoud
Shah, and the song that he sang was '*Dray wara yow dee*'—
'All three are one.' It was as though a heel-rope had been
slipped round my heart and all the Devils were drawing it
tight past endurance. I crept silently up the hill-road, but the
fuse of my matchlock was wetted with the rain, and I could
not slay Daoud Shah from afar. Moreover, it was in my mind
to kill the woman also. Thus he sang, sitting outside my
house, and, anon, the woman opened the door, and I came
nearer, crawling on my belly among the rocks. I had only my
knife to my hand. But a stone slipped under my foot, and the
two looked down the hillside, and he, leaving his matchlock,

fled from my anger, because he was afraid for the life that was
in him. But the woman moved not till I stood in front of her,
crying: 'O woman, what is this that thou hast done?' And
she, void of fear, though she knew my thought, laughed,
saying: 'It is a little thing. I loved him, and *thou* art a dog and
cattle-thief coming by night. Strike!' And I, being still
blinded by her beauty, for, O my friend, the women of the
Abazai are very fair, said: 'Hast thou no fear?' And she
answered: 'None—but only the fear that I do not die.' Then
said I: 'Have no fear.' And she bowed her head, and I smote it
off at the neck-bone so that it leaped between my feet.
Thereafter the rage of our people came upon me, and I
hacked off the breasts, that the men of Little Malikand might
know the crime, and cast the body into the watercourse that
flows to the Kabul River. *Dray wara yow dee! Dray wara yow
dee!* The body without the head, the soul without light, and
my own darkling heart—all three are one—all three are one!

That night, making no halt, I went to Ghor and demanded
news of Daoud Shah. Men said: 'He is gone to Pubbi for
horses. What wouldst thou of him? There is peace between
the villages.' I made answer: 'Ay! The peace of treachery and
the love that the Devil Atala bore to Gurel.' So I fired thrice
into the tower-gate and laughed and went my way.

In those hours, brother and friend of my heart's heart, the
moon and the stars were as blood above me, and in my mouth
was the taste of dry earth. Also, I broke no bread, and my
drink was the rain of the valley of Ghor upon my face.

At Pubbi I found Mahbub Ali, the writer, sitting upon his
charpoy,* and gave up my arms according to your Law. But I
was not grieved, for it was in my heart that I should kill
Daoud Shah with my bare hands thus—as a man strips a
bunch of raisins. Mahbub Ali said: 'Daoud Shah has even
now gone hot-foot to Peshawur, and he will pick up his
horses upon the road to Delhi, for it is said that the Bombay
Tramway Company are buying horses there by the truck-
load; eight horses to the truck.' And that was a true saying.

Then I saw that the hunting would be no little thing, for
the man was gone into your borders to save himself against
my wrath. And shall he save himself so? Am I not alive?

Though he run northward to the Dora and the snow, or
southerly to the Black Water,* I will follow him, as a lover
follows the footsteps of his mistress, and coming upon him I
will take him tenderly—Aho! so tenderly!—in my arms,
saying: 'Well hast thou done and well shalt thou be repaid.'
And out of that embrace Daoud Shah shall not go forth with
the breath in his nostrils. *Auggrh!* Where is the pitcher? I am
as thirsty as a mother mare in the first month.

Your Law! What is your Law to me? When the horses fight
on the runs do they regard the boundary pillars; or do the
kites of Ali Musjid forbear because the carrion lies under the
shadow of the Ghor Kuttri?* The matter began across the
Border. It shall finish where God pleases. Here; in my own
country; or in Hell. All three are one.

Listen now, sharer of the sorrow of my heart, and I will tell
of the hunting. I followed to Peshawur from Pubbi, and I
went to and fro about the streets of Peshawur like a houseless
dog, seeking for my enemy. Once I thought that I saw him
washing his mouth in the conduit in the big square, but when
I came up he was gone. It may be that it was he, and, seeing
my face, he had fled.

A girl of the bazar said that he would go to Nowshera. I
said: 'O heart's heart, does Daoud Shah visit thee?' And she
said: 'Even so.' I said: 'I would fain see him, for we be friends
parted for two years. Hide me, I pray, here in the shadow of
the window-shutter, and I will wait for his coming.' And the
girl said: 'O Pathan, look into my eyes!' And I turned,
leaning upon her breast, and looked into her eyes, swearing
that I spoke the very Truth of God. But she answered: 'Never
friend waited friend with such eyes. Lie to God and the
Prophet, but to a woman ye cannot lie. Get hence! There
shall no harm befall Daoud Shah by cause of me.'

I would have strangled that girl but for the fear of your
Police; and thus the hunting would have come to naught.
Therefore I only laughed and departed, and she leaned over
the window-bar in the night and mocked me down the street.
Her name is Jamun. When I have made my account with the
man I will return to Peshawur and—her lovers shall desire
her no more for her beauty's sake. She shall not be *Jamun*,
but *Ak*, the cripple among trees.* Ho! ho! *Ak* shall she be!

At Peshawur I bought the horses and grapes, and the almonds and dried fruits, that the reason of my wanderings might be open to the Government, and that there might be no hindrance upon the road. But when I came to Nowshera he was gone; and I knew not where to go. I stayed one day at Nowshera, and in the night a Voice spoke in my ears as I slept among the horses. All night it flew round my head and would not cease from whispering. I was upon my belly, sleeping as the Devils sleep, and it may have been that the Voice was the voice of a Devil. It said: 'Go south, and thou shalt come upon Daoud Shah.' Listen, my brother and chiefest among friends—listen! Is the tale a long one? Think how it was long to me. I have trodden every league of the road from Pubbi to this place; and from Nowshera my guide was only the Voice and the lust of vengeance.

To the Uttock I went, but that was no hindrance to me. Ho! ho! A man may turn the word twice, even in his trouble. The Uttock was no *uttock* [obstacle] to me; and I heard the Voice above the noise of the waters beating on the big rock, saying: 'Go to the right.' So I went to Pindigheb, and in those days my sleep was taken from me utterly, and the head of the woman of the Abazai was before me night and day, even as it had fallen between my feet. *Dray wara yow dee! Dray wara yow dee!* Fire, ashes, and my couch, all three are one—all three are one!

Now I was far from the winter path of the dealers who had gone to Sialkot, and so south by the rail and the Big Road to the line of cantonments; but there was a Sahib in camp at Pindigheb who bought from me a white mare at a good price, and told me that one Daoud Shah had passed to Shahpur with horses. Then I saw that the warning of the Voice was true, and made swift to come to the Salt Hills. The Jhelum was in flood, but I could not wait, and, in the crossing, a bay stallion was washed down and drowned. Herein was God hard to me—not in respect of the beast, of that I had no care—but in this snatching. While I was upon the right bank urging the horses into the water, Daoud Shah was upon the left; for—*Alghias! Alghias!*—the hoofs of my mare scattered the hot ashes of his fires when we came up the hither bank in the light of morning. But he had fled. His feet were made swift by the terror of Death. And I went south from Shahpur as the kite flies. I dared not turn aside lest I should miss my vengeance—which is my right. From Shahpur I skirted by the Jhelum, for I thought that he would avoid the Desert of the Rechna. But, presently, at Sahiwal, I turned away upon the road to Jhang, Samundri, and Gugera, till, upon a night, the mottled mare breasted the fence of the rail that runs to Montgomery. And that place was Okara, and the head of the woman of the Abazai lay upon the sand between my feet.

Thence I went to Fazilka, and they said that I was mad to bring starved horses there. The Voice was with me, and I was *not* mad, but only wearied, because I could not find Daoud Shah. It was written that I should not find him at Rania nor Bahadurgarh, and I came into Delhi from the west, and there also I found him not. My friend, I have seen many strange things in my wanderings. I have seen the Devils rioting across the Rechna as the stallions riot in spring. I have heard the *Djinns* calling to each other from holes in the sand, and I have seen them pass before my face. There are no Devils, say the Sahibs? They are very wise, but they do not know all things about Devils or—horses. Ho! ho! I say to you who are laughing at my misery, that I have seen the Devils at high noon whooping and leaping on the shoals of the Chenab. And was I afraid? My brother, when the desire of a man is set upon one thing alone, he fears neither God nor Man nor Devil. If my vengeance failed, I would splinter the Gates of Paradise with the butt of my gun, or I would cut my way into Hell with my knife, and I would call upon Those who Govern there for the body of Daoud Shah. What love so deep as hate?

Do not speak. I know the thought in your heart. Is the white of this eye clouded? How does the blood beat at the wrist? There is no madness in my flesh, but only the vehemence of the desire that has eaten me up. Listen!

South of Delhi I knew not the country at all. Therefore I cannot say where I went, but I passed through many cities. I knew only that it was laid upon me to go south. When the horses could march no more, I threw myself upon the earth and waited till the day. There was no sleep with me in that journeying; and that was a heavy burden. Dost thou know, brother of mine, the evil of wakefulness that cannot break—when the bones are sore for lack of sleep, and the skin of the temples twitches with weariness, and yet—there is no sleep—there is no sleep? *Dray wara yow dee! Dray wara yow dee!* The eye of the Sun, the eye of the Moon, and my own unrestful eyes—all three are one—all three are one!

There was a city the name whereof I have forgotten, and there the Voice called all night. That was ten days ago. It has cheated me afresh.

I have come hither from a place called Hamirpur, and, behold, it is my Fate that I should meet with thee to my comfort, and the increase of friendship. This is a good omen. By the joy of looking upon thy face the weariness has gone from my feet, and the sorrow of my so long travel is forgotten. Also my heart is peaceful; for I know that the end is near.

It may be that I shall find Daoud Shah in this city going northward, since a Hillman will ever head back to his Hills when the spring warns. And shall he see those hills of our country? Surely I shall overtake him! Surely my vengeance is safe! Surely God hath him in the hollow of His hand against my claiming! There shall no harm befall Daoud Shah till I come; for I would fain kill him quick and whole with the life sticking firm in his body. A pomegranate is sweetest when the cloves break away unwilling from the rind. Let it be in the daytime, that I may see his face, and my delight may be crowned.

And when I have accomplished the matter and my Honour is made clean, I shall return thanks unto God, the Holder of the Scales of the Law, and I shall sleep. From the night, through the day, and into the night again I shall sleep; and no dream shall trouble me.

And now, O my brother, the tale is all told. *Ahi! Ahi! Alghias! Ahi!*

The Judgment of Dungara

See the pale martyr with his shirt on fire.
*Printer's Error**

THEY tell the tale even now among the groves of the
Berbulda Hills, and for corroboration point to the roofless
and windowless Mission-house. The great God Dungara, the
God of Things as They Are, Most Terrible, One-eyed,
Bearing the Red Elephant Tusk, did it all; and he who refuses
to believe in Dungara will assuredly be smitten by the
Madness of Yat—the madness that fell upon the sons and the
daughters of the Buria Kol when they turned aside from
Dungara and put on clothes. So says Athon Dazé, who is
High Priest of the shrine and Warden of the Red Elephant
Tusk. But if you ask the Assistant Collector and Agent in
Charge of the Buria Kol, he will laugh—not because he bears
any malice against missions, but because he himself saw the
vengeance of Dungara executed upon the spiritual children
of the Reverend Justus Krenk, Pastor of the Tübingen
Mission, and upon Lotte, his virtuous wife.

Yet if ever a man merited good treatment of the Gods it was
the Reverend Justus, one time of Heidelberg, who, on the
faith of a call, went into the wilderness and took the blonde,
blue-eyed Lotte with him. 'We will these Heathen now by
idolatrous practices so darkened better make,' said Justus in
the early days of his career. 'Yes,' he added with conviction,
'they shall good be and shall with their hands to work learn.
For all good Christians must work.' And upon a stipend more
modest even than that of an English lay-reader, Justus Krenk
kept house beyond Kamala and the gorge of Malair, beyond
the Berbulda River close to the foot of the blue hill of Panth
on whose summit stands the Temple of Dungara—in the
heart of the country of the Buria Kol—the naked, good-
tempered, timid, shameless, lazy Buria Kol.

Do you know what life at a Mission outpost means? Try to
imagine a loneliness exceeding that of the smallest station to
which Government has ever sent you—isolation that weighs

upon the waking eyelids and drives you by force headlong into the labours of the day. There is no post, there is no one of your own colour to speak to, there are no roads: there is, indeed, food to keep you alive, but it is not pleasant to eat; and whatever of good or beauty or interest there is in your life, must come from yourself and the grace that may be planted in you.

In the morning, with a patter of soft feet, the converts, the doubtful, and the open scoffers troop up to the veranda. You must be infinitely kind and patient, and, above all, clear-sighted, for you deal with the simplicity of childhood, the experience of man, and the subtlety of the savage. Your congregation have a hundred material wants to be considered; and it is for you, as you believe in your personal responsibility to your Maker, to pick out of the clamouring crowd any grain of spirituality that may lie therein. If to the cure of souls you add that of bodies, your task will be all the more difficult, for the sick and the maimed will profess any and every creed for the sake of healing, and will laugh at you because you are simple enough to believe them.

As the day wears and the impetus of the morning dies away, there will come upon you an overwhelming sense of the uselessness of your toil. This must be striven against, and the only spur in your side will be the belief that you are playing against the Devil for the living soul. It is a great, a joyous belief. But he who can hold it unwavering for four-and-twenty consecutive hours must be blessed with an abundantly strong physique and equable nerve.

Ask the grey heads of the Bannockburn Medical Crusade what manner of life their preachers lead; speak to the Racine Gospel Agency, those lean Americans whose boast is that they go where no Englishman dare follow; get a Pastor of the Tübingen Mission to talk of his experiences—if you can. You will be referred to the printed reports, but these contain no mention of the men who have lost youth and health, all that a man may lose except faith, in the wilds; of English maidens who have gone forth and died in the fever-stricken jungle of the Panth Hills, knowing from the first that death was almost a certainty. Few Pastors will tell you of these things any more than they will speak of that young David of St Bees, who, set apart for the Lord's work, broke down in the utter desolation, and returned half distraught to the Head Mission, crying, 'There is no God, but I have walked with the Devil!'

The reports are silent here, because heroism, failure, doubt, despair, and self-abnegation on the part of a mere cultured white man are things of no weight as compared to the saving of one half-human soul from a fantastic faith in wood-spirits, goblins of the rock, and river-fiends.

And Gallio,* the Assistant Collector of the countryside, 'cared for none of these things.' He had been long in the District, and the Buria Kol loved him and brought him offerings of speared fish, orchids from the dim moist heart of the forests, and as much game as he could eat. In return, he gave them quinine, and with Athon Dazé, the High Priest, controlled their simple policies.

'When you have been some years in the country,' said Gallio at the Krenks' table, 'you get to find one creed as good as another. I'll give you all the assistance in my power, of course, but don't hurt my Buria Kol. They are a good people and they trust me.'

'I will them the Word of the Lord teach,' said Justus, his round face beaming with enthusiasm, 'and I will assuredly to their prejudices no wrong hastily without thinking make. But, O my friend, this in the mind impartiality-of-creed-judgment-belooking is very bad.'

'Heigh-ho!' said Gallio. 'I have their bodies and the District to see to, but you can try what you can do for their souls. Only don't behave as your predecessor did, or I'm afraid that I can't guarantee your life.'

'And that?' said Lotte sturdily, handing him a cup of tea.

'He went up to the Temple of Dungara—to be sure, he was new to the country—and began hammering old Dungara over the head with an umbrella; so the Buria Kol turned out and hammered *him* rather savagely. I was in the District, and he sent a runner to me with a note saying: "Persecuted for the Lord's sake. Send wing of regiment." The nearest troops were about two hundred miles off, but I guessed what he had been doing. I rode to Panth and talked to old Athon Dazé like

a father, telling him that a man of his wisdom ought to have
known that the Sahib had sunstroke and was mad. You never
saw a people more sorry in your life. Athon Dazé apologized,
sent wood and milk and fowls and all sorts of things; and I
gave five rupees to the shrine and told Macnamara that he had
been injudicious. He said that I had bowed down in the
House of Rimmon;* but if he had only just gone over the
brow of the hill and insulted Palin Deo, the idol of the Suria
Kol, he would have been impaled on a charred bamboo long
before I could have done anything, and then I should have
had to hang some of the poor brutes. Be gentle with them,
Padre—but I don't think you'll do much.'

'Not I,' said Justus, 'but my Master. We will with the little
children begin. Many of them will be sick—that is so. After
the children the mothers; and then the men. But I would
greatly prefer that you in internal sympathies with us were.'

Gallio departed to risk his life in mending the rotten
bamboo bridges of his people, in killing a too persistent tiger
here or there, in sleeping out in the reeking jungle, or in
tracking the Suria Kol raiders who had taken a few heads
from their brethren of the Buria clan. He was a knock-kneed,
shambling young man, naturally devoid of creed or
reverence, with a longing for absolute power which his
undesirable District gratified.

'No one wants my post,' he used to say grimly, 'and my
Collector only pokes his nose in when he's quite certain that
there is no fever. I'm monarch of all I survey, and Athon
Dazé is my viceroy.'

Because Gallio prided himself on his supreme disregard of
human life—though he never extended the theory beyond his
own—he naturally rode forty miles to the Mission with a tiny
brown girl-baby on his saddle-bow.

'Here is something for you, Padre,' said he. 'The Kols
leave their surplus children to die. Don't see why they
shouldn't, but you may rear this one. I picked it up beyond
the Berbulda forks. I've a notion that the mother has been
following me through the woods ever since.'

'It is the first of the fold,' said Justus, and Lotte caught up
the screaming morsel to her bosom and hushed it craftily;

while, as a wolf hangs in the field, Matui who had borne it, and in accordance with the law of her tribe had exposed it to die, panted weary and footsore in the bamboo-brake, watching the house with hungry mother-eyes. What would the omnipotent Assistant Collector do? Would the little man in the black coat eat her daughter alive, as Athon Dazé said was the custom of all men in black coats?

Matui waited among the bamboos through the long night; and, in the morning, there came forth a fair white woman, the like of whom Matui had never seen, and in her arms was Matui's daughter clad in spotless raiment. Lotte knew little of the tongue of the Buria Kol, but when mother calls to mother, speech is easy to follow. By the hands stretched timidly to the hem of her gown, by the passionate gutturals and the longing eyes, Lotte understood with whom she had to deal. So Matui took her child again—would be a servant, even a slave, to this wonderful white woman, for her own tribe would recognize her no more. And Lotte wept with her exhaustively, after the German fashion, which includes much blowing of the nose.

'First the Child, then the Mother, and last the Man, and to the Glory of God all,' said Justus the Hopeful. And the man came, with a bow and arrows, very angry indeed, for there was no one to cook for him.

But the tale of the Mission is a long one, and I have no space to show how Justus, forgetful of his injudicious predecessor, grievously smote Moto, the husband of Matui, for his brutality; how Moto was startled, but being released from the fear of instant death, took heart and became the faithful ally and first convert of Justus; how the little gathering grew, to the huge disgust of Athon Dazé; how the Priest of the God of Things as They Are argued subtilely with the Priest of the God of Things as They Should Be, and was worsted; how the dues of the Temple of Dungara fell away in fowls and fish and honeycomb; how Lotte lightened the Curse of Eve among the women, and how Justus did his best to introduce the Curse of Adam; how the Buria Kol rebelled at this, saying that their God was an idle God, and how Justus partially overcame their scruples against work, and taught them that the black earth was rich in other produce than pig-nuts only.

All these things belong to the history of many months, and throughout those months the white-haired Athon Dazé meditated revenge for the tribal neglect of Dungara. With savage cunning he feigned friendship towards Justus, even hinting at his own conversion; but to the congregation of Dungara he said darkly: 'They of the Padre's flock have put on clothes and worship a busy God. Therefore Dungara will afflict them grievously till they throw themselves, howling, into the waters of the Berbulda.' At night the Red Elephant Tusk boomed and groaned among the hills, and the faithful waked and said: 'The God of Things as They Are matures revenge against the backsliders. Be merciful, Dungara, to us Thy children, and give us all their crops!'

Late in the cold weather the Collector and his wife came into the Buria Kol country. 'Go and look at Krenk's Mission,' said Gallio. 'He is doing good work in his own way, and I think he'd be pleased if you opened the bamboo chapel that he has managed to run up. At any rate you'll see a civilized Buria Kol.'

Great was the stir in the Mission. 'Now he and the gracious lady will that we have done good work with their own eyes see, and—yes—we will him our converts in all their by their own hands constructed new clothes exhibit. It will a great day be—for the Lord always,' said Justus; and Lotte said 'Amen.'

Justus had, in his quiet way, felt jealous of the Basel Weaving Mission, his own converts being unhandy; but Athon Dazé had latterly induced some of them to hackle the glossy silky fibres of a plant that grew plenteously on the Panth Hills. It yielded a cloth white and smooth almost as the *tappa* of the South Seas, and that day the converts were to wear for the first time clothes made therefrom. Justus was proud of his work.

'They shall in white clothes clothed to meet the Collector and his well-born lady come down, singing "*Now thank we all our God*". Then he will the Chapel open, and—yes—even Gallio to believe will begin. Stand so, my children, two by two, and—Lotte, why do they thus themselves bescratch? It is not seemly to wriggle, Nala, my child. The Collector will be here and be pained.'

The Collector, his wife, and Gallio climbed the hill to the Mission-station. The converts were drawn up in two lines, a shining band nearly forty strong. 'Hah!' said the Collector, whose acquisitive bent of mind led him to believe that he had fostered the institution from the first. 'Advancing, I see, by leaps and bounds.'

Never was truer word spoken! The Mission was advancing exactly as he had said—at first by little hops and shuffles of shamefaced uneasiness, but soon by the leaps of fly-stung horses and the bounds of maddened kangaroos. From the hill of Panth the Red Elephant Tusk delivered a dry and anguished blare. The ranks of the converts wavered, broke, and scattered with yells and shrieks of pain, while Justus and Lotte stood horror-stricken.

'It is the Judgment of Dungara!' shouted a voice. 'I burn! I burn! To the river or we die!'

The mob wheeled and headed for the rocks that overhung the Berbulda, writhing, stamping, twisting, and shedding its garments as it ran, pursued by the thunder of the trumpet of Dungara. Justus and Lotte fled to the Collector almost in tears.

'I cannot understand! Yesterday,' panted Justus, 'they had the Ten Commandments.—What is this? Praise the Lord, all good spirits by land and by sea! Nala! Oh, shame!'

With a bound and a scream there alighted on the rocks above their heads, Nala, once the pride of the Mission, a maiden of fourteen summers, good, docile, and virtuous— now naked as the dawn and spitting like a wild-cat.

'Was it for this?' she raved, hurling her petticoat at Justus; 'was it for this I left my people and Dungara—for the fires of your Bad Place? Blind ape, little earth-worm, dried fish that you are, you said that I should never burn! O Dungara, I burn now! I burn now! Have mercy, God of Things as They Are!'

She turned and flung herself into the Berbulda, and the trumpet of Dungara bellowed jubilantly. The last of the converts of the Tübingen Mission had put a quarter of a mile of rapid river between herself and her teachers.

'Yesterday,' gulped Justus, 'she taught in the school A, B, C, D.—Oh! It is the work of Satan!'

But Gallio was curiously regarding the maiden's petticoat where it had fallen at his feet. He felt its texture, drew back his shirt-sleeve beyond the deep tan of his wrist and pressed a fold of the cloth against the flesh. A blotch of angry red rose on the white skin.

'Ah!' said Gallio calmly, 'I thought so.'

'What is it?' said Justus.

'I should call it the Shirt of Nessus,* but—where did you get the fibre of this cloth from?'

'Athon Dazé,' said Justus. 'He showed the boys how it should manufactured be.'

'The old fox! Do you know that he has given you the Nilgiri Nettle*—scorpion—*Girardenia heterophylla*—to work up. No wonder they squirmed! Why, it stings even when they make bridge-ropes of it unless it's soaked for six weeks. The cunning brute! It would take about half an hour to burn through their thick hides, and then——!'

Gallio burst into laughter, but Lotte was weeping in the arms of the Collector's wife, and Justus had covered his face with his hands.

'*Girardenia heterophylla!*' repeated Gallio. 'Krenk, why *didn't* you tell me? I could have saved you this. Woven fire! Anybody but a naked Kol would have known it, and, if I'm a judge of their ways, you'll never get them back.'

He looked across the river to where the converts were still wallowing and wailing in the shallows, and the laughter died out of his eyes, for he saw that the Tübingen Mission to the Buria Kol was dead.

Never again, though they hung mournfully round the deserted school for three months, could Lotte or Justus coax back even the most promising of their flock. No! The end of conversion was the fire of the Bad Place—fire that ran through the limbs and gnawed into the bones. Who dare a second time tempt the anger of Dungara? Let the little man and his wife go elsewhere. The Buria Kol would have none of them. An unofficial message to Athon Dazé that if a hair of their heads were touched, Athon Dazé and the priests of Dungara would be hanged by Gallio at the temple shrine, protected Justus and Lotte from the stumpy poisoned arrows of the Buria Kol, but neither fish nor fowl, honeycomb, salt, nor young pig were brought to their doors any more. And, alas! man cannot live by grace alone if meat be wanting.

'Let us go, mine wife,' said Justus; 'there is no good here, and the Lord has willed that some other man shall the work take—in good time—in His own good time. We will away go, and I will—yes—some botany bestudy.'

If any one is anxious to convert the Buria Kol afresh, there lies at least the core of a Mission-house under the hill of Panth. But the chapel and school have long since fallen back into jungle.

With the Main Guard

Der jungere Uhlanen
Sit round mit open mouth
While Breitmann tell dem sdories
Of fightin' in the South;
Und gif dem moral lessons,
How before der battle pops,
Take a little prayer to Himmel
Und a goot long drink of Schnapps.
*C. G. Leland**

'MARY, Mother av Mercy, fwhat the divil possist us to take an' kape this melancolious counthry? Answer me that, sorr.'

It was Mulvaney who was speaking. The time was one o'clock of a stifling June night, and the place was the main gate of Fort Amara,* most desolate and least desirable of all fortresses in India. What I was doing there at that hour is a question which only concerns M'Grath the Sergeant of the Guard, and the men on the gate.

'Slape,' said Mulvaney, 'is a shuparfluous necessity. This Gyard'll shtay lively till relieved.' He himself was stripped to the waist; Learoyd on the next bedstead was dripping from the skinful of water which Ortheris, clad only in white trousers, had just sluiced over his shoulders; and a fourth private was muttering uneasily as he dozed open-mouthed in the glare of the great guard-lantern. The heat under the bricked archway was terrifying.

'The worrst night that iver I remimber. Eyah! Is all Hell loose this tide?' said Mulvaney. A puff of burning wind lashed through the wicket-gate like a wave of the sea, and Ortheris swore.

'Are ye more heasy, Jock?' he said to Learoyd. 'Put yer 'ead between your legs. It'll go orf in a minute.'

'Ah doan't care. Ah would not care, but ma heart is plaayin' tivvy-tivvy on ma ribs. Let ma die! Oh, leave ma die!' groaned the huge Yorkshireman, who was feeling the heat acutely, being of fleshy build.

The sleeper under the lantern roused for a moment and

raised himself on his elbow. 'Die and be damned then!' he said. '*I*'m damned and I can't die!'

'Who's that?' I whispered, for the voice was new to me.

'Gentleman born,' said Mulvaney; 'Corp'ril wan year, Sargint nex'. Red-hot on his C'mission, but dhrinks like a fish. He'll be gone before the cowld weather's here. So!'

He slipped his boot, and with the naked toe just touched the trigger of his Martini. Ortheris misunderstood the movement, and the next instant the Irishman's rifle was dashed aside, while Ortheris stood before him, his eyes blazing with reproof.

'You!' said Ortheris. 'My Gawd, *you*! If it was you, wot would *we* do?'

'Kape quiet, little man,' said Mulvaney, putting him aside, but very gently; ''tis not me, nor will ut be me whoile Dinah Shadd's here. I was but showin' somethin'.'

Learoyd, bowed on his bedstead, groaned, and the gentleman-ranker sighed in his sleep. Ortheris took Mulvaney's tendered pouch, and we three smoked gravely for a space while the dust-devils danced on the glacis and scoured the red-hot plain.

'Pop?' said Ortheris, wiping his forehead.

'Don't tantalize wid talkin' av dhrink, or I'll shtuff you into your own breech-block an'—fire you off!' grunted Mulvaney.

Ortheris chuckled, and from a niche in the veranda produced six bottles of gingerade.

'Where did ye get ut, ye Machiavel?' said Mulvaney. ''Tis no bazar pop.'

''Ow do *I* know wot the orf'cers drink?' answered Ortheris. 'Arst the mess-man.'

'Ye'll have a Disthrict Coort-Martial settin' on ye yet, me son,' said Mulvaney, 'but'—he opened a bottle—'I will not report ye this time. Fwhat's in the mess-kid is mint for the belly, as they say, 'specially whin that mate is dhrink. Here's luck! A bloody war or a—no, we've got the sickly season. War, thin!'—he waved the innocent 'pop' to the four quarters of heaven. 'Bloody war! North, East, South, an' West! Jock, ye quakin' hayrick, come an' dhrink.'

But Learoyd, half mad with the fear of death presaged in the swelling veins of his neck, was begging his Maker to strike him dead, and fighting for more air between his prayers. A second time Ortheris drenched the quivering body with water, and the giant revived.

'An' Ah divn't see thot a mon is i' fettle for gooin' on to live; an' Ah divn't see thot there is owt for t' livin' for. Hear now, lads! Ah'm tired—tired. There's nobbut watter i' ma bones. Leave ma die!'

The hollow of the arch gave back Learoyd's broken whisper in a bass boom. Mulvaney looked at me hopelessly, but I remembered how the madness of despair had once fallen upon Ortheris, that weary, weary afternoon on the banks of the Khemi River, and how it had been exorcized by the skilful magician Mulvaney.*

'Talk, Terence!' I said, 'or we shall have Learoyd slinging loose, and he'll be worse than Ortheris was. Talk! He'll answer to your voice.'

Almost before Ortheris had deftly thrown all the rifles of the guard on Mulvaney's bedstead, the Irishman's voice was uplifted as that of one in the middle of a story, and, turning to me, he said:—

'In barricks or out av it, as *you* say, sorr, an Irish rig'mint is the divil an' more. 'Tis only fit for a young man wid eddicated fisteses. Oh, the crame av disrupshin is an Irish rig'mint, an' rippin', tearin', ragin' scattherers in the field av war! My first rig'mint was Irish—Faynians an' rebils to the heart av their marrow was they, an' *so* they fought for the Widdy* betther than most, bein' contrairy—Irish. They was the Black Tyrone.* You've heard av thim, sorr?'

Heard of them! I knew the Black Tyrone for the choicest collection of unmitigated blackguards, dog-stealers, robbers of hen-roosts, assaulters of innocent citizens, and recklessly daring heroes in the Army List. Half Europe and half Asia has had cause to know the Black Tyrone—good luck be with their tattered Colours as Glory has ever been!

'They *was* hot pickils an' ginger! I cut a man's head tu deep wid me belt in the days av me youth, an', afther some circumstances which I will oblitherate, I came to the Ould

Rig'mint, bearin' the character av a man wid hands an' feet. But, as I was goin' to tell you, I fell acrost the Black Tyrone agin wan day whin we wanted thim powerful bad. Orth'ris, me son, fwhat was the name av that place where they sint wan comp'ny av us an' wan av the Tyrone roun' a hill an' down agin, all for to tache the Paythans* something they'd niver learned before? Afther Ghuzni 'twas.'

'Don't know what the bloomin' Paythans called it. We called it Silver's Theayter.* You know that, sure!'

'Silver's Theatre—so 'twas. A gut betwix' two hills, as black as a bucket, an' as thin as a gurl's waist. There was over-many Paythans for our convaynience in the gut, an' begad they called thimsilves a Reserve—bein' impident by natur'! Our Scotchies an' lashin's av Gurkys* was poundin' into some Paythan rig'mints, I think 'twas. Scotchies an' Gurkys are twins bekaze they're so onlike, an' they get dhrunk together whin God plazes. As I was sayin', they sint wan comp'ny av the Ould an' wan av the Tyrone to double up the hill an' clane out the Paythan Reserve. Orf'cers was scarce in thim days, fwhat wid dysint'ry an' not takin' care av thimsilves, an' we was sint out wid only wan orf'cer for the comp'ny; but he was a Man that had his feet beneath him an' all his teeth in their sockuts.'

'Who was he?' I asked.

'Captain O'Neil—Old Crook—Cruik-na-bulleen—him that I tould ye that tale av whin he was in Burma.* Hah! He was a Man. The Tyrone tuk a little orf'cer bhoy, but divil a bit was he in command, as I'll dimonsthrate prisintly. We an' they came over the brow av the hill, wan on each side av the gut, an' there was that ondacint Reserve waitin' down below like rats in a pit.

'"Howld on, men," sez Crook, who tuk a mother's care av us always. "Rowl some rocks on thim by way av visitin'-kyards." We hadn't rowled more than twinty bowlders, an' the Paythans was beginnin' to swear tremenjus, whin the little orf'cer bhoy av the Tyrone shqueaks out acrost the valley: "Fwhat the divil an' all are you doin', shpoilin' the fun for my men? Do ye not see they'll stand?"

'"Faith, that's a rare pluckt wan!" sez Crook. "Niver

mind the rocks, men. Come along down an' take tay wid thim!"

'"There's damned little sugar in ut!" sez my rear-rank man; but Crook heard.

'"Have ye not all got spoons?" he sez, laughin', an' down we wint as fast as we cud. Learoyd bein' sick at the Base, he, av coorse, was not there.'

'Thot's a lie!' said Learoyd, dragging his bedstead nearer. 'Ah gotten *thot* theer, an' you knaw it, Mulvaaney.' He threw up his arms, and from the right armpit ran, diagonally through the fell of his chest, a thin white line terminating near the fourth left rib.

'My mind's goin',' said Mulvaney, the unabashed. 'Ye were there. Fwhat was I thinkin' av? 'Twas another man, av coorse. Well, you'll remimber thin, Jock, how we an' the Tyrone met wid a bang at the bottom an' got jammed past all movin' among the Paythans?'

'Ow! It *was* a tight 'ole. I was squeezed till I thought I'd bloomin' well bust,' said Ortheris, rubbing his stomach meditatively.

''Twas no place for a little man, but *wan* little man'—Mulvaney put his hand on Ortheris's shoulder—'saved the life av me. There we shtuck, for divil a bit did the Paythans flinch, an' divil a bit dare we; our business bein' to clear 'em out. An' the most exthryordinar' thing av all was that we an' they just rushed into each other's arrums, an' there was no firin' for a long time. Nothin' but knife an' bay'nit when we cud get our hands free: an' that was not often. We was breast-on to thim, an' the Tyrone was yelpin' behind av us in a way I didn't see the lean av at first. But I knew later, an' so did the Paythans.

'"Knee to knee!" sings out Crook, wid a laugh whin the rush av our comin' into the gut shtopped, an' he was huggin' a hairy great Paythan, neither bein' able to do anything to the other, tho' both was wishful.

'"Breast to breast!" he sez, as the Tyrone was pushin' us forward closer an' closer.

'"An' hand over back!" sez a Sargint that was behin'. I saw a sword lick out past Crook's ear, an' the Paythan was tuk in the apple av his throat like a pig at Dromeen Fair.

'"Thank ye, Brother Inner Guard,' sez Crook, cool as a cucumber widout salt. "I wanted that room." An' he wint forward by the thickness av a man's body, havin' turned the Paythan undher him. The man bit the heel off Crook's boot in his death-bite.

'"Push, men!" sez Crook. "Push, ye paper-backed beggars!" he sez. "Am *I* to pull ye through?" So we pushed, an' we kicked, an' we swung, an' we swore, an' the grass bein' slippery, our heels wudn't bite, an' God help the front-rank man that wint down that day!'

'' 'Ave you ever bin in the Pit hentrance o' the Vic.* on a thick night?' interrupted Ortheris. 'It was worse nor that, for they was goin' one way, an' we wouldn't 'ave it. Leastaways, I 'adn't much to say.'

'Faith, me son, ye said ut, thin. I kep' this little man betune my knees as long as I cud, but he was pokin' roun' wid his bay'nit, blindin' an' stiffin' feroshus. The divil of a man is Orth'ris in a ruction—aren't ye?' said Mulvaney.

'Don't make game!' said the Cockney. 'I knowed I wasn't no good then, but I guv 'em compot from the lef' flank when we opened out. No!' he said, bringing down his hand with a thump on the bedstead, 'a bay'nit ain't no good to a little man—might as well 'ave a bloomin' fishin'-rod! I 'ate a clawin', maulin' mess, but gimme a breech that's wore out a bit an' hamminition one year in store, to let the powder kiss the bullet, an' put me somewheres where I ain't trod on by 'ulking swine like you, an' s'elp me Gawd, I could bowl you over five times outer seven at height 'undred. Would yer try, you lumberin' Hirishman?'

'No, ye wasp. I've seen ye do ut. I say there's nothin' better than the bay'nit, wid a long reach, a double twist av ye can, an' a slow recover.'

'Dom the bay'nit,' said Learoyd, who had been listening intently. 'Look a-here!' He picked up a rifle an inch below the foresight with an underhanded action, and used it exactly as a man would use a dagger.

'Sitha,' said he softly, 'thot's better than owt, for a mon can bash t' faace wi' thot, an', if he divn't, he can breeak t' forearm o' t' guaard. 'Tis nut i' t' books, though. Gie me t' butt.'

'Each does ut his own way, like makin' love,' said Mulvaney quietly; 'the butt or the bay'nit or the bullet accordin' to the natur' av the man. Well, as I was sayin', we shtuck there breathin' in each other's faces an' swearin' powerful; Orth'ris cursin' the mother that bore him bekaze he was not three inches taller.

'Prisintly he sez: "Duck, ye lump, an' I can get at a man over your shoulther!"

'"You'll blow me head off," I sez, throwin' my arrum clear; "go through under my arrum-pit, ye bloodthirsty little scutt," sez I, "but don't shtick me or I'll wring your ears round."

'Fwhat was ut ye gave the Paythan man forninst me, him that cut at me whin I cudn't move hand or foot? Hot or cowld was ut?'

'Cold,' said Ortheris, 'up an' under the rib-jints. 'E come down flat. Best for you 'e did.'

'Thrue, me son! This jam thing that I'm talkin' about lasted for five minut's good, an' thin we got our arrums clear an' wint in. I misremimber exactly fwhat I did, but I didn't want Dinah to be a widdy at the depôt. Thin, afther some promishcuous hackin' we shtuck agin, an' the Tyrone behin' was callin' us dogs an' cowards an' all manner av names; we barrin' their way.

'"Fwhat ails the Tyrone?" thinks I. "They've the makin's av a most convanient fight here."

'A man behind me sez beseechful an' in a whisper: "Let me get at thim! For the love av Mary, give me room beside ye, ye tall man!"

'"An' who are you that's so anxious to be kilt?" sez I, widout turnin' my head, for the long knives was dancin' in front likc the sun on Donegal Bay whin ut's rough.

'"We've seen our dead,"* he sez, squeezin' into me; "our dead that was men two days gone! An' me that was his cousin by blood cud not bring Tim Coulan off! Let me get on," he sez, "let me get to thim or I'll run ye through the back!"

'"" My troth," thinks I, "if the Tyrone have seen their
dead, God help the Paythans this day!" An' thin I knew why
the Tyrone was ragin' behind us as they was.

'I gave room to the man, an' he ran forward wid the
Haymakers' Lift on his bay'nit an' swung a Paythan clear off
his feet by the belly-band av the brute, an' the iron bruk at
the lockin'-ring.

'"Tim Coulan 'll slape aisy to-night," sez he wid a grin; an'
the next minut' his head was in two halves and he wint down
grinnin' by sections.

'The Tyrone was pushin' an' pushin' in, an' our men was
swearin' at thim, an' Crook was workin' away in front av us
all, his sword-arrum swingin' like a pump-handle an' his
revolver spittin' like a cat. But the strange thing av ut was the
quiet that lay upon. 'Twas like a fight in a drame—excipt for
thim that was dead.

'Whin I gave room to the Irishman I was expinded an'
forlorn in my inside. 'Tis a way I have, savin' your presince,
sorr, in action. "Let me out, bhoys," sez I, backin' in among
thim. "I'm goin' to be onwell!" Faith, they gave me room at
the wurrud, though they wud not ha' given room for all Hell
wid the chill off. When I got clear, I was, savin' your
presince, sorr, outrajis sick bekaze I had dhrunk heavy that
day.

'Well an' far out av harm was a Sargint av the Tyrone sittin'
on the little orf'cer bhoy who had stopped Crook from
rowlin' the rocks. Oh, he was a beautiful bhoy, an' the long
black curses was slidin' out av his innocint mouth like
mornin'-jew from a rose!

'"Fwhat have you got there?" sez I to the Sargint.

'"Wan av Her Majesty's bantams wid his spurs up," sez
he. "He's goin' to Coort-Martial me."

'"Let me go!" sez the little orf'cer bhoy. "Let me go and
command me men!" manin' thereby the Black Tyrone which
was beyond any command—even av they had made the Divil
Field-Orf'cer.

'"His father howlds my mother's cow-feed in Clonmel,"
sez the man that was sittin' on him. "Will I go back to *his*
mother an' tell her that I've let him throw himsilf away? Lie

still, ye little pinch of dynamite, an' Coort-Martial me aftherwards."

'"Good," sez I; "'tis the likes av him makes the likes av the Commandher-in-Chief, but we must presarve thim. Fwhat d'you want to do, sorr?" sez I, very politeful.

'"Kill the beggars—kill the beggars!" he shqueaks, his big blue eyes brimmin' wid tears.

'"An' how'll ye do that?" sez I. "You've shquibbed off your revolver like a child wid a cracker; you can make no play wid that fine large sword av yours; an' your hand's shakin' like an asp on a leaf. Lie still and grow," sez I.

'"Get back to your comp'ny," sez he; "you're insolint!"

'"All in good time," sez I, "but I'll have a dhrink first."

'Just thin Crook comes up, blue an' white all over where he wasn't red.

'"Wather!" sez he; "I'm dead wid drouth! Oh, but it's a gran' day!"

'He dhrank half a skinful, and the rest he tilts into his chest, an' it fair hissed on the hairy hide av him. He sees the little orf'cer bhoy undher the Sargint.

'"Fwhat's yonder?" sez he.

'"Mutiny, sorr," sez the Sargint, an' the orf'cer bhoy begins pleadin' pitiful to Crook to be let go; but divil a bit wud Crook budge.

'"Kape him there," he sez; "'tis no child's work this day. By the same token," sez he, "I'll confishcate that iligant nickel-plated scent-sprinkler av yours, for my own has been vomitin' dishgraceful!"

'The fork av his hand was black wid the back-spit av the machine. So he tuk the orf'cer bhoy's revolver. Ye may look, sorr, but, by my faith, *there's a dale more done in the field than iver gets into Field Ordhers!*

'"Come on, Mulvaney," sez Crook; "is this a Coort-Martial?" The two av us wint back together into the mess an' the Paythans was still standin' up. They was not *too* impart'nint though, for the Tyrone was callin' wan to another to remimber Tim Coulan.

'Crook holted outside av the strife an' looked anxious, his eyes rowlin' roun'.

'"Fwhat is ut, sorr?" sez I; "can I get ye anything?"

'"Where's a bugler?" sez he.

'I wint into the crowd—our men was dhrawin' breath behin' the Tyrone, who was fightin' like sowls in tormint—an' prisintly I came acrost little Frehan, our bugler bhoy, pokin' roun' among the best wid a rifle an' bay'nit.

'"Is amusin' yoursilf fwhat you're paid for, ye limb?" sez I, catchin' him by the scruff. "Come out av that an' attind to your jooty," I sez; but the bhoy was not plazed.

'"I've got wan," sez he, grinnin', "big as you, Mulvaney, an' fair half as ugly. Let me go get another."

'I was dishplazed at the personality av that remark, so I tucks him under my arrum an' carries him to Crook, who was watchin' how the fight wint. Crook cuffs him till the bhoy cries, an' thin sez nothin' for a whoile.

'The Paythans began to flicker onaisy, an' our men roared. "Opin ordher! Double!" sez Crook. "Blow, child, blow for the honour av the British Arrmy!"

'That bhoy blew like a typhoon, an' the Tyrone an' we opind out as the Paythans bruk, an' I saw that fwhat had gone before wud be kissin' an' huggin' to fwhat was to come. We'd dhruv thim into a broad part av the gut whin they gave, an' thin we opind out an' fair danced down the valley, dhrivin' thim before us. Oh, 'twas lovely, an' stiddy, too! There was the Sargints on the flanks av what was left av us, kapin' touch, an' the fire was runnin' from flank to flank, an' the Paythans was dhroppin'. We opind out wid the widenin' av the valley, an' whin the valley narrowed we closed agin like the shticks on a lady's fan, an' at the far ind av the gut where they thried to stand, we fair blew them off their feet, for we had expinded very little ammunition by reason av the knife-work.'

'I used thirty rounds goin' down that valley,' said Ortheris, 'an' it was gentleman's work. Might 'a' done it in a white 'andkerchief an' pink silk stockin's, that part. Hi was on in that piece.'

'You cud ha' heard the Tyrone yellin' a mile away,' said Mulvaney, 'an' 'twas all their Sargints cud do to get thim off. They was mad—mad—mad! Crook sits down in the quiet that fell whin we had gone down the valley, an' covers his face wid his hands. Prisintly we all came back agin accordin' to our natur's and disposishins, for they, mark you, show through the hide av a man in that hour.

'"Bhoys! bhoys!" sez Crook to himsilf. "I misdoubt we cud ha' engaged at long range an' saved betther men than me." He looked at our dead an' said no more.

'"Captain dear," sez a man av the Tyrone, comin' up wid his mouth bigger than iver his mother kissed ut, spittin' blood like a whale; "Captain dear," sez he, "if wan or two in the shtalls have been dishcommoded, the gallery have enjoyed the performinces av a Roshus."*

'Thin I knew that man for the Dublin dock-rat he was— wan av the bhoys that made the lessee av Silver's Theatre grey before his time wid tearin' out the bowils av the benches an' throwin' thim into the pit. So I passed the wurrud that I knew whin I was in the Tyrone an' we lay in Dublin. "I don't know who 'twas," I whishpers, "an' I don't care, but anyways I'll knock the face av you, Tim Kelly."

'"Eyah!" sez the man, "was you there too? We'll call ut Silver's Theatre." Half the Tyrone, knowin' the ould place, tuk ut up: so we called ut Silver's Theatre.

'The little orf'cer bhoy av the Tyrone was thremblin' an' cryin'. He had no heart for the Coort-Martials that he talked so big upon. "Ye'll do well later," sez Crook, very quiet, "for not bein' allowed to kill yoursilf for amusemint."

'"I'm a dishgraced man!" sez the little orf'cer bhoy.

'"Put me undher arrest, sorr, if you will, but, by my sowl, I'd do ut agin sooner than face your mother wid you dead," sez the Sargint that had sat on his head, standin' to attenshin an' salutin'. But the young wan only cried as tho' his little heart was breakin'.

'Thin another man av the Tyrone came up, wid the fog av fightin' on him.'

'The what, Mulvaney?'

'Fog av fightin'. You know, sorr, that, like makin' love, ut takes each man diff'rint. Now, I can't help bein' powerful sick whin I'm in action. Orth'ris, here, niver stops swearin' from ind to ind, an' the only time that Learoyd opins his

mouth to sing is whin he is messin' wid other people's heads;
for he's a dhirty fighter is Jock. Recruities sometime cry, an'
sometime they don't know fwhat they do, an' sometime they
are all for cuttin' throats an' such-like dhirtiness; but some
men get heavy-dead-dhrunk on the fightin'. This man was.
He was staggerin', an' his eyes were half shut, an' we cud hear
him dhraw breath twinty yards away. He sees the little orf'cer
bhoy, an' comes up, talkin' thick an' drowsy to himsilf.
"Blood the young whelp!" he sez; "Blood the young whelp";
an' wid that he threw up his arrums, shpun roun', an'
dropped at our feet, dead as a Paythan, an' there was niver
sign or scratch on him. They said 'twas his heart was rotten,
but oh, 'twas a quare thing to see!

'Thin we wint to bury our dead, for we wud not lave thim
to the Paythans, an' in movin' among the haythen we nearly
lost that little orf'cer bhoy. He was for givin' wan divil wather
and layin' him aisy against a rock. "Be careful, sorr," sez I;
"a wounded Paythan's worse than a live wan." My troth,
before the words was out av me mouth, the man on the
ground fires at the orf'cer bhoy lanin' over him, an' I saw the
helmit fly. I dropped the butt on the face av the man an' tuk
his pistol. The little orf'cer bhoy turned very white, for the
hair av half his head was singed away.

'"I tould you so, sorr!" sez I; an', afther that, whin he
wanted to help a Paythan I stud wid the muzzle contagious to
the ear. They dared not do anythin' but curse. The Tyrone
was growlin' like dogs over a bone that has been taken away
too soon, for they had seen their dead an' they wanted to kill
ivry sowl on the ground. Crook tould thim that he'd blow the
hide off any man that misconducted himsilf; but, seeing that
ut was the first time the Tyrone had iver seen their dead, I do
not wondher they was on the sharp. 'Tis a shameful sight!
Whin I first saw ut I wud niver ha' given quarter to any man
north of the Khyber—no, nor woman either, for the wimmen
used to come out afther dhark—Auggrh!

'Well, evenshually we buried our dead an' tuk away our
wounded, an' come over the brow av the hills to see the
Scotchies an' the Gurkys takin' tay with the Paythans in
bucketsfuls. We were a gang av dissolute ruffians, for the

blood had caked the dust, an' the sweat had cut the cake, an' our bay'nits was hangin' like butchers' steels betune our legs, an' most av us was marked one way or another.

'A Staff Orf'cer man, clane as a new rifle, rides up an' sez: "What damned scarecrows are you?"

'"A comp'ny av Her Majesty's Black Tyrone an' wan av the Ould Rig'mint," sez Crook very quiet, givin' our visitors the flure as 'twas.

'"Oh!" sez the Staff Orf'cer. "Did you dislodge that Reserve?"

'"No!" sez Crook, an' the Tyrone laughed.

'"Thin fwhat the divil have ye done?"

'"Disthroyed ut," sez Crook, an' he took us on, but not before Toomey that was in the Tyrone sez aloud, his voice somewhere in his stummick: "Fwhat in the name av misfortune does this parrit widout a tail mane by shtoppin' the road av his betthers?"

'The Staff Orf'cer wint blue, an' Toomey makes him pink by changin' to the voice av a minowdherin' woman an' sayin': "Come an' kiss me, Major dear, for me husband's at the wars an' I'm all alone at the depôt."

'The Staff Orf'cer wint away, an' I cud see Crook's shoulthers shakin'.

'His Corp'ril checks Toomey. "Lave me alone," sez Toomey, widout a wink. "I was his batman before he was married an' he knows fwhat I mane, av you don't. There's nothin' like livin' in the hoight av society." D'you remimber that, Orth'ris?'

'Yuss. Toomey, 'e died in 'orspital, next week it was, 'cause I bought 'arf his kit; an' I remember after that——'

'GUARRD, TURN OUT!'

The Relief had come; it was four o'clock. 'I'll catch a kyart for you, sorr,' said Mulvaney, diving hastily into his accoutrements. 'Come up to the top av the Fort an' we'll pershue our invistigations into M'Grath's shtable.' The relieved guard strolled round the main bastion on its way to the swimming-bath, and Learoyd grew almost talkative. Ortheris looked into the Fort Ditch and across the plain. 'Ho! it's weary waitin' for Ma-ary!' he hummed; 'but I'd like to kill some more bloomin' Paythans before my time's up. War! Bloody war! North, East, South, and West.'

'Amen,' said Learoyd slowly.

'Fwhat's here?' said Mulvaney, checking at a blur of white by the foot of the old sentry-box. He stooped and touched it. 'It's Norah—Norah M'Taggart! Why, Nonie darlin', fwhat are ye doin' out av your mother's bed at this time?'

The two-year-old child of Sergeant M'Taggart must have wandered for a breath of cool air to the very verge of the parapet of the Fort Ditch. Her tiny nightshift was gathered into a wisp round her neck and she moaned in her sleep. 'See there!' said Mulvaney; 'poor lamb! Look at the heat-rash on the innocint shkin av her. 'Tis hard—crool hard even for us. Fwhat must it be for these? Wake up, Nonie, your mother will be woild about you. Begad, the child might ha' fallen into the Ditch!'

He picked her up in the growing light, and set her on his shoulder, and her fair curls touched the grizzled stubble of his temples. Ortheris and Learoyd followed snapping their fingers, while Norah smiled at them a sleepy smile. Then carolled Mulvaney, clear as a lark, dancing the baby on his arm:—

> 'If any young man should marry you,
>   Say nothin' about the joke;
> That iver ye slep' in a sinthry-box,
>   Wrapped up in a soldier's cloak.'*

'Though, on my sowl, Nonie,' he said gravely, 'there was not much cloak about you. Niver mind, you won't dhress like this ten years to come. Kiss your frinds an' run along to your mother.'

Nonie, set down close to the Married Quarters, nodded with the quiet obedience of the soldier's child, but, ere she pattered off over the flagged path, held up her lips to be kissed by the Three Musketeers. Ortheris wiped his mouth with the back of his hand and swore sentimentally! Learoyd turned pink; and the two walked away together. The York-shireman lifted up his voice and gave in thunder the chorus of *The Sentry-Box*, while Ortheris piped at his side.

'Bin to a bloomin' sing-song, you two?' said the Artillery-man, who was taking his cartridge down to the Morning Gun. 'You're over merry for these dashed days.'

> 'I bid ye take care o' the brat, said he,
> For it comes of a noble race,'

Learoyd bellowed. The voices died out in the swimming-bath.

'Oh, Terence!' I said, dropping into Mulvaney's speech, when we were alone, 'it's you that have the Tongue!'

He looked at me wearily; his eyes were sunk in his head, and his face was drawn and white. 'Eyah!' said he; 'I've blandandhered thim through the night somehow, but can thim that helps others help thimsilves? Answer me that, sorr!'

And over the bastions of Fort Amara broke the pitiless day.

In Flood Time

Tweed said tae Till:
'What gars ye rin sae still?'
Till said tae Tweed:
'Though ye rin wi' speed
An' I rin slaw—
Yet where ye droon ae man
I droon twa.'*

THERE is no getting over the river to-night, Sahib. They say
that a bullock-cart has been washed down already, and the
*ekka** that went over a half-hour before you came has not yet
reached the far side. Is the Sahib in haste? I will drive the
ford-elephant in to show him. Ohé, mahout there in the shed!
Bring out Ram Pershad, and if he will face the current, good.
An elephant never lies, Sahib, and Ram Pershad is separated
from his friend Kala Nag. He, too, wishes to cross to the far
side. Well done! Well done! my King! Go half-way across,
*mahoutji,** and see what the river says. Well done, Ram
Pershad! Pearl among elephants, go into the river! Hit him
on the head, fool! Was the goad made only to scratch thine
own fat back with, bastard? Strike! strike! What are the
boulders to thee, Ram Pershad, my Rustum,* my mountain
of strength? Go in! Go in!

No, Sahib! It is useless. You can hear him trumpet. He is
telling Kala Nag that he cannot come over. See! He has
swung round and is shaking his head. He is no fool. He
knows what the Barhwi means when it is angry. Aha! Indeed,
thou art no fool, my child! Salaam, Ram Pershad, Bahadur!*
Take him under the trees, mahout, and see that he gets his
spices. Well done, thou chiefest among tuskers! Salaam to
the Sirkar* and go to sleep.

What is to be done? The Sahib must wait till the river goes
down. It will shrink to-morrow morning, if God pleases, or
the day after at the latest! Now why does the Sahib get so
angry? I am his servant. Before God, *I* did not create this
stream! What can I do? My hut and all that is therein is at the
service of the Sahib, and it is beginning to rain. Come away,

my Lord. How will the river go down for your throwing abuse at it? In the old days the English people were not thus. The fire-carriage has made them soft. In the old days, when they drave behind horses by day or by night, they said naught if a river barred the way, or a carriage sat down in the mud. It was the will of God—not like a fire-carriage which goes and goes and goes, and would go though all the devils in the land hung on to its tail. The fire-carriage hath spoiled the English people. After all, what is a day lost, or, for that matter, what are two days? Is the Sahib going to his own wedding, that he is so mad with haste? Ho! ho! ho! I am an old man and see few Sahibs. Forgive me if I have forgotten the respect that is due to them. The Sahib is not angry?

His own wedding! Ho! ho! ho! The mind of an old man is like the *numah*-tree. Fruit, bud, blossom, and the dead leaves of all the years of the past flourish together. Old and new and that which is gone out of remembrance, all three are there! Sit on the bedstead, Sahib, and drink milk. Or—would the Sahib in truth care to drink my tobacco?* It is good. It is the tobacco of Nuklao. My son, who is in service there, sends it to me. Drink, then, Sahib, if you know how to handle the tube. The Sahib takes it like a Mussulman. Wah! Wah! Where did he learn that? His own wedding! Ho! ho! ho! The Sahib says that there is no wedding in the matter at all. Now *is* it likely that the Sahib would speak true talk to me who am only a black man? Small wonder, then, that he is in haste. Thirty years have I beaten the gong at this ford, but never have I seen a Sahib in such haste. Thirty years, Sahib! That is a very long time. Thirty years ago this ford was on the track of the *bunjaras*,* and I have seen two thousand pack-bullocks cross in one night. Now the rail has come, and the fire-carriage says *buz-buz-buz*, and a hundred lakhs of maunds* slide across that big bridge. It is very wonderful; but the ford is lonely now that there are no *bunjaras* to camp under the trees.

Nay, do not trouble to look at the sky without. It will rain till the dawn. Listen! The boulders are talking to-night in the bed of the river. Hear them! They would be husking your bones, Sahib, had you tried to cross. See, I will shut the door and no rain can enter. *Wahi! Ahi! Ugh!* Thirty years on the banks of the ford. An old man am I and—where is the oil for the lamp?

*   *.   *   *   *

Your pardon, but, because of my years, I sleep no sounder than a dog; and you moved to the door. Look then, Sahib. Look and listen. A full half *koss** from bank to bank is the stream now—you can see it under the stars—and there are ten feet of water therein. It will not shrink because of the anger in your eyes, and it will not be quiet on account of your curses. Which is louder, Sahib—your voice or the voice of the river? Call to it—perhaps it will be ashamed. Lie down and sleep afresh, Sahib. I know the anger of the Barhwi when there has fallen rain in the foot-hills. I swam the flood, once, on a night tenfold worse than this, and by the Favour of God I was released from Death when I had come to the very gates thereof.

May I tell the tale? Very good talk. I will fill the pipe anew.

Thirty years ago it was, when I was a young man and had but newly come to the ford. I was strong then, and the *bunjaras* had no doubt when I said: 'This ford is clear.' I have toiled all night up to my shoulder-blades in running water amid a hundred bullocks mad with fear, and have brought them across losing not a hoof. When all was done I fetched the shivering men, and they gave me for reward the pick of their cattle—the bell-bullock of the drove. So great was the honour in which I was held! But to-day, when the rain falls and the river rises, I creep into my hut and whimper like a dog. My strength is gone from me. I am an old man and the fire-carriage has made the ford desolate. They were wont to call me the Strong One of the Barhwi.

Behold my face, Sahib—it is the face of a monkey. And my arm—it is the arm of an old woman. I swear to you, Sahib, that a woman has loved this face and has rested in the hollow of this arm. Twenty years go, Sahib. Believe me, this was true talk—twenty years ago.

Come to the door and look across. Can you see a thin fire very far away down the stream? That is the temple-fire, in the shrine of Hanuman,* of the village of Pateera. North, under the big star, is the village itself, but it is hidden by a bend of the river. Is that far to swim, Sahib? Would you take off your clothes and adventure? Yet I swam to Pateera—not once, but many times; and there are *muggers** in the river too.

Love knows no caste; else why should I, a Mussulman and the son of a Mussulman, have sought a Hindu woman—a widow of the Hindus—the sister of the headman of Pateera? But it was even so. They of the headman's household came on a pilgrimage to Muttra when She was but newly a bride. Silver tyres were upon the wheels of the bullock-cart, and silken curtains hid the woman. Sahib, I made no haste in their conveyance, for the wind parted the curtains and I saw Her. When they returned from pilgrimage the boy that was Her husband had died, and I saw Her again in the bullock-cart. By God, these Hindus are fools! What was it to me whether She was Hindu or Jain—scavenger, leper, or whole? I would have married Her and made Her a home by the ford. The Seventh of the Nine Bars says that a man may not marry one of the idolaters? Is that truth? Both Shiahs and Sunnis* say that a Mussulman may not marry one of the idolaters? Is the Sahib a priest, then, that he knows so much? I will tell him something that he does not know. There is neither Shiah nor Sunni, forbidden nor idolater, in Love; and the Nine Bars are but nine little faggots that the flame of Love utterly burns away. In truth, I would have taken Her; but what could I do? The headman would have sent his men to break my head with staves. I am not—I was not—afraid of any five men; but against half a village who can prevail?

Therefore it was my custom, these things having been arranged between us twain, to go by night to the village of Pateera, and there we met among the crops, no man knowing aught of the matter. Behold, now! I was wont to cross here, skirting the jungle to the river bend where the railway bridge is, and thence across the elbow of land to Pateera. The light of the shrine was my guide when the nights were dark. That jungle near the river is very full of snakes—little *karaits* that sleep on the sand—and moreover, Her brothers would have slain me had they found me in the crops. But none knew—none knew save She and I; and the blown sand of the river-bed covered the track of my feet. In the hot months it was an easy thing to pass from the ford to Pateera, and in the first Rains, when the river rose slowly, it was an easy thing also. I set the strength of my body against the strength of the stream, and nightly I ate in my hut here and drank at Pateera yonder. She had said that one Hirnam Singh, a thief, had sought Her, and he was of a village up the river but on the same bank. All Sikhs are dogs, and they have refused in their folly that good gift of God—tobacco. I was ready to destroy Hirnam Singh that ever he had come nigh Her; and the more because he had sworn to Her that She had a lover, and that he would lie in wait and give the name to the headman unless She went away with him. What curs are these Sikhs!

After that news I swam always with a little sharp knife in my belt, and evil would it have been for a man had he stayed me. I knew not the face of Hirnam Singh, but I would have killed any who came between me and Her.

Upon a night in the beginning of the Rains I was minded to go across to Pateera, albeit the river was angry. Now the nature of the Barhwi is this, Sahib. In twenty breaths it comes down from the Hills a wall three feet high, and I have seen it, between the lighting of a fire and the cooking of a cake, grow from a runnel to a sister of the Jumna.*

When I left this bank there was a shoal a half-mile down, and I made shift to fetch it and draw breath there ere going forward; for I felt the hands of the river heavy upon my heels. Yet what will a young man not do for Love's sake? There was but little light from the stars, and midway to the shoal a branch of the stinking deodar* tree brushed my mouth as I swam. That was a sign of heavy rain in the foot-hills and beyond, for the deodar is a strong tree, not easily shaken from the hillsides. I made haste, the river aiding me, but ere I had touched the shoal, the pulse of the stream beat, as it were, within me and around, and, behold, the shoal was gone and I rode high on the crest of a wave that ran from bank to bank. Has the Sahib ever been cast into much water that fights and will not let a man use his limbs? To me, my head upon the water, it seemed as though there were naught but water to the world's end, and the river drave me with its driftwood. A man is a very little thing in the belly of a flood. And *this* flood, though I knew it not, was the Great Flood about which men talk still. My liver was dissolved and I lay like a log upon my back in the fear of Death. There were living things in the water, crying and howling grievously—beasts of the forest and cattle, and once the voice of a man asking for help. But the rain came and lashed the water white, and I heard no more save the roar of the boulders below and the roar of the rain above. Thus I was whirled downstream, wrestling for the breath in me. It is very hard to die when one is young. Can the Sahib, standing here, see the railway bridge? Look, there are the lights of the mail-train going to Peshawur! The bridge is now twenty feet above the river, but upon that night the water was roaring against the lattice-work, and against the lattice came I feet first. But much driftwood was piled there and upon the piers, and I took no great hurt. Only the river pressed me as a strong man presses a weaker. Scarcely could I take hold of the lattice-work and crawl to the upper boom.* Sahib, the water was foaming across the rails a foot deep! Judge therefore what manner of flood it must have been. I could not hear. I could not see. I could but lie on the boom and pant for breath.

After a while the rain ceased and there came out in the sky certain new-washed stars, and by their light I saw that there was no end to the black water as far as the eye could travel, and the water had risen upon the rails. There were dead beasts in the driftwood on the piers, and others caught by the neck in the lattice-work, and others not yet drowned who strove to find a foothold on the lattice-work—buffaloes and kine, and wild pig, and deer one or two, and snakes and jackals past all counting. Their bodies were black upon the left side of the bridge, but the smaller of them were forced through the lattice-work and whirled down-stream.

Thereafter the stars died and the rain came down afresh and the river rose yet more, and I felt the bridge begin to stir under me as a man stirs in his sleep ere he wakes. But I was not afraid, Sahib. I swear to you that I was not afraid, though I had no power in my limbs. I knew that I should not die till I had seen Her once more. But I was very cold, and I felt that the bridge must go.

There was a trembling in the water, such a trembling as

goes before the coming of a great wave, and the bridge lifted
its flank to the rush of that coming so that the right lattice
dipped under water and the left rose clear.* On my beard,
Sahib, I am speaking God's truth! As a Mirzapore stone-boat
careens to the wind, so the Barhwi Bridge turned. Thus and
in no other manner.

I slid from the boom into deep water, and behind me came
the wave of the wrath of the river. I heard its voice and the
scream of the middle part of the bridge as it moved from the
piers and sank, and I knew no more till I rose in the middle of
the great flood. I put forth my hand to swim, and lo! it fell
upon the knotted hair of the head of a man. He was dead, for
no one but I, the Strong One of Barhwi, could have lived in
that race. He had been dead full two days, for he rode high,
wallowing, and was an aid to me. I laughed then, knowing for
a surety that I should yet see Her and take no harm; and I
twisted my fingers in the hair of the man, for I was far spent,
and together we went down the stream—he the dead and I
the living. Lacking that help I should have sunk: the cold was
in my marrow, and my flesh was ribbed and sodden on my
bones. But *he* had no fear who had known the uttermost of
the power of the river; and I let him go where he chose. At last
we came into the power of a side-current that set to the right
bank, and I strove with my feet to draw with it. But the dead
man swung heavily in the whirl, and I feared that some
branch had struck him and that he would sink. The tops of
the tamarisks brushed my knees, so I knew we were come
into flood-water above the crops, and, after, I let down my
legs and felt bottom—the ridge of a field—and, after, the
dead man stayed upon a knoll under a fig-tree, and I drew my
body from the water rejoicing.

Does the Sahib know whither the backwash of the flood
had borne me? To the knoll which is the eastern boundary-
mark of the village of Pateera! No other place. I drew the
dead man up on the grass for the service that he had done me,
and also because I knew not whether I should need him
again. Then I went, crying thrice like a jackal, to the
appointed place, which was near the byre of the headman's
house. But my Love was already there, weeping. She feared

that the flood had swept my hut at the Barhwi Ford. When I came softly through the ankle-deep water, She thought it was a ghost and would have fled, but I put my arms round Her, and—I was no ghost in those days, though I am an old man now. Ho! ho! Dried corn, in truth. Maize without juice. Ho! ho!*

I told Her the story of the breaking of the Barhwi Bridge, and She said that I was greater than mortal man, for none may cross the Barhwi in full flood, and I had seen what never man had seen before. Hand in hand we went to the knoll where the dead lay, and I showed Her by what help I had made the ford. She looked also upon the body under the stars, for the latter end of the night was clear, and hid Her face in Her hands, crying: 'It is the body of Hirnam Singh!' I said: 'The swine is of more use dead than living, my Beloved,' and She said: 'Surely, for he has saved the dearest life in the world to my love. None the less, he cannot stay here, for that would bring shame upon me.' The body was not a gunshot from Her door.

Then said I, rolling the body with my hands: 'God hath judged between us, Hirnam Singh, that thy blood might not be upon my head. Now, whether I have done thee a wrong in keeping thee from the burning-ghat, do thou and the crows settle together.' So I cast him adrift into the flood-water, and he was drawn out to the open, ever wagging his thick black beard like a priest under the pulpit-board. And I saw no more of Hirnam Singh.

Before the breaking of the day we two parted, and I moved towards such of the jungle as was not flooded. With the full light I saw what I had done in the darkness, and the bones of my body were loosened in my flesh, for there ran two *koss* of raging water between the village of Pateera and the trees of the far bank, and, in the middle, the piers of the Barhwi Bridge showed like broken teeth in the jaw of an old man. Nor was there any life upon the waters—neither birds nor boats, but only an army of drowned things—bullocks and horses and men—and the river was redder than blood from the clay of the foot-hills. Never had I seen such a flood— never since that year have I seen the like—and, O Sahib, no

man living had done what I had done. There was no return
for me that day. Not for all the lands of the headman would I
venture a second time without the shield of darkness that
cloaks danger. I went a *koss* up the river to the house of a
blacksmith, saying that the flood had swept me from my hut,
and they gave me food. Seven days I stayed with the blacksmith, till a boat came and I returned to my house. There was
no trace of wall, or roof, or floor—naught but a patch of slimy
mud. Judge, therefore, Sahib, how far the river must have
risen.

It was written that I should not die either in my house, or in
the heart of the Barhwi, or under the wreck of the Barhwi
Bridge, for God sent down Hirnam Singh two days dead,
though I know not how the man died,* to be my buoy and
support. Hirnam Singh has been in Hell these twenty years,
and the thought of that night must be the flower of his
torment.

Listen, Sahib! The river has changed its voice. It is going
to sleep before the dawn, to which there is yet one hour. With
the light it will come down afresh. How do I know? Have I
been here thirty years without knowing the voice of the river
as a father knows the voice of his son? Every moment it is
talking less angrily. I swear that there will be no danger for
one hour or, perhaps, two. I cannot answer for the morning.
Be quick, Sahib! I will call Ram Pershad, and he will not turn
back this time. Is the paulin* tightly corded upon all the
baggage? Ohé, mahout with a mud head, the elephant for the
Sahib, and tell them on the far side that there will be no
crossing after daylight.

Money? Nay, Sahib. I am not of that kind. No, not even to
give sweetmeats to the baby-folk. My house, look you, is
empty, and I am an old man.

Dutt,* Ram Pershad! *Dutt! Dutt! Dutt!* Good luck go with
you, Sahib.

Only a Subaltern

... Not only to enforce by command, but to encourage by example the energetic discharge of duty and the steady endurance of the difficulties and privations inseparable from Military Service.—*Bengal Army Regulations*

THEY made Bobby Wick pass an examination at Sandhurst.*
He was a gentleman before he was gazetted, so, when the
Empress announced that 'Gentleman-Cadet Robert Hanna
Wick' was posted as Second Lieutenant to the Tyneside Tail-
Twisters* at Krab Bokhar,* he became an officer *and* a
gentleman, which is an enviable thing; and there was joy in
the house of Wick where Mamma Wick and all the little
Wicks fell upon their knees and offered incense to Bobby by
virtue of his achievements.

Papa Wick had been a Commissioner in his day, holding
authority over three millions of men in the Chota-Buldana
Division, building great works for the good of the land, and
doing his best to make two blades of grass grow where there
was but one before. Of course, nobody knew anything about
this in the little English village where he was just 'old Mr
Wick', and had forgotten that he was a Companion of the
Order of the Star of India.*

He patted Bobby on the shoulder and said: 'Well done, my
boy!'

There followed, while the uniform was being prepared, an
interval of pure delight, during which Bobby took brevet-
rank as a 'man' at the women-swamped tennis-parties and
tea-fights of the village, and, I daresay, had his joining-time
been extended, would have fallen in love with several girls at
once. Little country villages at Home are very full of nice
girls, because all the young men come out to India to make
their fortunes.

'India,' said Papa Wick, 'is the place. I've had thirty years
of it and, begad, I'd like to go back again. When you join the

Tail-Twisters you'll be among friends, if every one hasn't forgotten Wick of Chota-Buldana, and a lot of people will be kind to you for our sakes. The mother will tell you more about outfit than I can; but remember this. Stick to your Regiment, Bobby—stick to your Regiment. You'll see men all round you going into the Staff Corps, and doing every possible sort of duty but regimental, and you may be tempted to follow suit. Now so long as you keep within your allowance, and I haven't stinted you there, stick to the Line, the whole Line, and nothing but the Line.* Be careful how you back another young fool's bill, and if you fall in love with a woman twenty years older than yourself, don't tell *me* about it, that's all.'

With these counsels, and many others equally valuable, did Papa Wick fortify Bobby ere that last awful night at Portsmouth when the Officers' Quarters held more inmates than were provided for by the Regulations, and the liberty-men of the ships fell foul of the drafts for India, and the battle raged from the Dockyard Gates even to the slums of Long-port, while the drabs of Fratton came down and scratched the faces of the Queen's Officers.

Bobby Wick, with an ugly bruise on his freckled nose, a sick and shaky detachment to manœuvre inship, and the comfort of fifty scornful females to attend to, had no time to feel homesick till the *Malabar* reached mid-Channel, when he doubled his emotions with a little guard-visiting and a great many other matters.

The Tail-Twisters were a most particular Regiment. Those who knew them least said that they were eaten up with 'side'.* But their reserve and their internal arrangements generally were merely protective diplomacy. Some five years before, the Colonel commanding had looked into the fourteen fearless eyes of seven plump and juicy subalterns who had all applied to enter the Staff Corps, and had asked them why the three stars should he, a Colonel of the Line, command a dashed nursery for double-dashed bottle-suckers who put on condemned tin spurs and rode qualified mokes* at the hiatused heads of forsaken Black Regiments.* He was a rude man and a terrible. Wherefore the remnant took

measures (with the half-butt* as an engine of public opinion)
till the rumour went abroad that young men who used the
Tail-Twisters as a crutch to the Staff Corps had many and
varied trials to endure. However, a regiment has just as much
right to its own secrets as a woman.

When Bobby came up from Deolali and took his place
among the Tail-Twisters, it was gently but firmly borne in
upon him that the Regiment was his father and his mother
and his indissolubly wedded wife, and that there was no
crime under the canopy of heaven blacker than that of
bringing shame on the Regiment, which was the best-
shooting, best-drilled, best-set-up, bravest, most illustrious,
and in all respects most desirable Regiment within the
compass of the Seven Seas. He was taught the legends of the
Mess Plate, from the great grinning Golden Gods that had
come out of the Summer Palace in Pekin to the silver-
mounted markhor-horn snuff-mull presented by the last
C.O. (he who spake to the seven subalterns). And every one
of those legends told him of battles fought at long odds,
without fear as without support; of hospitality catholic as an
Arab's; of friendships deep as the sea and steady as the
fighting-line; of honour won by hard roads for honour's sake;
and of instant and unquestioning devotion to the Regiment—
the Regiment that claims the lives of all and lives for ever.

More than once, too, he came officially into contact with
the Regimental colours, which looked like the lining of a
bricklayer's hat on the end of a chewed stick. Bobby did not
kneel and worship them, because British subalterns are not
constructed in that manner. Indeed, he condemned them for
their weight at the very moment that they were filling him
with awe and other more noble sentiments.

But best of all was the occasion when he moved with the
Tail-Twisters in review order at the breaking of a November
day. Allowing for duty-men and sick, the Regiment was one
thousand and eighty strong, and Bobby belonged to them;
for was he not a Subaltern of the Line—the whole Line, and
nothing but the Line—as the tramp of two thousand one
hundred and sixty sturdy ammunition boots attested? He
would not have changed places with Deighton of the Horse

Battery, whirling by in a pillar of cloud to a chorus of 'Strong right! Strong left!' or Hogan-Yale of the White Hussars, leading his squadron for all it was worth, with the price of horseshoes thrown in; or 'Tick' Boileau, trying to live up to his fierce blue-and-gold turban while the wasps of the Bengal Cavalry stretched to a gallop in the wake of the long, lollopping Walers* of the White Hussars.

They fought through the clear cool day, and Bobby felt a little thrill run down his spine when he heard the *tinkle-tinkle-tinkle* of the empty cartridge-cases hopping from the breech-blocks after the roar of the volleys; for he knew that he should live to hear that sound in action. The review ended in a glorious chase across the plain—batteries thundering after cavalry to the huge disgust of the White Hussars, and the Tyneside Tail-Twisters hunting a Sikh Regiment, till the lean lathy Singhs panted with exhaustion. Bobby was dusty and dripping long before noon, but his enthusiasm was merely focused—not diminished.

He returned to sit at the feet of Revere, his 'skipper', that is to say, the Captain of his Company, and to be instructed in the dark art and mystery of managing men, which is a very large part of the Profession of Arms.

'If you haven't a taste that way,' said Revere between his puffs of his cheroot, 'you'll never be able to get the hang of it, but remember, Bobby, 'tisn't the best drill, though drill is nearly everything, that hauls a regiment through Hell and out on the other side. It's the man who knows how to handle men—goat-men, swine-men, dog-men, and so on.'

'Dormer, for instance,' said Bobby. 'I think he comes under the head of fool-men. He mopes like a sick owl.'

'That's where you make your mistake, my son. Dormer isn't a fool *yet*, but he's a dashed dirty soldier, and his Room Corporal makes fun of his socks before kit-inspection. Dormer, being two-thirds pure brute, goes into a corner and growls.'

'How do you know?' said Bobby admiringly.

'Because a Company Commander has to know these things—because, if he does *not* know, he may have crime—ay, murder—brewing under his very nose and yet not see that it's there. Dormer is being badgered out of his mind—big as

he is—and he hasn't intellect enough to resent it. He's taken
to quiet boozing, and, Bobby, when the butt of a room goes
on the drink, or takes to moping by himself, measures are
necessary to pull him out of himself.'

'What measures? Man can't run round coddling his men
for ever.'

'No. The men would precious soon show him that he was
not wanted. You've got to——'

Here the Colour-Sergeant entered with some papers;
Bobby reflected for a while as Revere looked through the
Company forms.

'Does Dormer do anything, Sergeant?' Bobby asked with
the air of one continuing an interrupted conversation.

'No, sir. Does 'is dooty like a hortomato,' said the
Sergeant, who delighted in long words. 'A dirty soldier and
'e's under full stoppages for new kit.* It's covered with
scales, sir.'

'Scales? What scales?'

'Fish-scales, sir. 'E's always pokin' in the mud by the river
an' a-cleanin' them *muchly*-fish* with 'is thumbs.' Revere was
still absorbed in the Company papers, and the Sergeant, who
was sternly fond of Bobby, continued—''E generally goes
down there when 'e's got 'is skinful, beggin' your pardon, sir,
an' they *do* say that the more lush—in-*he*-briated 'e is, the
more fish 'e catches. They call 'im the Looney Fishmonger in
the Comp'ny, sir.'

Revere signed the last paper, and the Sergeant retreated.

'It's a filthy amusement,' sighed Bobby to himself. Then
aloud to Revere: 'Are you really worried about Dormer?'

'A little. You see, he's never mad enough to send to
hospital, or drunk enough to run in, but at any minute he
may flare up, brooding and sulking as he does. He resents any
interest being shown in him, and the only time I took him out
shooting he all but shot *me* by accident.'

'I fish,' said Bobby with a wry face. 'I hire a country-boat
and go down the river from Thursday to Sunday, and the
amiable Dormer goes with me—if you can spare us both.'

'You blazing young fool!' said Revere, but his heart was
full of much more pleasant words.

Bobby, the captain of a *dhoni* [native boat], with Private

Dormer for mate, dropped down the river on Thursday morning—the Private at the bow, the Subaltern at the helm. The Private glared uneasily at the Subaltern, who respected the reserve of the Private.

After six hours, Dormer paced to the stern, saluted, and said: 'Beg y' pardon, sir, but *was* you ever on the Durh'm Canal?'

'No,' said Bobby Wick. 'Come and have some tiffin.'

They ate in silence. As the evening fell, Private Dormer broke forth, speaking to himself:—

'Hi was on the Durh'm Canal, jes' such a night, come next week twelve-month, a-trailin' *of* my toes in the water.' He smoked and said no more till bedtime.

The witchery of the dawn turned the grey river-reaches to purple, gold, and opal; and it was as though the lumbering *dhoni* crept across the splendours of a new heaven.

Private Dormer popped his head out of his blanket and gazed at the glory below and around.

'Well,—damn—my eyes!' said Private Dormer in an awed whisper. 'This 'ere is like a bloomin' gallanty-show!'* For the rest of the day he was dumb, but achieved an ensanguined filthiness through the cleaning of big fish.

The boat returned on Saturday evening. Dormer had been struggling with speech since noon. As the lines and luggage were being disembarked, he found tongue.

'Beg y' pardon, sir,' he said, 'but would you—would you min' shakin' 'ands with me, sir?'

'Of course not,' said Bobby, and he shook accordingly. Dormer returned to barracks and Bobby to Mess.

'He wanted a little quiet and some fishing, I think,' said Bobby. 'My aunt, but he's a filthy sort of animal! Have you ever seen him clean "them *muchly*-fish with 'is thumbs"?'

'Anyhow,' said Revere three weeks later, 'he's doing his best to keep his things clean.'

When the spring died, Bobby joined in the general scramble for Hill leave, and to his surprise and delight secured three months.

'As good a boy as I want,' said Revere, the admiring skipper.

'The best of the batch,' said the Adjutant to the Colonel. 'Keep back that young skrimshanker* Porkiss, sir, and let Revere make him sit up.'

So Bobby departed joyously to Simla Pahar* with a tin box of gorgeous raiment.

'Son of Wick—old Wick of Chota-Buldana? Ask him to dinner, dear,' said the aged men.

'What a nice boy!' said the matrons and the maids.

'First-class place, Simla. Oh, ri—ipping!' said Bobby Wick, and ordered new white cord breeches on the strength of it.

'We're in a bad way,' wrote Revere to Bobby at the end of two months. 'Since you left, the Regiment has taken to fever and is fairly rotten with it—two hundred in hospital, about a hundred in cells—drinking to keep off fever—and the Companies on parade fifteen file strong at the outside. There's rather more sickness in the out-villages than I care for, but then I'm so blistered with prickly-heat that I'm ready to hang myself. What's the yarn about your mashing a Miss Haverley up there? Not serious, I hope? You're over-young to hang millstones round your neck, and the Colonel will turf you out of it in double-quick time if you try.'

It was not the Colonel that brought Bobby out of Simla, but a much-more-to-be-respected Commandant. The sickness in the out-villages spread, the Bazar was put out of bounds, and then came the news that the Tail-Twisters must go into camp. The message flashed to the Hill stations.— 'Cholera—Leave stopped—Officers recalled.' Alas for the white gloves in the neatly-soldered boxes, the rides and the dances and picnics that were to be, the loves half spoken, and the debts unpaid! Without demur and without question, fast as tonga* could fly or pony gallop, back to their Regiments and their Batteries, as though they were hastening to their weddings, fled the subalterns.

Bobby received his orders on returning from a dance at Viceregal Lodge where he had—— But only the Haverley girl knows what Bobby had said, or how many waltzes he had claimed for the next ball. Six in the morning saw Bobby at the Tonga Office in the drenching rain, the whirl of the last waltz still in his ears, and an intoxication due neither to wine nor waltzing in his brain.

'Good man!' shouted Deighton of the Horse Battery through the mist. 'Whar you raise dat tonga? I'm coming with you. Ow! but I've a head and a half. *I* didn't sit out all night. They say the Battery's awful bad,' and he hummed dolorously:—

> Leave the what at the what's-its-name,
>   Leave the flock without shelter,
> Leave the corpse uninterred,
>   Leave the bride at the altar!*

'My faith! It'll be more bally corpse than bride, though, this journey. Jump in, Bobby. Get on, *Coachwan*!'

On the Umballa platform waited a detachment of officers discussing the latest news from the stricken cantonment, and it was here that Bobby learned the real condition of the Tail-Twisters.

'They went into camp,' said an elderly Major recalled from the whist-tables at Mussoorie to a sickly Native Regiment, 'they went into camp with two hundred and ten sick in carts. Two hundred and ten fever cases only, and the balance looking like so many ghosts with sore eyes. A Madras Regiment could have walked through 'em.'

'But they were as fit as be-damned when I left them!' said Bobby.

'Then you'd better make them as fit as be-damned when you rejoin,' said the Major brutally.

Bobby pressed his forehead against the rain-splashed window-pane as the train lumbered across the sodden Doab, and prayed for the health of the Tyneside Tail-Twisters. Naini Tal had sent down her contingent with all speed; the lathering ponies of the Dalhousie Road staggered into Pathânkot, taxed to the full stretch of their strength; while from cloudy Darjeeling the Calcutta Mail whirled up the last straggler of the little army that was to fight a fight in which was neither medal nor honour for the winning, against an enemy none other than 'the sickness that destroyeth in the noonday.'*

And as each man reported himself, he said: 'This is a bad business,' and went about his own forthwith, for every Regiment and Battery in the cantonment was under canvas, the sickness bearing them company.

Bobby fought his way through the rain to the Tail-Twisters' temporary Mess, and Revere could have fallen on the boy's neck for the joy of seeing that ugly, wholesome phiz once more.

'Keep 'em amused and interested,' said Revere. 'They went on the drink, poor fools, after the first two cases, and there was no improvement. Oh, it's good to have you back, Bobby! Porkiss is a—never mind.'

Deighton came over from the Artillery camp to attend a dreary Mess dinner, and contributed to the general gloom by nearly weeping over the condition of his beloved Battery. Porkiss so far forgot himself as to insinuate that the presence of the officers could do no earthly good, and that the best thing would be to send the entire Regiment into hospital and 'let the doctors look after them.' Porkiss was demoralized with fear, nor was his peace of mind restored when Revere said coldly: 'Oh! The sooner *you* go out the better, if that's your way of thinking. Any public school could send us fifty *good* men in your place, but it takes time, time, Porkiss, and money, and a certain amount of trouble, to make a Regiment. S'pose *you*'re the person we go into camp for, eh?'

Whereupon Porkiss was overtaken with a great and chilly fear which a drenching in the rain did not allay, and, two days later, quitted this world for another where, men do fondly hope, allowances are made for the weaknesses of the flesh. The Regimental Sergeant-Major looked wearily across the Sergeants' Mess tent when the news was announced.

'There goes the worst of them,' he said. 'It'll take the best, and then, please God, it'll stop.' The Sergeants were silent till one said: 'It couldn't be *him*!' and all knew of whom Travis was thinking.

Bobby Wick stormed through the tents of his Company, rallying, rebuking, mildly, as is consistent with the Regulations, chaffing the faint-hearted; haling the sound into the watery sunlight when there was a break in the weather, and bidding them be of good cheer for their trouble was nearly at an end; scuttling on his dun pony round the outskirts of the camp, and heading back men who, with the innate perversity of British soldiers, were always wandering into infected villages, or drinking deeply from rain-flooded marshes; comforting the panic-stricken with rude speech, and more than once tending the dying who had no friends—the men without 'townies'*; organizing, with banjos and burnt cork, Singsongs which should allow the talent of the Regiment full play; and generally, as he explained, 'playing the giddy gardengoat all round.'

'You're worth half-a-dozen of us, Bobby,' said Revere in a moment of enthusiasm. 'How the devil do you keep it up?'

Bobby made no answer, but had Revere looked into the breast-pocket of his coat he might have seen there a sheaf of badly-written letters which perhaps accounted for the power that possessed the boy. A letter came to Bobby every other day. The spelling was not above reproach, but the sentiments must have been most satisfactory, for on receipt Bobby's eyes softened marvellously, and he was wont to fall into a tender abstraction for a while ere, shaking his cropped head, he charged into his work.

By what power he drew after him the hearts of the roughest, and the Tail-Twisters counted in their ranks some rough diamonds indeed, was a mystery to both skipper and C.O., who learned from the Regimental Chaplain that Bobby was considerably more in request in the hospital tents than the Reverend John Emery.

'The men seem fond of you. Are you in the hospitals much?' said the Colonel, who did his daily round and ordered the men to get well with a hardness that did not cover his bitter grief.

'A little, sir,' said Bobby.

'Shouldn't go there too often if I were you. They say it's not contagious, but there's no use in running unnecessary risks. We can't afford to have you down, y'know.'

Six days later, it was with the utmost difficulty that the post-runner plashed his way out to the camp with the mailbags, for the rain was falling in torrents. Bobby received a letter, bore it off to his tent, and, the programme for the next week's Sing-song being satisfactorily disposed of, sat down to answer it. For an hour the unhandy pen toiled over the paper, and where sentiment rose to more than normal tide-level, Bobby Wick stuck out his tongue and breathed heavily. He was not used to letter-writing.

'Beg y' pardon, sir,' said a voice at the tent door; 'but Dormer's 'orrid bad, sir, an' they've taken him orf, sir.'

'Damn Private Dormer and you too!' said Bobby Wick, running the blotter over the half-finished letter. 'Tell him I'll come in the morning.'

''E's awful bad, sir,' said the voice hesitatingly. There was an undecided squelching of heavy boots.

'Well?' said Bobby impatiently.

'Excusin' 'imself before'and for takin' the liberty, 'e says it would be a comfort for to assist 'im, sir, if——'

'*Tattoo láo!** Get my pony! Here, come in out of the rain till I'm ready. What blasted nuisances you are! That's brandy. Drink some; you want it. Hang on to my stirrup and tell me if I go too fast.'

Strengthened by a four-finger 'nip' which he swallowed without a wink, the Hospital Orderly kept up with the slipping, mud-stained, and very disgusted pony as it shambled to the hospital tent.

Private Dormer was certainly ''orrid bad'. He had all but reached the stage of collapse and was not pleasant to look upon.

'What's this, Dormer?' said Bobby, bending over the man. 'You're not going out this time. You've got to come fishing with me once or twice more yet.'

The blue lips parted and in the ghost of a whisper said: 'Beg y' pardon, sir, disturbin' of you now, but would you min' 'oldin' my 'and, sir?'

Bobby sat on the side of the bed, and the icy-cold hand closed on his own like a vice, forcing a lady's ring which was on the little finger deep into the flesh. Bobby set his lips and waited, the water dripping from the hem of his trousers. An hour passed and the grasp of the hand did not relax, nor did the expression of the drawn face change. Bobby with infinite craft lit himself a cheroot with the left hand—his right arm was numbed to the elbow—and resigned himself to a night of pain.

Dawn showed a very white-faced subaltern sitting on the side of a sick man's cot, and a Doctor in the doorway using language unfit for publication.

'Have you been here all night, you young ass?' said the Doctor.

'There or thereabouts,' said Bobby ruefully. 'He's frozen on to me.'

Dormer's mouth shut with a click. He turned his head and sighed. The clinging hand opened, and Bobby's arm fell useless at his side.

'He'll do,' said the Doctor quietly. 'It must have been a toss-up all through the night. Think you're to be congratulated on this case.'

'Oh, bosh!' said Bobby. 'I thought the man had gone out long ago—only—only I didn't care to take my hand away. Rub my arm down, there's a good chap. What a grip the brute has! I'm chilled to the marrow.' He passed out of the tent shivering.

Private Dormer was allowed to celebrate his repulse of Death by strong waters. Four days later he sat on the side of his cot and said to the patients mildly: 'I'd 'a' liken to 'a' spoken to 'im—so I should.'

But at that time Bobby was reading yet another letter—he had the most persistent correspondent of any man in camp—and was even then about to write that the sickness had abated, and in another week at the outside would be gone. He did not intend to say that the chill of a sick man's hand seemed to have struck into the heart whose capacities for affection he dwelt on at such length. He did intend to enclose the illustrated programme of the forthcoming Sing-song whereof he was not a little proud. He also intended to write on many other matters which do not concern us, and doubtless would have done so but for the slight feverish headache which made him dull and unresponsive at Mess.

'You are overdoing it, Bobby,' said his skipper. 'Might give the rest of us credit of doing a little work. You go on as if you were the whole show rolled into one. Take it easy.'

'I will,' said Bobby. 'I'm feeling done up, somehow.'
Revere looked at him anxiously and said nothing.

There was a flickering of lanterns about the camp that
night, and a rumour that brought men out of their cots to the
tent doors, a paddling of the naked feet of doolie-bearers*
and the rush of a galloping horse.

'Wot's up?' asked twenty tents; and through twenty tents
ran the answer—'Wick, 'e's down.'

They brought the news to Revere and he groaned. 'Any
one but Bobby and I shouldn't have cared! The Sergeant-
Major was right.'

'Not going out this journey,' gasped Bobby, as he was
lifted from the doolie. 'Not going out this journey.' Then,
with an air of supreme conviction: 'I *can't*, you see.'

'Not if I can do anything!' said the Surgeon-Major, who
had hastened over from the Mess where he had been dining.

He and the Regimental Surgeon fought together with
Death for the life of Bobby Wick. Their work was interrupted by a hairy apparition in a blue-grey dressing-gown who
stared in horror at the bed and cried: 'Oh, my Gawd! It can't
be *'im!*' until an indignant Hospital Orderly whisked him
away.

If care of man and desire to live could have done aught,
Bobby would have been saved. As it was, he made a fight of
three days, and the Surgeon-Major's brow uncreased. 'We'll
save him yet,' he said; and the Surgeon, who, though he
ranked with the Captain, had a very youthful heart, went out
upon the word and pranced joyously in the mud.

'Not going out this journey,' whispered Bobby Wick
gallantly, at the end of the third day.

'Bravo!' said the Surgeon-Major. 'That's the way to look at
it, Bobby.'

As evening fell a grey shade gathered round Bobby's
mouth, and he turned his face to the tent wall wearily. The
Surgeon-Major frowned.

'I'm awfully tired,' said Bobby, very faintly. 'What's the
use of bothering me with medicine? I—don't—want—it. Let
me alone.'

The desire for life had departed, and Bobby was content to
drift away on the easy tide of Death.

'It's no good,' said the Surgeon-Major. 'He doesn't want to live. He's meeting it, poor child.' And he blew his nose.

Half a mile away the Regimental band was playing the overture to the Sing-song, for the men had been told that Bobby was out of danger. The clash of the brass and the wail of the horns reached Bobby's ears.

> Is there a single joy or pain,
>> That I should never kno—ow?
> You do not love me, 'tis in vain,
>> Bid me good-bye and go!*

An expression of hopeless irritation crossed the boy's face, and he tried to shake his head.

The Surgeon-Major bent down: 'What is it, Bobby?'— 'Not that waltz,' muttered Bobby. 'That's our own—our very ownest own. . . . Mummy dear.'

With this he sank into the stupor that gave place to death early next morning.

Revere, his eyes red at the rims and his nose very white, went into Bobby's tent to write a letter to Papa Wick which should bow the white head of the ex-Commissioner of Chota-Buldana in the keenest sorrow of his life. Bobby's little store of papers lay in confusion on the table, and among them a half-finished letter. The last sentence ran: 'So you see, darling, there is really no fear, because as long as I know you care for me and I care for you, nothing can touch me.'

Revere stayed in the tent for an hour. When he came out his eyes were redder than ever.

Private Conklin sat on a turned-down bucket, and listened to a not unfamiliar tune.* Private Conklin was a convalescent and should have been tenderly treated.

'Ho!' said Private Conklin. 'There's another bloomin' orf'cer da—ed.'

The bucket shot from under him, and his eyes filled with a smithyful of sparks. A tall man in a blue-grey bedgown was regarding him with deep disfavour.

'You ought to take shame for yourself, Conky! Orf'cer?— Bloomin' orf'cer? I'll learn you to misname the likes of 'im. Hangel! *Bloomin'* Hangel! That's wot 'e is!'

And the Hospital Orderly was so satisfied with the justice of the punishment that he did not even order Private Dormer back to his cot.

Baa Baa, Black Sheep

Baa Baa, Black Sheep,
Have you any wool?
Yes, Sir, yes, Sir, three bags full.
One for the Master, one for the Dame—
None for the Little Boy that cries down the lane.
Nursery Rhyme

THE FIRST BAG

When I was in my father's house, I was in a
better place.*

THEY were putting Punch to bed—*the *ayah* and the *hamal* and Meeta, the big *Surti* boy, with the red-and-gold turban. Judy, already tucked inside her mosquito-curtains, was nearly asleep. Punch had been allowed to stay up for dinner. Many privileges had been accorded to Punch within the last ten days, and a greater kindness from the people of his world had encompassed his ways and works, which were mostly obstreperous. He sat on the edge of his bed and swung his bare legs defiantly.

'Punch-*baba** going to bye-lo?' said the *ayah* suggestively.

'No,' said Punch. 'Punch-*baba* wants the story about the Ranee that was turned into a tiger. Meeta must tell it, and the *hamal* shall hide behind the door and make tiger-noises at the proper time.'

'But Judy-*baba* will wake up,' said the *ayah*.

'Judy-*baba* is waked,' piped a small voice from the mosquito-curtains. 'There was a Ranee that lived at Delhi. Go on, Meeta,' and she fell fast asleep again while Meeta began the story.

Never had Punch secured the telling of that tale with so little opposition. He reflected for a long time. The *hamal* made the tiger-noises in twenty different keys.

''Top!' said Punch authoritatively. 'Why doesn't Papa come in and say he is going to give me *put-put*?'*

'Punch-*baba* is going away,' said the *ayah*. 'In another week there will be no Punch-*baba* to pull my hair any more.' She sighed softly, for the boy of the household was very dear to her heart.

'Up the Ghauts* in a train?' said Punch, standing on his bed. 'All the way to Nassick where the Ranee-Tiger lives?'

'Not to Nassick this year, little Sahib,' said Meeta, lifting him on his shoulder. 'Down to the sea where the coconuts are thrown, and across the sea in a big ship. Will you take Meeta with you to *Belait*?'*

'You shall all come,' said Punch, from the height of Meeta's strong arms. 'Meeta and the *ayah* and the *hamal* and Bhini-in-the-Garden, and the salaam-Captain-Sahib-snake-man.'

There was no mockery in Meeta's voice when he replied: 'Great is the Sahib's favour,' and laid the little man down in the bed, while the *ayah*, sitting in the moonlight at the doorway, lulled him to sleep with an interminable canticle such as they sing in the Roman Catholic Church at Parel. Punch curled himself into a ball and slept.

Next morning Judy shouted that there was a rat in the nursery, and thus he forgot to tell her the wonderful news. It did not much matter, for Judy was only three and she would not have understood. But Punch was five; and he knew that going to England would be much nicer than a trip to Nassick.

*   *   *   *   *

Papa and Mamma sold the brougham* and the piano, and stripped the house, and curtailed the allowance of crockery for the daily meals, and took long counsel together over a bundle of letters bearing the Rocklington postmark.

'The worst of it is that one can't be certain of anything,' said Papa, pulling his moustache. 'The letters in themselves are excellent, and the terms are moderate enough.'

'The worst of it is that the children will grow up away from me,' thought Mamma; but she did not say it aloud.

'We are only one case among hundreds,' said Papa bitterly. 'You shall go Home again in five years, dear.'

'Punch will be ten then—and Judy eight. Oh, how long and long and long the time will be! And we have to leave them among strangers.'

'Punch is a cheery little chap. He's sure to make friends wherever he goes.'

'And who could help loving my Ju?'

They were standing over the cots in the nursery late at night, and I think that Mamma was crying softly. After Papa had gone away, she knelt down by the side of Judy's cot. The *ayah* saw her and put up a prayer that the Memsahib might never find the love of her children taken away from her and given to a stranger.

Mamma's own prayer was a slightly illogical one. Summarized it ran: 'Let strangers love my children and be as good to them as I should be, but let *me* preserve their love and their confidence for ever and ever. Amen.' Punch scratched himself in his sleep, and Judy moaned a little.

Next day they all went down to the sea, and there was a scene at the Apollo Bunder* when Punch discovered that Meeta could not come too, and Judy learned that the *ayah* must be left behind. But Punch found a thousand fascinating things in the rope, block, and steam-pipe line on the big P. & O.* steamer long before Meeta and the *ayah* had dried their tears.

'Come back, Punch-*baba*,' said the *ayah*.

'Come back,' said Meeta, 'and be a *Burra Sahib* [a big man].'

'Yes,' said Punch, lifted up in his father's arms to wave good-bye. 'Yes, I will come back, and I will be a *Burra Sahib Bahadur* [a very big man indeed]!'

At the end of the first day Punch demanded to be set down in England, which he was certain must be close at hand. Next day there was a merry breeze, and Punch was very sick. 'When I come back to Bombay,' said Punch on his recovery, 'I will come by the road—in a broom-*gharri*.* This is a very naughty ship.'

The Swedish boatswain consoled him, and he modified his opinions as the voyage went on. There was so much to see and to handle and ask questions about that Punch nearly forgot the *ayah* and Meeta and the *hamal*, and with difficulty remembered a few words of the Hindustani once his second speech.

But Judy was much worse. The day before the steamer reached Southampton, Mamma asked her if she would not like to see the *ayah* again. Judy's blue eyes turned to the stretch of sea that had swallowed all her tiny past, and she said: '*Ayah*! What *ayah*?'

Mamma cried over her and Punch marvelled. It was then that he heard for the first time Mamma's passionate appeal to him never to let Judy forget Mamma. Seeing that Judy was young, ridiculously young, and that Mamma, every evening for four weeks past, had come into the cabin to sing her and Punch to sleep with a mysterious rune that he called 'Sonny, my soul,'* Punch could not understand what Mamma meant. But he strove to do his duty; for, the moment Mamma left the cabin, he said to Judy: 'Ju, you bemember Mamma?'

'"Torse I do,' said Judy.

'Then *always* bemember Mamma, 'r else I won't give you the paper ducks that the red-haired Captain Sahib cut out for me.'

So Judy promised always to 'bemember Mamma'.

Many and many a time was Mamma's command laid upon Punch, and Papa would say the same thing with an insistence that awed the child.

'You must make haste and learn to write, Punch,' said Papa, 'and then you'll be able to write letters to us in Bombay.'

'I'll come into your room,' said Punch, and Papa choked.

Papa and Mamma were always choking in those days. If Punch took Judy to task for not 'bemembering,' they choked. If Punch sprawled on the sofa in the Southampton lodging-house and sketched his future in purple and gold, they choked; and so they did if Judy put up her mouth for a kiss.

Through many days all four were vagabonds on the face of the earth—Punch with no one to give orders to, Judy too young for anything, and Papa and Mamma grave, distracted, and choking.

'Where,' demanded Punch, wearied of a loathsome contrivance on four wheels with a mound of luggage atop—

'*where* is our broom-*gharri*? This thing talks so much that *I* can't talk. Where is our *own* broom-*gharri*? When I was at Bandstand before we comed away, I asked Inverarity Sahib why he was sitting in it, and he said it was his own. And I said, "I will *give* it to you"—I like Inverarity Sahib—and I said, "Can you put your legs through the pully-wag loops by the windows?" And Inverarity Sahib said No, and laughed. I can put my legs through the pully-wag loops. I can put my legs through *these* pully-wag loops. Look! Oh, Mamma's crying again! I didn't know I wasn't not to do *so*.'

Punch drew his legs out of the loops of the four-wheeler: the door opened and he slid to the earth, in a cascade of parcels, at the door of an austere little villa whose gates bore the legend 'Downe Lodge'. Punch gathered himself together and eyed the house with disfavour. It stood on a sandy road, and a cold wind tickled his knickerbockered legs.

'Let us go away,' said Punch. 'This is not a pretty place.'

But Mamma and Papa and Judy had left the cab, and all the luggage was being taken into the house. At the doorstep stood a woman in black, and she smiled largely, with dry chapped lips. Behind her was a man, big, bony, grey, and lame as to one leg—behind him a boy of twelve, black-haired and oily in appearance. Punch surveyed the trio, and advanced without fear, as he had been accustomed to do in Bombay when callers came and he happened to be playing in the veranda.

'How do you do?' said he. 'I am Punch.' But they were all looking at the luggage—all except the grey man, who shook hands with Punch, and said he was 'a smart little fellow'. There was much running about and banging of boxes, and Punch curled himself up on the sofa in the dining-room and considered things.

'I don't like these people,' said Punch. 'But never mind. We'll go away soon. We have always went away soon from everywhere. I wish we was gone back to Bombay *soon*.'

The wish bore no fruit. For six days Mamma wept at intervals, and showed the woman in black all Punch's clothes—a liberty which Punch resented. 'But p'raps she's a new white *ayah*,' he thought. 'I'm to call her Antirosa, but she doesn't call *me* Sahib. She says just Punch,' he confided to Judy. 'What is Antirosa?'

Judy didn't know. Neither she nor Punch had heard anything of an animal called an aunt. Their world had been Papa and Mamma, who knew everything, permitted everything, and loved everybody—even Punch when he used to go into the garden at Bombay and fill his nails with mould after the weekly nail-cutting, because, as he explained between two strokes of the slipper to his sorely-tried father, his fingers 'felt so new at the ends.'

In an undefined way Punch judged it advisable to keep both parents between himself and the woman in black and the boy with black hair. He did not approve of them. He liked the grey man, who had expressed a wish to be called 'Uncleharri'. They nodded at each other when they met, and the grey man showed him a little ship with rigging that took up and down.

'She is a model of the *Brisk*—the little *Brisk* that was sore exposed that day at Navarino.'* The grey man hummed the last words and fell into a reverie. 'I'll tell you about Navarino, Punch, when we go for walks together; and you mustn't touch the ship, because she's the *Brisk*.'

Long before that walk, the first of many, was taken, they roused Punch and Judy in the chill dawn of a February morning to say Good-bye; and of all people in the wide earth to Papa and Mamma—both crying this time. Punch was very sleepy and Judy was cross.

'Don't forget us,' pleaded Mamma. 'Oh, my little son, don't forget us, and see that Judy remembers too.'

'I've told Judy to bemember,' said Punch, wriggling, for his father's beard tickled his neck. 'I've told Judy—ten—forty—'leven thousand times. But Ju's so young—quite a baby—isn't she?'

'Yes,' said Papa, 'quite a baby, and you must be good to Judy, and make haste to learn to write and—and—and——'

Punch was back in his bed again. Judy was fast asleep, and there was the rattle of a cab below. Papa and Mamma had gone away. Not to Nassick; that was across the sea. To some place much nearer, of course, and equally of course they would return. They came back after dinner-parties, and Papa had come back after he had been to a place called 'The Snows', and Mamma with him, to Punch and Judy at Mrs Inverarity's house in Marine Lines. Assuredly they would come back again. So Punch fell asleep till the true morning, when the black-haired boy met him with the information that Papa and Mamma had gone to Bombay, and that he and Judy were to stay at Downe Lodge 'for ever'. Antirosa, tearfully appealed to for a contradiction, said that Harry had spoken the truth, and that it behoved Punch to fold up his clothes neatly on going to bed. Punch went out and wept bitterly with Judy, into whose fair head he had driven some ideas of the meaning of separation.

When a matured man discovers that he has been deserted by Providence, deprived of his God, and cast without help, comfort, or sympathy, upon a world which is new and strange to him, his despair, which may find expression in evil living, the writing of his experiences, or the more satisfactory diversion of suicide, is generally supposed to be impressive. A child, under exactly similar circumstances as far as its knowledge goes, cannot very well curse God and die. It howls till its nose is red, its eyes are sore, and its head aches. Punch and Judy, through no fault of their own, had lost all their world. They sat in the hall and cried; the black-haired boy looking on from afar.

The model of the ship availed nothing, though the grey man assured Punch that he might pull the rigging up and down as much as he pleased; and Judy was promised free entry into the kitchen. They wanted Papa and Mamma, gone to Bombay beyond the seas, and their grief while it lasted was without remedy.

When the tears ceased the house was very still. Antirosa had decided that it was better to let the children 'have their cry out', and the boy had gone to school. Punch raised his head from the floor and sniffed mournfully. Judy was nearly asleep. Three short years had not taught her how to bear sorrow with full knowledge. There was a distant, dull boom in the air—a repeated heavy thud. Punch knew that sound in Bombay in the monsoon. It was the sea—the sea that must be traversed before any one could get to Bombay.

'Quick, Ju!' he cried. 'We're close to the sea. I can hear it! Listen! That's where they've went. P'raps we can catch them if we was in time. They didn't mean to go without us. They've only forgot.'

'Iss,' said Judy. 'They've only forgotted. Less go to the sea.'

The hall-door was open and so was the garden-gate.

'It's very, very big, this place,' he said, looking cautiously down the road, 'and we will get lost. But *I* will find a man and order him to take me back to my house—like I did in Bombay.'

He took Judy by the hand, and the two ran hatless in the direction of the sound of the sea. Downe Lodge was almost the last of a range of newly-built houses running out, through a field of brick-mounds, to a heath where gipsies occasionally camped and where the Garrison Artillery of Rocklington practised. There were few people to be seen, and the children might have been taken for those of the soldiery who ranged far. Half an hour the wearied little legs tramped across heath, potato-patch, and sand-dune.

'I'se so tired,' said Judy, 'and Mamma will be angry.'

'Mamma's *never* angry. I suppose she is waiting at the sea now while Papa gets tickets. We'll find them and go along with them. Ju, you mustn't sit down. Only a little more and we'll come to the sea. Ju, if you sit down I'll *thmack* you!' said Punch.

They climbed another dune, and came upon the great grey sea at low tide. Hundreds of crabs were scuttling about the beach, but there was no trace of Papa and Mamma, not even of a ship upon the waters—nothing but sand and mud for miles and miles.

And 'Uncleharri' found them by chance—very muddy and very forlorn—Punch dissolved in tears, but trying to divert Judy with an 'ickle trab', and Judy wailing to the pitiless horizon for 'Mamma, Mamma!'—and again 'Mamma!'

THE SECOND BAG

Ah, well-a-day, for we are souls bereaved!
Of all the creatures under Heaven's wide cope
We are most hopeless, who had once most hope,
And most beliefless, who had most believed.
                                    *A. H. Clough**

ALL this time not a word about Black Sheep. He came later, and Harry, the black-haired boy, was mainly responsible for his coming.

Judy—who could help loving little Judy?—passed, by special permit, into the kitchen and thence straight to Aunty Rosa's heart. Harry was Aunty Rosa's one child, and Punch was the extra boy about the house. There was no special place for him or his little affairs, and he was forbidden to sprawl on sofas and explain his ideas about the manufacture of this world and his hopes for his future. Sprawling was lazy and wore out sofas, and little boys were not expected to talk. They were talked to, and the talking-to was intended for the benefit of their morals. As the unquestioned despot of the house at Bombay, Punch could not quite understand how he came to be of no account in this his new life.

Harry might reach across the table and take what he wanted; Judy might point and get what she wanted. Punch was forbidden to do either. The grey man was his great hope and stand-by for many months after Mamma and Papa left, and he had forgotten to tell Judy to 'bemember Mamma'.

This lapse was excusable, because in the interval he had been introduced by Aunty Rosa to two very impressive things—an abstraction called God, the intimate friend and ally of Aunty Rosa, generally believed to live behind the kitchen-range because it was hot there—and a dirty brown book filled with unintelligible dots and marks. Punch was always anxious to oblige everybody. He therefore welded the story of the Creation on to what he could recollect of his Indian fairy tales, and scandalized Aunty Rosa by repeating the result to Judy. It was a sin, a grievous sin, and Punch was talked to for a quarter of an hour. He could not understand where the iniquity came in, but was careful not to repeat the offence, because Aunty Rosa told him that God had heard every word he had said and was very angry. If this were true why didn't God come and say so, thought Punch, and dismissed the matter from his mind. Afterwards he learned to know the Lord as the only thing in the world more awful than Aunty Rosa—as a Creature that stood in the background and counted the strokes of the cane.

But the reading was, just then, a much more serious matter than any creed. Aunty Rosa sat him upon a table and told him that A B meant ab.

'Why?' said Punch. 'A is a and B is bee. *Why* does A B mean ab?'

'Because I tell you it does,' said Aunty Rosa, 'and you've got to say it.'

Punch said it accordingly, and for a month, hugely against his will, stumbled through the brown book, not in the least comprehending what it meant. But Uncle Harry, who walked much and generally alone, was wont to come into the nursery and suggest to Aunty Rosa that Punch should walk with him. He seldom spoke, but he showed Punch all Rocklington, from the mud-banks and the sand of the back-bay to the great harbours where ships lay at anchor, and the dockyards where the hammers were never still, and the marine-store shops, and the shiny brass counters in the Offices where Uncle Harry went once every three months with a slip of blue paper and received sovereigns in exchange; for he held a wound-pension. Punch heard, too, from his lips the story of the battle of Navarino, where the sailors of the Fleet, for three days afterwards, were deaf as posts and could only sign to each other. 'That was because of the noise of the guns,' said Uncle Harry, 'and I have got the wadding of a bullet somewhere inside me now.'

Punch regarded him with curiosity. He had not the least idea what wadding was, and his notion of a bullet was a dockyard cannon-ball bigger than his own head. How could Uncle Harry keep a cannon-ball inside him? He was afraid to ask, for fear Uncle Harry might be angry.

Punch had never known what anger—real anger—meant until one terrible day when Harry had taken his paint-box to paint a boat with, and Punch had protested. Then Uncle

Harry had appeared on the scene and, muttering something about 'strangers' children', had with a stick smitten the black-haired boy across the shoulders till he wept and yelled, and Aunty Rosa came in and abused Uncle Harry for cruelty to his own flesh and blood, and Punch shuddered to the tips of his shoes. 'It wasn't my fault,' he explained to the boy, but both Harry and Aunty Rosa said that it was, and that Punch had told tales, and for a week there were no more walks with Uncle Harry.

But that week brought a great joy to Punch.

He had repeated till he was thrice weary the statement that 'The Cat lay on the Mat and the Rat came in.'

'Now I can truly read,' said Punch, 'and now I will never read anything in the world.'

He put the brown book in the cupboard where his school-books lived and accidentally tumbled out a venerable volume, without covers, labelled *Sharpe's Magazine*.* There was the most portentous picture of a Griffin on the first page, with verses below. The Griffin carried off one sheep a day from a German village, till a man came with a 'falchion' and split the Griffin open. Goodness only knew what a falchion was, but there was the Griffin and his history was an improvement upon the eternal Cat.

'This,' said Punch, 'means things, and now I will know all about everything in all the world.' He read till the light failed, not understanding a tithe of the meaning, but tantalized by glimpses of new worlds hereafter to be revealed.

'What is a "falchion"? What is a "e-wee lamb"? What is a "base *us*surper"? What is a "verdant mead"?' he demanded, with flushed cheeks, at bedtime, of the astonished Aunty Rosa.

'Say your prayers and go to sleep,' she replied, and that was all the help Punch then or afterwards found at her hands in the new and delightful exercise of reading.

'Aunty Rosa only knows about God and things like that,' argued Punch. 'Uncle Harry will tell me.'

The next walk proved that Uncle Harry could not help either; but he allowed Punch to talk, and even sat down on a bench to hear about the Griffin. Other walks brought other

stories as Punch ranged farther afield, for the house held
large store of old books that no one ever opened—from *Frank
Fairlegh* in serial numbers, and the earlier poems of Tennyson, contributed anonymously to *Sharpe's Magazine*, to
'62 Exhibition Catalogues, gay with colours and delightfully
incomprehensible, and odd leaves of *Gulliver's Travels*.

As soon as Punch could string a few pot-hooks together he
wrote to Bombay, demanding by return of post 'all the books
in all the world'. Papa could not comply with this modest
indent, but sent *Grimm's Fairy Tales* and a *Hans Andersen*.
That was enough. If he were only left alone Punch could
pass, at any hour he chose, into a land of his own, beyond
reach of Aunty Rosa and her God, Harry and his teasements,
and Judy's claims to be played with.

'Don't disturve me, I'm reading. Go and play in the
kitchen,' grunted Punch. 'Aunty Rosa lets *you* go there.'
Judy was cutting her second teeth and was fretful. She
appealed to Aunty Rosa, who descended on Punch.

'I was reading,' he explained, 'reading a book. I *want* to
read.'

'You're only doing that to show off,' said Aunty Rosa. 'But
we'll see. Play with Judy now, and don't open a book for a
week.'

Judy did not pass a very enjoyable playtime with Punch,
who was consumed with indignation. There was a pettiness
at the bottom of the prohibition which puzzled him.

'It's what I like to do,' he said, 'and she's found out that
and stopped me. Don't cry, Ju—it wasn't your fault—*please*
don't cry, or she'll say I made you.'

Ju loyally mopped up her tears, and the two played in their
nursery, a room in the basement and half underground, to
which they were regularly sent after the mid-day dinner
while Aunty Rosa slept. She drank wine—that is to say,
something from a bottle in the cellaret—for her stomach's
sake, but if she did not fall asleep she would sometimes come
into the nursery to see that the children were really playing.
Now bricks, wooden hoops, ninepins, and chinaware cannot
amuse for ever, especially when all Fairyland is to be won by
the mere opening of a book, and, as often as not, Punch

would be discovered reading to Judy or telling her interminable tales. That was an offence in the eyes of the law, and Judy would be whisked off by Aunty Rosa, while Punch was left to play alone, 'and be sure that I hear you doing it.'

It was not a cheering employ, for he had to make a playful noise. At last, with infinite craft, he devised an arrangement whereby the table could be supported as to three legs on toy bricks, leaving the fourth clear to bring down on the floor. He could work the table with one hand and hold the book with the other. This he did till an evil day when Aunty Rosa pounced upon him unawares and told him that he was 'acting a lie'.

'If you're old enough to do that,' she said—her temper was always worst after dinner—'you're old enough to be beaten.'

'But—I'm—I'm not a animal!' said Punch aghast. He remembered Uncle Harry and the stick, and turned white. Aunty Rosa had hidden a light cane behind her, and Punch was beaten then and there over the shoulders. It was a revelation to him. The room-door was shut, and he was left to weep himself into repentance and work out his own gospel of life.

Aunty Rosa, he argued, had the power to beat him with many stripes. It was unjust and cruel, and Mamma and Papa would never have allowed it. Unless perhaps, as Aunty Rosa seemed to imply, they had sent secret orders. In which case he was abandoned indeed. It would be discreet in the future to propitiate Aunty Rosa, but then again, even in matters in which he was innocent, he had been accused of wishing to 'show off'. He had 'shown off' before visitors when he had attacked a strange gentleman—Harry's uncle, not his own— with requests for information about the Griffin and the falchion, and the precise nature of the Tilbury* in which Frank Fairlegh rode—all points of paramount interest which he was bursting to understand. Clearly it would not do to pretend to care for Aunty Rosa.

At this point Harry entered and stood afar off, eyeing Punch, a dishevelled heap in the corner of the room, with disgust.

'You're a liar—a young liar,' said Harry, with great

unction, 'and you're to have tea down here because you're not fit to speak to us. And you're not to speak to Judy again till Mother gives you leave. You'll corrupt her. You're only fit to associate with the servant. Mother says so.'

Having reduced Punch to a second agony of tears, Harry departed upstairs with the news that Punch was still rebellious.

Uncle Harry sat uneasily in the dining-room. 'Damn it all, Rosa,' said he at last, 'can't you leave the child alone? He's a good enough little chap when I meet him.'

'He puts on his best manners with you, Henry,' said Aunty Rosa, 'but I'm afraid, I'm very much afraid, that he is the Black Sheep of the family.'

Harry heard and stored up the name for future use. Judy cried till she was bidden to stop, her brother not being worth tears; and the evening concluded with the return of Punch to the upper regions and a private sitting at which all the blinding horrors of Hell were revealed to Punch with such store of imagery as Aunty Rosa's narrow mind possessed.

Most grievous of all was Judy's round-eyed reproach, and Punch went to bed in the depths of the Valley of Humiliation. He shared his room with Harry and knew the torture in store. For an hour and a half he had to answer that young gentleman's questions as to his motives for telling a lie, and a grievous lie, the precise quantity of punishment inflicted by Aunty Rosa, and had also to profess his deep gratitude for such religious instruction as Harry thought fit to impart.

From that day began the downfall of Punch, now Black Sheep.

'Untrustworthy in one thing, untrustworthy in all,' said Aunty Rosa, and Harry felt that Black Sheep was delivered into his hands. He would wake him up in the night to ask him why he was such a liar.

'I don't know,' Punch would reply.

'Then don't you think you ought to get up and pray to God for a new heart?'

'Y-yess.'

'Get out and pray, then!' And Punch would get out of bed with raging hate in his heart against all the world, seen and unseen. He was always tumbling into trouble. Harry had a knack of cross-examining him as to his day's doings, which seldom failed to lead him, sleepy and savage, into half-a-dozen contradictions—all duly reported to Aunty Rosa next morning.

'But it *wasn't* a lie,' Punch would begin, charging into a laboured explanation that landed him more hopelessly in the mire. 'I said that I didn't say my prayers *twice* over in the day, and *that* was on Tuesday. *Once* I did. I *know* I did, but Harry said I didn't,' and so forth, till the tension brought tears, and he was dismissed from the table in disgrace.

'You usen't to be as bad as this,' said Judy, awestricken at the catalogue of Black Sheep's crimes. 'Why are you so bad now?'

'I don't know,' Black Sheep would reply. 'I'm not, if I only wasn't bothered upside-down. I knew what I *did*, and I want to say so; but Harry always makes it out different somehow, and Aunty Rosa doesn't believe a word I say. Oh, Ju! Don't *you* say I'm bad too.'

'Aunty Rosa says you are,' said Judy. 'She told the Vicar so when he came yesterday.'

'Why does she tell all the people outside the house about me? It isn't fair,' said Black Sheep. 'When I was in Bombay, and was bad—*doing* bad, not made-up bad like this—Mamma told Papa, and Papa told me he knew, and that was all. *Outside* people didn't know too—even Meeta didn't know.'

'I don't remember,' said Judy wistfully. 'I was all little then. Mamma was just as fond of you as she was of me, wasn't she?'

''Course she was. So was Papa. So was everybody.'

'Aunty Rosa likes me more than she does you. She says that you are a Trial and a Black Sheep, and I'm not to speak to you more than I can help.'

'Always? Not outside of the times when you mustn't speak to me at all?'

Judy nodded her head mournfully. Black Sheep turned away in despair, but Judy's arms were round his neck.

'Never mind, Punch,' she whispered. 'I *will* speak to you just the same as ever and ever. You're my own own brother

though you are—though Aunty Rosa says you're bad, and
Harry says you are a little coward. He says that if I pulled
your hair hard, you'd cry.'

'Pull, then,' said Punch.

Judy pulled gingerly.

'Pull harder—as hard as you can! There! I don't mind how
much you pull it *now*. If you'll speak to me same as ever I'll let
you pull it as much as you like—pull it out if you like. But I
know if Harry came and stood by and made you do it I'd cry.'

So the two children sealed the compact with a kiss, and
Black Sheep's heart was cheered within him, and by extreme
caution and careful avoidance of Harry he acquired virtue,
and was allowed to read undisturbed for a week. Uncle Harry
took him for walks, and consoled him with rough tenderness,
never calling him Black Sheep. 'It's good for you, I suppose,
Punch,' he used to say. 'Let us sit down. I'm getting tired.'
His steps led him now not to the beach, but to the Cemetery
of Rocklington, amid the potato-fields. For hours the grey
man would sit on a tombstone, while Black Sheep would read
epitaphs, and then with a sigh would stump home again.

'I shall lie there soon,' said he to Black Sheep, one winter
evening, when his face showed white as a worn silver coin
under the light of the lych gate. 'You needn't tell Aunty
Rosa.'

A month later he turned sharp round, ere half a morning
walk was completed, and stumped back to the house. 'Put me
to bed, Rosa,' he muttered. 'I've walked my last. The
wadding has found me out.'

They put him to bed, and for a fortnight the shadow of his
sickness lay upon the house, and Black Sheep went to and fro
unobserved. Papa had sent him some new books, and he was
told to keep quiet. He retired into his own world, and was
perfectly happy. Even at night his felicity was unbroken. He
could lie in bed and string himself tales of travel and
adventure while Harry was downstairs.

'Uncle Harry's going to die,' said Judy, who now lived
almost entirely with Aunty Rosa.

'I'm very sorry,' said Black Sheep soberly. 'He told me
that a long time ago.'

Aunty Rosa heard the conversation. 'Will nothing check

your wicked tongue?' she said angrily. There were blue circles round her eyes.

Black Sheep retreated to the nursery and read *Cometh up as a Flower** with deep and uncomprehending interest. He had been forbidden to open it on account of its 'sinfulness', but the bonds of the Universe were crumbling, and Aunty Rosa was in great grief.

'I'm glad,' said Black Sheep. 'She's unhappy now. It wasn't a lie, though. *I* knew. He told me not to tell.'

That night Black Sheep woke with a start. Harry was not in the room, and there was a sound of sobbing on the next floor. Then the voice of Uncle Harry, singing the song of the Battle of Navarino, came through the darkness:—

> 'Our vanship was the *Asia*—
> The *Albion* and *Genoa*!'

'He's getting well,' thought Black Sheep, who knew the song through all its seventeen verses. But the blood froze at his little heart as he thought. The voice leapt an octave, and ran shrill as a boatswain's pipe:—

> 'And next came on the lovely *Rose*,
> The *Philomel*, her fire-ship, closed,
> And the little *Brisk* was sore exposed
> That day at Navarino.'*

'That day at Navarino, Uncle Harry!' shouted Black Sheep, half wild with excitement and fear of he knew not what.

A door opened, and Aunty Rosa screamed up the staircase: 'Hush! For God's sake hush, you little devil! Uncle Harry is *dead*!'

THE THIRD BAG

> Journeys end in lovers' meeting,
> Every wise man's son doth know.*

'I WONDER what will happen to me now,' thought Black Sheep, when semi-pagan rites peculiar to the burial of the Dead in middle-class houses had been accomplished, and

Aunty Rosa, awful in black crape, had returned to this life. 'I don't think I've done anything bad that she knows of. I suppose I will soon. She will be very cross after Uncle Harry's dying, and Harry will be cross too. I'll keep in the nursery.'

Unfortunately for Punch's plans, it was decided that he should be sent to a day-school which Harry attended. This meant a morning walk with Harry, and perhaps an evening one; but the prospect of freedom in the interval was refreshing. 'Harry'll tell everything I do, but I won't do anything,' said Black Sheep. Fortified with this virtuous resolution, he went to school only to find that Harry's version of his character had preceded him, and that life was a burden in consequence. He took stock of his associates. Some of them were unclean, some of them talked in dialect, many dropped their h's, and there were two Jews and a negro, or some one quite as dark, in the assembly. 'That's a *hubshi*,' said Black Sheep to himself. 'Even Meeta used to laugh at a *hubshi*.* I don't think this is a proper place.' He was indignant for at least an hour, till he reflected that any expostulation on his part would be by Aunty Rosa construed into 'showing off', and that Harry would tell the boys.

'How do you like school?' said Aunty Rosa at the end of the day.

'I think it is a very nice place,' said Punch quietly.

'I suppose you warned the boys of Black Sheep's character?' said Aunty Rosa to Harry.

'Oh yes,' said the censor of Black Sheep's morals. 'They know all about him.'

'If I was with my father,' said Black Sheep, stung to the quick, 'I shouldn't *speak* to those boys. He wouldn't let me. They live in shops. I saw them go into shops—where their fathers live and sell things.'

'You're too good for that school, are you?' said Aunty Rosa, with a bitter smile. 'You ought to be grateful, Black Sheep, that those boys speak to you at all. It isn't every school that takes little liars.'

Harry did not fail to make much capital out of Black Sheep's ill-considered remark; with the result that several boys, including the *hubshi*, demonstrated to Black Sheep the eternal equality of the human race by smacking his head, and his consolation from Aunty Rosa was that it 'served him right for being vain'. He learned, however, to keep his opinions to himself, and by propitiating Harry in carrying books and the like to get a little peace. His existence was not too joyful. From nine till twelve he was at school, and from two to four, except on Saturdays. In the evenings he was sent down into the nursery to prepare his lessons for the next day, and every night came the dreaded cross-questionings at Harry's hand. Of Judy he saw but little. She was deeply religious—at six years of age Religion is easy to come by—and sorely divided between her natural love for Black Sheep and her love for Aunty Rosa, who could do no wrong.

The lean woman returned that love with interest, and Judy, when she dared, took advantage of this for the remission of Black Sheep's penalties. Failures in lessons at school were punished at home by a week without reading other than schoolbooks, and Harry brought the news of such a failure with glee. Further, Black Sheep was then bound to repeat his lessons at bedtime to Harry, who generally succeeded in making him break down, and consoled him by gloomiest forebodings for the morrow. Harry was at once spy, practical joker, inquisitor, and Aunty Rosa's deputy executioner. He filled his many posts to admiration. From his actions, now that Uncle Harry was dead, there was no appeal. Black Sheep had not been permitted to keep any self-respect at school: at home he was, of course, utterly discredited, and grateful for any pity that the servant-girls—they changed frequently at Downe Lodge because they, too, were liars—might show. 'You're just fit to row in the same boat with Black Sheep,' was a sentiment that each new Jane or Eliza might expect to hear, before a month was over, from Aunty Rosa's lips; and Black Sheep was used to ask new girls whether they had yet been compared to him. Harry was 'Master Harry' in their mouths; Judy was officially 'Miss Judy'; but Black Sheep was never anything more than Black Sheep *tout court*.*

As time went on and the memory of Papa and Mamma became wholly overlaid by the unpleasant task of writing them letters, under Aunty Rosa's eye, each Sunday, Black

Sheep forgot what manner of life he had led in the beginning of things. Even Judy's appeals to 'try and remember about Bombay' failed to quicken him.

'I can't remember,' he said. 'I know I used to give orders and Mamma kissed me.'

'Aunty Rosa will kiss you if you are good,' pleaded Judy.

'Ugh! I don't want to be kissed by Aunty Rosa. She'd say I was doing it to get something more to eat.'

The weeks lengthened into months, and the holidays came; but just before the holidays Black Sheep fell into deadly sin.

Among the many boys whom Harry had incited to 'punch Black Sheep's head because he daren't hit back', was one more aggravating than the rest, who, in an unlucky moment, fell upon Black Sheep when Harry was not near. The blows stung, and Black Sheep struck back at random with all the power at his command. The boy dropped and whimpered. Black Sheep was astounded at his own act, but, feeling the unresisting body under him, shook it with both his hands in blind fury and then began to throttle his enemy; meaning honestly to slay him. There was a scuffle, and Black Sheep was torn off the body by Harry and some colleagues, and cuffed home tingling but exultant. Aunty Rosa was out. Pending her arrival, Harry set himself to lecture Black Sheep on the sin of murder—which he described as the offence of Cain.

'Why didn't you fight him fair? What did you hit him when he was down for, you little cur?'

Black Sheep looked up at Harry's throat and then at a knife on the dinner-table.

'I don't understand,' he said wearily. 'You always set him on me and told me I was a coward when I blubbed. Will you leave me alone until Aunty Rosa comes in? She'll beat me if you tell her I ought to be beaten; so it's all right.'

'It's all wrong,' said Harry magisterially. 'You nearly killed him, and I shouldn't wonder if he dies.'

'Will he die?' said Black Sheep.

'I daresay,' said Harry, 'and then you'll be hanged, and go to Hell.'

'All right,' said Black Sheep, picking up the table-knife. 'Then I'll kill *you* now. You say things and do things and— and *I* don't know how things happen, and you never leave me alone—and I don't care *what* happens!'

He ran at the boy with the knife, and Harry fled upstairs to his room, promising Black Sheep the finest thrashing in the world when Aunty Rosa returned. Black Sheep sat at the bottom of the stairs, the table-knife in his hand, and wept for that he had not killed Harry. The servant-girl came up from the kitchen, took the knife away, and consoled him. But Black Sheep was beyond consolation. He would be badly beaten by Aunty Rosa; then there would be another beating at Harry's hands; then Judy would not be allowed to speak to him; then the tale would be told at school, and then—

There was no one to help and no one to care, and the best way out of the business was by death. A knife would hurt, but Aunty Rosa had told him, a year ago, that if he sucked paint he would die. He went into the nursery, unearthed the now disused Noah's Ark, and sucked the paint off as many animals as remained. It tasted abominably, but he had licked Noah's Dove clean by the time Aunty Rosa and Judy returned. He went upstairs and greeted them with: 'Please, Aunty Rosa, I believe I've nearly killed a boy at school, and I've tried to kill Harry, and when you've done all about God and Hell, will you beat me and get it over?'

The tale of the assault as told by Harry could only be explained on the ground of possession by the Devil. Wherefore Black Sheep was not only most excellently beaten, once by Aunty Rosa, and once, when thoroughly cowed down, by Harry, but he was further prayed for at family prayers, together with Jane, who had stolen a cold rissole from the pantry, and snuffled audibly as her sin was brought before the Throne of Grace. Black Sheep was sore and stiff but triumphant. He would die that very night and be rid of them all. No, he would ask for no forgiveness from Harry, and at bed-time would stand no questioning at Harry's hands, even though addressed as 'Young Cain'.

'I've been beaten,' said he, 'and I've done other things. I don't care what I do. If you speak to me to-night, Harry, I'll get out and try to kill you. Now you can kill me if you like.'

Harry took his bed into the spare room, and Black Sheep lay down to die.

It may be that the makers of Noah's Arks know that their animals are likely to find their way into young mouths, and paint them accordingly. Certain it is that the common, weary next morning broke through the windows and found Black Sheep quite well and a good deal ashamed of himself, but richer by the knowledge that he could, in extremity, secure himself against Harry for the future.

When he descended to breakfast on the first day of the holidays, he was greeted with the news that Harry, Aunty Rosa, and Judy were going away to Brighton, while Black Sheep was to stay in the house with the servant. His latest outbreak suited Aunty Rosa's plans admirably. It gave her good excuse for leaving the extra boy behind. Papa in Bombay, who really seemed to know a young sinner's wants to the hour, sent, that week, a package of new books. And with these, and the society of Jane on board-wages, Black Sheep was left alone for a month.

The books lasted for ten days. They were eaten too quickly in long gulps of twelve hours at a time. Then came days of doing absolutely nothing, of dreaming dreams and marching imaginary armies up and down stairs, of counting the number of banisters, and of measuring the length and breadth of every room in handspans—fifty down the side, thirty across, and fifty back again. Jane made many friends, and, after receiving Black Sheep's assurance that he would not tell of her absences, went out daily for long hours. Black Sheep would follow the rays of the sinking sun from the kitchen to the dining-room and thence upward to his own bedroom until all was grey dark, and he ran down to the kitchen fire and read by its light. He was happy in that he was left alone and could read as much as he pleased. But, later, he grew afraid of the shadows of window curtains and the flapping of doors and the creaking of shutters. He went out into the garden, and the rustling of the laurel-bushes frightened him.

He was glad when they all returned—Aunty Rosa, Harry, and Judy—full of news, and Judy laden with gifts. Who could help loving loyal little Judy? In return for all her merry babblement, Black Sheep confided to her that the distance from the hall-door to the top of the first landing was exactly one-hundred and eighty-four handspans. He had found it out himself!

Then the old life recommenced; but with a difference, and a new sin. To his other iniquities Black Sheep had now added a phenomenal clumsiness—was as unfit to trust in action as he was in word. He himself could not account for spilling everything he touched, upsetting glasses as he put his hand out, and bumping his head against doors that were manifestly shut. There was a grey haze upon all his world, and it narrowed month by month, until at last it left Black Sheep almost alone with the flapping curtains that were so like ghosts, and the nameless terrors of broad daylight that were only coats on pegs after all.

Holidays came and holidays went, and Black Sheep was taken to see many people whose faces were all exactly alike; was beaten when occasion demanded, and tortured by Harry on all possible occasions; but defended by Judy through good and evil report, though she hereby drew upon herself the wrath of Aunty Rosa.

The weeks were interminable and Papa and Mamma were clean forgotten. Harry had left school and was a clerk in a Banking-Office. Freed from his presence, Black Sheep resolved that he should no longer be deprived of his allowance of pleasure-reading. Consequently when he failed at school he reported that all was well, and conceived a large contempt for Aunty Rosa as he saw how easy it was to deceive her. 'She says I'm a little liar when I don't tell lies, and now I do, she doesn't know,' thought Black Sheep. Aunty Rosa had credited him in the past with petty cunning and stratagem that had never entered into his head. By the light of the sordid knowledge that she had revealed to him he paid her back full tale. In a household where the most innocent of his motives, his natural yearning for a little affection, had been interpreted into a desire for more bread and jam, or to ingratiate himself with strangers and so put Harry into the background, his work was easy. Aunty Rosa could penetrate certain kinds of hypocrisy, but not all. He set his child's wits against hers and was no more beaten. It grew monthly more and more of a trouble to read the school-books, and even the pages of the open-print story-books danced and were dim. So Black Sheep brooded in the shadows that fell about him and cut him off from the world, inventing horrible punishments for 'dear Harry', or plotting another line of the tangled web of deception that he wrapped round Aunty Rosa.

Then the crash came and the cobwebs were broken. It was impossible to foresee everything. Aunty Rosa made personal inquiries as to Black Sheep's progress and received information that startled her. Step by step, with a delight as keen as when she convicted an underfed housemaid of the theft of cold meats, she followed the trail of Black Sheep's delinquencies. For weeks and weeks, in order to escape banishment from the book-shelves, he had made a fool of Aunty Rosa, of Harry, of God, of all the world! Horrible, most horrible, and evidence of an utterly depraved mind.

Black Sheep counted the cost. 'It will only be one big beating and then she'll put a card with "Liar" on my back, same as she did before. Harry will whack me and pray for me, and she will pray for me at prayers and tell me I'm a Child of the Devil and give me hymns to learn. But I've done all my reading and she never knew. She'll say she knew all along. She's an old liar too,' said he.

For three days Black Sheep was shut in his own bed-room—to prepare his heart. 'That means two beatings. One at school and one here. *That* one will hurt most.' And it fell even as he thought. He was thrashed at school before the Jews and the *hubshi* for the heinous crime of carrying home false reports of progress. He was thrashed at home by Aunty Rosa on the same count, and then the placard was produced. Aunty Rosa stitched it between his shoulders and bade him go for a walk with it upon him.

'If you make me do that,' said Black Sheep very quietly, 'I shall burn this house down, and perhaps I'll kill you. I don't know whether I *can* kill you—you're so bony—but I'll try.'

No punishment followed this blasphemy, though Black Sheep held himself ready to work his way to Aunty Rosa's withered throat, and grip there till he was beaten off. Perhaps Aunty Rosa was afraid, for Black Sheep, having reached the Nadir of Sin, bore himself with a new recklessness.

In the midst of all the trouble there came a visitor from

over the seas to Downe Lodge, who knew Papa and Mamma, and was commissioned to see Punch and Judy. Black Sheep was sent to the drawing-room and charged into a solid tea-table laden with china.

'Gently, gently, little man,' said the visitor, turning Black Sheep's face to the light slowly. 'What's that big bird on the palings?'

'What bird?' asked Black Sheep.

The visitor looked deep down into Black Sheep's eyes for half a minute, and then said suddenly: 'Good God, the little chap's nearly blind!'

It was a most businesslike visitor. He gave orders, on his own responsibility, that Black Sheep was not to go to school or open a book until Mamma came home. 'She'll be here in three weeks, as you know, of course,' said he, 'and I'm Inverarity Sahib. I ushered you into this wicked world, young man, and a nice use you seem to have made of your time. You must do nothing whatever. Can you do that?'

'Yes,' said Punch in a dazed way. He had known that Mamma was coming. There was a chance, then, of another beating. Thank Heaven, Papa wasn't coming too. Aunty Rosa had said of late that he ought to be beaten by a man.

For the next three weeks Black Sheep was strictly allowed to do nothing. He spent his time in the old nursery looking at the broken toys, for all of which account must be rendered to Mamma. Aunty Rosa hit him over the hands if even a wooden boat were broken. But that sin was of small importance compared to the other revelations, so darkly hinted at by Aunty Rosa. 'When your Mother comes, and hears what I have to tell her, she may appreciate you properly,' she said grimly, and mounted guard over Judy lest that small maiden should attempt to comfort her brother, to the peril of her soul.

And Mamma came—in a four-wheeler—fluttered with tender excitement. Such a Mamma! She was young, frivolously young, and beautiful, with delicately flushed cheeks, eyes that shone like stars, and a voice that needed no appeal of outstretched arms to draw little ones to her heart. Judy ran straight to her, but Black Sheep hesitated. Could this wonder be 'showing off'? She would not put out her arms when she knew of his crimes. Meantime was it possible that by fondling she wanted to get anything out of Black Sheep? Only all his love and all his confidence; but that Black Sheep did not know. Aunty Rosa withdrew and left Mamma, kneeling between her children, half laughing, half crying, in the very hall where Punch and Judy had wept five years before.

'Well, chicks, do you remember me?'

'No,' said Judy frankly, 'but I said, "God bless Papa and Mamma" ev'vy night.'

'A little,' said Black Sheep. 'Remember I wrote to you every week, anyhow. That isn't to show off, but 'cause of what comes afterwards.'

'What comes after? What should come after, my darling boy?' And she drew him to her again. He came awkwardly, with many angles. 'Not used to petting,' said the quick Mother-soul. 'The girl is.'

'She's too little to hurt any one,' thought Black Sheep, 'and if I said I'd kill her, she'd be afraid. I wonder what Aunty Rosa will tell.'

There was a constrained late dinner, at the end of which Mamma picked up Judy and put her to bed with endearments manifold. Faithless little Judy had shown her defection from Aunty Rosa already. And that lady resented it bitterly. Black Sheep rose to leave the room.

'Come and say good-night,' said Aunty Rosa, offering a withered cheek.

'Huh!' said Black Sheep. 'I never kiss you, and I'm not going to show off. Tell that woman what I've done, and see what she says.'

Black Sheep climbed into bed feeling that he had lost Heaven after a glimpse through the gates. In half an hour 'that woman' was bending over him. Black Sheep flung up his right arm. It wasn't fair to come and hit him in the dark. Even Aunty Rosa never tried that. But no blow followed.

'Are you showing off? I won't tell you anything more than Aunty Rosa has, and *she* doesn't know everything,' said Black Sheep as clearly as he could for the arms round his neck.

'Oh, my son—my little, little son! It was my fault—*my*

fault, darling—and yet how could we help it? Forgive me, Punch.' The voice died out in a broken whisper, and two hot tears fell on Black Sheep's forehead.

'Has she been making you cry too?' he asked. 'You should see Jane cry. But you're nice, and Jane is a Born Liar—Aunty Rosa says so.'

'Hush, Punch, hush! My boy, don't talk like that. Try to love me a little bit—a little bit. You don't know how I want it. Punch-*baba*, come back to me! I am your Mother—your own Mother—and never mind the rest. I know—yes, I know, dear. It doesn't matter now. Punch, won't you care for me a little?'

It is astonishing how much petting a big boy of ten can endure when he is quite sure that there is no one to laugh at him. Black Sheep had never been made much of before, and here was this beautiful woman treating him—Black Sheep, the Child of the Devil and the inheritor of undying flame—as though he were a small God.

'I care for you a great deal, Mother dear,' he whispered at last, 'and I'm glad you've come back; but are you sure Aunty Rosa told you everything?'

'Everything. What *does* it matter? But——' the voice broke with a sob that was also laughter—'Punch, my poor, dear, half-blind darling, don't you think it was a little foolish of you?'

'*No*. It saved a lickin'.'

Mamma shuddered and slipped away in the darkness to write a long letter to Papa. Here is an extract:—

'. . . Judy is a dear, plump little prig who adores the woman, and wears with as much gravity as her religious opinions—only eight, Jack!—a venerable horse-hair atrocity which she calls her Bustle! I have just burnt it, and the child is asleep in my bed as I write. She will come to me at once. Punch I cannot quite understand. He is well nourished, but seems to have been worried into a system of small deceptions which the woman magnifies into deadly sins. Don't you recollect our own upbringing, dear, when the Fear of the Lord was so often the beginning of falsehood? I shall win

Punch to me before long. I am taking the children away into the country to get them to know me, and, on the whole, I am content, or shall be when you come home, dear boy, and then, thank God, we shall be all under one roof again at last!'

Three months later, Punch, no longer Black Sheep, has discovered that he is the veritable owner of a real, live, lovely Mamma, who is also a sister, comforter, and friend, and that he must protect her till the Father comes home. Deception does not suit the part of a protector, and, when one can do anything without question, where is the use of deception?

'Mother would be awfully cross if you walked through that ditch,' says Judy, continuing a conversation.

'Mother's never angry,' says Punch. 'She'd just say, "You're a little *pagal* [idiot]"; and that's not nice, but I'll show.'

Punch walks through the ditch and mires himself to the knees. 'Mother dear,' he shouts, 'I'm just as dirty as I can pos-*sib*-ly be!'

'Then change your clothes as quickly as you pos-*sib*-ly can!' Mother's clear voice rings out from the house. 'And don't be a little *pagal*!'

'There! Told you so,' says Punch. 'It's all different now, and we are just as much Mother's as if she had never gone.'

Not altogether, O Punch, for when young lips have drunk deep of the bitter waters of Hate, Suspicion, and Despair, all the Love in the world will not wholly take away that knowledge; though it may turn darkened eyes for a while to the light, and teach Faith where no Faith was.

At the Pit's Mouth

Men say it was a stolen tide—
   The Lord that sent it He knows all,
But in mine ear will aye abide
   The message that the bells let fall,
And awesome bells they were to me,
That in the dark rang 'Enderby.'
                  *Jean Ingelow**

ONCE upon a time there was a Man and his Wife and a Tertium Quid.*

All three were unwise, but the Wife was the unwisest. The Man should have looked after his Wife, who should have avoided the Tertium Quid, who, again, should have married a wife of his own, after clean and open flirtations, to which nobody can possibly object, round Jakko or Observatory Hill. When you see a young man with his pony in a white lather and his hat on the back of his head, flying downhill at fifteen miles an hour to meet a girl who will be properly surprised to meet him, you naturally approve of that young man, and wish him Staff appointments, and take an interest in his welfare, and, as the proper time comes, give them sugar-tongs or side-saddles according to your means and generosity.

The Tertium Quid flew downhill on horseback, but it was to meet the Man's Wife; and when he flew uphill it was for the same end. The Man was in the Plains, earning money for his Wife to spend on dresses and four-hundred-rupee bracelets, and inexpensive luxuries of that kind. He worked very hard, and sent her a letter or a postcard daily. She also wrote to him daily, and said that she was longing for him to come up to Simla. The Tertium Quid used to lean over her shoulder and laugh as she wrote the notes. Then the two would ride to the Post Office together.

Now, Simla is a strange place and its customs are peculiar; nor is any man who has not spent at least ten seasons there qualified to pass judgment on circumstantial evidence, which is the most untrustworthy in the Courts. For these reasons, and for others which need not appear, I decline to state positively whether there was anything irretrievably wrong in the relations between the Man's Wife and the Tertium Quid. If there was, and hereon you must form your own opinion, it was the Man's Wife's fault. She was kittenish in her manners, wearing generally an air of soft and fluffy innocence. But she was deadlily learned and evil-instructed; and, now and again, when the mask dropped, men saw this, shuddered and— almost drew back. Men are occasionally particular, and the least particular men are always the most exacting.

Simla is eccentric in its fashion of treating friendships. Certain attachments which have set and crystallized through half-a-dozen seasons acquire almost the sanctity of the marriage bond, and are revered as such. Again, certain attachments equally old, and, to all appearance, equally venerable, never seem to win any recognized official status; while a chance-sprung acquaintance, not two months born, steps into the place which by right belongs to the senior. There is no law reducible to print which regulates these affairs.

Some people have a gift which secures them infinite toleration, and others have not. The Man's Wife had not. If she looked over the garden wall, for instance, women taxed her with stealing their husbands. She complained patheti- cally that she was not allowed to choose her own friends. When she put up her big white muff to her lips, and gazed over it and under her eyebrows at you as she said this thing, you felt that she had been infamously misjudged, and that all the other women's instincts were all wrong. Which was absurd. She was not allowed to own the Tertium Quid in peace; and was so strangely constructed that she would not have enjoyed peace had she been so permitted. She preferred some semblance of intrigue to cloak even her most common- place actions.

After two months of riding, first round Jakko, then Elysium, then Summer Hill, then Observatory Hill, then under Jutogh, and lastly up and down the Cart Road, as far as the Tara Devi gap in the dusk, she said to the Tertium Quid,

'Frank, people say we are too much together, and people are
so horrid.'

The Tertium Quid pulled his moustache, and replied that
horrid people were unworthy of the consideration of nice
people.

'But they have done more than talk—they have written—
written to my hubby—I'm sure of it,' said the Man's Wife,
and she pulled a letter from her husband out of her saddle-
pocket and gave it to the Tertium Quid.

It was an honest letter, written by an honest man, then
stewing in the Plains on two hundred rupees a month (for he
allowed his wife eight hundred and fifty), and in a silk singlet
and cotton trousers. It said that, perhaps, she had not
thought of the unwisdom of allowing her name to be so
generally coupled with the Tertium Quid's; that she was too
much of a child to understand the dangers of that sort of
thing; that he, her husband, was the last man in the world to
interfere jealously with her little amusements and interests,
but that it would be better were she to drop the Tertium Quid
quietly and for her husband's sake. The letter was sweetened
with many pretty little pet names, and it amused the Tertium
Quid considerably. He and She laughed over it, so that you,
fifty yards away, could see their shoulders shaking while the
horses slouched along side by side.

Their conversation was not worth repeating. The upshot
of it was that, next day, no one saw the Man's Wife and the
Tertium Quid together. They had both gone down to the
Cemetery, which, as a rule, is only visited officially by the
inhabitants of Simla.

A Simla funeral with the clergyman riding, the mourners
riding, and the coffin creaking as it swings between the
bearers, is one of the most depressing things on this earth,
particularly when the procession passes under the wet, dank
dip beneath the Rockcliffe Hotel, where the sun is shut out,
and all the hill streams are wailing and weeping together as
they go down the valleys.

Occasionally folk tend the graves, but we in India shift and
are transferred so often that, at the end of the second year, the
Dead have no friends—only acquaintances who are far too
busy amusing themselves up the hill to attend to old partners.

The idea of using a Cemetery as a rendezvous is distinctly a feminine one. A man would have said simply, 'Let people talk. We'll go down the Mall.' A woman is made differently, especially if she be such a woman as the Man's Wife. She and the Tertium Quid enjoyed each other's society among the graves of men and women whom they had known and danced with aforetime.

They used to take a big horse-blanket and sit on the grass a little to the left of the lower end, where there is a dip in the ground, and where the occupied graves stop short and the ready-made ones are not ready. Each well-regulated Indian Cemetery keeps half-a-dozen graves permanently open for contingencies and incidental wear and tear. In the Hills these are more usually baby's size, because children who come up weakened and sick from the Plains often succumb to the effects of the Rains in the Hills or get pneumonia from their *ayahs** taking them through damp pinewoods after the sun has set. In cantonments, of course, the man's size is more in request; these arrangements varying with the climate and population.

One day when the Man's Wife and the Tertium Quid had just arrived in the Cemetery, they saw some coolies breaking ground. They had marked out a full-size grave, and the Tertium Quid asked them whether any Sahib was sick. They said that they did not know; but it was an order that they should dig a Sahib's grave.

'Work away,' said the Tertium Quid, 'and let's see how it's done.'

The coolies worked away, and the Man's Wife and the Tertium Quid watched and talked for a couple of hours while the grave was being deepened. Then a coolie, taking the earth in baskets as it was thrown up, jumped over the grave.

'That's queer,' said the Tertium Quid. 'Where's my ulster?'

'What's queer?' said the Man's Wife.

'I have got a chill down my back—just as if a goose had walked over my grave.'

'Why do you look at the thing, then?' said the Man's Wife. 'Let us go.'

The Tertium Quid stood at the head of the grave, and

stared without answering for a space. Then he said, dropping a pebble down, 'It is nasty—and cold: horribly cold. I don't think I shall come to the Cemetery any more. I don't think grave-digging is cheerful.'

The two talked and agreed that the Cemetery was depressing. They also arranged for a ride next day out from the Cemetery through the Mashobra Tunnel up to Fagoo and back, because all the world was going to a garden-party at Viceregal Lodge, and all the people of Mashobra would go too.

Coming up the Cemetery road, the Tertium Quid's horse tried to bolt uphill, being tired with standing so long, and managed to strain a back sinew.

'I shall have to take the mare to-morrow,' said the Tertium Quid, 'and she will stand nothing heavier than a snaffle.'*

They made their arrangements to meet in the Cemetery, after allowing all the Mashobra people time to pass into Simla. That night it rained heavily, and, next day, when the Tertium Quid came to the trysting-place, he saw that the new grave had a foot of water in it, the ground being a tough and sour clay.

'Jove! That looks beastly,' said the Tertium Quid. 'Fancy being boarded up and dropped into that well!'

They then started off to Fagoo, the mare playing with the snaffle and picking her way as though she were shod with satin, and the sun shining divinely. The road below Mashobra to Fagoo is officially styled the Himalayan-Tibet Road; but in spite of its name it is not much more than six feet wide in most places, and the drop into the valley below may be anything between one and two thousand feet.

'Now we're going to Tibet,' said the Man's Wife merrily, as the horses drew near to Fagoo. She was riding on the cliff side.

'Into Tibet,' said the Tertium Quid, 'ever so far from people who say horrid things, and hubbies who write stupid letters. With you—to the end of the world!'

A coolie carrying a log of wood came round a corner, and the mare went wide to avoid him—forefeet in and haunches out, as a sensible mare should go.

'To the world's end,' said the Man's Wife, and looked

unspeakable things over her near shoulder at the Tertium Quid.

He was smiling, but, while she looked, the smile froze stiff, as it were, on his face, and changed to a nervous grin— the sort of grin men wear when they are not quite easy in their saddles. The mare seemed to be sinking by the stern, and her nostrils cracked while she was trying to realize what was happening. The rain of the night before had rotted the drop-side of the Himalayan-Tibet Road, and it was giving way under her. 'What are you doing?' said the Man's Wife. The Tertium Quid gave no answer. He grinned nervously and set his spurs into the mare, who rapped with her forefeet on the road, and the struggle began. The Man's Wife screamed, 'Oh, Frank, get off!'

But the Tertium Quid was glued to the saddle—his face blue and white—and he looked into the Man's Wife's eyes. Then the Man's Wife clutched at the mare's head and caught her by the nose instead of the bridle. The brute threw up her head and went down with a scream, the Tertium Quid upon her, and the nervous grin still set on his face.

The Man's Wife heard the tinkle-tinkle of little stones and loose earth falling off the roadway, and the sliding roar of the man and horse going down. Then everything was quiet, and she called on Frank to leave his mare and walk up. But Frank did not answer. He was underneath the mare, nine hundred feet below, spoiling a patch of Indian corn.

As the revellers came back from Viceregal Lodge in the mists of the evening, they met a temporarily insane woman, on a temporarily mad horse, swinging round the corners, with her eyes and her mouth open, and her head like the head of a Medusa.* She was stopped by a man at the risk of his life, and taken out of the saddle, a limp heap, and put on the bank to explain herself. This wasted twenty minutes, and then she was sent home in a lady's 'rickshaw, still with her mouth open and her hands picking at her riding-gloves.

She was in bed through the following three days, which were rainy; so she missed attending the funeral of the Tertium Quid, who was lowered into eighteen inches of water, instead of the twelve to which he had first objected.

Black Jack

To the wake av Tim O'Hara
Came company,
All St Patrick's Alley
Was there to see.
*Robert Buchanan**

As the Three Musketeers share their silver, tobacco, and liquor together, as they protect each other in barracks or camp, and as they rejoice together over the joy of one, so do they divide their sorrows. When Ortheris's irrepressible tongue has brought him into cells for a season, or Learoyd has run amok through his kit and accoutrements, or Mulvaney has indulged in strong waters, and under their influence reproved his Commanding Officer, you can see the trouble in the faces of the untouched two. And the rest of the Regiment know that comment or jest is unsafe. Generally the three avoid Orderly-Room and the Corner Shop* that follows, leaving both to the young bloods who have not sown their wild oats; but there are occasions——

For instance, Ortheris was sitting on the drawbridge of the main gate of Fort Amara,* with his hands in his pockets and his pipe, bowl down, in his mouth. Learoyd was lying at full length on the turf of the glacis, kicking his heels in the air, and I came round the corner and asked for Mulvaney.

Ortheris spat into the Ditch and shook his head. 'No good seein' 'im now,' said Ortheris; ''e's a bloomin' camel. Listen.'

I heard on the flags of the veranda opposite to the cells, which are close to the Guard-Room, a measured step that I could have identified out of the tramp of an army. There were twenty paces *crescendo*, a pause, and then twenty *diminuendo*.

'That's 'im,' said Ortheris; 'my Gawd, that's 'im! All for a bloomin' button you could see your face in an' a bit o' lip that a bloomin' Harkangel would 'a' guv back.'

Mulvaney was doing pack-drill—was compelled, that is to say, to walk up and down for certain hours in full marching order, with rifle, bayonet, ammunition, knapsack, and over-coat. And his offence was being dirty on parade! I nearly fell into the Fort Ditch with astonishment and wrath, for Mulvaney is the smartest man that ever mounted guard, and would as soon think of turning out uncleanly as of dispensing with his trousers.

'Who was the Sergeant that checked him?' I asked.

'Mullins, o' course,' said Ortheris. 'There ain't no other man would whip 'im on the peg so. But Mullins ain't a man. 'E's a dirty little pig-scraper, that's wot 'e is.'

'What did Mulvaney say? He's not the make of man to take that quietly.'

'Say! Bin better for 'im if 'e'd shut 'is mouth. Lord, 'ow we laughed! "Sargint," 'e sez, "ye say I'm dirty. Well," sez 'e, "when your wife lets you blow your own nose for yourself, perhaps you'll know wot dirt is. You're himperfec'ly eddi-cated, Sargint," sez 'e, an' then we fell in. But after p'rade, 'e was up an' Mullins was swearin' 'imself black in the face at Ord'ly-Room that Mulvaney 'ad called 'im a swine an' Lord knows wot all. You know Mullins. 'E'll 'ave 'is 'ead broke in one o' these days. 'E's too big a bloomin' liar for ord'nary consumption. "Three hours' can an' kit," sez the Colonel; "not for bein' dirty on p'rade, but for 'avin' said somethin' to Mullins, tho' I do not believe," sez 'e, "you said wot 'e said you said." An' Mulvaney fell away sayin' nothin'. You know 'e never speaks to the Colonel for fear o' gettin' 'imself fresh copped.'

Mullins, a very young and very much married Sergeant, whose manners were partly the result of innate depravity and partly of imperfectly digested Board School, came over the bridge, and most rudely asked Ortheris what he was doing.

'Me?' said Ortheris. 'Ow! I'm waiting for my C'mission. Seed it comin' along yit?'

Mullins turned purple and passed on. There was the sound of a gentle chuckle from the glacis where Learoyd lay.

''E expects to get his C'mission some day,' explained Ortheris. 'Gawd 'elp the Mess that 'ave to put their 'ands into the same kiddy* as 'im! Wot time d'you make it, sir? Fower! Mulvaney'll be out in 'arf an hour. You don't want to buy a dorg, sir, do you? A pup you can trust—'arf Rampur* by the Colonel's grey'ound.'

'Ortheris,' I answered sternly, for I knew what was in his mind, 'do you mean to say that——'

'I didn't mean to arx money o' you, any'ow,' said Ortheris. 'I'd 'a' sold you the dorg good an' cheap, but—but—I know Mulvaney'll want somethin' after we've walked 'im orf, an' I ain't got nothin', nor 'e 'asn't neither. I'd sooner sell you the dorg, sir. 'Strewth I would!'

A shadow fell on the drawbridge, and Ortheris began to rise into the air, lifted by a huge hand upon his collar.

'Onnything but t'braass,' said Learoyd quietly, as he held the Londoner over the Ditch. 'Onnything but t' braass, Orth'ris, ma son! Ah've got one rupee eight annas ma own.' He showed two coins, and replaced Ortheris on the drawbridge rail.

'Very good,' I said; 'where are you going to?'

'Goin' to walk 'im orf w'en 'e comes out—two miles or three or fower,' said Ortheris.

The footsteps within ceased. I heard the dull thud of a knapsack falling on a bedstead, followed by the rattle of arms. Ten minutes later, Mulvaney, faultlessly dressed, his lips tight and his face as black as a thunderstorm, stalked into the sunshine on the drawbridge. Learoyd and Ortheris sprang from my side and closed in upon him, both leaning towards him as horses lean upon the pole. In an instant they had disappeared down the sunken road to the cantonments, and I was left alone. Mulvaney had not seen fit to recognize me; so I knew that his trouble must be heavy upon him.

I climbed one of the bastions and watched the figures of the Three Musketeers grow smaller and smaller across the plain. They were walking as fast as they could put foot to the ground, and their heads were bowed. They fetched a great compass round the parade-ground, skirted the Cavalry lines, and vanished in the belt of trees that fringes the low land by the river.

I followed slowly, and sighted them—dusty, sweating, but still keeping up their long, swinging tramp—on the river bank. They crashed through the Forest Reserve,* headed

towards the Bridge of Boats, and presently established themselves on the bow of one of the pontoons. I rode cautiously till
I saw three puffs of white smoke rise and die out in the clear
evening air, and knew that peace had come again. At the
bridge-head they waved me forward with gestures of
welcome.

'Tie up your 'orse,' shouted Ortheris, 'an' come on, sir.
We're all goin' 'ome in this 'ere bloomin' boat.'

From the bridge-head to the Forest Officer's bungalow is
but a step. The mess-man was there, and would see that a
man held my horse. Did the Sahib require aught else—a
peg,* or beer? Ritchie Sahib had left half-a-dozen bottles of
the latter, but since the Sahib was a friend of Ritchie Sahib,
and he, the mess-man, was a poor man——

I gave my order quietly, and returned to the bridge.
Mulvaney had taken off his boots, and was dabbling his toes
in the water; Learoyd was lying on his back on the pontoon;
and Ortheris was pretending to row with a big bamboo.

'I'm an ould fool,' said Mulvaney reflectively, 'dhraggin'
you two out here bekaze I was undher the Black Dog*—
sulkin' like a child. Me that was sodgerin' when Mullins, an'
be damned to him, was shquealin' on a counterpin for five
shillin' a week—an' that not paid! Bhoys, I've tuk you five
miles out av natural pivarsity. Phew!'

'Wot's the odds as long as you're 'appy?'* said Ortheris,
applying himself afresh to the bamboo. 'As well 'ere as
anywhere else.'

Learoyd held up a rupee and an eight-anna bit, and shook
his head sorrowfully. 'Five miles from t' Canteen, all along o'
Mulvaaney's blaasted pride.'

'I know ut,' said Mulvaney penitently. 'Why will ye come
wid me? An' yet I wud be mortial sorry av ye did not—any
time—though I am ould enough to know betther. But I will
do penance. I will take a dhrink av wather.'

Ortheris squeaked shrilly. The butler of the Forest
bungalow was standing near the railings with a basket,
uncertain how to clamber down to the pontoon.

'Might 'a' know'd you'd 'a' got liquor out o' bloomin'
desert, sir,' said Ortheris gracefully to me. Then to the mess-

man: 'Easy with them there bottles. They're worth their weight in gold. Jock, ye long-armed beggar, get out o' that an' hike 'em down.'

Learoyd had the basket on the pontoon in an instant, and the Three Musketeers gathered round it with dry lips. They drank my health in due and ancient form, and thereafter tobacco tasted sweeter than ever. They absorbed all the beer, and disposed themselves in picturesque attitudes to admire the setting sun—no man speaking for a while.

Mulvaney's head dropped upon his chest, and we thought that he was asleep.

'What on earth did you come so far for?' I whispered to Ortheris.

'To walk 'im orf, o' course. When 'e's been checked we allus walks 'im orf. 'E ain't fit to be spoke to those times—nor 'e ain't fit to leave alone neither. So we takes 'im till 'e is.'

Mulvaney raised his head, and stared straight into the sunset. 'I had my rifle,' said he dreamily, 'an' I had my bay'nit, an' Mullins came round the corner, an' he looked in my face an' grinned dishpiteful. "*You* can't blow your own nose," sez he. Now, I cannot tell fwhat Mullins's expayrience may ha' been, but, Mother av God, he was nearer to his death that minut' than I have iver been to mine—and that's less than the thicknuss av a hair!'

'Yes,' said Ortheris calmly,* 'you'd look fine with all your buttons took orf, an' the Band in front o' you, walkin' roun' slow time. We're both front-rank men, me an' Jock, when the Rig'ment's in 'ollow square. Bloomin' fine you'd look. "The Lord giveth an' the Lord taketh awai,—Heasy with that there drop!—Blessed be the naime o' the Lord."' He gulped in a quaint and suggestive fashion.

'Mullins! What's Mullins?' said Learoyd slowly. 'Ah'd taake a coomp'ny o' Mullinses—ma hand behind me. Sitha, Mulvaaney, don't be a fool.'

'*You* were not checked for fwhat you did not do, an' made a mock av afther. 'Twas for less than that the Tyrone wud ha' sent O'Hara* to Hell, instid av lettin' him go by his own choosin', whin Rafferty shot him,' retorted Mulvaney.

'And who stopped the Tyrone from doing it?' I asked.

'This ould fool who's sorry he did not shtick that pig Mullins.' His head dropped again. When he raised it he shivered and put his hands on the shoulders of his two companions.

'Ye've walked the Divil out av me, bhoys,' said he.

Ortheris shot out the red-hot dottle of his pipe on the back of the hairy fist. 'They say 'Ell's 'otter than that,' said he, as Mulvaney swore aloud. 'You be warned so. Look yonder!'— he pointed across the river to a ruined temple—'Me an' you an' '*im*'—he indicated me by a jerk of his head—'was there one day when Hi made a bloomin' show o' myself. You an' 'im stopped me doin' such—an' Hi was on'y wishful for to desert.* You are makin' a bigger bloomin' show o' yourself now.'

'Don't mind him, Mulvaney,' I said; 'Dinah Shadd* won't let you hang yourself yet awhile, and you don't intend to try it either. Let's hear about the Tyrone and O'Hara. Rafferty shot him for fooling with his wife. What happened before that?'

'There's no fool like an ould fool. Ye know ye can do anythin' wid me whin I'm talkin'. Did I say I wud like to cut Mullins's liver out? I deny the imputashin, for fear that Orth'ris here wud report me—Ah! You wud tip me into the river, wud you? Set quiet, little man. Anyways, Mullins is not worth the throuble av an extry p'rade, an' I will trate him wid outrajis contimpt. The Tyrone an' O'Hara! O'Hara an' the Tyrone, begad! Ould days are hard to bring back into the mouth, but they're always inside the head.'

Followed a long pause.

'O'Hara was a Divil. Though I saved him, for the honour av the Rig'mint, from his death that time, I say it now. He was a Divil—a long, bould, black-haired Divil.'

'Which way?' asked Ortheris.

'Wimmen.'

'Then I know another.'

'Not more than in reason, if you manc me, ye warped walkin'-shtick. I have been young, an' for why shud I not have tuk what I cud? Did I iver, whin I was Corp'ril, use the rise av my rank—wan step an' that taken away, more's the sorrow an' the fault av me!—to prosecute nefarious inthrigues, as O'Hara did? Did I, whin I was Corp'ril, lay my spite upon a man an' make his life a dog's life from day to day? Did I lie, as O'Hara lied, till the young wans in the Tyrone turned white wid the fear av the Judgment av God killin' thim all in a lump, as ut killed the woman at Devizes?* I did not! I have sinned my sins an' I have made my confesshin, an' Father Victor knows the worst av me. O'Hara was tuk, before he cud spake, on Rafferty's doorstip, an' no man knows the worst av him. But this much I know!

'The Tyrone was recruited any fashion in the ould days. A draf' from Connemara—a draf' from Portsmouth—a draf' from Kerry, an' that was a blazin' bad draf'—here, there, and ivrywhere—but the large av thim was Irish—Black Irish. Now there are Irish an' Irish. The good are good as the best, but the bad are wurrse than the wurrst. 'Tis this way. They clog together in pieces as fast as thieves, an' no wan knows fwhat they will do till wan turns informer an' the gang is bruk. But ut begins agin, a day later, meetin' in holes an' corners an' swearin' bloody oaths an' shtickin' a man in the back an' runnin' away, an' thin waitin' for the blood-money on the reward papers—to see if ut's worth enough. Those are the Black Irish, an' 'tis they that bring dishgrace upon the name av Ireland, an' thim I wud kill—as I nearly killed wan wanst.

'But to reshume. My room—'twas before I was married—was wid twelve av the scum av the earth—the pickin's av the gutther—mane men that wud neither laugh nor talk nor yet get dhrunk as a man shud. They thried some av their dog's thricks on me, but I dhrew a line round my cot, an' the man that thransgressed ut wint into hospital for three days good.

'O'Hara had put his spite on the room—he was my Colour-Sargint—an' nothing cud we do to plaze him. I was younger than I am now, an' I tuk fwhat I got in the way av dhressing-down and punishmint-dhrill wid me tongue in me cheek. But it was diff'rint wid the others, an' why I cannot say, excipt that some men are borrun mane an' go to dhirty murther where a fist is more than enough. Afther a whoile, they changed their chune to me an' was desp'rit frien'ly—all twelve av thim cursin' O'Hara in chorus.

'"Eyah!" sez I, "O'Hara's a divil and I'm not for denyin'
ut, but is he the only man in the wurruld? Let him go. He'll
get tired av findin' our kit foul an' our 'coutrements onproperly kep'."

'"We will *not* let him go," sez they.

'"Thin take him," sez I, "an' a dashed poor yield you will
get for your throuble."

'"Is he not misconductin' himsilf wid Slimmy's wife?" sez
another.

'"She's common to the Rig'mint," sez I. "Fwhat has made
ye this partic'lar on a suddint?"

'"Has he not put his spite on the roomful av us? Can we do
anythin' that he will not check us for?" sez another.

'"That's thrue," sez I.

'"Will ye not help us to do aught," sez another—"a big
bould man like you?"

'"I will break his head upon his shoulthers av he puts hand
on me," sez I. "I will give him the lie av he says that I'm
dhirty, an' I wud not mind duckin' him in the Artillery
troughs if ut was not that I'm thryin' for me shtripes."

'"Is that all ye will do?" sez another. "Have ye no more
spunk than that, ye blood-dhrawn calf?"*

'"Blood-dhrawn I may be," says I, gettin' back to my cot
an' makin' my line round ut; "but ye know that the man who
comes acrost this mark will be more blood-dhrawn than me.
No man gives me the name in my mouth," I sez. "Ondhersthand, I will have no part wid you in anythin' ye do, nor will I
raise my fist to my shuperior. Is any wan comin' on?" sez I.

'They made no move, tho' I gave thim full time, but stud
growlin' an' snarlin' together at wan ind av the room. I tuk up
my cap and wint out to Canteen, thinkin' no little av mesilf,
an' there I grew most ondacintly dhrunk in my legs. My head
was all reasonable.

'"Houligan," I sez to a man in E Comp'ny that was by way
av bein' a frind av mine; "I'm overtuk from the belt down.
Do you give me the touch av your shoulther to presarve me
formashin* an' march me acrost the ground into the high
grass. I'll sleep ut off there," sez I; an' Houligan—he's dead
now, but good he was whoile he lasted—walked wid me,
givin' me the touch whin I wint wide, ontil we came to the

high grass, an', my faith, sky an' earth was fair rowlin'
undher me. I made for where the grass was thickust, an' there
I slep' off my liquor wid an aisy conscience. I did not desire to
come on the books too frequint; my characther havin' been
shpotless for the good half av a year.

'Whin I roused, the dhrink was dyin' out in me, an' I felt as
though a she-cat had littered in me mouth. I had not learned
to hould my liquor wid comfort in thim days. 'Tis little
betther I am now. "I will get Houligan to pour a bucket over
my head," thinks I, an' I wud ha' risen, but I heard some wan
say: "Mulvaney can take the blame av ut for the backslidin'
hound he is."

'"Oho!" sez I, an' me head ringing like a guard-room
gong: "fwhat is the blame that this young man must take to
oblige Tim Vulmea?" For 'twas Tim Vulmea that shpoke.

'I turned on me belly an' crawled through the grass, a bit at
a time, to where the spache came from. There was the twelve
av my room sittin' down in a little patch, the dhry grass
wavin' above their heads an' the sin av black murther in their
hearts. I put the stuff aside to get clear view.

'"Fwhat's that?" sez wan man, jumpin' up.

'"A dog," says Vulmea. "You're a nice hand to this job! As
I said, Mulvaney will take the blame—av ut comes to a
pinch."

'"'Tis harrd to swear a man's life away," sez a young wan.

'"Thank ye for that," thinks I. "Now, fwhat the divil are
you paragins conthrivin' agin' me?"

'"'Tis as aisy as dhrinkin' your quart," sez Vulmea. "At
sivin or thereon, O'Hara will come acrost to the Married
Quarters, goin' to call on Slimmy's wife, the swine! Wan av
us'll pass the wurrud to the room an' we shtart the divil an' all
av a shine—laughin' an' crackin' on an' t'rowin' our boots
about. Thin O'Hara will come to give us the ordher to be
quiet, the more by token bekaze the room lamp will be
knocked over in the larkin'. He will take the straight road to
the ind door where there's the lamp in the veranda, an' that'll
bring him clear agin' the light as he shtands. He will not be
able to look into the dhark. Wan av us will loose off, an' a
close shot ut will be, an' shame to the man that misses. 'Twill
be Mulvaney's rifle, she that is at the head av the rack—

there's no mishtakin' that long-shtocked, cross-eyed bitch even in the dhark.''

'The thief misnamed my ould firin'-piece out av jealousy— I was pershuaded av that—an' ut made me more angry than all.

'But Vulmea goes on: "O'Hara will dhrop, an' by the time the light's lit agin, there'll be some six av us on the chest av Mulvaney, cryin' murther an' rape. Mulvaney's cot is near the ind door, an' the shmokin' rifle will be lyin' undher him whin we've knocked him over. We know, an' all the Rig'mint knows, that Mulvaney has given O'Hara more lip than any man av us. Will there be any doubt at the Coort-Martial? Wud twelve honust sodger-bhoys swear away the life av a dear, quiet, swate-timpered man such as is Mulvaney—wid his line av pipe-clay roun' his cot, threatenin' us wid murther av we overshtepped ut, as we can truthful testify?"

'"Mary, Mother av Mercy!" thinks I to mesilf; "ut is this to have an unruly mimber* an' fistes fit to use! The hounds!"

'The big dhrops ran down my face, for I was wake wid the liquor an' had not the full av my wits about me. I laid shtill an' heard thim workin' thimsilves up to swear me life away by tellin' tales av ivry time I had put my mark on wan or another; an', my faith, they was few that was not so dishtinguished. 'Twas all in the way av fair fight, though, for niver did I raise my hand excipt whin they had provoked me to ut.

'"'Tis all well," sez wan av thim, "but who's to do this shootin'?"

'"Fwhat matther?" sez Vulmea. "'Tis Mulvaney will do that—at the Coort-Martial."

'"He will so," sez the man, "but whose hand is put to the thrigger—*in the room*?"

'"Who'll do ut?" sez Vulmea, lookin' round, but divil a man answered. They began to dishpute till Kiss, that was always playin' Shpoil Five, sez: "Thry the kyards!" Wid that he opind his tunic an' tuk out the greasy palammers, an' they all fell in wid the notion.

'"Deal on!" sez Vulmea, wid a big rattlin' oath, "an' the Black Curse av Shielygh come to the man that will not do his jooty as the kyards say. Amin!"

'"Black Jack is the masther," sez Kiss, dealin'. Black

Jack, sorr, I shud expaytiate to you, is the Ace av Shpades which from time immimorial has been intimately connect wid battle, murther, an' suddin death.

'*Wanst* Kiss dealt, an' there was no sign, but the men was whoite wid the workin's av their sowls. *Twice* Kiss dealt, an' there was a grey shine on their cheeks like the mess av an egg. *Three* times Kiss dealt, an' they was blue. "Have ye not lost him?" sez Vulmea, wipin' the sweat on him; "let's ha' done quick!" "Quick ut is," sez Kiss, throwin' him the kyard; an' ut fell face up on his knee—Black Jack!

'Thin they all cackled wid laughin'. "Jooty thrippence,"* sez wan av thim, "an' damned cheap at that price!" But I cud see they all dhrew a little away from Vulmea an' lef' him sittin' playin' wid the kyard. Vulmea sez no wurrud for a whoile but licked his lips—cat-ways. Thin he threw up his head an' made the men swear by ivry oath known to stand by him not alone in the room but at the Coort-Martial that was to set on *me*! He tould off five av the biggest to stretch me on my cot whin the shot was fired, an' another man he tould off to put out the light, an' yet another to load my rifle. He wud not do that himsilf; an' that was quare, for 'twas but a little thing considherin'.

'Thin they swore over agin that they wud not bethray wan another, an' crep' out av the grass in diff'rint ways, two by two. A mercy ut was that they did not come on me. I was sick wid fear in the pit av me stummick—sick, sick, sick! Afther they was all gone, I wint back to Canteen an' called for a quart to put a thought in me. Vulmea was there, dhrinkin' heavy, an' politeful to me beyond reason. "Fwhat will I do?—fwhat will I do?" thinks I to mesilf whin Vulmea wint away.

'Prisintly the Arm'rer-Sargint comes in stiffin' an' crackin' on,* not plazed wid any wan, bekaze the Martini-Henry bein' new to the Rig'mint in those days we used to play the mischief wid her arrangemints. 'Twas a long time before I cud get out av the way av thryin' to pull back the backsight an' turnin' her over afther firin'—as if she was a Snider.*

'"Fwhat tailor-men do they give me to work wid?" sez the Arm'rer-Sargint. "Here's Hogan, his nose flat as a table, laid by for a week, an' ivry Comp'ny sendin' their arrums in knocked to small shivreens."

'"Fwhat's wrong wid Hogan, Sargint?" sez I.

'"Wrong!" sez the Arm'rer-Sargint; "I showed him, as though I had been his mother, the way av shtrippin' a 'Tini, an' he shtrup her clane an' aisy.* I tould him to put her to agin an' fire a blank into the blow-pit to show how the dhirt hung on the groovin'. He did that, but he did not put in the pin av the fallin'-block, an' av coorse whin he fired he was strook by the block jumpin' clear. Well for him 'twas but a blank—a full charge wud ha' cut his eye out."

'I looked a thrifle wiser than a boiled sheep's head. "How's that, Sargint?" sez I.

'"This way, ye blundherin' man, an' don't you be doin' ut," sez he. Wid that he shows me a Waster action—the breech av her all cut away to show the inside—an' so plazed he was to grumble that he dimonsthrated fwhat Hogan had done twice over. "An' that comes av not knowin' the wepping you're provided wid," sez he.

'"Thank ye, Sargint," sez I; "I will come to you agin for further informashin."

'"Ye will not," sez he. "Kape your clanin'-rod away from the breech-pin or you will get into throuble."

'I wint outside an' I cud ha' danced wid delight for the grandeur av ut. "They will load my rifle, good luck to thim, whoile I'm away," thinks I, and back I wint to the Canteen to give thim their clear chanst.

'The Canteen was fillin' wid men at the ind av the day. I made feign to be far gone in dhrink, an', wan by wan, all my roomful came in wid Vulmea. I wint away, walkin' thick an' heavy, but not so thick an' heavy that any wan cud ha' tuk me. Sure an' thrue, there was a kyartridge gone from my pouch an' lyin' snug in my rifle. I was hot wid rage agin' thim all, and I worried the bullet out wid me teeth as fast as I cud, the room bein' empty. Then I tuk my boot an' the clanin'-rod and knocked out the pin av the fallin'-block. Oh, 'twas music whin that pin rowled on the flure! I put ut into my pouch an' shtuck a dab av dhirt on the holes in the plate, puttin' the fallin'-block back. "That'll do your business, Vulmea," sez

I, lyin' aisy on me cot. "Come an' sit on me chest, the whole
room av you, an' I will take you to me bosom for the biggest
divils that iver cheated halter." I wud have no mercy on
Vulmea. His eye or his life—little I cared!

'At dusk they came back, the twelve av thim, an' they had
all been dhrinkin'. I was shammin' sleep on the cot. Wan
man wint outside in the veranda. Whin he whishtled they
began to rage roun' the room an' carry on tremenjus. But I
niver want to hear men laugh as they did—sky-larkin' too!
'Twas like mad jackals.

'"Shtop that blasted noise!" sez O'Hara in the dark, an'
pop goes the room lamp. I cud hear O'Hara runnin' up an'
the rattlin' av my rifle in the rack an' the men breathin' heavy
as they stud roun' my cot. I cud see O'Hara in the light av the
veranda lamp, an' thin I heard the crack av my rifle. She cried
loud, poor darlint, bein' mishandled. Next minut' five men
were houldin' me down. "Go aisy," I sez; "fwhat's ut all
about?"

'Thin Vulmea, on the flure, raised a howl you cud hear
from wan ind av cantonmints to the other. "I'm dead, I'm
butchered, I'm blind!" sez he. "Saints have mercy on my
sinful sowl! Sind for Father Constant! Oh, sind for Father
Constant an' let me go clane!" By that I knew he was not so
dead as I cud ha' wished.

'O'Hara picks up the lamp in the veranda wid a hand as
stiddy as a rest. "Fwhat damned dog's thrick is this av
yours?" sez he, and turns the light on Tim Vulmea that was
shwimmin' in blood from top to toe. The fallin'-block had
sprung free behin' a full charge av powther—good care I tuk
to bite down the brass afther takin' out the bullet, that there
might be somethin' to give ut full worth—an' had cut Tim
from the lip to the corner av the right eye, lavin' the eyelid in
tatthers, an' so up an' along by the forehead to the hair. 'Twas
more av a rakin' plough, if you will ondhersthand, than a
clane cut; an' niver did I see a man bleed as Vulmea did. The
dhrink an' the stew that he was in pumped the blood strong.
The minut' the men sittin' on my chest heard O'Hara spakin'
they scatthered each wan to his cot, an' cried out very
politeful: "Fwhat is ut, Sargint?"

'"Fwhat is ut!" sez O'Hara, shakin' Tim. "Well an' good

do you know fwhat ut is, ye skulkin' ditch-lurkin' dogs! Get a *dooli*,* an' take this whimperin' scutt away. There will be more heard av ut than any av you will care for."

'Vulmea sat up rockin' his head in his hand an' moanin' for Father Constant.

'"Be done!" sez O'Hara, dhraggin' him up by the hair. "You're none so dead that you cannot go fifteen years for thryin' to shoot me."

'"I did not," sez Vulmea; "I was shootin' mesilf."

'"That's quare," sez O'Hara, "for the front av my jackut is black wid your powther." He tuk up the rifle that was still warm an' began to laugh. "I'll make your life Hell to you," sez he, "for attempted murther an' kapin' your rifle onproperly. You'll be hanged first an' thin put undher stoppages for four fifteen.* The rifle's done for," sez he.

'"Why, 'tis *my* rifle!" sez I, comin' up to look. "Vulmea, ye divil, fwhat were you doin' wid her—answer me that?"

'"Lave me alone," sez Vulmea; "I'm dyin'!"

'"I'll wait till you're betther," sez I, "an' thin we two will talk ut out umbrageous."

'O'Hara pitched Tim into the *dooli*, none too tinder, but all the bhoys kep' by their cots, which was not the sign av innocint men. I was huntin' ivrywhere for my fallin'-block, but not findin' ut at all. I niver found ut.

'"*Now* fwhat will I do?" sez O'Hara, swinging the veranda light in his hand an' lookin' down the room. I had hate and contimpt av O'Hara an' I have now, dead tho' he is, but for all that will I say he was a brave man. He is baskin' in Purgathory this tide, but I wish he cud hear that, whin he stud lookin' down the room an' the bhoys shivered before the eye av him, I knew him for a brave man an' I liked him *so*.

'"Fwhat will I do?" sez O'Hara agin, an' we heard the voice av a woman low an' sof' in the veranda. 'Twas Slimmy's wife, come over at the shot, sittin' on wan av the benches an' scarce able to walk.

'"O Denny!—Denny, dear," sez she, "have they kilt you?"

'O'Hara looked down the room agin an' showed his teeth to the gum. Thin he spat on the flure.

'"You're not worth ut," sez he. "Light that lamp, ye

dogs," an' wid that he turned away, an' I saw him walkin' off
wid Slimmy's wife; she thryin' to wipe off the powther-black
on the front av his jackut wid her handkerchief. "A brave
man you are," thinks I—"a brave man an' a bad woman."

'No wan said a wurrud for a time. They was all ashamed,
past spache.

'"Fwhat d'you think he will do?" sez wan av thim at last.
"He knows we're all in ut."

'"Are we so?" sez I from my cot. "The man that sez that to
me will be hurt. I do not know," sez I, "fwhat ondherhand
divilmint you have conthrived, but by fwhat I've seen I know
that you cannot commit murther wid another man's rifle—
such shakin' cowards you are. I'm goin' to slape," I sez, "an'
you can blow my head off whoile I lay." I did not slape,
though, for a long time. Can ye wonder?

'Next morn the news was through all the Rig'mint, an'
there was nothin' that the men did not tell. O'Hara reports,
fair an' aisy, that Vulmea was come to grief through
tamperin' wid his rifle in barricks, all for to show the
mechanism. An', by my sowl, he had the impart'nince to say
that he was on the shpot at the time an' cud certify that ut was
an accidint! You might ha' knocked my roomful down wid a
straw whin they heard that. 'Twas lucky for thim that the
bhoys were always thryin' to find out how the new rifle was
made, an' a lot av thim had come up for aisin' the pull by
shtickin' bits av grass an' such in the part av the lock that
showed near the thrigger. The first issues of the 'Tinis was
not covered in, an' I mesilf have aised the pull av mine time
an' agin. A light pull is ten points on the range to me.

'"I will not have this foolishness!" sez the Colonel. "I will
twist the tail off Vulmea!" sez he; but whin he saw him, all
tied up an' groanin' in hospital, he changed his will. "Make
him an early convalescint," sez he to the Doctor, an' Vulmea
was made so for a warnin'. His big bloody bandages an' face
puckered up to wan side did more to kape the bhoys from
messin' wid the insides av their rifles than any punishment.

'O'Hara gave no reason for fwhat he'd said, an' all my
roomful were too glad to ask, tho' he put his spite upon thim
more wearin' than before. Wan day, howiver, he tuk me
apart very polite, for he cud be that at his choosin'.

'"You're a good sodger, tho' you're a damned insolint man," sez he.

'"Fair wurruds, Sargint," sez I, "or I may be insolint agin."

'"'Tis not like you," sez he, "to lave your rifle in the rack widout the breech-pin, for widout the breech-pin she was whin Vulmea fired. I shud ha' found the break av ut in the eyes av the holes, else," he sez.

'"Sargint," sez I, "fwhat wud your life ha' been worth av the breech-pin had been in place, for, on my sowl, my life wud be worth just as much to me av I tould you whether ut was or was not? Be thankful the bullet was not there," I sez.

'"That's thrue," sez he, pulling his moustache; "but I do not believe that you, for all your lip, were in that business."

'"Sargint," sez I, "I cud hammer the life out av a man in ten minut's wid my fistes if that man dishplazed me; for I am a good sodger, an' I will be threated as such, an' whoile my fistes are my own they're strong enough for all the work I have to do. *They* do not fly back towards me!" sez I, lookin' him betune the eyes.

'"You're a good man," sez he, lookin' me betune the eyes—an' oh, he was a gran'-built man to see!—"you're a good man," he sez, "an' I cud wish, for the pure frolic av ut, that I was not a Sargint, or that you were not a Privit; an' you will think me no coward whin I say this thing."

'"I do not," sez I. "I saw you whin Vulmea mishandled the rifle. But, Sargint," I sez, "take the wurrud from me now, spakin' as man to man wid the shtripes off, tho' 'tis little right I have to talk, me bein fwhat I am by natur'. This time ye tuk no harm, an' next time ye may not, but, in the ind, so sure as Slimmy's wife came into the veranda, so sure will ye take harm—an' bad harm. Have thought, Sargint," sez I. "Is ut worth ut?"

'"Ye're a bould man," sez he, breathin' harrd. "A very bould man. But I am a bould man tu. Do you go your ways, Privit Mulvaney, an' I will go mine."

'We had no further spache thin or afther, but, wan by another, he drafted the twelve av my room out into other rooms an' got thim spread among the Comp'nies, for they was not a good breed to live together, an' the Comp'ny

Orf'cers saw ut. They wud ha' shot me in the night av they had known fwhat I knew; but that they did not.

'An', in the ind, as I said, O'Hara met his death from Rafferty for foolin' wid his wife. He wint his own way too well—Eyah, too well! Shtraight to that affair, widout turnin' to the right or to the lef', he wint, an' may the Lord have mercy on his sowl. Amin!'

''Ear! 'ear!' said Ortheris, pointing the moral with a wave of his pipe. 'An' this is 'im 'oo would be a bloomin' Vulmea all for the sake of Mullins an' a bloomin' button! Mullins never went after a woman in his life. Mrs Mullins, she saw 'im one day——'

'Ortheris,' I said hastily, for the romances of Private Ortheris are all too daring for publication, 'look at the sun. It's a quarter past six!'

'Oh, Lord! Three-quarters of an hour for five an' a 'arf miles! We'll 'ave to run like Jimmy O.'

The Three Musketeers clambered on to the bridge, and departed hastily in the direction of the cantonment road. When I overtook them I offered them two stirrups and a tail, which they accepted enthusiastically. Ortheris held the tail, and in this manner we trotted steadily through the shadows by an unfrequented road.

At the turn into the cantonments we heard carriage wheels. It was the Colonel's barouche,* and in it sat the Colonel's wife and daughter. I caught a suppressed chuckle, and my beast sprang forward with a lighter step.

The Three Musketeers had vanished into the night.

On the City Wall

Then she let them down by a cord through
the window; for her house was upon the
town wall, and she dwelt upon the wall.—
Joshua ii. 15*

LALUN is a member of the most ancient profession in the
world.* Lilith was her very-great-grandmamma, and that
was before the days of Eve, as every one knows.* In the West,
people say rude things about Lalun's profession, and write
lectures about it, and distribute the lectures to young persons
in order that Morality may be preserved. In the East, where
the profession is hereditary, descending from mother to
daughter, nobody writes lectures or takes any notice; and
that is a distinct proof of the inability of the East to manage its
own affairs.

Lalun's real husband, for even ladies of Lalun's profession
in the East must have husbands, was a big jujube-tree. Her
Mamma, who had married a fig-tree, spent ten thousand
rupees on Lalun's wedding, which was blessed by forty-
seven clergymen of Mamma's Church, and distributed five
ythousand rupees in charity to the poor. And that was the
custom of the land. The advantages of having a jujube-tree
for a husband are obvious. You cannot hurt his feelings, and
he looks imposing.

Lalun's husband stood on the plain outside the City
walls,* and Lalun's house was upon the east wall facing the
river. If you fell from the broad window-seat you dropped
thirty feet sheer into the City Ditch. But if you stayed where
you should and looked forth, you saw all the cattle of the City
being driven down to water, the students of the Government
College playing cricket, the high grass and trees that fringed
the river-bank, the great sand-bars that ribbed the river, the
red tombs of dead Emperors beyond the river, and very far
away through the blue heat-haze a glint of the snows of the
Himalayas.

Wali Dad used to lie in the window-seat for hours at a time

watching this view. He was a young Mohammedan who was
suffering acutely from education of the English variety and
knew it. His father had sent him to a Mission-school to get
wisdom, and Wali Dad had absorbed more than ever his
father or the Missionaries intended he should. When his
father died, Wali Dad was independent and spent two years
experimenting with the creeds of the Earth and reading
books that are of no use to anybody.

After he had made an unsuccessful attempt to enter the
Roman Catholic Church and the Presbyterian fold at the
same time (the Missionaries found him out and called him
names; but they did not understand his trouble), he discovered Lalun on the City wall and became the most constant
of her few admirers. He possessed a head that English artists
at home would rave over and paint amid impossible surroundings—a face that female novelists would use with
delight through nine hundred pages. In reality he was only a
clean-bred young Mohammedan, with pencilled eyebrows,
small-cut nostrils, little feet and hands, and a very tired look
in his eyes. By virtue of his twenty-two years he had grown a
neat black beard which he stroked with pride and kept
delicately scented. His life seemed to be divided between
borrowing books from me and making love to Lalun in the
window-seat. He composed songs about her, and some of the
songs are sung to this day in the City from the Street of the
Mutton-Butchers to the Copper-Smiths' ward.

One song, the prettiest of all, says that the beauty of Lalun
was so great that it troubled the hearts of the British Government and caused them to lose their peace of mind. That is the
way the song is sung in the streets; but, if you examine it
carefully and know the key to the explanation, you will find
that there are three puns in it—on 'beauty', 'heart', and
'peace of mind',—so that it runs: 'By the subtlety of Lalun
the administration of the Government was troubled and it
lost such-and-such a man.' When Wali Dad sings that song
his eyes glow like hot coals, and Lalun leans back among the
cushions and throws bunches of jasmine-buds at Wali Dad.

But first it is necessary to explain something about the
Supreme Government which is above all and below all and

behind all. Gentlemen come from England, spend a few weeks in India, walk round this great Sphinx of the Plains, and write books upon its ways and its works, denouncing or praising it as their own ignorance prompts. Consequently all the world knows how the Supreme Government conducts itself. But no one, not even the Supreme Government, knows everything about the administration of the Empire. Year by year England sends out fresh drafts for the first fighting-line, which is officially called the Indian Civil Service. These die, or kill themselves by overwork, or are worried to death, or broken in health and hope in order that the land may be protected from death and sickness, famine and war, and may eventually become capable of standing alone. It will never stand alone, but the idea is a pretty one, and men are willing to die for it, and yearly the work of pushing and coaxing and scolding and petting the country into good living goes forward. If an advance be made all credit is given to the native, while the Englishmen stand back and wipe their foreheads. If a failure occurs the Englishmen step forward and take the blame. Overmuch tenderness of this kind has bred a strong belief among many natives that the native is capable of administering the country, and many devout Englishmen believe this also, because the theory is stated in beautiful English with all the latest political colours.

There are other men who, though uneducated, see visions and dream dreams, and they, too, hope to administer the country in their own way—that is to say, with a garnish of Red Sauce. Such men must exist among two hundred million people, and, if they are not attended to, may cause trouble and even break the great idol called *Pax Britannica*, which, as the newspapers say, lives between Peshawur and Cape Comorin. Were the Day of Doom to dawn to-morrow, you would find the Supreme Government 'taking measures to allay popular excitement', and putting guards upon the graveyards that the Dead might troop forth orderly. The youngest Civilian would arrest Gabriel on his own responsibility if the Archangel could not produce a Deputy-Commissioner's permission to 'make music or other noises' as the licence says.

Whence it is easy to see that mere men of the flesh who would create a tumult must fare badly at the hands of the Supreme Government. And they do. There is no outward sign of excitement; there is no confusion; there is no knowledge. When due and sufficient reasons have been given, weighed and approved, the machinery moves forward, and the dreamer of dreams and the seer of visions is gone from his friends and following. He enjoys the hospitality of Government; there is no restriction upon his movements within certain limits; but he must not confer any more with his brother dreamers. Once in every six months the Supreme Government assures itself that he is well and takes formal acknowledgment of his existence. No one protests against his detention, because the few people who know about it are in deadly fear of seeming to know him; and never a single newspaper 'takes up his case' or organizes demonstrations on his behalf, because the newspapers of India have got behind that lying proverb which says the Pen is mightier than the Sword, and can walk delicately.

So now you know as much as you ought about Wali Dad, the educational mixture, and the Supreme Government.

Lalun has not yet been described. She would need, so Wali Dad says, a thousand pens of gold, and ink scented with musk. She has been variously compared to the Moon, the Dil Sagar Lake, a spotted quail, a gazelle, the Sun on the Desert of Kutch, the Dawn, the Stars, and the young bamboo. These comparisons imply that she is beautiful exceedingly according to the native standards, which are practically the same as those of the West. Her eyes are black and her hair is black, and her eyebrows are black as leeches; her mouth is tiny and says witty things; her hands are tiny and have saved much money; her feet are tiny and have trodden on the naked hearts of many men. But, as Wali Dad sings: 'Lalun *is* Lalun, and when you have said that, you have only come to the Beginnings of Knowledge.'

The little house on the City wall was just big enough to hold Lalun, and her maid, and a pussy-cat with a silver collar. A big pink-and-blue cut-glass chandelier hung from the ceiling of the reception room. A petty Nawab had given

Lalun the horror, and she kept it for politeness' sake. The
floor of the room was of polished chunam,* white as curds. A
lattice window of carved wood was set in one wall; there was a
profusion of squabby pluffy cushions and fat carpets
everywhere, and Lalun's silver hookah, studded with
turquoises, had a special little carpet all to its shining self.
Wali Dad was nearly as permanent a fixture as the chandelier.
As I have said, he lay in the window-seat and meditated on
Life and Death and Lalun—'specially Lalun. The feet of the
young men of the City tended to her doorways and then—
retired, for Lalun was a particular maiden, slow of speech,
reserved of mind, and not in the least inclined to orgies which
were nearly certain to end in strife. 'If I am of no value, I am
unworthy of this honour,' said Lalun. 'If I am of value, they
are unworthy of Me.' And that was a crooked sentence.

In the long hot nights of latter April and May all the City
seemed to assemble in Lalun's little white room to smoke and
to talk.* Shiahs of the grimmest and most uncompromising
persuasion; Sufis who had lost all belief in the Prophet and
retained but little in God; wandering Hindu priests passing
southward on their way to the Central India fairs and other
affairs; Pundits in black gowns, with spectacles on their
noses and undigested wisdom in their insides; bearded head-
men of the wards; Sikhs with all the details of the latest
ecclesiastical scandal in the Golden Temple; red-eyed priests
from beyond the Border, looking like trapped wolves and
talking like ravens; M.A.'s of the University, very superior
and very voluble—all these people and more also you might
find in the white room. Wali Dad lay in the window-seat and
listened to the talk.

'It is Lalun's *salon*,' said Wali Dad to me, 'and it is
electic—is not that the word? Outside of a Freemasons'
Lodge I have never seen such gatherings. *There* I dined once
with a Jew—a Yahoudi!' He spat into the City Ditch with
apologies for allowing national feelings to overcome him.
'Though I have lost every belief in the world,' said he, 'and
try to be proud of my losing, I cannot help hating a Jew.
Lalun admits no Jews here.'

'But what in the world do all these men do?' I asked.

'The curse of our country,' said Wali Dad. 'They talk. It is like the Athenians—always hearing and telling some new thing.* Ask the Pearl and she will show you how much she knows of the news of the City and the Province. Lalun knows everything.'

'Lalun,' I said at random—she was talking to a gentleman of the Kurd persuasion who had come in from God-knows-where—'when does the 175th Regiment go to Agra?'

'It does not go at all,' said Lalun, without turning her head. 'They have ordered the 118th to go in its stead. That Regiment goes to Lucknow in three months, unless they give a fresh order.'

'That is so,' said Wali Dad, without a shade of doubt. 'Can you, with your telegrams and your newspapers, do better? Always hearing and telling some new thing,' he went on. 'My friend, has your God ever smitten a European nation for gossiping in the bazars? India has gossiped for centuries— always standing in the bazars until the soldiers go by. Therefore—you are here to-day instead of starving in your own country, and I am not a Mohammedan—I am a Prod-uct—a Demnition Product.* *That* also I owe to you and yours: that I cannot make an end to my sentence without quoting from your authors.' He pulled at the hookah and mourned, half feelingly, half in earnest, for the shattered hopes of his youth. Wali Dad was always mourning over something or other—the country of which he despaired, or the creed in which he had lost faith, or the life of the English which he could by no means understand.

Lalun never mourned. She played little songs on the *sitar*,* and to hear her sing,'O Peacock, cry again,' was always a fresh pleasure. She knew all the songs that have ever been sung, from the war-songs of the South, that make the old men angry with the young men and the young men angry with the State, to the love-songs of the North, where the swords whinny-whicker like angry kites in the pauses between the kisses, and the Passes fill with armed men, and the Lover is torn from his Beloved and cries *Ai! Ai! Ai!* evermore. She knew how to make up tobacco for the pipe so that it smelt like the Gates of Paradise and wafted you gently through them. She could embroider strange things in gold and silver, and dance softly with the moonlight when it came in at the window. Also she knew the hearts of men, and the heart of the City, and whose wives were faithful and whose untrue, and more of the secrets of the Government Offices than are good to be set down in this place. Nasiban, her maid, said that her jewelry was worth ten thousand pounds, and that, some night, a thief would enter and murder her for its possession; but Lalun said that all the City would tear that thief limb from limb, and that he, whoever he was, knew it.

So she took her *sitar* and sat in the window-seat, and sang a song of old days that had been sung by a girl of her profession in an armed camp on the eve of a great battle—the day before the Fords of the Jumna ran red and Sivaji fled fifty miles to Delhi with a Toorkh stallion at his horse's tail and another Lalun on his saddle-bow.* It was what men call a Mahratta *laonee*, and it said:—

> Their warrior forces Chimnajee
> Before the Peishwa led,
> The Children of the Sun and Fire
> Behind him turned and fled.

And the chorus said:—

> With them there fought who rides so free
> With sword and turban red,
> The warrior-youth who earns his fee
> At peril of his head.

'At peril of his head,' said Wali Dad in English to me. 'Thanks to your Government, all our heads are protected, and with the educational facilities at my command'—his eyes twinkled wickedly—'I might be a distinguished member of the local administration. Perhaps, in time, I might even be a member of a Legislative Council.'

'Don't speak English,' said Lalun, bending over her *sitar* afresh. The chorus went out from the City wall to the blackened wall of Fort Amara which dominates the City. No man knows the precise extent of Fort Amara. Three kings built it hundreds of years ago, and they say that there are miles of underground rooms beneath its walls. It is peopled with many ghosts, a detachment of Garrison Artillery, and a Company of Infantry. In its prime it held ten thousand men and filled its ditches with corpses.

'At peril of his head,' sang Lalun again and again.

A head moved on one of the ramparts—the grey head of an old man—and a voice, rough as shark-skin on a sword-hilt, sent back the last line of the chorus and broke into a song that I could not understand, though Lalun and Wali Dad listened intently.

'What is it?' I asked. 'Who is it?'

'A consistent man,'* said Wali Dad. 'He fought you in '46, when he was a warrior-youth; refought you in '57, and he tried to fight you in '71, but you had learned the trick of blowing men from guns too well. Now he is old; but he would still fight if he could.'

'Is he a Wahabi,* then? Why should he answer to a Mahratta *laonee* if he be Wahabi—or Sikh?' said I.

'I do not know,' said Wali Dad. 'He has lost, perhaps, his religion. Perhaps he wishes to be a King. Perhaps he *is* a King. I do not know his name.'

'That is a lie, Wali Dad. If you know his career you must know his name.'

'That is quite true. I belong to a nation of liars. I would rather not tell you his name. Think for yourself.'

Lalun finished her song, pointed to the Fort, and said simply: 'Khem Singh.'

'Hm,' said Wali Dad. 'If the Pearl chooses to tell you, the Pearl is a fool.'

I translated to Lalun, who laughed. 'I choose to tell what I choose to tell. They kept Khem Singh in Burma,' said she. 'They kept him there for many years until his mind was changed in him. So great was the kindness of the Government. Finding this, they sent him back to his own country that he might look upon it before he died. He is an old man, but when he looks upon this his country his memory will come. Moreover, there be many who remember him.'

'He is an Interesting Survival,' said Wali Dad, pulling at the pipe. 'He returns to a country now full of educational and political reform, but, as the Pearl says, there are many who remember him. He was once a great man. There will never be any more great men in India. They will all, when they are boys, go whoring after strange gods, and they will become citizens—"fellow-citizens"—"illustrious   fellow-citizens". What is it that the native papers call them?'

Wali Dad seemed to be in a very bad temper. Lalun looked out of the window and smiled into the dust-haze. I went away thinking about Khem Singh, who had once made history with a thousand followers, and would have been a princeling but for the power of the Supreme Government aforesaid.

The Senior Captain Commanding Fort Amara was away on leave, but the Subaltern, his Deputy, had drifted down to the Club, where I found him and inquired of him whether it was really true that a political prisoner had been added to the attractions of the Fort. The Subaltern explained at great length, for this was the first time that he had held command of the Fort, and his glory lay heavy upon him.

'Yes,' said he, 'a man was sent in to me about a week ago from down the line—a thorough gentleman, whoever he is. Of course I did all I could for him. He had his two servants and some silver cooking-pots, and he looked for all the world like a native officer. I called him Subadar Sahib.* Just as well to be on the safe side, y'know. "Look here, Subadar Sahib," I said, "you're handed over to my authority, and I'm sup-posed to guard you. Now I don't want to make your life hard, but you must make things easy for me. All the Fort is at your disposal, from the flagstaff to the dry Ditch, and I shall be happy to entertain you in any way I can, but you mustn't take advantage of it. Give me your word that you won't try to escape, Subadar Sahib, and I'll give you my word that you shall have no heavy guard put over you." I thought the best way of getting at him was by going at him straight, y'know; and it was, by Jove! The old man gave me his word, and moved about the Fort as contented as a sick crow. He's a rummy chap—always asking to be told where he is and what the buildings about him are. I had to sign a slip of blue paper when he turned up, acknowledging receipt of his body and all that, and I'm responsible, y'know, that he doesn't get away. Queer thing, though, looking after a Johnnie old enough to be your grandfather, isn't it? Come to the Fort one of these days and see him.'

For reasons which will appear, I never went to the Fort while Khem Singh was then within its walls. I knew him only as a grey head seen from Lalun's window—a grey head and a harsh voice. But natives told me that, day by day, as he looked upon the fair lands round Amara, his memory came back to him and, with it, the old hatred against the Government that had been nearly effaced in far-off Burma. So he raged up and down the West face of the Fort from morning till noon and from evening till the night, devising vain things in his heart, and croaking war-songs when Lalun sang on the City wall. As he grew more acquainted with the Subaltern he unburdened his old heart of some of the passions that had withered it. 'Sahib,' he used to say, tapping his stick against the parapet, 'when I was a young man I was one of twenty thousand horsemen who came out of the City and rode round the plain here. Sahib, I was the leader of a hundred, then of a thousand, then of five thousand, and now!'—he pointed to his two servants. 'But from the beginning to to-day I would cut the throats of all the Sahibs in the land if I could. Hold me fast, Sahib, lest I get away and return to those who would follow me. I forgot them when I was in Burma, but now that I am in my own country again, I remember everything.'

'Do you remember that you have given me your Honour not to make your tendance a hard matter?' said the Subaltern.

'Yes, to you, only to you, Sahib,' said Khem Singh. 'To you because you are of a pleasant countenance. If my turn comes again, Sahib, I will not hang you nor cut your throat.'

'Thank you,' said the Subaltern gravely, as he looked along the line of guns that could pound the City to powder in half an hour. 'Let us go into our own quarters, Khem Singh. Come and talk with me after dinner.'

Khem Singh would sit on his own cushion at the Subaltern's feet, drinking heavy, scented aniseed brandy in great gulps, and telling strange stories of Fort Amara, which had been a palace in the old days, of Begums and Ranees tortured to death—in the very vaulted chamber that now served as a mess-room; would tell stories of Sobraon* that made the Subaltern's cheeks flush and tingle with pride of race, and of the Kuka rising* from which so much was expected and the fore-knowledge of which was shared by a hundred thousand souls. But he never told tales of '57 because, as he said, he was the Subaltern's guest, and '57 is a year that no man, Black or White, cares to speak of. Once only, when the aniseed brandy had slightly affected his head, he said: 'Sahib, speaking now of a matter which lay between Sobraon and the affair of the Kukas, it was ever a wonder to us that you stayed your hand at all, and that, having stayed it, you did not make the land one prison. Now I hear from without that you do great honour to all men of our country and by your own hands are destroying the Terror of your Name which is your strong rock and defence. This is a foolish thing. Will oil and water mix? Now in '57—'

'I was not born then, Subadar Sahib,' said the Subaltern, and Khem Singh reeled to his quarters.

The Subaltern would tell me of these conversations at the Club, and my desire to see Khem Singh increased. But Wali Dad, sitting in the window-seat of the house on the City wall, said that it would be a cruel thing to do, and Lalun pretended that I preferred the society of a grizzled old Sikh to hers.

'Here is tobacco, here is talk, here are many friends and all the news of the City, and, above all, here is myself. I will tell you stories and sing you songs, and Wali Dad will talk his English nonsense in your ears. Is that worse than watching the caged animal yonder? Go to-morrow then, if you must, but to-day such-and-such an one will be here, and he will speak of wonderful things.'

It happened that To-morrow never came, and the warm heat of the latter Rains gave place to the chill of early October almost before I was aware of the flight of the year. The Captain Commanding the Fort returned from leave and took over charge of Khem Singh according to the laws of seniority. The Captain was not a nice man. He called all natives 'niggers', which, besides being extreme bad form, shows gross ignorance.

'What's the use of telling off two Tommies to watch that old nigger?' said he.

'I fancy it soothes his vanity,' said the Subaltern. 'The men are ordered to keep well out of his way, but he takes them as a tribute to his importance, poor old chap.'

'I won't have Line men taken off regular guards in this way. Put on a couple of Native Infantry.'

'Sikhs?' said the Subaltern, lifting his eyebrows.

'Sikhs, Pathans, Dogras*—they're all alike, these black people,' and the Captain talked to Khem Singh in a manner which hurt that old gentleman's feelings. Fifteen years before, when he had been caught for the second time, every one looked upon him as a sort of tiger. He liked being regarded in this light. But he forgot that the world goes forward in fifteen years, and many Subalterns are promoted to Captaincies.

'The Captain-pig is in charge of the Fort?' said Khem Singh to his native guard every morning. And the native guard said: 'Yes, Subadar Sahib,' in deference to his age and his air of distinction; but they did not know who he was.

In those days the gathering in Lalun's little white room was always large and talked more than before.

'The Greeks,' said Wali Dad, who had been borrowing my books, 'the inhabitants of the city of Athens, where they were always hearing and telling some new thing, rigorously secluded their women—who were fools. Hence the glorious institution of the heterodox* women—is it not?—who were amusing and *not* fools. All the Greek philosophers delighted in their company. Tell me, my friend, how it goes now in Greece and the other places upon the Continent of Europe. Are your women-folk also fools?'

'Wali Dad,' I said, 'you never speak to us about your women-folk and we never speak about ours to you. That is the bar between us.'

'Yes,' said Wali Dad, 'it is curious to think that our common meeting-place should be here, in the house of a common—how do you call *her*?' He pointed with the pipe-mouth to Lalun.

'Lalun is nothing but Lalun,' I said, and that was perfectly true. 'But if you took your place in the world, Wali Dad, and gave up dreaming dreams——'

'I might wear an English coat and trousers. I might be a

leading Mohammedan pleader.* I might be received even at the Commissioner's tennis-parties where the English stand on one side and the natives on the other, in order to promote social intercourse throughout the Empire. Heart's Heart,' said he to Lalun quickly, 'the Sahib says that I ought to quit you.'

'The Sahib is always talking stupid talk,' returned Lalun with a laugh. 'In this house I am a Queen and thou art a King. The Sahib'—she put her arms above her head and thought for a moment—'the Sahib shall be our Vizier*—thine and mine, Wali Dad—because he has said that thou shouldst leave me.'

Wali Dad laughed immoderately, and I laughed too. 'Be it so,' said he. 'My friend, are you willing to take this lucrative Government appointment? Lalun, what shall his pay be?'

But Lalun began to sing, and for the rest of the time there was no hope of getting a sensible answer from her or Wali Dad. When the one stopped, the other began to quote Persian poetry with a triple pun in every other line. Some of it was not strictly proper, but it was all very funny, and it only came to an end when a fat person in black, with gold pince-nez, sent up his name to Lalun, and Wali Dad dragged me into the twinkling night to walk in a big rose-garden and talk heresies about Religion and Governments and a man's career in life.

The Mohurrum, the great mourning-festival of the Mohammedans, was close at hand, and the things that Wali Dad said about religious fanaticism would have secured his expulsion from the loosest-thinking Muslim sect. There were the rose-bushes round us, the stars above us, and from every quarter of the City came the boom of the big Mohurrum drums. You must know that the City is divided in fairly equal proportions between the Hindus and the Mussulmans, and where both creeds belong to the fighting races, a big religious festival gives ample chance for trouble. When they can—that is to say, when the authorities are weak enough to allow it— the Hindus do their best to arrange some minor feast-day of their own in time to clash with the period of general mourning for the martyrs Hasan and Hussain, the heroes of the

Mohurrum. Gilt and painted paper representations of their tombs are borne with shouting and wailing, music, torches, and yells, through the principal thoroughfares of the City; which fakements are called *tazias*. Their passage is rigorously laid down beforehand by the Police, and detachments of Police accompany each *tazia*, lest the Hindus should throw bricks at it and the peace of the Queen and the heads of Her loyal subjects should thereby be broken. Mohurrum time in a 'fighting' town means anxiety to all the officials, because, if a riot breaks out, the officials and not the rioters are held responsible. The former must foresee everything, and while not making their precautions ridiculously elaborate, must see that they are at least adequate.

'Listen to the drums!' said Wali Dad. 'That is the heart of the people—empty and making much noise. How, think you, will the Mohurrum go this year? *I* think that there will be trouble.'

He turned down a side-street and left me alone with the stars and a sleepy Police patrol. Then I went to bed and dreamed that Wali Dad had sacked the City and I was made Vizier, with Lalun's silver pipe for mark of office.

All day the Mohurrum drums beat in the City, and all day deputations of tearful Hindu gentlemen besieged the Deputy-Commissioner with assurances that they would be murdered ere next dawning by the Mohammedans. 'Which,' said the Deputy-Commissioner, in confidence to the Head of Police, 'is a pretty fair indication that the Hindus are going to make 'emselves unpleasant. I think we can arrange a little surprise for them. I have given the heads of both Creeds fair warning. If they choose to disregard it, so much the worse for them.'

There was a large gathering in Lalun's house that night, but of men that I had never seen before, if I except the fat gentleman in black with the gold pince-nez. Wali Dad lay in the window-seat, more bitterly scornful of his Faith and its manifestations than I had ever known him. Lalun's maid was very busy cutting up and mixing tobacco for the guests. We could hear the thunder of the drums as the processions accompanying each *tazia* marched to the central gathering-place in the plain outside the City, preparatory to their triumphant re-entry and circuit within the walls. All the streets seemed ablaze with torches, and only Fort Amara was black and silent.

When the noise of the drums ceased, no one in the white room spoke for a time. 'The first *tazia* has moved off,' said Wali Dad, looking to the plain.

'That is very early,' said the man with the pince-nez. 'It is only half-past eight.' The company rose and departed.

'Some of them were men from Ladakh,' said Lalun, when the last had gone. 'They brought me brick-tea such as the Russians sell, and a tea-urn from Peshawur. Show me, now, how the English Memsahibs make tea.'

The brick-tea was abominable. When it was finished Wali Dad suggested going into the streets. 'I am nearly sure that there will be trouble to-night,' he said. 'All the City thinks so, and *Vox Populi* is *Vox Dei*,* as the Babus say. Now I tell you that at the corner of the Padshahi Gate you will find my horse all this night if you want to go about and to see things. It is a most disgraceful exhibition. Where is the pleasure of saying "*Ya Hasan! Ya Hussain!*" twenty thousand times in a night?'

All the processions—there were two-and-twenty of them—were now well within the City walls. The drums were beating afresh, the crowd were howling '*Ya Hasan! Ya Hussain!*' and beating their breasts, the brass bands were playing their loudest, and at every corner where space allowed, Mohammedan preachers were telling the lamentable story of the death of the Martyrs. It was impossible to move except with the crowd, for the streets were not more than twenty feet wide. In the Hindu quarters the shutters of all the shops were up and cross-barred. As the first *tazia*, a gorgeous erection, ten feet high, was borne aloft on the shoulders of a score of stout men into the semi-darkness of the Gully of the Horsemen, a brickbat crashed through its talc and tinsel sides.

'Into thy hands, O Lord!' murmured Wali Dad profanely,* as a yell went up from behind, and a native officer of Police jammed his horse through the crowd. Another brickbat followed, and the *tazia* staggered and swayed where it had stopped.

'Go on! In the name of the Sirkar,* go forward!' shouted

the Policeman, but there was an ugly cracking and splinter-
ing of shutters, and the crowd halted, with oaths and growl-
ings, before the house whence the brickbat had been thrown.

Then, without any warning, broke the storm—not only in
the Gully of the Horsemen, but in half-a-dozen other places.
The *tazias* rocked like ships at sea, the long pole-torches
dipped and rose round them while the men shouted: 'The
Hindus are dishonouring the *tazias*! Strike! strike! Into their
temples for the Faith!' The six or eight Policemen with each
tazia drew their batons, and struck as long as they could in
the hope of forcing the mob forward, but they were overpowered, and as contingents of Hindus poured into the
streets, the fight became general. Half a mile away where the
tazias were yet untouched the drums and the shrieks of '*Ya
Hasan! Ya Hussain!*' continued, but not for long. The priests
at the corners of the streets knocked the legs from the
bedsteads that supported their pulpits and smote for the
Faith, while stones fell from the silent houses upon friend
and foe, and the packed streets bellowed: '*Din! Din! Din!*'* A
tazia caught fire, and was dropped for a flaming barrier
between Hindu and Mussulman at the corner of the Gully.
Then the crowd surged forward, and Wali Dad drew me
close to the stone pillar of a well.

'It was intended from the beginning!' he shouted in my
ear, with more heat than blank unbelief should be guilty of.
'The bricks were carried up to the houses beforehand. These
swine of Hindus! We shall be killing kine in their temples
to-night!'

Tazia after *tazia*, some burning, others torn to pieces,
hurried past us and the mob with them, howling, shrieking,
and striking at the house doors in their flight. At last we saw
the reason of the rush. Hugonin, the Assistant District Superintendent of Police, a boy of twenty, had got together thirty
constables and was forcing the crowd through the streets. His
old grey Police-horse showed no sign of uneasiness as it was
spurred breast-on into the crowd, and the long dog-whip
with which he had armed himself was never still.

'They know we haven't enough Police to hold 'em,' he
cried as he passed me, mopping a cut on his face. 'They *know*

we haven't! Aren't any of the men from the Club coming down to help? Get on, you sons of burnt fathers!' The dog-whip cracked across the writhing backs, and the constables smote afresh with baton and gun-butt. With these passed the lights and the shouting, and Wali Dad began to swear under his breath. From Fort Amara shot up a single rocket; then two side by side. It was the signal for troops.

Petitt, the Deputy-Commissioner, covered with dust and sweat, but calm and gently smiling, cantered up the clean-swept street in rear of the main body of the rioters. 'No one killed yet,' he shouted. 'I'll keep 'em on the run till dawn! Don't let 'em halt, Hugonin! Trot 'em about till the troops come.'

The science of the defence lay solely in keeping the mob on the move. If they had breathing-space they would halt and fire a house, and then the work of restoring order would be more difficult, to say the least of it. Flames have the same effect on a crowd as blood has on a wild beast.

Word had reached the Club, and men in evening-dress were beginning to show themselves and lend a hand in heading off and breaking up the shouting masses with stirrup-leathers, whips, or chance-found staves. They were not very often attacked, for the rioters had sense enough to know that the death of a European would not mean one hanging but many, and possibly the appearance of the thrice-dreaded Artillery. The clamour in the City redoubled. The Hindus had descended into the streets in real earnest and ere long the mob returned. It was a strange sight. There were no *tazias*—only their riven platforms—and there were no Police. Here and there a City dignitary, Hindu or Moham-medan, was vainly imploring his co-religionists to keep quiet and behave themselves—advice for which his white beard was pulled. Then a native officer of Police, unhorsed but still using his spurs with effect, would be borne along, warning all the crowd of the danger of insulting the Government. Everywhere men struck aimlessly with sticks, grasping each other by the throat, howling and foaming with rage, or beat with their bare hands on the doors of the houses.

'It is a lucky thing that they are fighting with natural

weapons,' I said to Wali Dad, 'else we should have half the City killed.'

I turned as I spoke and looked at his face. His nostrils were distended, his eyes were fixed, and he was smiting himself softly on the breast. The crowd poured by with renewed riot—a gang of Mussulmans hard pressed by some hundred Hindu fanatics. Wali Dad left my side with an oath, and shouting: '*Ya Hasan! Ya Hussain!*' plunged into the thick of the fight, where I lost sight of him.

I fled by a side alley to the Padshahi Gate, where I found Wali Dad's horse, and thence rode to the Fort. Once outside the City wall, the tumult sank to a dull roar, very impressive under the stars and reflecting great credit on the fifty thousand angry able-bodied men who were making it. The troops who, at the Deputy-Commissioner's instance, had been ordered to rendezvous quietly near the Fort, showed no signs of being impressed. Two companies of Native Infantry,* a squadron of Native Cavalry, and a company of British Infantry were kicking their heels in the shadow of the East face, waiting for orders to march in. I am sorry to say that they were all pleased, unholily pleased, at the chance of what they called 'a little fun'. The senior officers, to be sure, grumbled at having been kept out of bed, and the English troops pretended to be sulky, but there was joy in the hearts of all the subalterns, and whispers ran up and down the line: 'No ball-cartridge—what a beastly shame!' 'D'you think the beggars will really stand up to us?' 'Hope I shall meet my money-lender there. I owe him more than I can afford.' 'Oh, they won't let us even unsheath swords.' 'Hurrah! Up goes the fourth rocket. Fall in, there!'

The Garrison Artillery, who to the last cherished a wild hope that they might be allowed to bombard the City at a hundred yards' range, lined the parapet above the East gateway and cheered themselves hoarse as the British Infantry doubled along the road to the Main Gate of the City. The Cavalry cantered on to the Padshahi Gate, and the Native Infantry marched slowly to the Gate of the Butchers. The surprise was intended to be of a distinctly unpleasant nature, and to come on top of the defeat of the Police, who had been just able to keep the Mohammedans from firing the houses of a few leading Hindus. The bulk of the riot lay in the north and north-west wards. The east and south-east were by this time dark and silent, and I rode hastily to Lalun's house, for I wished to tell her to send some one in search of Wali Dad. The house was unlighted, but the door was open, and I climbed upstairs in the darkness. One small lamp in the white room showed Lalun and her maid leaning half out of the window, breathing heavily and evidently pulling at something that refused to come.

'Thou art late—very late,' gasped Lalun without turning her head. 'Help us now, O Fool, if thou hast not spent thy strength howling among the *tazias*. Pull! Nasiban and I can do no more! O Sahib, is it you? The Hindus have been hunting an old Mohammedan round the Ditch with clubs. If they find him again they will kill him. Help us to pull him up.'

I put my hands to the long red silk waist-cloth that was hanging out of the window, and we three pulled and pulled with all the strength at our command. There was something very heavy at the end, and it swore in an unknown tongue as it kicked against the City wall.

'Pull, oh, pull!' said Lalun at the last. A pair of brown hands grasped the window-sill and a venerable Mohammedan tumbled upon the floor, very much out of breath. His jaws were tied up, his turban had fallen over one eye, and he was dusty and angry.

Lalun hid her face in her hands for an instant and said something about Wali Dad that I could not catch.

Then, to my extreme gratification, she threw her arms round my neck and murmured pretty things. I was in no haste to stop her; and Nasiban, being a handmaiden of tact, turned to the big jewel-chest that stands in the corner of the white room and rummaged among the contents. The Mohammedan sat on the floor and glared.

'One service more, Sahib, since thou hast come so opportunely,' said Lalun. 'Wilt thou'—it is very nice to be thou-ed by Lalun—'take this old man across the City—the troops are everywhere, and they might hurt him, for he is old—to the

Kumharsen Gate? There I think he may find a carriage to take him to his house. He is a friend of mine, and thou art—more than a friend—therefore I ask this.'

Nasiban bent over the old man, tucked something into his belt, and I raised him up and led him into the streets. In crossing from the east to the west of the City there was no chance of avoiding the troops and the crowd. Long before I reached the Gully of the Horsemen I heard the shouts of the British Infantry crying cheerily: '*Hutt*, ye beggars! *Hutt*, ye devils! Get along! Go forward, there!' Then followed the ringing of rifle-butts and shrieks of pain. The troops were banging the bare toes of the mob with their gun-butts—for not a bayonet had been fixed. My companion mumbled and jabbered as we walked on until we were carried back by the crowd and had to force our way to the troops. I caught him by the wrist and felt a bangle there—the iron bangle of the Sikhs—but I had no suspicions, for Lalun had only ten minutes before put her arms round me. Thrice we were carried back by the crowd, and when we made our way past the British Infantry it was to meet the Sikh Cavalry driving another mob before them with the butts of their lances.

'What are these dogs?' said the old man.

'Sikhs of the Cavalry, Father,' I said, and we edged our way up the line of horses two abreast and found the Deputy-Commissioner, his helmet smashed on his head, surrounded by a knot of men who had come down from the Club as amateur constables and had helped the Police mightily.

'We'll keep 'em on the run till dawn,' said Petitt. 'Who's your villainous friend?'

I had only time to say: 'The Protection of the Sirkar!' when a fresh crowd flying before the Native Infantry carried us a hundred yards nearer to the Kumharsen Gate, and Petitt was swept away like a shadow.

'I do not know—I cannot see—this is all new to me!' moaned my companion. 'How many troops are there in the City?'

'Perhaps five hundred,' I said.

'A lakh* of men beaten by five hundred—and Sikhs among them! Surely, surely, I am an old man, but—the Kumharsen Gate is new. Who pulled down the stone lions? Where is the conduit? Sahib, I am a very old man, and, alas, I—I cannot stand.' He dropped in the shadow of the Kumharsen Gate where there was no disturbance. A fat gentleman wearing gold pince-nez came out of the darkness.

'You are most kind to bring my old friend,' he said suavely. 'He is a landholder of Akala. He should not be in a big City when there is religious excitement. But I have a carriage here. You are quite truly kind. Will you help me to put him into the carriage? It is very late.'

We bundled the old man into a hired victoria that stood close to the gate, and I turned back to the house on the City wall. The troops were driving the people to and fro, while the Police shouted, 'To your houses! Get to your houses!' and the dog-whip of the Assistant District Superintendent cracked remorselessly. Terror-stricken *bunnias** clung to the stirrups of the Cavalry, crying that their houses had been robbed (which was a lie), and the burly Sikh horsemen patted them on the shoulder and bade them return to those houses lest a worse thing should happen. Parties of five or six British soldiers, joining arms, swept down the side-gullies, their rifles on their backs, stamping, with shouting and song, upon the toes of Hindu and Mussulman. Never was religious enthusiasm more systematically squashed; and never were poor breakers of the peace more utterly weary and footsore. They were routed out of holes and corners, from behind well-pillars and byres, and bidden to go to their houses. If they had no houses to go to, so much the worse for their toes.

On returning to Lalun's door I stumbled over a man at the threshold. He was sobbing hysterically and his arms flapped like the wings of a goose. It was Wali Dad, Agnostic and Unbeliever, shoeless, turbanless, and frothing at the mouth, the flesh on his chest bruised and bleeding from the vehemence with which he had smitten himself. A broken torch-handle lay by his side, and his quivering lips murmured, '*Ya Hasan! Ya Hussain!*' as I stooped over him. I pushed him a few steps up the staircase, threw a pebble at Lalun's City window and hurried home.

Most of the streets were very still, and the cold wind that comes before the dawn whistled down them. In the centre of the Square of the Mosque a man was bending over a corpse. The skull had been smashed in by gun-butt or bamboo-stave.

'It is expedient that one man should die for the people,'* said Petitt grimly, raising the shapeless head. 'These brutes were beginning to show their teeth too much.'

And from afar we could hear the soldiers singing 'Two Lovely Black Eyes'* as they drove the remnant of the rioters within doors.

*   *   *   *   *

Of course you can guess what happened? I was not so clever. When the news went abroad that Khem Singh had escaped from the Fort, I did not, since I was then living this story, not writing it, connect myself, or Lalun, or the fat gentleman of the gold pince-nez, with his disappearance. Nor did it strike me that Wali Dad was the man who should have convoyed him across the City, or that Lalun's arms round my neck were put there to hide the money that Nasiban gave to Khem Singh, and that Lalun had used me and my white face as even a better safeguard than Wali Dad who proved himself so untrustworthy. All that I knew at the time was that, when Fort Amara was taken up with the riots, Khem Singh profited by the confusion to get away, and that his two Sikh guards also escaped.

But later on I received full enlightenment; and so did Khem Singh. He fled to those who knew him in the old days, but many of them were dead and more were changed, and all knew something of the Wrath of the Government. He went to the young men, but the glamour of his name had passed away, and they were entering native regiments or Government offices, and Khem Singh could give them neither pension, decorations, nor influence—nothing but a glorious death with their back to the mouth of a gun. He wrote letters and made promises, and the letters fell into bad hands, and a wholly insignificant subordinate officer of Police tracked them down and gained promotion thereby. Moreover, Khem Singh was old, and aniseed brandy was scarce, and he had left his silver cooking-pots in Fort Amara with his nice warm bedding, and the gentleman with the gold pince-nez was told by Those who had employed him that Khem Singh as a popular leader was not worth the money paid.

'Great is the mercy of these fools of English!' said Khem Singh when the situation was put before him. 'I will go back to Fort Amara of my own free will and gain honour. Give me good clothes to return in.'

So, at his own time, Khem Singh knocked at the wicket-gate of the Fort and walked to the Captain and the Subaltern, who were nearly grey-headed on account of correspondence that daily arrived from Simla marked 'Private'.

'I have come back, Captain Sahib,' said Khem Singh. 'Put no more guards over me. It is no good out yonder.'

A week later I saw him for the first time to my knowledge, and he made as though there were an understanding between us.

'It was well done, Sahib,' said he, 'and greatly I admired your astuteness in thus boldly facing the troops when I, whom they would have doubtless torn to pieces, was with you. Now there is a man in Fort Ooltagarh whom a bold man could with ease help to escape. This is the position of the Fort as I draw it on the sand——'

But I was thinking how I had become Lalun's Vizier after all.

The Man who would be King

Brother to a Prince and fellow to a beggar if
he be found worthy.*

THE Law, as quoted, lays down a fair conduct of life, and one
not easy to follow. I have been fellow to a beggar again and
again under circumstances which prevented either of us
finding out whether the other was worthy. I have still to be
brother to a Prince, though I once came near to kinship with
what might have been a veritable King, and was promised the
reversion of a Kingdom—army, law-courts, revenue, and
policy all complete. But, to-day, I greatly fear that my King is
dead, and if I want a crown I must go hunt it for myself.

The beginning of everything was in a railway train upon
the road to Mhow from Ajmir. There had been a Deficit in
the Budget, which necessitated travelling, not Second-class,
which is only half as dear as First-class, but by Intermediate,
which is very awful indeed. There are no cushions in the
Intermediate class, and the population are either Intermediate, which is Eurasian, or Native, which for a long night
journey is nasty, or Loafer,* which is amusing though
intoxicated. Intermediates do not buy from refreshment-
rooms. They carry their food in bundles and pots, and buy
sweets from the native sweetmeat-sellers, and drink the
roadside water. That is why in the hot weather Intermediates
are taken out of the carriages dead, and in all weathers are
most properly looked down upon.

My particular Intermediate happened to be empty till I
reached Nasirabad, when a big black-browed gentleman in
shirt-sleeves entered, and, following the custom of Intermediates, passed the time of day. He was a wanderer and a
vagabond like myself, but with an educated taste for whisky.
He told tales of things he had seen and done, of out-of-the-
way corners of the Empire into which he had penetrated, and
of adventures in which he risked his life for a few days' food.

'If India was filled with men like you and me, not knowing
more than the crows where they'd get their next day's

rations, it isn't seventy millions of revenue the land would be paying—it's seven hundred millions,' said he; and as I looked at his mouth and chin I was disposed to agree with him.

We talked politics—the politics of Loaferdom, that sees things from the underside where the lath and plaster is not smoothed off—and we talked postal arrangements because my friend wanted to send a telegram back from the next station to Ajmir, the turning-off place from the Bombay to the Mhow line as you travel westward. My friend had no money beyond eight annas, which he wanted for dinner, and I had no money at all, owing to the hitch in the Budget before mentioned. Further, I was going into a wilderness where, though I should resume touch with the Treasury, there were no telegraph offices. I was, therefore, unable to help him in any way.

'We might threaten a Station-master, and make him send a wire on tick,' said my friend, 'but that'd mean inquiries for you and for me, and *I*'ve got my hands full these days. Did you say you are travelling back along this line within any days?'

'Within ten,' I said.

'Can't you make it eight?' said he. 'Mine is rather urgent business.'

'I can send your telegram within ten days if that will serve you,' I said.

'I couldn't trust the wire to fetch him, now I think of it. It's this way. He leaves Delhi on the 23rd for Bombay. That means he'll be running through Ajmir about the night of the 23rd.'

'But I'm going into the Indian Desert,' I explained.

'Well *and* good,' said he. 'You'll be changing at Marwar Junction to get into Jodhpore territory—you must do that— and he'll be coming through Marwar Junction in the early morning of the 24th by the Bombay Mail. Can you be at Marwar Junction on that time? 'Twon't be inconveniencing you because I know that there's precious few pickings to be got out of these Central India States—even though you pretend to be correspondent of the *Backwoodsman*.'*

'Have you ever tried that trick?' I asked.

'Again and again, but the Residents* find you out, and then you get escorted to the border before you've time to get your knife into them. But about my friend here. I *must* give him a word o' mouth to tell him what's come to me or else he won't know where to go. I would take it more than kind of you if you was to come out of Central India in time to catch him at Marwar Junction, and say to him: "He has gone South for the week." He'll know what that means. He's a big man with a red beard, and a great swell he is. You'll find him sleeping like a gentleman with all his luggage round him in a second-class compartment. But don't you be afraid. Slip down the window, and say: "He has gone South for the week," and he'll tumble. It's only cutting your time of stay in those parts by two days. I ask you as a stranger—going to the West,'* he said with emphasis.

'Where have *you* come from?' said I.

'From the East,' said he, 'and I am hoping that you will give him the message on the Square—for the sake of my Mother as well as your own.'

Englishmen are not usually softened by appeals to the memory of their mothers, but for certain reasons, which will be fully apparent, I saw fit to agree.

'It's more than a little matter,' said he, 'and that's why I asked you to do it—and now I know that I can depend on you doing it. A second-class carriage at Marwar Junction, and a red-haired man asleep in it. You'll be sure to remember. I get out at the next station, and I must hold on there till he comes or sends me what I want.'

'I'll give the message if I catch him,' I said, 'and for the sake of your Mother as well as mine I'll give you a word of advice. Don't try to run the Central India States just now as the correspondent of the *Backwoodsman*. There's a real one knocking about there, and it might lead to trouble.'

'Thank you,' said he simply, 'and when will the swine be gone? I can't starve because he's ruining my work. I wanted to get hold of the Degumber Rajah down here about his father's widow, and give him a jump.'

'What did he do to his father's widow, then?'

'Filled her up with red pepper and slippered her to death as she hung from a beam. I found that out myself, and I'm the only man that would dare going into the State to get hush-money for it. They'll try to poison me, same as they did in Chortumna when I went on the loot there. But you'll give the man at Marwar Junction my message?'

He got out at a little roadside station, and I reflected. I had heard, more than once, of men personating correspondents of newspapers and bleeding small Native States with threats of exposure, but I had never met any of the caste before. They lead a hard life, and generally die with great sudden-ness. The Native States have a wholesome horror of English newspapers which may throw light on their peculiar methods of government, and do their best to choke correspondents with champagne, or drive them out of their mind with four-in-hand barouches.* They do not understand that nobody cares a straw for the internal administration of Native States so long as oppression and crime are kept within decent limits, and the ruler is not drugged, drunk, or diseased from one end of the year to the other. They are the dark places of the earth, full of unimaginable cruelty, touching the Railway and the Telegraph on one side, and, on the other, the days of Harun-al-Raschid.* When I left the train I did business with divers Kings, and in eight days passed through many changes of life. Sometimes I wore dress-clothes and consorted with Princes and Politicals,* drinking from crystal and eating from silver. Sometimes I lay out upon the ground and devoured what I could get, from a plate made of leaves, and drank the running water, and slept under the same rug as my servant. It was all in the day's work.

Then I headed for the Great Indian Desert upon the proper date, as I had promised, and the night mail set me down at Marwar Junction, where a funny, little, happy-go-lucky, native-managed railway runs to Jodhpore. The Bombay Mail from Delhi makes a short halt at Marwar. She arrived as I got in, and I had just time to hurry to her platform and go down the carriages. There was only one second-class on the train. I slipped the window and looked down upon a flaming red beard, half covered by a railway rug. That was my man, fast asleep, and I dug him gently in the ribs. He woke with a grunt, and I saw his face in the light of the lamps. It was a great and shining face.

'Tickets again?' said he.

'No,' said I. 'I am to tell you that he has gone South for the week. He has gone South for the week!'

The train had begun to move out. The red man rubbed his eyes. 'He has gone South for the week,' he repeated. 'Now that's just like his impidence. Did he say that I was to give you anything? Cause I won't.'

'He didn't,' I said, and dropped away, and watched the red lights die out in the dark. It was horribly cold because the wind was blowing off the sands. I climbed into my own train—not an Intermediate carriage this time—and went to sleep.

If the man with the beard had given me a rupee I should have kept it as a memento of a rather curious affair. But the consciousness of having done my duty was my only reward.

Later on I reflected that two gentlemen like my friends could not do any good if they forgathered and personated correspondents of newspapers, and might, if they black-mailed one of the little rat-trap states of Central India or Southern Rajputana, get themselves into serious difficulties. I therefore took some trouble to describe them as accurately as I could remember to people who would be interested in deporting them; and succeeded, so I was later informed, in having them headed back from the Degumber borders.

Then I became respectable, and returned to an office where there were no Kings and no incidents outside the daily manufacture of a newspaper. A newspaper office seems to attract every conceivable sort of person, to the prejudice of discipline. Zenana-mission* ladies arrive, and beg that the Editor will instantly abandon all his duties to describe a Christian prize-giving in a back-slum of a perfectly inaccess-ible village; Colonels who have been overpassed for com-mand sit down and sketch the outline of a series of ten, twelve, or twenty-four leading articles on Seniority *versus* Selection; Missionaries wish to know why they have not been permitted to escape from their regular vehicles of abuse and swear at a brother-missionary under special patronage of the editorial We; stranded theatrical companies troop up to explain that they cannot pay for their advertisements, but on their return from New Zealand or Tahiti will do so with interest; inventors of patent punkah-pulling machines,* carriage couplings, and unbreakable swords and axle-trees, call with specifications in their pockets and hours at their disposal; tea-companies enter and elaborate their prospectuses with the office pens; secretaries of ball-committees clamour to have the glories of their last dance more fully described; strange ladies rustle in and say, 'I want a hundred lady's cards printed *at once*, please,' which is manifestly part of an Editor's duty; and every dissolute ruffian that ever tramped the Grand Trunk Road makes it his business to ask for employment as a proof-reader. And, all the time, the telephone-bell is ringing madly, and Kings are being killed on the Continent, and Empires are saying, 'You're another,' and Mister Gladstone* is calling down brimstone upon the British Dominions and the little black copy-boys are whining, '*kaa-pi chay-ha-yeh*' [copy wanted] like tired bees, and most of the paper is as blank as Modred's shield.*

But that is the amusing part of the year. There are six other months when none ever comes to call, and the thermometer walks inch by inch up to the top of the glass, and the office is darkened to just above reading-light, and the press-machines are red-hot of touch, and nobody writes anything but accounts of amusements in the Hill-stations or obituary notices. Then the telephone becomes a tinkling terror, because it tells you of the sudden deaths of men and women that you knew intimately, and the prickly-heat covers you with a garment, and you sit down and write: 'A slight increase of sickness is reported from the Khuda Janta Khan District.* The outbreak is purely sporadic in its nature, and, thanks to the energetic efforts of the District authorities, is now almost at an end. It is, however, with deep regret we record the death, etc.'

Then the sickness really breaks out, and the less recording and reporting the better for the peace of the subscribers. But the Empires and the Kings continue to divert themselves as selfishly as before, and the Foreman thinks that a daily paper really ought to come out once in twenty-four hours, and all the people at the Hill-stations in the middle of their amusements say: 'Good gracious! Why can't the paper be sparkling? I'm sure there's plenty going on up here.'

That is the dark half of the moon, and, as the advertisements say, 'must be experienced to be appreciated'.

It was in that season, and a remarkably evil season, that the paper began running the last issue of the week on Saturday night, which is to say Sunday morning, after the custom of a London paper. This was a great convenience, for immediately after the paper was put to bed, the dawn would lower the temperature from 96° to almost 84° for half an hour, and in that chill—you have no idea how cold is 84° on the grass until you begin to pray for it—a very tired man could get off to sleep ere the heat roused him.

One Saturday night it was my pleasant duty to put the paper to bed alone. A King or a courtier or courtesan or a Community was going to die or get a new Constitution, or do something that was important on the other side of the world, and the paper was to be held open till the latest possible minute in order to catch the telegram.

It was a pitchy black night, as stifling as a June night can be, and the *loo*, the red-hot wind from the westward, was booming among the tinder-dry trees and pretending that the rain was on its heels. Now and again a spot of almost boiling water would fall on the dust with the flop of a frog, but all our weary world knew that was only pretence. It was a shade cooler in the press-room than the office, so I sat there, while the type ticked and clicked, and the night-jars hooted at the windows, and the all but naked compositors wiped the sweat from their foreheads, and called for water. The thing that was keeping us back, whatever it was, would not come off, though the *loo* dropped and the last type was set, and the whole round earth stood still in the choking heat, with its finger on its lip, to wait the event. I drowsed, and wondered whether the telegraph was a blessing, and whether this dying man, or struggling people, might be aware of the inconvenience the delay was causing. There was no special reason beyond the heat and worry to make tension, but, as the clock-hands crept up to three o'clock, and the machines spun their fly-wheels two or three times to see that all was in order before I said the word that would set them off, I could have shrieked aloud.

Then the roar and rattle of the wheels shivered the quiet into little bits. I rose to go away, but two men in white clothes stood in front of me. The first one said: 'It's him!' The second said: 'So it is!' And they both laughed almost as loudly as the machinery roared, and mopped their foreheads. 'We seed there was a light burning across the road, and we were sleeping in that ditch there for coolness, and I said to my friend here, "The office is open. Let's come along and speak to him as turned us back from the Degumber State,"' said the smaller of the two. He was the man I had met in the Mhow train, and his fellow was the red-haired man of Marwar Junction. There was no mistaking the eyebrows of the one or the beard of the other.

I was not pleased, because I wished to go to sleep, not to squabble with loafers. 'What do you want?' I asked.

'Half an hour's talk with you, cool and comfortable, in the office,' said the red-bearded man. 'We'd *like* some drink—the Contrack doesn't begin yet, Peachey, so you needn't look—but what we really want is advice. We don't want money. We ask you as a favour, because we found out you did us a bad turn about Degumber State.'

I led from the press-room to the stifling office with the maps on the walls, and the red-haired man rubbed his hands. 'That's something like,' said he. 'This was the proper shop to come to. Now, sir, let me introduce to you Brother Peachey Carnehan,* that's him, and Brother Daniel Dravot, that is *me*, and the less said about our professions the better, for we have been most things in our time. Soldier, sailor, compositor, photographer, proof-reader, street-preacher, *and* correspondent of the *Backwoodsman* when we thought the paper wanted one. Carnehan is sober, and so am I. Look at us first, and see that's sure. It will save you cutting into my talk. We'll take one of your cigars apiece, and you shall see us light up.'

I watched the test. The men were absolutely sober, so I gave them each a tepid whisky and soda.

'Well *and* good,' said Carnehan of the eyebrows, wiping

the froth from his moustache. 'Let *me* talk now, Dan. We have been all over India, mostly on foot. We have been boiler-fitters, engine-drivers, petty contractors, and all that, and we have decided that India isn't big enough for such as us.'

They certainly were too big for the office. Dravot's beard seemed to fill half the room and Carnehan's shoulders the other half, as they sat on the big table. Carnehan continued: 'The country isn't half worked out because they that governs it won't let you touch it. They spend all their blessed time in governing it, and you can't lift a spade, nor chip a rock, nor look for oil, nor anything like that, without all the Government saying, "Leave it alone, and let us govern." Therefore, such *as* it is, we will let it alone, and go away to some other place where a man isn't crowded and can come to his own. We are not little men, and there is nothing that we are afraid of except Drink, and we have signed a Contrack on that. *Therefore*, we are going away to be Kings.'

'Kings in our own right,' muttered Dravot.

'Yes, of course,' I said. 'You've been tramping in the sun, and it's a very warm night, and hadn't you better sleep over the notion? Come to-morrow.'

'Neither drunk nor sunstruck,' said Dravot. 'We have slept over the notion half a year, and require to see Books and Atlases, and we have decided that there is only one place now in the world that two strong men can Sar-a-*whack*.* They call it Kafiristan.* By my reckoning it's the top right-hand corner of Afghanistan, not more than three hundred miles from Peshawur. They have two-and-thirty heathen idols there, and we'll be the thirty-third and fourth. It's a mountainous country, and the women of those parts are very beautiful.'

'But that is provided against in the Contrack,' said Carnehan. 'Neither Woman nor Liqu-or, Daniel.'

'And that's all we know, except that no one has gone there, and they fight; and in any place where they fight, a man who knows how to drill men can always be a King. We shall go to those parts and say to any King we find—"D'you want to vanquish your foes?" and we will show him how to drill men; for that we know better than anything else. Then we will subvert that King and seize his Throne and establish a Dy-nasty.'

'You'll be cut to pieces before you're fifty miles across the Border,' I said. 'You have to travel through Afghanistan to get to that country. It's one mass of mountains and peaks and glaciers, and no Englishman has been through it. The people are utter brutes, and even if you reached them you couldn't do anything.'

'That's more like,' said Carnehan. 'If you could think us a little more mad we would be more pleased. We have come to you to know about this country, to read a book about it, and to be shown maps. We want you to tell us that we are fools and to show us your books.' He turned to the bookcases.

'Are you at all in earnest?' I said.

'A little,' said Dravot sweetly. 'As big a map as you have got, even if it's all blank where Kafiristan is, and any books you've got. We can read, though we aren't very educated.'

I uncased the big thirty-two-miles-to-the-inch map of India, and two smaller Frontier maps, hauled down volume INF-KAN* of the *Encyclopædia Britannica*, and the men consulted them.

'See here!' said Dravot, his thumb on the map. 'Up to Jagdallak, Peachey and me know the road. We was there with Roberts' Army.* We'll have to turn off to the right at Jagdallak through Laghman territory. Then we get among the hills—fourteen thousand feet—fifteen thousand—it will be cold work there, but it don't look very far on the map.'

I handed him Wood on the *Sources of the Oxus*. Carnehan was deep in the *Encyclopædia*.

'They're a mixed lot,' said Dravot reflectively; 'and it won't help us to know the names of their tribes. The more tribes the more they'll fight, and the better for us. From Jagdallak to Ashang—H'mm!'

'But all the information about the country is as sketchy and inaccurate as can be,' I protested. 'No one knows anything about it really. Here's the file of the *United Services' Institute*. Read what Bellew says.'

'Blow Bellew!' said Carnehan. 'Dan, they're a stinkin' lot

of heathens, but this book here says they think they're related to us English.'

I smoked while the men pored over Raverty, Wood, the maps, and the *Encyclopædia*.

'There is no use your waiting,' said Dravot politely. 'It's about four o'clock now. We'll go before six o'clock if you want to sleep, and we won't steal any of the papers. Don't you sit up. We're two harmless lunatics, and if you come to-morrow evening down to the Serai we'll say goodbye to you.'

'You *are* two fools,' I answered. 'You'll be turned back at the Frontier or cut up the minute you set foot in Afghanistan. Do you want any money or a recommendation down-country? I can help you to the chance of work next week.'

'Next week we shall be hard at work ourselves, thank you,' said Dravot. 'It isn't so easy being a King as it looks. When we've got our Kingdom in going order we'll let you know, and you can come up and help us to govern it.'

'Would two lunatics make a Contrack like that?' said Carnehan, with subdued pride, showing me a greasy half-sheet of notepaper on which was written the following. I copied it, then and there, as a curiosity:—

This Contract between me and you persuing witnesseth in the name of God—Amen and so forth.

    (One)   That me and you will settle this matter together; i.e. to be
            Kings of Kafiristan.

    (Two)   That you and me will not, while this matter is being settled,
            look at any Liquor, nor any Woman black, white, or brown,
            so as to get mixed up with one or the other harmful.

    (Three)   That we conduct ourselves with Dignity and Discretion, and
            if one of us gets into trouble the other will stay by him.

   Signed by you and me this day.

      Peachey Taliaferro Carnehan.
      Daniel Dravot.
      Both Gentlemen at Large.

'There was no need for the last article,' said Carnehan, blushing modestly; 'but it looks regular. Now you know the sort of men that loafers are—we *are* loafers, Dan, until we get out of India—and *do* you think that we would sign a Contrack like that unless we was in earnest? We have kept away from the two things that make life worth having.'

'You won't enjoy your lives much longer if you are going to try this idiotic adventure. Don't set the office on fire,' I said, 'and go away before nine o'clock.'

I left them still poring over the maps and making notes on the back of the 'Contrack'. 'Be sure to come down to the Serai* to-morrow,' were their parting words.

The Kumharsen Serai is the great four-square sink of humanity where the strings of camels and horses from the North load and unload. All the nationalities of Central Asia may be found there, and most of the folk of India proper. Balkh and Bokhara there meet Bengal and Bombay, and try to draw eye-teeth. You can buy ponies, turquoises, Persian pussy-cats, saddle-bags, fat-tailed sheep and musk in the Kumharsen Serai, and get many strange things for nothing. In the afternoon I went down to see whether my friends intended to keep their word or were lying there drunk.

A priest attired in fragments of ribbons and rags stalked up to me, gravely twirling a child's paper whirligig.* Behind him was his servant bending under the load of a crate of mud toys. The two were loading up two camels, and the inhabitants of the Serai watched them with shrieks of laughter.

'The priest is mad,' said a horse-dealer to me. 'He is going up to Kabul to sell toys to the Amir. He will either be raised to honour or have his head cut off. He came in here this morning and has been behaving madly ever since.'

'The witless are under the protection of God,' stammered a flat-cheeked Uzbeg in broken Hindi. 'They foretell future events.'

'Would they could have foretold that my caravan would have been cut up by the Shinwaris almost within shadow of the Pass!' grunted the Yusufzai agent of a Rajputana trading-house whose goods had been diverted into the hands of other robbers just across the Border, and whose misfortunes were the laughing-stock of the bazar. 'Ohé, priest, whence come you and whither do you go?'

'From Roum* have I come,' shouted the priest, waving his

whirligig; 'from Roum, blown by the breath of a hundred devils across the sea! O thieves, robbers, liars, the blessing of Pir Khan on pigs, dogs, and perjurers! Who will take the Protected of God to the North to sell charms that are never still to the Amir?* The camels shall not gall, the sons shall not fall sick, and the wives shall remain faithful while they are away, of the men who give me place in their caravan. Who will assist me to slipper the King of the Roos* with a golden slipper with a silver heel? The protection of Pir Khan be upon his labours!' He spread out the skirts of his gaberdine and pirouetted between the lines of tethered horses.

'There starts a caravan from Peshawur to Kabul in twenty days, *Huzrut*,'* said the Yusufzai trader. 'My camels go therewith. Do thou also go and bring us good luck.'

'I will go even now!' shouted the priest. 'I will depart upon my winged camels, and be at Peshawur in a day! Ho! Hazar* Mir Khan,' he yelled to his servant, 'drive out the camels, but let me first mount my own.'

He leaped on the back of his beast as it knelt, and, turning to me, cried: 'Come thou also, Sahib, a little along the road, and I will sell thee a charm—an amulet that shall make thee King of Kafiristan.'

Then the light broke upon me, and I followed the two camels out of the Serai till we reached open road and the priest halted.

'What d'you think o' that?' said he in English. 'Carnehan can't talk their patter, so I've made him my servant. He makes a handsome servant. 'Tisn't for nothing that I've been knocking about the country for fourteen years. Didn't I do that talk neat? We'll hitch onto a caravan at Peshawur till we get to Jagdallak, and then we'll see if we can get donkeys for our camels, and strike into Kafiristan. Whirligigs for the Amir, oh, Lor! Put your hand under the camel-bags and tell me what you feel.'

I felt the butt of a Martini*, and another and another.

'Twenty of 'em,' said Dravot placidly. 'Twenty of 'em and ammunition to correspond, under the whirligigs and the mud dolls.'

'Heaven help you if you are caught with those things!' I

said. 'A Martini is worth her weight in silver among the Pathans.'*

'Fifteen hundred rupees of capital—every rupee we could beg, borrow, or steal—are invested on these two camels,' said Dravot. 'We won't get caught. We're going through the Khyber with a regular caravan. Who'd touch a poor mad priest?'

'Have you got everything you want?' I asked, overcome with astonishment.

'Not yet, but we shall soon. Give us a memento of your kindness, *Brother*. You did me a service, yesterday, and that time in Marwar. Half my Kingdom shall you have, as the saying is.' I slipped a small charm compass from my watch-chain and handed it up to the priest.

'Good-bye,' said Dravot, giving me hand cautiously. 'It's the last time we'll shake hands with an Englishman these many days. Shake hands with him, Carnehan,' he cried, as the second camel passed me.

Carnehan leaned down and shook hands. Then the camels passed away along the dusty road, and I was left alone to wonder. My eye could detect no failure in the disguises. The scene in the Serai proved that they were complete to the native mind. There was just the chance, therefore, that Carnehan and Dravot would be able to wander through Afghanistan without detection. But, beyond, they would find death—certain and awful death.

Ten days later a native correspondent, giving me the news of the day from Peshawur, wound up his letter with: 'There has been much laughter here on account of a certain mad priest who is going in his estimation to sell petty gauds and insignificant trinkets which he ascribes as great charms to H.H. the Amir of Bokhara. He passed through Peshawur and associated himself to the Second Summer caravan that goes to Kabul. The merchants are pleased because through superstition they imagine that such mad fellows bring good fortune.'

The two, then, were beyond the Border. I would have prayed for them, but, that night, a real King died in Europe, and demanded an obituary notice.

*   *   *   *   *

The wheel of the world swings through the same phases again and again. Summer passed and winter thereafter, and came and passed again. The daily paper continued and I with it, and upon the third summer there fell a hot night, a night-issue, and a strained waiting for something to be telegraphed from the other side of the world, exactly as had happened before. A few great men had died in the past two years, the machines worked with more clatter, and some of the trees in the office garden were a few feet taller. But that was all the difference.

I passed over to the press-room, and went through just such a scene as I have already described. The nervous tension was stronger than it had been two years before, and I felt the heat more acutely. At three o'clock I cried, 'Print off,' and turned to go, when there crept to my chair what was left of a man. He was bent into a circle, his head was sunk between his shoulders, and he moved his feet one over the other like a bear. I could hardly see whether he walked or crawled—this rag-wrapped, whining cripple who addressed me by name, crying that he was come back. 'Can you give me a drink?' he whimpered. 'For the Lord's sake, give me a drink!'

I went back to the office, the man following with groans of pain, and I turned up the lamp.

'Don't you know me?' he gasped, dropping into a chair, and he turned his drawn face, surmounted by a shock of grey hair, to the light.

I looked at him intently. Once before had I seen eyebrows that met over the nose in an inch-broad black band, but for the life of me I could not recall where.

'I don't know you,' I said, handing him the whisky. 'What can I do for you?'

He took a gulp of the spirit raw, and shivered in spite of the suffocating heat.

'I've come back,' he repeated; 'and I was the King of Kafiristan—me and Dravot—crowned Kings we was! In this office we settled it—you setting there and giving us the books. I am Peachey—Peachey Taliaferro Carnehan, and you've been setting here ever since—oh, Lord!'

I was more than a little astonished, and expressed my feelings accordingly.

'It's true,' said Carnehan, with a dry cackle, nursing his feet, which were wrapped in rags. 'True as gospel. Kings we were, with crowns upon our heads—me and Dravot—poor Dan—oh, poor, poor Dan, that would never take advice, not though I begged of him!'

'Take the whisky,' I said, 'and take your own time. Tell me all you can recollect of everything from beginning to end. You got across the Border on your camels, Dravot dressed as a mad priest and you his servant. Do you remember that?'

'I ain't mad—yet, but I shall be that way soon. Of course I remember. Keep looking at me, or maybe my words will go all to pieces. Keep looking at me in my eyes and don't say anything.'

I leaned forward and looked into his face as steadily as I could. He dropped one hand upon the table and I grasped it by the wrist. It was twisted like a bird's claw, and upon the back was a ragged red diamond-shaped scar.

'No, don't look there. Look at *me*,' said Carnehan. 'That comes afterwards, but for the Lord's sake don't distrack me. We left with that caravan, me and Dravot playing all sorts of antics to amuse the people we were with. Dravot used to make us laugh in the evenings when all the people was cooking their dinners—cooking their dinners, and . . . what did they do then? They lit little fires with sparks that went into Dravot's beard, and we all laughed—fit to die. Little red fires they was, going into Dravot's big red beard—so funny.' His eyes left mine and he smiled foolishly.

'You went as far as Jagdallak with that caravan,' I said at a venture, 'after you had lit those fires. To Jagdallak where you turned off to try to get into Kafiristan.'

'No, we didn't neither. What are you talking about? We turned off before Jagdallak, because we heard the roads was good. But they wasn't good enough for our two camels—mine and Dravot's. When we left the caravan, Dravot took off all his clothes and mine too, and said we would be heathen, because the Kafirs* didn't allow Mohammedans to talk to them. So we dressed betwixt and between, and such a

sight as Daniel Dravot I never saw yet nor expect to see again.
He burned half his beard, and slung a sheep-skin over his
shoulder, and shaved his head into patterns. He shaved
mine, too, and made me wear outrageous things to look like a
heathen. That was in a most mountainous country, and our
camels couldn't go along any more because of the mountains.
They were tall and black, and coming home I saw them fight
like wild goats—there are lots of goats in Kafiristan. And
these mountains, they never keep still, no more than the
goats. Always fighting they are, and don't let you sleep at
night.'

'Take some more whisky,' I said very slowly. 'What did
you and Daniel Dravot do when the camels could go no
farther because of the rough roads that led into Kafiristan?'

'What did which do? There was a party called Peachey
Taliaferro Carnehan that was with Dravot. Shall I tell you
about him? He died out there in the cold. Slap from the
bridge fell old Peachey, turning and twisting in the air like a
penny whirligig that you can sell to the Amir.—No; they was
two for three-ha'pence, those whirligigs, or I am much
mistaken and woeful sore. . . . And then these camels were no
use, and Peachey said to Dravot—"For the Lord's sake let's
get out of this before our heads are chopped off," and with
that they killed the camels all among the mountains, not
having anything in particular to eat, but first they took off the
boxes with the guns and the ammunition, till two men came
along driving four mules. Dravot up and dances in front of
them, singing: "Sell me four mules." Says the first man: "If
you are rich enough to buy, you are rich enough to rob"; but
before ever he could put his hand to his knife, Dravot breaks
his neck over his knee, and the other party runs away. So
Carnehan loaded the mules with the rifles that was taken off
the camels, and together we starts forward into those bitter
cold mountaineous parts, and never a road broader than the
back of your hand.'

He paused for a moment, while I asked him if he could
remember the nature of the country through which he had
journeyed.

'I am telling you as straight as I can, but my head isn't as good as it might be. They drove nails through it to make me hear better how Dravot died. The country was mountaineous, and the mules were most contrary, and the inhabitants was dispersed and solitary. They went up and up, and down and down, and that other party, Carnehan, was imploring of Dravot not to sing and whistle so loud, for fear of bringing down the tremenjus avalanches. But Dravot says that if a King couldn't sing it wasn't worth being King, and whacked the mules over the rump, and never took no heed for ten cold days. We came to a big level valley all among the mountains, and the mules were near dead, so we killed them, not having anything in special for them or us to eat. We sat upon the boxes, and played odd and even with the cartridges that was jolted out.

'Then ten men with bows and arrows ran down that valley, chasing twenty men with bows and arrows, and the row was tremenjus. They was fair men—fairer than you or me—with yellow hair and remarkable well built.* Says Dravot, unpacking the guns: "This is the beginning of the business. We'll fight for the ten men," and with that he fires two rifles at the twenty men, and drops one of them at two hundred yards from the rock where he was sitting. The other men began to run, but Carnehan and Dravot sits on the boxes picking them off at all ranges, up and down the valley. Then we goes up to the ten men that had run across the snow too, and they fires a footy little arrow at us. Dravot he shoots above their heads and they all falls down flat. Then he walks over them and kicks them, and then he lifts them up and shakes hands all round to make them friendly like. He calls them and gives them the boxes to carry, and waves his hand for all the world as though he was King already. They takes the boxes and him across the valley and up the hill into a pine wood on the top, where there was half-a-dozen big stone idols. Dravot he goes to the biggest—a fellow they call Imbra*—and lays a rifle and a cartridge at his feet, rubbing his nose respectful with his own nose, patting him on the head, and saluting in front of it. He turns round to the men and nods his head and says: "That's all right. I'm in the know too, and all these old jim-jams are my friends." Then he opens his mouth and points down it, and when the first man brings him food, he says: "No"; and when the second man brings him food, he says: "No"; but when one of the old priests and the boss of the village brings him food, he says: "Yes," very haughty, and eats it slow. That was how we came to our first village, without any trouble, just as though we had tumbled from the skies. But we tumbled from one of those damned rope-bridges, you see, and—you couldn't expect a man to laugh much after that?'

'Take some more whisky and go on,' I said. 'That was the first village you came into. How did you get to be King?'

'I wasn't King,' said Carnehan. 'Dravot he was the King, and a handsome man he looked with the gold crown on his head and all. Him and the other party stayed in that village, and every morning Dravot sat by the side of old Imbra, and the people came and worshipped. That was Dravot's order. Then a lot of men came into the valley, and Carnehan and Dravot picks them off with the rifles before they knew where they was, and runs down into the valley and up again the other side and finds another village, same as the first one, and the people all falls down flat on their faces, and Dravot says: "Now what is the trouble between you two villages?" and the people points to a woman, as fair as you or me, that was carried off, and Dravot takes her back to the first village and counts up the dead—eight there was. For each dead man Dravot pours a little milk on the ground and waves his arms like a whirligig, and "That's all right," says he. Then he and Carnehan takes the big boss of each valley by the arm and walks them down into the valley, and shows them how to scratch a line with a spear right down the valley, and gives each a sod of turf from both sides of the line. Then all the people comes down and shouts like the devil and all, and Dravot says: "Go and dig the land, and be fruitful and multiply,"* which they did, though they didn't understand. Then we asks the names of things in their lingo—bread and water and fire and idols and such, and Dravot leads the priest of each village up to the idol, and says he must sit there and judge the people, and if anything goes wrong he is to be shot.

'Next week they was all turning up the land in the valley as quiet as bees and much prettier, and the priests heard all the complaints and told Dravot in dumb show what it was about. "That's just the beginning," says Dravot. "They think we're Gods." He and Carnehan picks out twenty good men and shows them how to click off a rifle, and form fours, and advance in line, and they was very pleased to do so, and clever to see the hang of it. Then he takes out his pipe and his baccy-pouch and leaves one at one village, and one at the other, and off we two goes to see what was to be done in the next valley. That was all rock, and there was a little village there, and Carnehan says: "Send 'em to the old valley to plant," and takes 'em there, and gives 'em some land that wasn't took before. They were a poor lot, and we blooded 'em with a kid before letting 'em into the new Kingdom. That was to impress the people, and then they settled down quiet, and Carnehan went back to Dravot, who had got into another valley, all snow and ice and most mountaineous. There was no people there and the Army got afraid, so Dravot shoots one of them, and goes on till he finds some people in a village, and the Army explains that unless the people wants to be killed they had better not shoot their little matchlocks; for they had matchlocks.* We makes friends with the priest, and I stays there alone with two of the Army, teaching the men how to drill, and a thundering big Chief comes across the snow with kettle-drums and horns twanging, because he heard there was a new God kicking about. Carnehan sights for the brown* of the men half a mile across the snow and wings one of them. Then he sends a message to the Chief that, unless he wished to be killed, he must come and shake hands with me and leave his arms behind. The Chief comes alone first, and Carnehan shakes hands with him and whirls his arms about, same as Dravot used, and very much surprised that Chief was, and strokes my eyebrows. Then Carnehan goes alone to the Chief, and asks him in dumb show if he had an enemy he hated. "I have," says the Chief. So Carnehan weeds out the pick of his men, and sets the two of the Army to show them drill, and at the end of two weeks the men can manœuvre about as well as Volunteers. So he marches with the Chief to a great big plain on the top of a mountain, and the Chief's men rushes into a village and takes it; we three Martinis firing into the brown of the enemy. So we took that village too, and I gives the Chief a rag from my coat and says, "Occupy till I come";* which was scriptural. By way of a reminder, when me and the Army was eighteen hundred yards away, I drops a bullet near him standing on the snow, and all the people falls flat on their faces. Then I sends a letter to Dravot wherever he be by land or by sea.'

At the risk of throwing the creature out of train I interrupted: 'How could you write a letter up yonder?'

'The letter?—Oh!—The letter! Keep looking at me between the eyes, please. It was a string-talk letter, that we'd learned the way of it from a blind beggar in the Punjab.'

I remembered that there had once come to the office a blind man with a knotted twig and a piece of string which he wound round the twig according to some cipher of his own. He could, after the lapse of days or weeks, repeat the sentence which he had reeled up. He had reduced the alphabet to eleven primitive sounds, and tried to teach me his method, but I could not understand.

'I sent that letter to Dravot,' said Carnehan; 'and told him to come back because this Kingdom was growing too big for me to handle, and then I struck for the first valley, to see how the priests were working. They called the village we took along with the Chief, Bashkai, and the first village we took, Er-Heb. The priests at Er-Heb was doing all right, but they had a lot of pending cases about land to show me, and some men from another village had been firing arrows at night. I went out and looked for that village, and fired four rounds at it from a thousand yards. That used all the cartridges I cared to spend, and I waited for Dravot, who had been away two or three months, and I kept my people quiet.

'One morning I heard the devil's own noise of drums and horns, and Dan Dravot marches down the hill with his Army and a tail of hundreds of men, and, which was the most amazing, a great gold crown on his head. "My Gord, Carnehan," says Daniel, "this is a tremenjus business, and we've got the whole country as far as it's worth having. I am the son of Alexander by Queen Semiramis,* and you're my younger brother and a God too! It's the biggest thing we've ever seen. I've been marching and fighting for six weeks with the Army, and every footy little village for fifty miles has come in rejoiceful; and more than that, I've got the key of the whole show, as you'll see, and I've got a crown for you! I told 'em to make two of 'em at a place called Shu, where the gold lies in the rock like suet in mutton. Gold I've seen, and turquoise I've kicked out of the cliffs, and there's garnets in the sands of the river, and here's a chunk of amber that a man brought me. Call up all the priests and, here, take your crown."

'One of the men opens a black hair bag, and I slips the crown on. It was too small and too heavy, but I wore it for the glory. Hammered gold it was—five pound weight, like a hoop of a barrel.

'"Peachey," says Dravot, "we don't want to fight no more. The Craft's the trick, so help me!"* and he brings forward that same Chief that I left at Bashkai—Billy Fish we called him afterwards, because he was so like Billy Fish that drove the big tank-engine at Mach on the Bolan in the old days. "Shake hands with him," says Dravot, and I shook hands and nearly dropped, for Billy Fish gave me the Grip. I said nothing, but tried him with the Fellow Craft Grip. He answers all right, and I tried the Master's Grip, but that was a slip. "A Fellow Craft he is!" I says to Dan. "Does he know the Word?"—"He does," says Dan, "and all the priests know. It's a miracle! The Chiefs and the priests can work a Fellow Craft Lodge in a way that's very like ours, and they've cut the marks on the rocks, but they don't know the Third Degree, and they've come to find out. It's Gord's Truth! I've known these long years that the Afghans knew up to the Fellow Craft Degree, but this is a miracle. A God and a Grand-Master of the Craft am I, and a Lodge in the Third Degree I will open, and we'll raise the head priests and the Chiefs of the villages."

'"It's against all the law," I says, "holding a Lodge without warrant from any one; and you know we never held office in any Lodge."

'"It's a master-stroke o' policy," says Dravot. "It means running the country as easy as a four-wheeled bogie* on a down grade. We can't stop to inquire now, or they'll turn against us. I've forty Chiefs at my heel, and passed and raised according to their merit they shall be. Billet these men on the villages, and see that we run up a Lodge of some kind. The temple of Imbra will do for the Lodge-room. The women must make aprons as you show them. I'll hold a levee of Chiefs to-night and Lodge to-morrow."

'I was fair run off my legs, but I wasn't such a fool as not to see what a pull this Craft business gave us. I showed the priests' families how to make aprons of the degrees, but for Dravot's apron the blue border and marks was made of turquoise lumps on white hide, not cloth. We took a great square stone in the temple for the Master's chair, and little stones for the officers' chairs, and painted the black pavement with white squares, and did what we could to make things regular.

'At the levee which was held that night on the hillside with big bonfires, Dravot gives out that him and me were Gods and sons of Alexander, and Past Grand-Masters in the Craft, and was come to make Kafiristan a country where every man should eat in peace and drink in quiet, and 'specially obey us. Then the Chiefs come round to shake hands, and they were so hairy and white and fair it was just shaking hands with old friends. We gave them names according as they was like men we had known in India—Billy Fish, Holly Dilworth, Pikky Kergan, that was Bazar-master when I was at Mhow, and so on, and so on.

The most amazing miracles was at Lodge next night. One of the old priests was watching us continuous, and I felt uneasy, for I knew we'd have to fudge the Ritual, and I didn't know what the men knew. The old priest was a stranger come in from beyond the village of Bashkai. The minute Dravot puts on the Master's apron that the girls had made for him, the priest fetches a whoop and a howl, and tries to overturn the stone that Dravot was sitting on. "It's all up now," I says. "That comes of meddling with the Craft without warrant!" Dravot never winked an eye, not when ten priests took and tilted over the Grand-Master's chair—which was to say the stone of Imbra. The priest begins rubbing the bottom end of it to clear away the black dirt, and presently he shows all the other priests the Master's Mark, same as was on Dravot's apron, cut into the stone. Not even the priests of the temple of Imbra knew it was there. The old chap falls flat on his face at Dravot's feet and kisses 'em. "Luck again," says Dravot, across the Lodge to me; "they say it's the missing Mark that no one could understand the why of. We're more than safe now." Then he bangs the butt of his gun for a gavel and says: "By virtue of the authority vested in me by my own right hand and the help of Peachey, I declare myself Grand-Master of all Freemasonry in Kafiristan in this the Mother Lodge o' the country, and King of Kafiristan equally with Peachey!" At that he puts on his crown and I puts on mine—I was doing Senior Warden—and we opens the Lodge in most ample form. It was a amazing miracle! The priests moved in Lodge through the first two degrees almost without telling, as if the memory was coming back to them. After that, Peachey and Dravot raised such as was worthy—high priests and Chiefs of far-off villages. Billy Fish was the first, and I can tell you we scared the soul out of him. It was not in any way according to Ritual, but it served our turn. We didn't raise more than ten of the biggest men, because we didn't want to make the Degree common. And they was clamouring to be raised.

'"In another six months," says Dravot, "we'll hold another Communication, and see how you are working." Then he asks them about their villages, and learns that they was fighting one against the other, and was sick and tired of it. And when they wasn't doing that they was fighting with the Mohammedans. "You can fight those when they come into our country," says Dravot. "Tell off every tenth man of your tribes for a Frontier guard, and send two hundred at a time to this valley to be drilled. Nobody is going to be shot or speared any more so long as he does well, and I know that you won't cheat me, because you're white people—sons of Alexander—and not like common, black Mohammedans. You are *my* people, and by God," says he, running off into English at the end, "I'll make a damned fine Nation of you, or I'll die in the making!"

'I can't tell all we did for the next six months, because

Dravot did a lot I couldn't see the hang of, and he learned their lingo in a way I never could. My work was to help the people plough, and now and again go out with some of the Army and see what the other villages were doing, and make 'em throw rope-bridges across the ravines which cut up the country horrid. Dravot was very kind to me, but when he walked up and down in the pine-wood pulling that bloody red beard of his with both fists I knew he was thinking plans I could not advise about, and I just waited for orders.

'But Dravot never showed me disrespect before the people. They were afraid of me and the Army, but they loved Dan. He was the best of friends with the priests and the Chiefs; but any one could come across the hills with a complaint, and Dravot would hear him out fair, and call four priests together and say what was to be done. He used to call in Billy Fish from Bashkai, and Pikky Kergan from Shu, and an old Chief we called Kafoozelum*—it was like enough to his real name—and hold councils with 'em when there was any fighting to be done in small villages. That was his Council of War, and the four priests of Bashkai, Shu, Khawak, and Madora was his Privy Council. Between the lot of 'em they sent me, with forty men and twenty rifles and sixty men carrying turquoises, into the Ghorband country to buy those hand-made Martini rifles, that come out of the Amir's workshops at Kabul, from one of the Amir's Herati regiments that would have sold the very teeth out of their mouths for turquoises.

'I stayed in Ghorband a month, and gave the Governor there the pick of my baskets for hush-money, and bribed the Colonel of the regiment some more, and, between the two and the tribes-people, we got more than a hundred hand-made Martinis, a hundred good Kohat *jezails** that'll throw to six hundred yards, and forty man-loads of very bad ammunition for the rifles. I came back with what I had, and distributed 'em among the men that the Chiefs sent in to me to drill. Dravot was too busy to attend to those things, but the old Army that we first made helped me, and we turned out five hundred men that could drill, and two hundred that knew how to hold arms pretty straight. Even those cork-screwed, handmade guns was a miracle to them. Dravot talked big about powder-shops and factories, walking up and down in the pine-wood when the winter was coming on.

'"I won't make a Nation," says he. "I'll make an Empire! These men aren't niggers; they're English! Look at their eyes—look at their mouths. Look at the way they stand up. They sit on chairs in their own houses. They're the Lost Tribes, or something like it, and they've grown to be English. I'll take a census in the spring if the priests don't get frightened. There must be a fair two million of 'em in these hills. The villages are full o' little children. Two million people—two hundred and fifty thousand fighting men—and all English! They only want the rifles and a little drilling. Two hundred and fifty thousand men, ready to cut in on Russia's right flank when she tries for India! Peachey, man," he says, chewing his beard in great hunks, "we shall be Emperors—Emperors of the Earth! Rajah Brooke* will be a suckling to us. I'll treat with the Viceroy on equal terms. I'll ask him to send me twelve picked English—twelve that I know of—to help us govern a bit. There's Mackray, Sergeant-pensioner at Segowli—many's the good dinner he's given me, and his wife a pair of trousers. There's Donkin, the Warder of Tounghoo Jail. There's hundreds that I could lay my hand on if I was in India. The Viceroy shall do it for me. I'll send a man through in the spring for those men, and I'll write for a Dispensation from the Grand Lodge for what I've done as Grand-Master. That—and all the Sniders that'll be thrown out when the native troops in India take up the Martini.* They'll be worn smooth, but they'll do for fighting in these hills. Twelve English, a hundred thousand Sniders run through the Amir's country in driblets—I'd be content with twenty thousand in one year—and we'd be an Empire. When everything was shipshape, I'd hand over the crown—this crown I'm wearing now—to Queen Victoria on my knees, and she'd say: 'Rise up, Sir Daniel Dravot.' Oh, it's big! It's big, I tell you! But there's so much to be done in every place—Bashkai, Khawak, Shu, and everywhere else."

'"What is it?" I says. "There are no more men coming in to be drilled this autumn. Look at those fat, black clouds. They're bringing the snow."

'"It isn't that," says Daniel, putting his hand very hard on my shoulder; "and I don't wish to say anything that's against you, for no other living man would have followed me and made me what I am as you have done. You're a first-class Commander-in-Chief, and the people know you; but—it's a big country, and somehow you can't help me, Peachey, in the way I want to be helped."

'"Go to your blasted priests, then!" I said, and I was sorry when I made that remark, but it did hurt me sore to find Daniel talking so superior, when I'd drilled all the men, and done all he told me.

'"Don't let's quarrel, Peachey," says Daniel without cursing. "You're a King too, and the half of this Kingdom is yours; but can't you see, Peachey, we want cleverer men than us now—three or four of 'em, that we can scatter about for our Deputies. It's a hugeous great State, and I can't always tell the right thing to do, and I haven't time for all I want to do, and here's winter coming on and all." He stuffed half his beard into his mouth, all red like the gold of his crown.

'"I'm sorry, Daniel," says I. "I've done all I could. I've drilled the men and shown the people how to stack their oats better; and I've brought in those tinware rifles from Ghor-band—but I know what you're driving at. I take it Kings always feel oppressed that way."

'"There's another thing too," says Dravot, walking up and down. "The winter's coming and these people won't be giving much trouble, and if they do we can't move about. I want a wife."

'"For Gord's sake, leave the women alone!" I says. "We've both got all the work we can, though I *am* a fool. Remember the Contrack, and keep clear o' women."

'"The Contrack only lasted till such time as we was Kings; and Kings we have been these months past," says Dravot, weighing his crown in his hand. "You go get a wife, too, Peachey—a nice, strappin', plump girl that'll keep you warm in the winter. They're prettier than English girls, and we can take the pick of 'em. Boil 'em once or twice in hot water and they'll come out like chicken and ham."

'"Don't tempt me!" I says. "I will not have any dealings with a woman not till we are a dam' sight more settled than we

are now. I've been doing the work o' two men, and you've
been doing the work o' three. Let's lie off a bit, and see if we
can get some better tobacco from Afghan country and run in
some good liquor; but no women."

'"Who's talking o' *women*?" says Dravot. "I said *wife*—a
Queen to breed a King's son for the King. A Queen out of the
strongest tribe, that'll make them your blood-brothers, and
that'll lie by your side and tell you all the people thinks about
you and their own affairs. That's what I want."

'"Do you remember that Bengali woman I kept at Mogul
Serai when I was a platelayer?"* says I. "A fat lot o' good she
was to me. She taught me the lingo and one or two other
things; but what happened? She ran away with the Station-
master's servant and half my month's pay. Then she turned
up at Dadur Junction in tow of a half-caste, and had the
impidence to say I was her husband—all among the drivers in
the running-shed too!"

'"We've done with that," says Dravot; "these women are
whiter than you or me, and a Queen I will have for the winter
months."

'"For the last time o' asking, Dan, do *not*," I says. "It'll
only bring us harm. The Bible says that Kings ain't to waste
their strength on women,* 'specially when they've got a raw
new Kingdom to work over."

'"For the last time of answering, I will," said Dravot, and
he went away through the pine-trees looking like a big red
devil, the sun being on his crown and beard and all.

'But getting a wife was not as easy as Dan thought. He put
it before the Council, and there was no answer till Billy Fish
said that he'd better ask the girls. Dravot damned them all
round. "What's wrong with me?" he shouts, standing by the
idol Imbra. "Am I a dog or am I not enough of a man for your
wenches? Haven't I put the shadow of my hand over this
country? Who stopped the last Afghan raid?" It was me
really, but Dravot was too angry to remember. "Who bought
your guns? Who repaircd the bridges? Who's the Grand-
Master of the Sign cut in the stone?" says he, and he thumped
his hand on the block that he used to sit on in Lodge, and at
Council, which opened like Lodge always. Billy Fish said

nothing and no more did the others. "Keep your hair on, Dan," said I; "and ask the girls. That's how it's done at Home, and these people are quite English."

'"The marriage of the King is a matter of State," says Dan, in a red-hot rage, for he could feel, I hope, that he was going against his better mind. He walked out of the Council-room, and the others sat still, looking at the ground.

'"Billy Fish," says I to the Chief of Bashkai, "what's the difficulty here? A straight answer to a true friend."

'"You know," says Billy Fish. "How should a man tell you who knows everything? How can daughters of men marry Gods or Devils? It's not proper."

'I remembered something like that in the Bible*; but if, after seeing us as long as they had, they still believed we were Gods, 'twasn't for me to undeceive them.

'"A God can do anything," says I. "If the King is fond of a girl he'll not let her die."—"She'll have to," says Billy Fish. "There are all sorts of Gods and Devils in these mountains, and now and again a girl marries one of them and isn't seen any more. Besides, you two know the Mark cut in the stone. Only the Gods know that. We thought you were men till you showed the Sign of the Master."

'I wished then that we had explained about the loss of the genuine secrets of a Master-Mason at the first go-off; but I said nothing. All that night there was a blowing of horns in a little dark temple half-way down the hill, and I heard a girl crying fit to die. One of the priests told us that she was being prepared to marry the King.

'"I'll have no nonsense of that kind," says Dan. "I don't want to interfere with your customs, but I'll take my own wife."—"The girl's a little bit afraid," says the priest. "She thinks she's going to die, and they are a-heartening of her up down in the temple."

'"Hearten her very tender, then," says Dravot, "or I'll hearten you with the butt of a gun so you'll never want to be heartened again." He licked his lips, did Dan, and stayed up walking about more than half the night, thinking of the wife that he was going to get in the morning. I wasn't any means comfortable, for I knew that dealings with a woman in foreign parts, though you was a crowned King twenty times over, could not but be risky. I got up very early in the morning while Dravot was asleep, and I saw the priests talking together in whispers, and the Chiefs talking together too, and they looked at me out of the corners of their eyes.

'"What is up, Fish?" I says to the Bashkai man, who was wrapped up in his furs and looking splendid to behold.

'"I can't rightly say," says he; "but if you can make the King drop all this nonsense about marriage, you'll be doing him and me and yourself a great service."

'"That I do believe," says I. "But sure, you know, Billy, as well as me, having fought against and for us, that the King and me are nothing more than two of the finest men that God Almighty ever made. Nothing more, I do assure you."

'"That may be," says Billy Fish, "and yet I should be sorry if it was." He sinks his head upon his great fur cloak for a minute and thinks. "King," says he, "be you man or God or Devil, I'll stick by you to-day. I have twenty of my men with me, and they will follow me. We'll go to Bashkai until the storm blows over."

'A little snow had fallen in the night, and everything was white except them greasy fat clouds that blew down and down from the north. Dravot came out with his crown on his head, swinging his arms and stamping his feet, and looking more pleased than Punch.

'"For the last time, drop it, Dan," says I in a whisper. "Billy Fish here says that there will be a row."

'"A row among my people!" says Dravot. "Not much. Peachey, you're a fool not to get a wife too. Where's the girl?" says he with a voice as loud as the braying of a jackass. "Call up all the Chiefs and priests, and let the Emperor see if his wife suits him."

'There was no need to call any one. They were all there leaning on their guns and spears round the clearing in the centre of the pine-wood. A lot of priests went down to the little temple to bring up the girl, and the horns blew fit to wake the dead. Billy Fish saunters round and gets as close to Daniel as he could, and behind him stood his twenty men with matchlocks. Not a man of them under six feet. I was

next to Dravot, and behind me was twenty men of the regular
Army. Up comes the girl, and a strapping wench she was,
covered with silver and turquoises, but white as death, and
looking back every minute at the priests.

'"She'll do," said Dan, looking her over. "What's to be
afraid of, lass? Come and kiss me." He puts his arm round
her. She shuts her eyes, gives a bit of a squeak, and down goes
her face in the side of Dan's flaming red beard.

'"The slut's bitten me!" says he, clapping his hand to his
neck, and, sure enough, his hand was red with blood. Billy
Fish and two of his matchlock-men catches hold of Dan by
the shoulders and drags him into the Bashkai lot, while the
priests howls in their lingo: "Neither God nor Devil but a
man!" I was all taken aback, for a priest cut at me in front,
and the Army behind began firing into the Bashkai men.

'"God A'mighty!" says Dan. "What is the meaning o'
this?"

'"Come back! Come away!" says Billy Fish. "Ruin and
Mutiny's the matter. We'll break for Bashkai if we can."

'I tried to give some sort of orders to my men—the men o'
the regular Army—but it was no use, so I fired into the brown
of 'em with an English Martini and drilled three beggars in a
line. The valley was full of shouting, howling people, and
every soul was shrieking, "Not a God nor a Devil but only a
man!" The Bashkai troops stuck to Billy Fish all they were
worth, but their matchlocks wasn't half as good as the Kabul
breech-loaders, and four of them dropped. Dan was bellow-
ing like a bull, for he was very wrathy; and Billy Fish had a
hard job to prevent him running out at the crowd.

'"We can't stand," says Billy Fish. "Make a run for it
down the valley! The whole place is against us." The matchlock-men ran, and we went down the valley in spite of
Dravot. He was swearing horrible and crying out he was a
King. The priests rolled great stones on us, and the regular
Army fired hard, and there wasn't more than six men, not
counting Dan, Billy Fish, and me, that came down to the
bottom of the valley alive.

'Then they stopped firing and the horns in the temple blew
again. "Come away—for God's sake come away!" says Billy

Fish. "They'll send runners out to all the villages before ever we get to Bashkai. I can protect you there, but I can't do anything now."

'My own notion is that Dan began to go mad in his head from that hour. He stared up and down like a stuck pig. Then he was all for walking back alone and killing the priests with his bare hands; which he could have done. "An Emperor am I," says Daniel, "and next year I shall be a Knight of the Queen."

'"All right, Dan," says I; "but come along now while there's time."

'"It's your fault," says he, "for not looking after your Army better. There was mutiny in the midst, and you didn't know—you damned engine-driving, plate-laying, mission-ary's-pass-hunting hound!" He sat upon a rock and called me every name he could lay tongue to. I was too heart-sick to care, though it was all his foolishness that brought the smash.

'"I'm sorry, Dan," says I, "but there's no accounting for natives. This business is our 'Fifty-Seven.* Maybe we'll make something out of it yet, when we've got to Bashkai."

'"Let's get to Bashkai, then," says Dan, "and, by God, when I come back here again I'll sweep the valley so there isn't a bug in a blanket left!"

'We walked all that day, and all that night Dan was stumping up and down on the snow, chewing his beard and muttering to himself.

'"There's no hope o' getting clear," said Billy Fish. "The priests will have sent runners to the villages to say that you are only men. Why didn't you stick on as Gods till things was more settled? I'm a dead man," says Billy Fish, and he throws himself down on the snow and begins to pray to his Gods.

'Next morning we was in a cruel bad country—all up and down, no level ground at all, and no food either. The six Bashkai men looked at Billy Fish hungry-ways as if they wanted to ask something, but they said never a word. At noon we came to the top of a flat mountain all covered with snow, and when we climbed up into it, behold, there was an Army in position waiting in the middle!

'"The runners have been very quick," says Billy Fish, with a little bit of a laugh. "They are waiting for us."

'Three or four men began to fire from the enemy's side, and a chance shot took Daniel in the calf of the leg. That brought him to his senses. He looks across the snow at the Army, and sees the rifles that we had brought into the country.

'"We're done for," says he. "They are Englishmen, these people,—and it's my blasted nonsense that has brought you to this. Get back, Billy Fish, and take your men away. You've done what you could, and now cut for it. Carnehan," says he, "shake hands with me and go along with Billy. Maybe they won't kill you. I'll go and meet 'em alone. It's me that did it. Me, the King!"

'"Go!" says I. "Go to Hell, Dan! I'm with you here. Billy Fish, you clear out, and we two will meet those folk."

'"I'm a Chief," says Billy Fish, quite quiet. "I stay with you. My men can go."

'The Bashkai fellows didn't wait for a second word, but ran off, and Dan and me and Billy Fish walked across to where the drums were drumming and the horns were horning. It was cold—awful cold. I've got that cold in the back of my head now. There's a lump of it there.'

The punkah-coolies had gone to sleep. Two kerosene lamps were blazing in the office, and the perspiration poured down my face and splashed on the blotter as I leaned forward. Carnehan was shivering, and I feared that his mind might go. I wiped my face, took a fresh grip of the piteously mangled hands, and said: 'What happened after that?'

The momentary shift of my eyes had broken the clear current.

'What was you pleased to say?' whined Carnehan. 'They took them without any sound. Not a little whisper all along the snow, not though the King knocked down the first man that set hand on him—not though old Peachey fired his last cartridge into the brown of 'em. Not a single solitary sound did those swines make. They just closed up tight, and I tell you their furs stunk. There was a man called Billy Fish, a good friend of us all, and they cut his throat, sir, then and there, like a pig; and the King kicks up the bloody snow and says: "We've had a dashed fine run for our money. What's coming next?" But Peachey, Peachey Taliaferro, I tell you, sir, in confidence as betwixt two friends, he lost his head, sir. No, he didn't neither. The King lost his head, so he did, all along o' one of those cunning rope-bridges. Kindly let me have the paper-cutter, sir. It tilted this way. They marched him a mile across that snow to a rope-bridge over a ravine with a river at the bottom. You may have seen such. They prodded him behind like an ox. "Damn your eyes!" says the King. "D'you suppose I can't die like a gentleman?" He turns to Peachey—Peachey that was crying like a child. "I've brought you to this, Peachey," says he. "Brought you out of your happy life to be killed in Kafiristan, where you was late Commander-in-Chief of the Emperor's forces. Say you forgive me, Peachey."—"I do," says Peachey. "Fully and freely do I forgive you, Dan."—"Shake hands, Peachey," says he. "I'm going now." Out he goes, looking neither right nor left, and when he was plumb in the middle of those dizzy dancing ropes—"Cut, you beggars," he shouts; and they cut, and old Dan fell, turning round and round and round, twenty thousand miles, for he took half an hour to fall till he struck the water, and I could see his body caught on a rock with the gold crown close beside.

'But do you know what they did to Peachey between two pine-trees? They crucified him, sir, as Peachey's hands will show. They used wooden pegs for his hands and his feet; and he didn't die. He hung there and screamed, and they took him down next day, and said it was a miracle that he wasn't dead. They took him down—poor old Peachey that hadn't done them any harm—that hadn't done them any—'

He rocked to and fro and wept bitterly, wiping his eyes with the back of his scarred hands and moaning like a child for some ten minutes.

'They was cruel enough to feed him up in the temple, because they said he was more of a God than old Daniel that was a man. Then they turned him out on the snow, and told him to go home, and Peachey came home in about a year, begging along the roads quite safe; for Daniel Dravot he

walked before and said: "Come along, Peachey. It's a big
thing we're doing." The mountains they danced at night, and
the mountains they tried to fall on Peachey's head, but Dan
he held up his hand, and Peachey came along bent double.
He never let go of Dan's hand, and he never let go of Dan's
head. They gave it to him as a present in the temple, to
remind him not to come again, and though the crown was
pure gold, and Peachey was starving, never would Peachey
sell the same. You knew Dravot, sir! You knew Right
Worshipful Brother Dravot! Look at him now!'

He fumbled in the mass of rags round his bent waist;
brought out a black horsehair bag embroidered with silver
thread, and shook therefrom on to my table—the dried,
withered head of Daniel Dravot! The morning sun that had
long been paling the lamps struck the red beard and blind
sunken eyes; struck, too, a heavy circlet of gold studded with
raw turquoises, that Carnehan placed tenderly on the bat-
tered temples.

'You behold now,' said Carnehan, 'the Emperor in his
habit as he lived*—the King of Kafiristan with his crown
upon his head. Poor old Daniel that was a monarch once!'

I shuddered, for, in spite of defacements manifold, I
recognized the head of the man of Marwar Junction. Carnehan rose to go. I attempted to stop him. He was not fit to walk
abroad. 'Let me take away the whisky, and give me a little
money,' he gasped. 'I was a King once. I'll go to the Deputy-
Commissioner and ask to set in the Poorhouse till I get my
health. No, thank you, I can't wait till you get a carriage for
me. I've urgent private affairs—in the South—at Marwar.'

He shambled out of the office and departed in the direction
of the Deputy-Commissioner's house. That day at noon I had
occasion to go down the blinding hot Mall, and I saw a
crooked man crawling along the white dust of the roadside,
his hat in his hand, quavering dolorously after the fashion of
street-singers at Home. There was not a soul in sight, and he
was out of all possible earshot of the houses. And he sang
through his nose, turning his head from right to left:—

> 'The Son of God goes forth to war,
>   A kingly crown to gain;

His blood-red banner streams afar!
Who follows in his train?'*

I waited to hear no more, but put the poor wretch into my carriage and drove him to the nearest missionary for eventual transfer to the Asylum. He repeated the hymn twice while he was with me, whom he did not in the least recognize, and I left him singing it to the missionary.

Two days later I inquired after his welfare of the Superintendent of the Asylum.

'He was admitted suffering from sunstroke. He died early yesterday morning,' said the Superintendent. 'Is it true that he was half an hour bare-headed in the sun at mid-day?'

'Yes,' said I, 'but do you happen to know if he had anything upon him by any chance when he died?'

'Not to my knowledge,' said the Superintendent.

And there the matter rests.

EXPLANATORY NOTES

IN an effort to keep the number of notes within reasonable bounds, I have in most cases excluded the following categories:

Rare words that can be found in standard British and American dictionaries are not glossed: exceptions are obsolete slang, words with significant changes of meaning, and some technical terms, mostly military.

Place names. Writing with an eye on his Anglo-Indian public, Kipling worked local place names into the texture of his stories in order to emphasize the ordinariness of their settings. To avoid a plethora of 'gazetteer' entries, I have annotated only place names that carry particular significance in their fictional context.

Biographical sources. As Kipling was writing directly from his own experience during the Indian years, there has been much speculation concerning the identity of his sources and models. I have called attention to this background material only in cases where it appears to illuminate the meaning of the fiction.

Every editor of Kipling's writings owes an incalculable debt to R. E. Harbord and the members of the Kipling Society who collaborated on *The Readers' Guide to Rudyard Kipling's Work* (Canterbury and Bournemouth, 1961–72). I have borrowed freely from this wonderful compendium of Kipling lore and, for the most part, silently. In one or two places I have cited the *Readers' Guide*, usually where I have been unable to verify the reference, or where the older work includes a body of scholarship too significant to pass over but too extensive to reproduce.

3 *The Strange Ride of Morrowbie Jukes*: first published December 1885 in *Quartette*, a Christmas annual written by the four members of the Kipling family and produced by the *Civil and Military Gazette*.

A manuscript diary now in the possession of Harvard University reveals that Kipling was at work on the story as early as August 1884: together with two other very early stories— 'The Gate of the Hundred Sorrows' (*Plain Tales from the Hills*) and 'The Dream of Duncan Parrenness' (*Life's Handicap*)—it reflects the dominant influence of Poe's tales of the fantastic.

Like 'The Phantom 'Rickshaw', its companion-piece in *Quartette*, 'Morrowbie Jukes' was significantly altered by the addition of an introductory paragraph when it was reprinted in the Indian Railway Library series. The place-names locate the City of the Dead on the bank of the Sutlej River, in a desolate region about one hundred miles from Lahore.

3 *Minton*: fine English porcelain produced in Stoke-on-Trent.

4 *in terrorem*: as an object of fear.

 persuaders: spurs.

6 *Martini-Henry*: rifle issued to the British Army after 1875.

 picket: rifle bullet.

7 *local self-government*: a controversial policy introduced by Lord Ripon as Viceroy to help the political education of Indians.

8 *Deccanee Brahmin*: Hindu of the highest caste, from the Deccan Plateau in South Central India and therefore far from home in the Punjab.

 continuations: trousers (slang).

11 *chapatti*: round flat cake of unleavened bread, the common food of the Indian poor.

12 *Heaven*: in his reproof of the Sadducees, who ask him about a woman multiply widowed, Jesus replies, 'In the resurrection they neither marry, nor are given in marriage, but are as the angels of God in heaven' (Matthew 22: 23–30).

16 *Mignonette*: a *cause célèbre* of 1884. Cast away in a storm, the crew of the yacht *Mignonette* escaped the wreck with scant rations; after nearly three weeks of atrocious suffering they were driven to murder and cannibalism.

18 *Feringhi*: European.

19 *Vishnu*: one of the three chief gods in Hindu mythology.

22 *seven back*: it has been pointed out that, whether or not Kipling so intended it, the path across the quicksand is unnecessarily complicated—of the fifteen movements given, ten are superfluous, as the track crosses itself twice (*Readers' Guide*).

26 *The Phantom 'Rickshaw*: first published December 1885 in *Quartette*; reprinted in *The Phantom 'Rickshaw* December 1888.

 Kipling associated the tale with the first appearance of his 'Personal Daemon', an inner voice which 'came to me early when I sat bewildered among other notions, and said: "Take this and no other." I obeyed, and was rewarded . . . Some of it was weak, much was bad and out of key; but it was my first serious attempt to think in another man's skin' (*Something of Myself*, pp. 208–9).

Among the revisions Kipling made in the text when the story was reprinted, the most striking was the addition of the introductory material; in its original form the story began with Pansay's opening words, 'My doctor tells me that I need rest and change of air' (p. 28).

'Rickshaw: in the early 1880s the Japanese *jinrikisha*, a two-wheeled carriage drawn by a single coolie, had only recently been imported to the Indian hill stations. The liveried *jhampanis*, or bearers, who attended Mrs Wessington must have been a holdover from the days of the litter or sedan chair, which would have required a team of four.

Evening Hymn: 'Glory to thee, my God, this night', by Bishop Thomas Ken (1637–1711).

Civilians: officials of the Indian Civil Service.

loose-box: a stall large enough to give the horse freedom of movement; American *box stall*.

27　*tale of bricks*: daily quota of bricks demanded by Pharaoh of the Israelites (Exodus 5: 7–9).

　　P. & O.: Peninsula and Oriental Steamship Company, the principal means of transport between India and Europe.

28　*from Peshawur to the sea*: Peshawur, now in Pakistan, represented the far north-west corner of India; hence, the length and breadth of the land.

30　*Jakko*: mountain at Simla, the road round which was a favourite ride.

32　*Waler*: big horse imported from Australia for the use of the British cavalry in India; originally bred in New South Wales, whence the name.

　　Peliti's: famous café and confectioners at Simla, much used as a rendezvous.

33　*sais*: groom.

40　*lakh*: 100,000, with 'rupees' understood.

41　*Singing and murmuring*: Tennyson's 'Place of Art', slightly altered ('your' for 'her'; 'yourself' for 'herself').

46　*I seemed to move*: Tennyson's *Princess*, part I, line 17, slightly misquoted ('amid' for 'among').

　　mashing: making love to.

49 *Gemini*: first published 14 January 1888 in the *Week's News*; reprinted in December 1888 in *In Black and White*.

The series of tales Kipling published nearly every week in the *Week's News* had begun on 7 January. The first of the stories—'The God from the Machine'—is one of the least memorable of Mulvaney's adventures. 'Gemini', however, the second of the series and the earliest of the dramatic monologues delivered by Indian speakers, represents a striking new departure.

Gemini: the twins; especially Castor and Pollux, twin sons of Leda and Zeus.

Mahajun: an important banker (literally 'great person'); to the villagers the brothers are merely *bunnias* (small merchants, money-lenders).

pice: smallest unit of currency, equivalent of a farthing.

50 *Nawab*: originally a deputy under the Mughal emperors, later a title of rank or respect, not necessarily implying territorial authority. Muslims, of course, are forbidden alcohol.

lakh: 100,000 (of rupees).

51 *Phagun*: eleventh month, which falls in February and March.

lac-bangles: cheap lacquer ornaments for wrists and ankles.

52 *the Sirkar*: the Government of India.

sons of Belial: devil-worshippers, idolaters (Deuteronomy 13: 13).

54 *Mahadeo*: the great god; another name for Shiva in Hindu mythology.

the baba Stunt Sahib: the young 'Stunt' is an inexperienced Assistant Collector; *baba*, traditionally a title of veneration, came to be used as a form of address by Indians to English children (perhaps under the influence of 'baby').

55 *Kirpa Ram, the Jat*: the Jats were one of several ethnic groups that made up the population of the Punjab; chiefly farmers, they were known as a slow and heavy race.

57 *Dipty Sahib*: Deputy (Commissioner) for the province.

58 *A Wayside Comedy*: first published 21 January 1888 in the *Week's News*; reprinted December 1888 in *Under the Deodars*. *Kashima* and its surroundings are invented.

jhils: marshy ponds.

61 *dâk*: day's journey, stage; hence, means of transportation.

62 *terai hat*: wide-brimmed hat with double crown and special ventilation, named for the *terai*, a belt of marshy jungle at the foot of the Himalayas.

Queen: popular London periodical, still in existence.

63 *purdah*: here with its literal meaning of 'curtain'.

66 *sais*: groom.

70 *At Twenty-Two*: first published 18 February 1888 in the *Week's News*; reprinted December 1888 in *In Black and White*.

The story alludes, both implicitly and explicitly, to *Germinal*, Emile Zola's sombre novel of the French coalfields, which appeared in 1885. Though Zola's books were banned in England on account of their sexual explicitness, his name occurs several times in Kipling's Indian writings. English translations were available in British India; at the same time, Kipling's knowledge of French and interest in contemporary French literature may have led him to read Zola in the original.

Sonthal: race of non-Aryan hill folk.

Meah: tribal rather than personal name; the Meahs were low-caste Hindus converted to Islam.

72 *Babuji*: originally a title of respect, 'Babu' came to be used—often with overtones of disparagement—to refer to Indian (especially Bengali) clerks with a knowledge of written English; the untranslatable *-ji* is honorific.

beck: stream, in North of England dialects.

79 *Geordie*: native of Newcastle.

80 *Germinal upside-down*: At the climax of Zola's novel, Catherine and her two lovers are imprisoned together in the flooded mine; Etienne, the protagonist, is driven to kill his enemy, but the girl dies before the arrival of the rescuers, and Etienne alone survives.

81 *The Education of Otis Yeere*: Part I was originally published 10 March 1888 in the *Week's News* under the subtitle 'Showing how the great idea was born'; Part II, subtitled 'Showing what was born of the great idea', first appeared in the *Week's News* on 17 March; both parts were reprinted in *Under the Deodars* in December 1888.

Mrs Hauksbee, the central figure in nine of Kipling's stories, was based on a number of his lively and strong-minded Simla acquaintances: among the models were a Mrs Burton and, almost certainly, his own witty and popular mother.

A companion piece to 'Otis Yeere' is 'A Supplementary Chapter'; first published 19 May 1888 in the *Week's News*, the tale was reprinted without Kipling's authorization in *Abaft the Funnel* (1909) and finally collected in the Sussex and Burwash editions. In it we meet Trewinnard, the 'Platonic' friend of Mrs Mallowe, to whom he owes his career; here he makes the mistake of deserting her for Mrs Reiver, with dire consequences.

epigraph: opening lines of 'The Lost Bower', by E. B. Browning.

The Fallen Angel: not identified.

the New Gaiety Theatre: opened at Simla in June 1887.

82 *Mussuck*: goatskin sack used by an Indian water-bearer.

83 *the other two things*: that is, the flesh and the devil. (See the Ministration of Holy Baptism, in the Book of Common Prayer.)

Baruch: name of Jeremiah's secretary and putative author of one of the books of the Apocrypha. The source of Mrs Mallowe's words has not been identified; probably they are meant to be taken as a careless or humorous misquotation.

84 *teapoy*: three-legged table.

85 *khud*: precipitous hillside.

George Eliot: because Polly is uttering sententious generalities?

86 *kala juggahs*: dark corners (for 'sitting out' in).

I have preached: the allusion is to the book of Ecclesiastes, though the exact words do not appear there; see note to *Baruch*, p. 83 above.

Abana and Pharpar: rivers of Damascus, which failed to cure Naaman of his leprosy; they are proverbial for anything convenient but insufficient, as opposed to the distant but efficacious Jordan (2 Kings 5: 12).

87 *gharri*: carriage.

list: cloth border or binding, selvage.

88 *Theosophists*: theosophy, a mystical movement founded in the 1870s, had become popular at Simla shortly before Kipling's first visit there.

90 *Verse epigraph*: presumably by Kipling.

St Simon Stylites: early Christian hermit (390–459) who retired to the top of a pillar.

in manner most ironical: W. S. Gilbert's *Patience*, Act II, slightly misquoted ('in manner most' for 'with compliment').

91 *Milton Wellings*: composer of popular songs.

burra-khana: big dinner.

the Pioneer: Allahabad newspaper of which Kipling was an employee.

à la Gibbon: According to an unflattering anecdote retailed by Mme de Genlis, the historian Edward Gibbon fell on his knees to propose marriage to Mme de Crousaz. When she gently refused and invited him to rise, her suitor—whose corpulence was legendary—replied, 'Madame, je ne peux pas,' and she was forced to call the servants to help him. (G. B. Hill dismisses the story as a fabrication; see his edition of Gibbon's *Memoirs* [London, 1900], Appendix 66.)

92 *Stunt*: slang for Assistant (Commissioner).

ryot: peasant.

94 *Punjabis*: Indian Civil Service, on duty in the Punjab; their self-esteem was proverbial.

Ditcher: contemptuous name for a member of the Bengal Civil Service, so called from the Marattha Ditch at Calcutta.

95 *Jeshurun*: see Deuteronomy 32: 15.

96 *Gullals*: the name is invented.

Darjeeling: the hill station most convenient to Calcutta and other places in Bengal; summer location for the Government of Bengal.

native pleader: Indian lawyer.

101 *. . . a fair woman's foot*: 'A False Step', by E. B. Browning.

103 *The Hill of Illusion*: first published 21 April 1888 in the *Week's News*; reprinted December 1888 in *Under the Deodars*.

The form of 'The Hill of Illusion'—a tale told entirely through dialogue—shows the influence of 'Gyp' (the Comtesse de Martel de Janville), a French novelist then popular though now forgotten. Her *Autour du mariage* Kipling identified in his autobiography as the model for his *Story of the Gadsbys*, which began to run in the *Week's News* a month after 'The Hill of Illusion' appeared. The latter is thematically related to an unpublished version of 'At the Pit's Mouth': for a discussion of the 1884 manuscript of 'At the Pit's Mouth', see the headnotes to that story.

epigraph: from 'To Marguerite—Continued', slightly misquoted. Line 1 should read 'Who renders'; line 3, 'betwixt'.

jhampanis: bearers; see 'The Phantom 'Rickshaw', note to p. 26.

tonga: small, light carriage, commonly used as transport between the hill stations and the plains.

106 *Kind Sir . . .*: source not identified.

Keek into the draw-well, Janet, Janet: attributed to 'My Jo Janet', a Scottish folk-song (*Readers' Guide*).

kutcha: temporary, not properly finished; opposite of *pukka*.

109 *La Chanson du Colonel*: source not identified. The verses may be translated:

> For a whole year
> The regiment didn't turn up.
> At the War Ministry
> It was reported lost.
>
> The search was abandoned
> When suddenly one morning
> It reappeared in the square,
> The Colonel still at its head.

110 *Keene*: Probably H. G. Keene (1781–1864), a popular satirist of British India.

112 *See-Saw! Margery Daw!*: traditional nursery rhyme.

113 *Dray Wara Yow Dee*: first published 28 April 1888 in the *Week's News*; reprinted December 1888 in *In Black and White*.

113 *thirteen-three*: thirteen hands three inches high at the shoulder.

114 *Kashmir Serai*: A *serai* is a place or building for the accommodation of travellers and their pack animals, usually an enclosed yard with chambers around it. Located within the city walls of Lahore, the Kashmir Serai was a meeting place for pilgrims and caravans from the north.

Amir: ruler of Afghanistan.

115 *Thana*: police post, jail.

blackened my face: insulted me.

Pathan: member of a tribal group widespread through Afghanistan and northern Pakistan. Sunni Muslims, the Pathans are known for fierce individualism and a tradition of blood feuds.

116 *Rahman*: probably the seventeenth-century Pathan philosopher Abdur Rahman.

the Pindi camp: Kipling had visited Rawalpindi in 1885 as a
Special Correspondent reporting on the Durbar at which the
Viceroy received a state visit from the Amir of Afghanistan.

117 *charpoy*: bedstead.

118 *Black Water*: the sea.

Ali Musjid, Ghor Kuttri: a Mohammedan mosque and a Hindu
temple.

Jamun, Ak: the *jamun* is a handsome fruit-tree, the *ak* a twisted
shrub known for its acrid juice.

122 *The Judgment of Dungara*: first published 28 July 1888 in the
Week's News as 'The Peculiar Embarrassment of Justus
Krenk'; reprinted December 1888 in *In Black and White*. The
geography and ethnology are invented.

epigraph: the 'misprinted' line should read 'Like a pale martyr
in his shirt of fire'; see Alexander Smith, *A Life Drama* (1853).

124 *Gallio*: Deputy of Achaia, he refused to intervene in the dispute
between St Paul and the Jews of Corinth, hence became, for
Kipling, the type of the administrator unconcerned with the
theological side of missionary activity in his district (Acts 18).

125 *House of Rimmon*: Naaman, cured of his leprosy by the inter-
vention of Elisha, asked and was granted God's pardon for
having to continue to bow before the idol of his master, the king
of Syria (2 Kings 5: 18). The phrase, one of Kipling's
favourites, is proverbial for having to pay lip service to a
despised or superseded authority.

129 *Shirt of Nessus*: fatally wounded by Hercules, the Centaur
Nessus managed to trick the hero into wearing a poisoned shirt;
the effect of the venom was so agonizing that Hercules chose
death by fire in preference.

Nilgiri Nettle: according to Balfour's *Cyclopaedia of India*,
Girardenia is frequent among the Nilgiri Hills. 'The bark
yields a fine, strong, white, flax-like fibre, which the hill people
obtain by plunging the plant into hot water, to deprive it of its
virulently stinging properties, and then peeling the stalks.'

131 *With the Main Guard*: first published 4 August 1888 in the
Week's News; reprinted December 1888 in *Soldiers Three*.
This was the tenth story to feature Privates Terence

Mulvaney, Stanley Ortheris, and Jock Learoyd: they had been introduced in 'The Three Musketeers', published 11 March 1887 as one of the 'Plain Tales from the Hills' series in the *Civil and Military Gazette*.

epigraph: from 'Breitmann in Bivouac' by Charles Godfrey Leland (1824–1903). Kipling was an admirer and imitator of this American humorist's dialect verses.

Fort Amara: historic citadel of Lahore, garrisoned by a detachment stationed at the nearby cantonment of Mian Mir.

133 *Khemi River . . . magician Mulvaney*: allusion to 'The Madness of Private Ortheris' (*Plain Tales from the Hills*), though in that story it is the narrator, not Mulvaney, who persuades Ortheris not to desert.

the Widdy: Queen Victoria.

Black Tyrone: first of the two regiments with which Mulvaney served in India, the second being the 'Ould Rig'mint'. They have been identified with the 18th Royal Irish and the 59th East Lancashires, respectively, but Kipling is probably drawing on his contacts with several different regiments.

134 *Paythans*: see note to 'Dray Wara Yow Dee', p. 287.

Silver's Theatre: this skirmish may be based on the battle of Ahmed Khel, fought in 1880 in the course of the Second Afghan War.

Gurkys: Gurkhas, hill tribesmen from Nepal noted for their ferocity in battle; recruited by Britain for service in the Indian Army.

Burma: 'Now first of the foemen of Boh Da Thone / Was Captain O'Neil of the Black Tyrone.' *The Ballad of Boh Da Thone* [Kipling's footnote]. Though the author assigns O'Neil to the Black Tyrone, observe that in the present story he is commanding the men of the Ould Rig'mint: the Black Tyrone are in the charge of the 'little orf'cer bhoy'.

136 *the Vic.*: the present Old Vic was the Victoria Music Hall in Ortheris's youth.

137 *'We've seen our dead'*: presumably, mutilated by the Afghans.

141 *a Roshus*: Roscius, a famous actor of ancient Rome, proverbial for Thespian accomplishment.

144 *. . . in a soldier's cloak*: the ballad of 'The Sentry-Box' has not been identified.

146 *In Flood Time*: first published 11 August 1888 in the *Week's News*; reprinted December 1888 in *In Black and White*.

The setting of the story has not been conclusively identified. The name of the Barhwi River is invented, but Kipling did spend a night talking to the ford-keeper on the banks of the flooded Gugger, on the road from Simla to Allahabad, and may have based the present story on that experience. Cf. '"In Forma Pauperis"', *Pioneer* (28 July 1888). The geographical layout of the ford, bridge, and village is discussed at some length in the *Readers' Guide*.

epigraph: has been attributed to an old Scottish poem entitled 'Two Rivers' (*Readers' Guide*).

ekka: small one-horse carriage.

mahoutji: polite way of addressing the *mahout*, or elephant-driver.

Rustum: hero of Persian epic.

Bahadur: honorific form of address, literally 'hero' or 'champion'.

Sirkar: Government of India.

147 *drink my tobacco*: the guardian is offering to share his hookah, or water-pipe. To take it 'like a Mussulman' is to inhale through a clenched fist, so that the lips do not touch the mouthpiece.

bunjaras: carters.

a hundred lakhs of maunds: the maund was a common measure of weight, variable from region to region; ten million of them would add up to an impossibly heavy load of freight.

148 *koss*: variable measure of distance, usually between one and two miles.

Hanuman: monkey-god of the Hindu pantheon.

149 *muggers*: crocodiles.

Shiahs and Sunnis: the two chief Islamic sects.

150 *Jumna*: one of the great rivers of North India.

deodar: cedar.

151 *lattice-work . . . upper boom*: the network of girders for stiffening the bridge must be imagined as *above* the line of the rails, as if the tracks were laid upon the lower surface of a tube of oblong cross-section. The keeper looks down from the upper boom on the waters foaming across the rails a foot deep.

152 *the left rose clear*: perched on the boom, the keeper is looking along the line of the rails, so that upstream is to his left, downstream to his right.

153 *Ho! ho!*: 'I grieve to say the Warden of the Barhwi Ford is responsible here for two very bad puns in the vernacular.—R.K.' [Kipling's footnote]. The present editor regrets that he is unable to elucidate the puns.

154 *how the man died*: Hirnam Singh has been dead two full days; thus, when the keeper learns the identity of the corpse, he realizes that the flood could not have been the cause of his rival's death, as he had earlier assumed.

paulin: evidently a waterproof sheet; may be Kipling's own coinage, a back-formation from *tarpaulin*.

Dutt: Kneel!

155 *Only a Subaltern*: first published 25 August 1888 in the *Week's News*; reprinted December 1888 in *Under the Deodars*.

In the British army, a *subaltern* is any commissioned officer below the rank of Captain (i.e. a lieutenant or second lieutenant). The corresponding term in American usage would be 'junior officer'.

Sandhurst: site of the Royal Military College.

Tyneside Tail-Twisters: Kipling's affectionate nickname for The Royal Northumberland Fusiliers (5th Foot), stationed at Lahore from 1886 to 1888.

Krab Bokhar: the Mian Mir Cantonment, literally 'bad fever'.

Star of India: senior Order of British India.

156 *the Line*: regular infantry, as opposed to Guards, staff, auxiliaries, etc.

'side': conceit.

mokes: donkeys.

Black Regiments: the British military presence in India comprised regiments of the Indian Army, together with British regiments on Indian service. The former were staffed by British officers holding the Queen's commission and Indian officers holding a commission from the Viceroy, the rank and file all being natives of India or of neighbouring territories such as Nepal.

157 *half-butt*: billiard-cue.

158 *Walers*: big Australian chargers issued to British cavalry regi-

ments stationed in India (see note to 'The Phantom 'Rick-shaw', p. 32). The 'wasps of the Bengal Cavalry', as troops of the Indian Army, would have been mounted on smaller animals.

159 *under full stoppages for new kit*: the cost of new kit is being taken out of his pay.

muchly-fish: literally, 'fishy fish'.

160 *gallanty-show*: shadow pantomime or puppet show (Cockney slang).

161 *skrimshanker*: shirker.

Simla Pahar: literally, 'Simla the mountain refuge'.

tonga: small, light carriage commonly used as transport between the hill stations and the plains.

162 *Leave the bride at the altar*: adapted from Sir Walter Scott's 'Pibroch of Donald Dhu' (1816): 'Leave untended the herd,/ The flock without shelter;/Leave the corpse uninterr'd,/The bride at the altar.'

'the sickness that destroyeth in the noonday': cf. Psalms 91: 6.

164 *townies*: men from the same town, hence buddies.

165 *Tattoo láo*: bring 'Tattoo' (the pony).

167 *doolie-bearers*: stretcher-bearers.

168 *Bid me good-bye and go!*: from *The Lady Slavey*, by Eleanor Robinson.

a not unfamiliar tune: that is, the Dead March from Handel's *Saul*.

170 *Baa Baa, Black Sheep*: first published 21 December 1888 in the Christmas Supplement to the *Week's News*; reprinted early in 1889 in *Wee Willie Winkie*.

   The autobiographical basis of the story has never been in doubt. Kipling returned to this unhappy period of his child-hood twice more, producing somewhat different versions of the experience in *The Light that Failed* (1890) and *Something of Myself* (1937). Mrs Edmonia Hill, whom Rudyard was visiting when he wrote 'Baa Baa, Black Sheep', mentioned in her diary the intensity of his feelings as he revived the memory of those years. 'It was pitiful to see Kipling living over the experience, pouring out his soul in the story, as the drab life was worse than he could possibly describe it . . . When he was writing this he was a sorry guest, as he was in a towering rage at the recollec-tion of those days.'

Given Kipling's strong feelings and exceptional powers of recall, it is not surprising that many of the details of the story have been corroborated by later research. Proposed connections to real places, persons, books, and events are fully set forth in the *Readers' Guide*.

epigraphs: the nursery rhyme is traditional. The second epigraph is a slightly altered line from *As You Like It*: Touchstone's words are 'When I was at home, I was in a better place.' (II, iv. 17)

ayah, *hamal*; *Surti*: nursemaid, porter; Meeta is from Surat.

baba: this form of address, traditionally connoting respect, was commonly used by Indians to English children; cf. the '*baba Stunt Sahib*' in 'Gemini', p. 54 and note.

put-put: smack-smack.

171 *the Ghauts*: range of mountains near Bombay, en route to the hill station of Nassick.

Belait: Europe, England, the 'Blighty' of the World War I Tommies.

brougham: one-horse, closed carriage; pronounced like 'broom'.

172 *Apollo Bunder*: chief dock at Bombay.

P. & O.: see note to 'The Phantom 'Rickshaw', p. 27.

broom-gharri: i.e., brougham carriage.

173 *Sonny, my soul*: evening hymn by John Keble (1792–1866)— 'Sun of my soul.'

175 *Navarino*: naval battle fought on 27 October 1827, in which the British fleet under Admiral Sir Edward Codrington defeated the Turks and secured the liberation of Greece.

178 *epigraph*: from 'Easter Day. Naples, 1849' by A. H. Clough (1819–61), slightly misquoted ('Ah, well-a-day' is substituted for 'Eat, drink, and die', 'who had' for 'that had').

180 *Sharpe's Magazine*: this and the other readings that so delighted Punch have been identified by patient detective work: see Roger Lancelyn Green, *Kipling and the Children*, 1965.

182 *Tilbury*: a kind of gig for two.

186 *Cometh up as a Flower*: popular romantic novel by Rhoda Broughton (1840–1920).

That day at Navarino: Uncle Harry's song has not been identified.

187 *epigraph*: Feste's song from *Twelfth Night*, II, iii. 44f.

hubshi: Negro.

188 *tout court*: without anything else added.

198 *At the Pit's Mouth*: first published December 1888 in *Under the Deodars*.

The Berg Collection at the New York Public Library possesses an interesting manuscript with the same title. Dated 1884, it contains the draft of a story about an adulterous couple on the eve of an elopement: the man dreams of a riding accident that overtakes himself and his mistress; then, as ghosts, the two observe the aftermath. Kipling never finished the tale: instead, he returned to the theme of adultery and mutual distrust in 'The Hill of Illusion', the ghostly lover in 'The Phantom 'Rickshaw', the prophetic nightmare in 'The Dream of Duncan Parrenness', and the fatal accident in the present story.

epigraph: a composite of scattered lines from Jean Ingelow's 'The High Tide on the Coast of Lincolnshire'. In the poem the bells warn of the impending flood that overtakes 'my son's wife, Elizabeth'.

Tertium Quid: in philosophy, a third thing, distinct from two others. Possibly a contemporary slang term for the lover of a married woman.

201 *ayahs*: nursemaids.

202 *snaffle*: simplified bit, with less restraining power than one fitted with a curb.

203 *Medusa*: one of the Gorgons, demon women of Greek mythology, whose hair was snakes and whose hideous expression turned the beholders to stone.

Black Jack: first published December 1888 in *Soldiers Three*.

204 *epigraph*: from 'The Wake of Tim O'Hara', by Robert Buchanan (1841–1901).

Orderly-Room and the Corner Shop: military equivalent of police court and jail cells.

Fort Amara: see note to 'With the Main Guard', p. 131.

205 *kiddy*: box or tub for mess stores.

206 *'arf Rampur*: its mother was a Rampur hound.

Forest Reserve: land set aside for plantation, fenced or hedged to protect the young trees from being browsed.

207 *peg*: drink of whisky and soda. Anglo-Indian slang (*c*.1860) of obscure origin, not derived from any Indian language.

undher the Black Dog: to have the black dog on one's back is to be depressed, out of temper.

'*Wot's the odds as long as you're 'appy?*': evidently a catch-phrase of the period, as it is found in other contemporary texts.

208 '*Yes,' said Ortheris*: as he goes on to describe a military execution.

O'Hara: the feud with Rafferty is first mentioned in 'The Solid Muldoon' (9 June 1888, *Week's News*, and *Soldiers Three*). For the (Black) Tyrone, see note to 'With the Main Guard', p. 133.

209 *wishful for to desert*: see 'The Madness of Private Ortheris', first published in *Plain Tales from the Hills*.

Dinah Shadd: Mulvaney's wife.

210 *the woman at Devizes*: a monument in this Wiltshire market town marks the spot where she fell dead in 1753 after committing perjury.

211 *blood-dhrawn calf*: allusion to the practice of bleeding calves to improve the quality of the veal.

presarve me formashin: 'preserve my formation', keep me walking in a straight line.

213 *an unruly mimber*: i.e., an unbridled tongue; cf. James 3: 5–8, of which this is a more or less proverbial misquotation.

214 *Jooty thrippence*: until recent times a duty of three pence was levied on every deck of playing cards; the stamp is stuck to the face of the 'Black Jack'.

stiffin' an' crackin' on: cursing.

turnin' her over: the Martini-Henry ejected but the older Snider did not, so had to be turned over after every shot to clear the chamber of the spent cartridge.

215 *he shtrup her clane an' aisy*: it has been pointed out that Kipling's account of the disabling of the Martini is not accurate in every particular; the result, however, is clear enough. (Cf. *Readers' Guide*.)

217 *dooli*: stretcher.

put undher stoppages for four fifteen: the cost of the rifle (rupees 4 annas 15) will be taken out of Vulmea's pay.

220 *barouche*: four-wheeled carriage seating a driver and four passengers.

221 *On the City Wall*: first published December 1888 in *In Black and White*.

Three years earlier Kipling had experienced a night of communal rioting like the one he describes in 'On the City Wall': he wrote it up for the *Civil and Military Gazette* as 'The City of Two Creeds' (19 and 20 October 1885).

Kipling's public would have been aware of the historical background against which this tale unfolds. The fierce wars against the Sikhs that led to the annexation of the Punjab in 1849; the Indian Mutiny of 1857; the Kuka Rising of 1871: these were chapters in a history of struggle for communal and national autonomy that continues to the present day. Specific allusions to this background are explained in several of the notes below.

epigraph: the second chapter of the Book of Joshua tells the story of Rahab the harlot, whose house was upon the wall of Jericho, and how she sheltered the two men sent by Joshua to spy out the defences of the city.

Lalun: the name is borrowed from a historical romance—*Lalun the Beragun: Or The Battle of Paniput* (Bombay, 1884)—by an otherwise unknown writer named Mirza Murad Ali Beg. Kipling was a great admirer of the book, copies of which are now extremely rare; McIntosh Jellaludin praises it in 'To Be Filed for Reference' (*Plain Tales from the Hills*) as the finest of all studies of Indian life.

Lilith: first wife of Adam, in Talmudic tradition.

the City walls: the City is Lahore, though Kipling has altered the geography somewhat for the sake of the plot.

225 *chunam*: a fine polished plaster.

to smoke and to talk: Lalun's visitors include Shiite and Sufi Muslims; Hindu priests and scholars; Sikhs, for whom the Golden Temple in Amritsar is the Holy of Holies; and red-eyed mullahs from Afghanistan 'beyond the Border': men, that is, who would be at each other's throats anywhere else.

226 *hearing and telling some new thing*: the Athenians are so described in Acts 17: 21.

a Demnition Product: allusion, perhaps, to Mr Mantalini and his 'gone to the demnition bow wows' (Dickens, *Nicholas Nickleby*, chapter 64).

sitar: long-necked, plucked stringed instrument.

227 *on his saddle-bow*: that is, the Battle of Panipat in the Punjab
(1761), when the Marathas were defeated by the Afghans. The
tale is told in *Lalun the Beragun* and retold by Kipling in his
poem 'With Scindia to Delhi' (1890). The *laonee* is a strophic
verse form of the Marathas: Kipling lifted the chorus almost
word for word from a *laonee* composed by Mirza Murad Ali
Beg.

228 *A consistent man*: 1846—the First Sikh War; 1857—the Indian
Mutiny; 1871—the Kuka rising (see below).

Wahabi: member of a puritanical Moslem sect, with a reputation for militancy and fanaticism.

229 *Subadar*: a rank held by Indians in the Indian Army, equivalent
to Captain.

Sobraon: decisive defeat of the Sikhs by the British in 1846.

231 *Kuka rising*: an attempt on the part of Sikh fundamentalists to
restore political independence, which had been lost with the
annexation of the Punjab in 1849. The rising was defeated in
1872; sixty-six conspirators were blown from cannon, and their
leader, Ram Singh, was exiled to Burma, where he died in
1885.

232 *Sikhs, Pathans, Dogras*: tribal group of the Punjab. Kipling's
point, of course, is that the three warrior races the Captain
mentions are the reverse of 'all alike'.

heterodox: Wali Dad uses the English word (not altogether
accurately) to refer to the *hetairai*, or courtesans, of ancient
Athens.

233 *pleader*: lawyer.

Vizier: prime minister.

235 *Vox Populi, Vox Dei*: the Voice of the People, the Voice of God.

profanely: 'Father, into thy hands I commend my spirit' are
Jesus's last words from the Cross (Luke 23: 46).

Sirkar: Government of India.

236 *Din*: the Faith (a Moslem cry).

238 *Native Infantry*: see note to 'Only a Subaltern', p. 156.

240 *lakh*: 100,000.

241 *bunnias*: Hindu shopkeepers, money-lenders.

242 *It is expedient . . . people*: Caiaphas, the high priest, uses these
words when he advises the Pharisees to sacrifice Jesus in order
'that the whole nation perish not'. See John 11: 47–50.

Two Lovely Black Eyes: music-hall song of the 1880s, by Charles Coborn (1852–1946).

244 *The Man who would be King*: first published December 1888 in *The Phantom 'Rickshaw*. A more complete elucidation of the geographical and Masonic references will be found in the *Readers' Guide*.

epigraph: meant to suggest the spirit of Freemasonry—probably not from Masonic ritual.

Loafer: in the Anglo-Indian slang of Kipling's time, any European at large in India with no official attachments or visible means of support, a vagabond. This would better fit the energetic Dan and Peachey than the word's original and current American sense of an idler or lounger.

245 *the Backwoodsman*: that is, the Allahabad *Pioneer*, which in 1888 employed Kipling as a roving correspondent.

246 *Residents*: a Resident was a British political officer assigned to oversee affairs at the court of one of the quasi-independent Native States.

going to the West: this and the phrases that follow are Masonic.

247 *barouches*: tempt them, perhaps, with the Victorian equivalent of Rolls-Royce limousines.

Harun-al-Raschid: Caliph of Baghdad (763–809) who figures largely in the *Thousand and One Nights*.

Politicals: that is, Residents.

248 *Zenana-mission*: pertaining to missionary work among Indian women, traditionally secluded from contact with strangers.

249 *punkah*: large swinging fan, worked by hand labour.

Gladstone: Liberal Prime Minister to Queen Victoria, noted for his hostility to British overseas expansion.

Modred's shield: the shield of King Arthur's traitorous nephew was blank because he had won no device through deeds of valour.

Khuda Janta Khan: 'Nowheresville'; literally, 'God Knows Town'.

251 *Brother Peachey*: Dravot reminds the narrator of the Masonic connection.

252 *Sar-a-whack*: allusion to Sir James Brooke (1803–68), the 'White Rajah', an English soldier who in 1841 was made ruler

of Sarawak by the Sultan of Borneo as a reward for his military exploits.

Kafiristan: literally 'land of the unbelievers', a desolate region of north-eastern Afghanistan, now officially called Nuristan; Dan's sense of its location is deliberately made a bit vague and inaccurate.

253 *INF-KAN*: that is, volume XII of the ninth edition, where Dan and Peachey would have found Sir Henry Yule's article on Kafiristan.

Roberts' Army: Dan refers to an incident of the Second Afghan War (1878–80), when a force under the command of General Frederick Roberts made a difficult forced march of 300 miles from Kabul to Kandahar.

255 *Serai*: see note to 'Dray Wara Yow Dee', p. 114.

whirligig: pinwheel.

Roum: Turkey (Constantinople).

256 *Amir*: ruler of Afghanistan.

King of the Roos: Tsar of Russia.

Huzrut: 'Presence', an honorific.

Hazar: get ready.

Martini: regulation rifle issued to British infantry and therefore valuable contraband.

257 *Pathans*: members of the predominant (Moslem) tribe of Afghanistan.

259 *Kafirs*: non-Moslems, unbelievers.

261 *fair men . . . well built*: an old tradition held that there still existed descendants of the Greek colonists left at Charikar, north of Kabul, by Alexander the Great.

Imbra: the name is taken from Yule's *Britannica* article.

262 '*Be fruitful and multiply*': God's command to Adam and Eve (Genesis 1: 28).

263 *matchlock*: primitive type of musket.

sights for the brown: in shooting, to fire into the middle of a covey of game birds, rather than picking one out as a specific target.

264 *Occupy till I come*: the nobleman's instructions to his servants in Jesus's parable of the talents (Luke 19: 13).

Queen Semiramis: legendary Assyrian Queen, like Alexander the Great associated with an invasion of India from the West.

265 *the Craft*: Freemasonry.

four-wheeled bogie: railway truck.

268 *Kafoozelum*: the Harlot of Jerusalem in a well-known ribald song.

jezail: long, heavy Afghan musket.

269 *Rajah Brooke*: of Sarawak. See above, note to p. 252.

Sniders . . . Martini: Sniders were being replaced with Martini-Henrys; the old rifles, the rifling worn out of their barrels, would be a drug on the market.

271 *platelayer*: before the introduction of rails early trams ran on metal plates; hence, anyone who lays railway tracks.

women: 'Give not thy strength unto women, nor thy ways to that which destroyeth kings' (Proverbs 31: 3).

272 *something like that in the Bible*: 'The sons of God saw the daughters of men that they were fair; and they took them wives of all which they chose' (Genesis 6: 1–4).

275 *our 'Fifty-Seven*: allusion to the Mutiny of 1857, when the soldiers of the Bengal Army rebelled against their British officers.

278 *the Emperor in his habit as he lived*: compare Hamlet to Gertrude on the appearance of the Ghost—'My father, in his habit as he lived!' (III. iv. 135).

279 *The Son of God goes forth to war*: early editions show 'The Son of Man' as a variant; the latest editions, however, alter 'Man' to 'God', bringing the text into line with the words of Bishop Heber's familiar hymn. The alternative version is probably due to Kipling's habit of quoting erroneously from memory.

GEORGE ELIOT	Daniel Deronda
	The Lifted Veil and Brother Jacob
	Middlemarch
	The Mill on the Floss
	Silas Marner
SUSAN FERRIER	Marriage
ELIZABETH GASKELL	Cranford
	The Life of Charlotte Brontë
	Mary Barton
	North and South
	Wives and Daughters
GEORGE GISSING	New Grub Street
	The Odd Woman
THOMAS HARDY	Far from the Madding Crowd
	Jude the Obscure
	The Mayor of Casterbridge
	The Return of the Native
	Tess of the d'Urbervilles
	The Woodlanders
WILLIAM HAZLITT	Selected Writings
JAMES HOGG	The Private Memoirs and Confessions of a Justified Sinner
JOHN KEATS	The Major Works
	Selected Letters
CHARLES MATURIN	Melmoth the Wanderer
WALTER SCOTT	The Antiquary
	Ivanhoe
	Rob Roy
MARY SHELLEY	Frankenstein
	The Last Man

TROLLOPE IN   **OXFORD WORLD'S CLASSICS**

Anthony Trollope   An Autobiography

The American Senator

Barchester Towers

Can You Forgive Her?

The Claverings

Cousin Henry

Doctor Thorne

The Duke's Children

The Eustace Diamonds

Framley Parsonage

He Knew He Was Right

Lady Anna

The Last Chronicle of Barset

Orley Farm

Phineas Finn

Phineas Redux

The Prime Minister

Rachel Ray

The Small House at Allington

The Warden

The Way We Live Now

The Oxford World's Classics Website

www.worldsclassics.co.uk

- Information about new titles
- Explore the full range of Oxford World's Classics
- Links to other literary sites and the main OUP webpage
- Imaginative competitions, with bookish prizes
- Peruse the Oxford World's Classics Magazine
- Articles by editors
- Extracts from Introductions
- A forum for discussion and feedback on the series
- Special information for teachers and lecturers

www.worldsclassics.co.uk

American Literature

British and Irish Literature

Children's Literature

Classics and Ancient Literature

Colonial Literature

Eastern Literature

European Literature

History

Medieval Literature

Oxford English Drama

Poetry

Philosophy

Politics

Religion

The Oxford Shakespeare

A complete list of Oxford Paperbacks, including Oxford World's Classics, Oxford Shakespeare, Oxford Drama, and Oxford Paperback Reference, is available in the UK from the Academic Division Publicity Department, Oxford University Press, Great Clarendon Street, Oxford OX2 6DP.

In the USA, complete lists are available from the Paperbacks Marketing Manager, Oxford University Press, 198 Madison Avenue, New York, NY 10016.

Oxford Paperbacks are available from all good bookshops. In case of difficulty, customers in the UK can order direct from Oxford University Press Bookshop, Freepost, 116 High Street, Oxford OX1 4BR, enclosing full payment. Please add 10 per cent of published price for postage and packing.